"THE WAVE, WELL, IT SEEMED TO COME OUT OF NOWHERE, THIS GREAT RUSH OF WATER, LIKE A GREEN WALL."

"It pulled both children into the sea, I take it," I said.

Reverend Wilson nodded. "Cody managed to get out again. Brittany didn't."

"I'm sorry to hear that."

Wilson choked back a sob. "The oddest thing, though." He glanced at the huddled group behind him, as if reassuring himself they were still safe. "The wave, it was like it had tentacles or hands. It was reaching for our kids, I swear it, with strands of seawater. I could feel a malignancy in that wave. Satan, I suppose, bent on murder." He gave me an odd twisted smile, all pain and black humor. "The police think I'm crazy. Do you?"

"No," I said. "I don't think it was Satan, but if you say you felt something malignant, you could be right. I don't know yet, but I'm not dismissing what you say."

"Thanks." He gulped for breath, then turned away. "It meant to take them. I swear it."

I let him go back to his flock. Ari rejoined me.

"I've seen enough," I said. "Let's get out of everyone's way."

We crossed the highway, but at the head of the path down, I glanced back at the ocean. I saw, just for a brief moment, the figure of an enormous woman standing on the sea. The fog wrapped her with gray mourning clothes, and a dead child lay across her outstretched arms. I knew then that the girl had drowned.

KATHARINE KERR

WATER TO BURN

A NOLA O'GRADY NOVEL

DAW BOOKS, INC.

DONALD A. WOLLHEIM, FOUNDER

375 Hudson Street, New York, NY 10014

ELIZABETH R. WOLLHEIM
SHEILA E. GILBERT
PUBLISHERS
www.dawbooks.com

First Printing, August 2011
1   2   3   4   5   6   7   8   9

In memoriam
Michael Plotts
1960–2009
an honorable officer of the law

Acknowledgments

Many thanks to Howard Dunstan, Kate Elliott, JD Glass, Jo Kasper, Madeleine Robins, Karen Williams, and Cliff Winnig for sage advice during the writing of this book. And a special thanks to Rebecca Caccavo for her research into the arcane matter of Bay Area teenage slang.

CHAPTER I

I KNEW THAT SOMETHING WAS WRONG with that fog the minute I saw it. When you live in western San Francisco, as I have for many years, you come to know fog in all its aspects—the chilly blankets of late summer, the soft-focus mists of autumn, the near-rains of winter, the delicate wisps of spring—but none of them have faces. This one did. A dark gray face, about three feet high, pressed against my kitchen window and stared at me while I drank my breakfast coffee.

"What do you want?" I said to it, as politely as I could manage. "Got something to tell me?"

It shook its huge head no, then mouthed a word.

"Help?" I said. "You need help?"

It nodded yes, then pulled back. I got up from the table and took a long look out of the window at the ground, three stories below my apartment. Fog hung low over the roof-tops of the local shops and the Persian restaurant across the street. Long tendrils of gray damp swayed in the wind and wrapped themselves around the electric cables above the streetcar tracks like ocean kelp on a slow tide.

Fog Face kept drifting back and forth outside. Yet no one walking by or waiting at the streetcar stop seemed to notice anything unusual, even though a sudden flood of water lapped around the concrete island out in the middle of the street. One of my IOIs again, I figured. That's slang for "Image Objectification of Insight," where a psychic like me sees intuitions or flashes of data as literal things or events outside of herself.

It pays, however, to treat them as real, because sometimes they are.

"Look," I said, "I'll be glad to help, but I don't know what you need."

I heard the sound of waves, breaking on a shore, a rocky shore or a graveled beach, because the sound rumbled and chattered. It turned into the noise of the N Judah streetcar, screeching to a halt at the passenger island, which had become dry again. For a moment more Fog Face looked up at me. It frayed out into normal fog and disappeared.

I'd gotten an answer, even though I had no idea of what it meant. Most people assume that when you're a psychic investigator, information and messages bombard your mind with no effort on your part. Once in a great while they do, but you've still got to interpret the ambiguities. Ambiguities always abound.

I picked up my coffee mug and sat back down to think. The message pointed to the ocean, possibly as a source of the Chaos eruption I was tracking. That's my job, tracking down outbreaks of Chaos into the normal world and then dealing with them.

My name is Nola O'Grady. I won't name the government agency I work for; it's so secret that even the CIA doesn't know it exists, and a good thing, too, because they'd probably try to snag some of our funding. Only two outsiders have access to the Agency, and they both work for a top-secret office inside the State Department. Technically I was the head of the new San Francisco bureau, the Apocalypse Squad. My staff at that time consisted of two stringers and a bodyguard, nothing, in short, to pump up anyone's ego, especially since the bodyguard was probably spying for the Israeli government on the side.

"Nola?" Ari Nathan, the bodyguard cum spy in question, stood in the kitchen doorway. "Who were you talking to?"

"I'm not sure," I said. "It only had a face, no body." I considered its silent plea for help. "I don't think it was a Chaos creature, but I'm not sure."

"What are those things you throw at your apparitions?"

"Wards, you mean? The face was outside. You can't throw a ward through glass."

Ari opened his mouth and shut it again.

"You'll get used to all this after a while," I said. "I know there's a lot to learn."

Ari gave me the look of droop-eyed reproach he does so well. He isn't movie star handsome but macho attractive, with his athletic body and thick curly dark hair. He has gorgeous eyes, jet black and as large and straightforward as those on a Byzantine icon, even though that's the wrong religion. Despite his British accent, he's an Israeli national.

He poured himself coffee and sat down opposite me at the small table. We'd begun our relationship a month or so earlier, only to have it interrupted when he'd been called back to Israel to appear at a legal hearing. He'd just returned, and now our fire was burning white-hot again. The clock over the stove read noon. We'd had an athletic night and slept late.

"Speaking of windows," he said, "why is there still plywood over the window in the lounge? I was gone what? Almost a fortnight, and your sodding landlady still hasn't fixed it."

"She wants me out, is why. I've already given her my notice."

I couldn't really blame her, either. The living room window had shattered when someone tried to shoot me through it. This kind of thing does not get you a top rating on a landlord's list of desirable tenants.

"Good," Ari said. "With my salary and yours combined, surely we can find something better."

"I guess that means you're assuming we're going to live together."

"Of course. Aren't you?"

I hesitated, torn because I liked living alone almost as much as I liked sleeping with him. He gulped some coffee and considered me for a moment.

"I can hardly be your bodyguard from a distance," he said. "And I gather that you're in considerable danger."

"I don't know about that. My handler at the Agency keeps

sending me warnings about Chaos masters on the prowl, but I never received any ASTAs while you were gone."

"What?"

"Automatic Survival Threat Awareness. Sorry. It's Agency slang."

"Very well, but the Chaotics could be just biding their time. Scheming. I suppose Chaos masters would scheme."

"Constantly. It's their bread and butter, scheming." I couldn't stop myself from smiling. "They have devoted themselves to darkness and the evils it brings."

"I wish you'd take the threat a little more seriously." He glared at me over his coffee mug.

"You're right. Sorry, again."

"You know what's wrong with you?" Ari waved a finger at me. "You trust your sodding talents too much. You don't feel any danger, so you assume there isn't any."

"What else am I supposed to assume?"

"That the danger's too far away for your talents to pick it up. That doesn't mean it isn't there." He paused for a sip of coffee. "When you depend on your talents, you turn off your common sense. It's a kind of blindness."

I started to snarl but made myself think instead. "You know something?" I said. "You're right. Thanks."

"Well, it's my job to keep you safe."

"One of your jobs, anyway."

Ari froze with his mug halfway to the table, just for a second, but I knew I'd hit pay dirt. He set the cup down carefully before he said, "Just what do you mean by that?"

"Oh, come on," I said. "Do you think I'm stupid or something? I'll bet your real agency sent you here to keep an eye on more things than me. Why else would they make this weird arrangement with Interpol?"

For a long moment he stared at me. His Subliminal Psychological Profile was giving off a welter of vibrations: irritation, mostly, but with a certain grudging admiration mixed in. Eventually he sighed, looked put upon, and picked up his coffee mug again.

"Oh, very well," Ari said. "I should have known. What is it that your brother says you have?"

"X-ray vision. One of Dan's favorite phrases: my kid sister with the X-ray vision."

"Yes, that's it." He had a pensive sip of coffee. "But they didn't make the arrangement. Interpol did. Someone requested I be posted to San Francisco, so it all worked out."

"Someone?"

"I don't know who. Someone at the NCB level."

"The what?"

"The National Central Bureau."

"Ah. Thanks. But even if you did know, I bet you wouldn't tell me."

"Quite right I wouldn't, but I don't."

"So you really do work for them? I've always wondered."

"Yes, in the antiterrorism unit. You Americans seem to think that your country's the only target of terrorists, but it's a real problem internationally, too. Of course Interpol's involved. It's perfectly compatible with my other job."

"You're right. Sorry. So okay, someone high up wanted you here."

"Yes. I think I know the reason. I'm authorized to share intel. It might have a direct bearing on this question of Chaos masters. Reb Ezekiel's been spotted here in San Francisco."

I nearly dropped my mug. "I thought he was dead. Cardiac arrest in a whorehouse, wasn't it?"

"Yes, just that. The body was properly identified at the time by reliable witnesses. He was buried on his wretched retro kibbutz. But an IT person at one of the big banks is convinced he's seen him twice, at two different locations here in San Francisco. Both times Ezekiel turned and ran when he realized that he'd been spotted."

"Did this tech know Zeke well enough to be sure?"

"Oh, yes. I know the fellow who saw him. Itzak Stein's his name. He was a fellow sufferer in the sodding kibbutz, but his family returned to the States."

"Reb Ezekiel had some American converts, huh?"

"Yes. Itzak was born in New York, and he retrieved his American citizenship once he was old enough. I'm not surprised, considering what we went through." Ari paused and looked away, probably to repress memories from his childhood. After two minutes by the kitchen clock, he turned back to me. "So yes, he's quite sure."

"Okay then. Have you considered that this Ezekiel might be a doppelgänger?"

"From one of those deviant world levels? That's my current assumption. The question is why he's here. I had my agency send yours a dossier. Haven't you received it yet?

"Not yet. It takes a while to get things cleared."

Ari made the noise I call his growl, a sort of low-frequency clearing of his throat accompanied by a scowl.

"So you were sent back," I went on, "because both agencies know you can recognize this fake holy man. It makes sense."

"Yes. I was glad to get the assignment."

"Why?"

"Nola, don't be dense."

We were edging toward a subject I didn't want opened. Ari leaned back in his chair and watched me, waiting, while it was my turn for the meaningless smile. Eventually he gave up. With a sigh he finished his coffee and got up. When he held out a hand for my mug, I gave it to him. He went to the stove and refilled both from the carafe. He handed me mine, then stayed standing by the stove to gulp his down.

"I'm going to shower and shave," Ari said. "I suppose I should unpack some clothes, but not the rest, if we're going to move—" He let the sentence dangle.

I merely smiled for an answer. He finished the coffee and left me alone to think.

I felt like sulking over this new problem that the Agency and Interpol had dumped onto the Apocalypse Squad. I already had a complex problem sitting in my metaphoric inbox. Recently we'd broken up a dangerous Chaos group. Two of their members, now dead, had dealt in heroin. A third member had been murdered, probably for knowing too much about their racket.

The question: were the two dead perps the leaders of the group? I had some evidence that they were only part of the problem. In that case, where were the rest of them? I knew of four other people in their occult circle, and they were still on the loose. The two dead members, Johnson and Doyle by name, had devoted themselves to the cult of the Peacock Angel, Tawsi Melek. Islamic clerics identified this figure with Satan, which was not good news.

So possibly a stronger force lay behind the group—and possibly behind whatever trouble had brought me Fog Face. The mystery mist might also have seen some completely other criminal mischief brewing. That's what I mean by ambiguity: two problems or one, I didn't know.

I got up and walked into the living room, dark and gloomy at the moment from the plywood over the bay window. A mound of Ari's luggage, a couple of kelvar suitcases and some cardboard cartons, sat on my old Persian rug between my computer desk and the blue couch. He'd put one leather case, marked "fragile" in big red letters, on the coffee table. The floor was apparently good enough for the rest.

Ari came back in and zipped open one of the suitcases to pull out his shaving kit.

"What is all this stuff, anyway?" I said.

"Things I'm going to need for my job. A crime kit, that sort of thing, standard police issue. In locked containers."

"Ah. I wondered if you'd been sent to blow something up."

He scowled at me and retreated back to the bathroom.

I returned to the kitchen and saw Venus hovering a few feet above the black-and-white tile floor, over by the refrigerator. She wore a simple straight white dress, pinned with gold brooches at each shoulder, all the adornment she needed, since she also radiated a dazzling golden light.

"I admire your bedroom techniques, honey." She sounded a lot like Mae West. "But you've got to get a better mirror."

"Yes, your divineness," I said. You don't argue with goddesses when they give you beauty tips. "What should I look for?"

"The boyfriend's right. You're too thin." She smiled at me and raised one hand in blessing. "Remember! A better mirror." With that she disappeared.

Ari reappeared in the doorway, this time with his razor in his hand. Shaving soap covered half of his face.

"Who were you talking to now?" he said.

"Venus," I said. "The Roman goddess, y'know?"

He rolled his eyes. "I see that nothing's changed while I've been gone." He went back into the bathroom and slammed the door behind him.

While he cleaned up, I checked some Agency files on our protected site, TranceWeb, which has its own encryption system. Since the cross-agency file on Reb Ezekiel had yet to come through, I hunted for archived intel on sea creatures such as kelpies, nereids, and mermaids in the hopes of finding out more about Fog Face.

None of these creatures—whether Chaotic or Orderly—have the same kind of reality as an actual animal like a seal or a fish. Most sightings fall under the heading of IOIs or outright hallucinations. A few, however, of these "things seen" have a quasi-reality, because they're manifestations of the hidden forces of the universe. Solid they're not, but those who observe them are seeing something real, not mere illusions.

The trick is knowing the difference. I felt a gut response to Fog Face strong enough to assume he emanated from the forces of Order and Harmony. Since I found nothing about mist creatures in the archives, I'd have to test the assumption as I went along.

While I finished my search, Ari unpacked his clothes, then went into the kitchen and began rummaging around in the refrigerator. We'd stopped at a local grocery the night before and stocked up on a number of staples, like coffee, lettuce, and tomatoes for me.

"I don't suppose you'll eat breakfast," he called out.

"No," I said. "I won't."

In a minute or two he appeared in the kitchen doorway. He was eating a half round of pita bread filled with something.

"What's in that?" I said.

"Peanut butter," he said. "And sweet gherkins."

"And what?"

"Pickles, you'd call them."

I gagged. He returned to the kitchen to eat it out of my sight.

After he ate this evidence that breakfast is a miserable meal, he began stowing the other luggage. In particular he worked from his salesman's sample case, a big tan leather holdover from his previous cover story, when he'd posed as an importer of prayer shawls as well as some souvenir goods from the Holy Land. It actually held gadgets, among them a detection device for bugs in the walls, something he called an "interference generator" to protect our cell phone connections, and a gizmo that checked my landline and answering machine for wiretaps. At one point, when the case stood open, I glimpsed a long narrow bundle, wrapped in black.

"What's that in the prayer shawl?" I asked.

"The name is tallit." He looked up and scowled at me. "Not prayer shawl."

"Sorry, but you called them that when you came to my office—the first time, if you remember."

"I had to use the sodding password I was given. That was just the kind of insensitive gaffe your State Department is known for." He glanced into the case. "As for this, it's just a bit of cloth. You never wrap things in a tallit."

"Okay. I didn't realize. But what's the thing in the cloth?"

"None of your business." He gave me the smile I call his tiger's smile, tight-lipped and narrow-eyed. "But it's in two pieces at the moment. Perfectly harmless."

"You mean it's some kind of gun."

"You don't want to know." He shut the case and stood up.

I could recognize a change of subject when I saw one. "How do you get this stuff through Customs?" I said.

"Someone calls ahead. The security forces are waiting for me when I get off the plane."

I knew better than to ask who the "someone" was.

"That reminds me," he went on. "The next time you call your Aunt Eileen? Tell her I brought her a gift from Jerusalem."

"It's not a gun, is it?" I said.

"Don't be silly! It's a rosary. The beads were carved from wood grown in the Holy Land."

"She'll love that. Michael will be glad you're back, too. He's been badgering me about eating more. On your orders."

"Not orders. A simple request. He's a good kid, or he will be with a little supervision."

"Which you're planning on supplying."

"Will you mind?"

"Of course not. You're right about my little brother. He needs it."

About three minutes later, my Aunt Eileen called. In my family, this kind of "mental overlap," as we call it, is not coincidence. The first thing she said after hello was, "I dreamt last night that your Ari came back to San Francisco."

"He's not mine, exactly," I said, "but he did, yeah. He's here now."

"Oh, good! Why don't you come over for dinner tonight? Michael will be so glad to see him."

"I'll ask."

Ari agreed so fast and so happily to accept the invitation that the truth washed over me: he liked my family. He actually liked the peculiar collection of my relatives that he'd met, the same people who had made my previous boyfriends all run like hell in the opposite direction. I'd have a better chance of stopping a tidal wave than of talking Ari out of our moving in together.

"Six o'clock then," Eileen said. "Your uncle likes to eat when he gets home from work. Besides, he has less time to drink that way."

"We'll be there," I said.

During the call, Ari had been hovering nearby. I clicked off and slipped the phone back into my jeans pocket.

"About that apartment," he began.

I sighed and surrendered. "I want to move down near the ocean."

Ari's grin disappeared. "It'll be cold and foggy."

"I know, but that's where I need to live." I got up and put my hands on his shoulders. "You'll have me to keep you warm."

"Oh, very well, then." He bent his head for a quick kiss. "Near the ocean it is."

My landlady, Mrs. Zukovski, wasted no time when it came to speeding the parting tenant. Just as we were about to leave to start apartment hunting, the glazier, a certain Mr. Hansen, arrived to give an estimate on the window. Mrs. Zukovski escorted him up; she'd put on actual clothes for the occasion, a pink polyester tracksuit almost as baggy as the muumuus she usually favored. It clashed, however, every bit as badly as they did with her purple hair.

Hansen himself, a tall man with a shaved head and arms bulging with muscles, began by discussing the available types of glass. Every time he gave a by-the-square-foot price, Mrs. Z moaned softly. Trailing behind them was a young man in denim coveralls carrying a clipboard and measuring tape, Hansen's assistant, I assumed at first, though oddly enough, Hansen carried a clipboard and tape of his own.

While Hansen measured the central window, the assistant stood to one side and looked around him, so carefully and slowly that I realized he was studying the apartment. He was a skinny little guy with a narrow face and some kind of adenoid problem, apparently, since his mouth hung slightly open. He had pale gray eyes that appeared too big for their sockets—fish eyes, I thought.

"That estimate's for the big window," Hansen was saying, "but you should have the side panels refitted, too. Look, the framing's warped right clear off the glass." He moved to the side window in question and nearly stepped on the assistant, who scuttled out of the way.

That's when I realized no one but me could see him. I raised my hand to sketch a ward. He noticed and began edging sideways toward the open door, but not fast enough. I drew the ward with a sweep of my hand and flung it straight for him. It hit with a pale blue flash of light. He disappeared, and the clipboard and tape vanished with him, though a faint odor of fried fish lingered in the air.

Neither Hansen nor Mrs. Z noticed because they were arguing about money, which they continued to do as they left the apartment. Ari, however, had been watching the proceedings from the kitchen. As soon as I shut the door, he came in and stood looking at the spot where Fish Guy had been standing.

"What was that?" he said.

"Did you see him?"

"It was a him? No, of course not. But I did see you draw some kind of symbol in the air and gesture toward the wall."

"The target was a Chaos creature dressed up to look like a human being. Huh. I've never seen that before. I'd better report in to my handler. I need to go into trance."

I flopped down on the couch, rested my head against the upholstery, and let my mind slip below the consciousness level. As soon as I sent out the emergency signal, Y responded. That's the only name I have for him, Y, even though he's been my handler ever since I took the job. I do know what he looks like, however. Since my promotion he's appeared in these trance meetings as himself, or so he's assured me: a Japanese-American man with glasses, streaks of gray in his thick hair, and distinguished features. In his youth, he must have been really handsome.

"I've been meaning to contact you," Y thought to me. "What's the problem?"

"I've had an unpleasant visitor."

I extruded an image of Fish Guy, that is, I visualized him so clearly that the image picked up Qi and became visible to other psychics. As I described what had happened, Y examined this 3-D picture.

"The ward dispatched him?" Y said. "This bodes ill."

"Very ill," I said. "I've never heard of a Chaos critter appearing human before, not even a real dorky human like this guy."

"Neither have I. I wonder if he was the usual creature, or if he was some new type of projection."

"Projection? You mean a direct link back to a Chaos master's mind?"

"I'm not sure what I mean. The thought just came to me. That's the trouble with running on intuition."

"Yeah, 'fraid so. Look, some old magical texts talk about astral projections—"

"I wish you'd stop referring to those. There's nothing scientific about them."

I bit my inner tongue and shielded my thoughts to keep

from snapping at him. There's nothing scientific about ignoring evidence, either, is what I wanted to say, even though the evidence needs to be sorted through.

"I think he was a totally new kind of apparition," I said, "because when he vanished he left nothing behind. An ordinary Chaos creature would have popped like a balloon and left a skin or pieces on the floor for a couple of seconds."

"That's very true." Y paused to remove his glasses and wipe them on a white handkerchief that materialized in his image's hand. "It bears investigating." He put the glasses back on. "But be very careful."

"I will. You can bet on that."

"I need to sign off and go to a meeting, but quickly, is there anything else you need to report?"

"I have a question. What about that gate between worlds? The one in my aunt's house."

"I'm afraid I don't have anything new to tell you. The higher-ups are still making up their minds what to do."

"They'd better make them up faster. It's beginning to wear on the family, wondering if some radioactive weirdo's going to come charging in one night."

"I could possibly put in a requisition for a Marine squad to stand guard—"

"That would be worse. Never mind. Just try to drop a few of the right words in the right ears, will you?"

"I'll do my best."

Y's image flickered and disappeared.

I swam back up to the surface of my mind and opened my eyes. Ari was sitting on my computer chair on the other side of the coffee table and staring at me.

"I'm fine," I said. "I'm back."

"You need to eat something." Ari glowered at me.

"No, I don't. Aunt Eileen's going to fix a massive meal to welcome you back. I'll wait."

I changed into a dark green corduroy skirt, brown boots, and a rust sweater, so I could look respectable if, by some miracle, we saw a workable apartment for rent. Since the day looked cold, I added my raincoat. I also carried my cross-agency government ID, which is not precisely fake— that group knows I have it even though I don't work for them. Ari wore the navy-blue pinstriped suit he calls his police outfit, a move that turned out to be prescient, even though he has no psychic talents.

Since I wanted to live by the ocean, we drove to the outer Sunset district, one of the least interesting parts of San Francisco. It stretches from the big crosstown artery, 19th Avenue, down to the Great Highway and Ocean Beach on the western edge of the city. The neighborhood features street after street of jam-packed houses, painted in pastels, most of them built in the late '30s and '40s by the same company. The typical house is your basic cube, set above a garage and fronted by a tiny square of lawn.

After an hour or so of cruising for "for rent" signs, Ari turned glum. We were heading north on 37th Avenue when I realized that he was staring out the window with a hopeless sort of expression on his face.

"I know this isn't the coolest architecture in the world," I said.

"It's not the architecture. It's the sodding fog. Look at it! Doesn't it ever leave?"

Since we'd paused at a stop sign, and no other cars moved on the gray and windswept street, I looked. In the sky to the west a hovering Fog Face stared at me with a hopeless expression that matched Ari's.

"Uh, yeah, it does sometimes," I said and hung a left onto Rivera. "We're going to the beach."

Fog Face smiled and disappeared.

As we drove west on Rivera, I heard the thuck thuck thuck of a helicopter passing overhead, going in the same direction as we were. Ari rolled down his window and stuck his head out to look.

"It's a police chopper." He had to yell over the noise.

At that point we heard sirens, too, racing ahead of us. I drove faster. When we reached the end of the street, which stops at the Great Highway, we parked the car and got out. Just across Rivera I noticed a small yellow school bus. Inside, maybe a dozen kids sat oddly quietly for kids waiting to go somewhere. A pair of adults walked up and down the aisle. Above us the helicopter headed out to sea. The noise dimmed, and I could hear myself think again.

The Great Highway runs on a semi-artificial surface, built of reinforced dunes and a seawall, some ten to twelve feet above street level. We headed up the path that leads through moribund freeway daisies to a crosswalk and a stoplight. At the top we saw a pair of squad cars and an ambulance blocking one lane of the highway. Ari pulled his Interpol ID out of his shirt pocket. A uniformed officer, a skinny white guy, jogged across the crosswalk with one hand raised in the universal "stop" sign. When Ari showed him the ID, he lowered his arm.

I glanced back at the Great Highway. Despite the "great" in its name, nobody drives on this roadway much because it tends to be blocked by blowing sand from the beach. That afternoon a few cars came speeding along, only to slow down as they approached the police presence. Most slowed further to rubberneck, then sped up once they passed. A white luxury sedan approached at a steady speed and zipped on by in the outer lane. I caught a glimpse of a blond man at the wheel before it sped out of sight. I turned my attention back to the police.

"What happened here?" Ari said.

"A drowning," the officer said. "Well, we're pretty sure the poor kid drowned. The Coast Guard's sending a rescue unit, but the water's pretty damn cold this time of year, and the girl's only twelve. Not a strong swimmer, they tell us."

He jerked his head in the direction of the "them," a huddle of seven people, standing on the cement half circle at the top of the seawall. I got my cross-agency ID out of my shoulder bag and held it out. "Mind if I have a word with them?" I said.

He glanced at the ID, whistled under his breath, and shrugged again. "No problem, sure. The mother's real broken up, though."

"Yeah, I bet. I'll talk to someone else."

The officer escorted us across the road to the concrete esplanade. A sergeant, a formidable-looking African-American guy of about forty, met us. We showed our IDs again.

On the half circle of view area, near the steps that led down to the actual sand and water, two women had their arms around a third, who stood hunched over, sobbing, with her hands covering her face. Two men stood protectively on either side of a teenage boy, who was shivering despite the heavy blanket wrapped around him. His red hair hung in wet tendrils around his face. Everyone wore heavy jeans or slacks and sensible thick jackets.

"It doesn't look like anyone planned on going into the water for a swim," I said.

"They didn't," the sergeant said. "A rogue wave."

"What?" Ari said. "It's high tide, but the sea looks calm enough."

"Yeah. It's strange, all around. Here, I'll let you talk to the preacher."

A youngish white man, wearing jeans and a parka, open at the throat to display a black shirt with a churchman's white collar, hurried over when the sergeant beckoned to him. He introduced himself as the Reverend Tom Wilson of a local Baptist church. He had a long narrow face and pale blue eyes that at the moment looked half full of tears.

"Can you stand to tell me what happened?" I said.

"The Lord giveth, the Lord taketh away," Wilson said, but his voice shook. "Blessed be the name of the Lord! It's a terrible thing. I can't believe it happened, and here I saw it myself."

I made a sympathetic noise.

"Our church also runs a Christian school," Wilson went on. "We brought a group of kids out here for a nature walk."

"Those are the children waiting in the bus?" I said.

"Yes. The police agreed that they didn't need to stand out in the cold. Anyway, we kept everyone on the sand, no wading allowed, even." He swallowed heavily. "I've lived in the Bay Area all my life. I know what the riptides and such are like."

"Very dangerous, yeah," I said. "Did the missing girl run into the water?"

"No, not at all. Brittany and Cody there—" He nodded in the direction of the shivering boy, "— had gotten a few yards ahead of the rest of us, but only a few. The wave, well, it seemed to come out of nowhere, this great rush of water, like a green wall. Look, you can see the damp patch on the sand, over there to the south of us."

I looked and noted the darker sand, a stretch maybe twenty feet long and a good ten feet beyond the soaked firm sand of the tide line. Ari pulled out his cell phone and walked a couple of yards away to snap photos of it.

"It pulled both children into the sea, I take it," I said.

Wilson nodded. "Cody managed to get out again. Brittany didn't."

"I'm sorry to hear that."

Wilson choked back a sob. "The oddest thing, though." He glanced at the huddled group behind him, as if reassuring himself they were still safe. "The wave, it was like it had tentacles or hands. It was reaching for our kids, I swear it, with strands of seawater. I could feel a malignancy in that wave. Satan, I suppose, bent on murder." He gave me an odd twisted smile, all pain and black humor. "The police think I'm crazy. Do you?"

"No," I said. "I don't think it was Satan, but if you say you felt something malignant, you could be right. I don't know yet, but I'm not dismissing what you say."

"Thanks." He gulped for breath, then turned away. "It meant to take them. I swear it."

I let him go back to his flock. Ari rejoined me.

"I've seen enough," I said. "Let's get out of everyone's way."

We crossed the highway, but at the head of the path down, I glanced back at the ocean. I saw, just for a brief moment, the figure of an enormous woman standing on the sea. The fog wrapped her with gray mourning clothes, and a dead child lay across her outstretched arms. I knew then that the girl had drowned.

CHAPTER 2

BY THE TIME WE RETURNED TO OUR PARKED CAR, I was so cold that just getting into the driver's seat felt like putting on a fur coat. I slid the keys into the ignition, then sat rubbing my icy hands to warm them up before I tried to drive.

"That wasn't a coincidence, was it?" Ari said.

"What wasn't?"

"Our happening on this accident."

I contemplated the question while I buckled my seat belt. "I'm not sure," I said. "It's just luck that we were so close when the chopper went over. But something's been prompting me to get down to the water all day."

Ari stared out the windshield for a moment. "I see," he said. "You know, I've had quite enough of flat hunting."

"So have I. Let's go over to Eileen's. She won't mind if we're early."

"I need to go back to the apartment first and change."

"Why? You're already wearing a suit. You look fine."

"That's not it. I can't keep this jacket on all evening to hide the shoulder holster. I need to get a smaller weapon."

Some men change their clothes to suit an occasion. Ari changes his gun.

While Ari rummaged through his half-unpacked luggage, I checked my messages on both my landline and my cell phone, and a good thing I did. My sister Kathleen had called to tell me that I could bring Ari to the party on Sunday, since he was back in town. Either Eileen had called her, or we'd mentally overlapped. My immediate reaction: Party? What party? A frantic search of my memory turned up the data that Kathleen had, a couple of weeks before, when I was enmeshed in the most dangerous case of my career, invited me to a pool party. Kathleen has never been known for her good timing.

I walked into the bedroom to see Ari putting his shoulder holster and semiautomatic pistol away in the bottom drawer of my dresser, where I kept my underwear.

"Symbolism?" I said.

He looked at me as if I'd spoken in Martian. "What?" he said. "This is the only drawer that locks."

"Just a joke," I said. "Don't let it bother you."

He had a tiny pistol that fit into a holster that slid under the waistband of his slacks. Before he stowed it, though, he held up the gun.

"This is a Sig Sauer P232." Ari sounded like a parent introducing a child. "It carries seven shots. Not many, but adequate in an emergency."

"Gosh, that makes me feel so much safer."

"No need for sarcasm! This holster's specially made for the Israeli army." He stroked the nasty little thing. "You should carry a weapon like this in your bag. I'll get one for you."

"I will not carry a firearm. Sorry. No way."

"I know you have another way to protect yourself, but—"

"There are no buts. No guns."

He rolled his eyes, then picked up his suit coat. For a moment he frowned at it.

"What's wrong?" I said.

"Do you have a sewing kit?"

"Uh, no. Why?"

"The lining in my jacket's torn again." He held up the jacket and demonstrated by turning the left sleeve inside out. The lining had frayed badly right at the seam shared by the sleeve and shoulder.

"I usually just take stuff like that to the seamstress at the dry cleaner's," I said.

"I need to do it myself."

"Why?"

"Because they always ask questions. The fraying's from the hammer of the Beretta in the shoulder holster. It rubs. I don't like to advertise that I carry a firearm."

"Oh. Well, when we're at Aunt Eileen's, ask her. She'll mend it for you, and she's good at keeping secrets."

"She'd have to be, in your family. Which reminds me. Does everyone in your family know about your real job?"

"No, just the trustworthy ones. Eileen and Jim, obviously, and the two boys. And Sean and Al. Father Keith. I think Dan suspects."

"You trust Brian and Michael?"

"Of course. Michael has plenty to hide himself, and Brian's a closemouthed kid by nature as well as nurture. He knows better than to blab family secrets. We all learned that young."

"Good," Ari said. "I should certainly hope you've not told Kathleen."

"I haven't, no. She never makes sure her brain's engaged before she puts her mouth in gear. And there's no reason for Jack to know anything. Ditto Maureen and her kids."

"But you trust the Houlihans."

A slight edge to his tone of voice put me in warning mode. He was probing, I suddenly realized, though I didn't know why or for what.

"Sure," I said. "Why wouldn't I?"

"I was just wondering how much I could say in front of them. They seem like the sort of people who can keep a secret, but I wanted to verify that."

"Okay. I wouldn't tell them anything about your other job, though."

"I certainly wasn't planning on it. No need to burden them. Oh, by the way, what does Jim do? I'd like to be able to chat with him."

"He works for the Muni, the bus system. He started out as a driver, but he's a supervisor now. He's a lot smarter than he acts, you know."

"I rather suspected that. Good. I know something about the underground and things of that sort from my time in London."

He smiled so blandly that my suspicions deepened. He had a logical reason to ask about the Houlihans, I supposed, but I changed the subject anyway. "Do you have something in that sample case of yours that measures radioactivity levels?"

"Yes, as a matter of fact. Why?"

"Is it small enough to take along to Aunt Eileen's? I'm worried about Michael sneaking through that world gate. He's got a girlfriend over in the trashed version of the United States."

"The hooker?"

"Yeah."

"And she'll have sex with him?"

"Yeah."

"Then I don't need the rad counter." Ari paused for a smile. "Of course he's going over to see her. I'd be more worried about diseases than radiation. I'll talk to him about condoms."

"Good idea. Better you than me." And damned if I didn't blush.

Aunt Eileen and her family, which now included my brother Michael, lived on the other side of the city, about halfway up the main hill of the Excelsior district, which slopes up from the outer reaches of Mission Street. It's a neighborhood of single-family homes built on top of long-ago truck gardens and small farms. Eileen and Jim Houlihan's house started life as a cottage on one of the farms, then expanded over the years with the neighborhood. Unlike most of the solid two-story stucco houses around it, it faced the street on a double lot and spread out in a weird formation. The north end had three stories, the south end, two, but the middle, the orginal construction, only one.

Various neighbors had made snide comments over the years about this ramshackle, pulling-down-the-property-values place, but little did they know just how peculiar a construction it was. Just as well, too. Knowing they lived next to a psychic gate to some other level of the universe wouldn't have done much for their peace of mind.

I found a spot to park the rental car right in front of the Houlihan house, or to be precise, at the foot of the steep slope that led up to the house. When we got out, I glanced across the street and saw a youngish man standing on the sidewalk and looking our way. One of the neighbors, or another Chaos spy? On the pretense of stretching, I sketched a Chaos ward and sent it sailing across the street. It hit him with absolutely no effect. Only one of the neighbors, then, idly curious. Dealing with Fish Guy had left me paranoid. If the Chaos forces could generate spies that looked like ordinary human beings, they could be lurking anywhere, in crowds, wandering down the street, standing around in grocery stores, anywhere.

"What's wrong?" Ari said. "You've gone a little pale."

"Just some evil thoughts. I'll explain later."

As we climbed the brick steps up from the street, I could hear faint rock music leaking from the upper story of the house. When Aunt Eileen opened the front door, the music blasted out. She was wearing one of her typical outfits, a bright red circle skirt with a fuzzy poodle applique at the bottom, a white blouse with a Peter Pan collar, and leopard-print flats.

"Both boys are home, huh?" I had to yell to be heard.

"Yes," she yelled back. "I'll tell them to turn it down, not that they will—much."

"I'll go do it," Ari said in a too-brief pause in the music. "They'll listen to me."

"It's so nice having you back." Eileen reached up and patted him on the cheek. "Thank you."

The music cranked up again. Ari smiled at her fondly, then strode across the long white living room to head for the stairway up. The exchange of smiles bothered me. I took it as another stake in the picket fence of domesticity that the family kept trying to build around me. Still, the music upstairs stopped, suddenly and permanently after a single bellow from Ari.

"He does have his uses," I said.

"I'd say so," Aunt Eileen said. "Come into the kitchen, dear. I'm just putting the finishing touches on dinner."

"Okay. Ari wanted to talk to Mike about something, so they may not be down for a while."

"Oh, good! We can gossip."

We went into the kitchen. Aunt Eileen put on a yellow calico bib apron, then stood at the counter by the sink to fuss with the food. I sat down in one of the captain's chairs at the round maple table, which she kept covered with a matching round of glass. She'd already set it for six with the family china, pale blue stoneware with green rims, and blue paper napkins.

"I wanted to tell you," Aunt Eileen said, "that I got a letter from Wally and Rose. They're coming to San Francisco for a visit."

"Cool!" I said. "Are they traveling in their RV?"

"Your aunt can't really travel any other way these days, I gather. Her knees, you know, and now they're talking about a hip replacement, too. Besides, she told me she has a special present for Kathleen."

"Oh, lord! Another damn dog."

"Oh, yes. A Russian wolfhound. And it's pregnant."

I could barely visualize hefty Aunt Rose, her equally hefty second husband, and a pregnant wolfhound all crammed into a small RV. Well, small as RVs go, anyway.

"Which reminds me," I said. "Have you heard from Kathleen lately?"

"Yes, she called me a couple of days ago." Aunt Eileen looked into a glass bowl of tomatoes and frowned. "You know how she is. She talked mostly about her animals, but I got the impression that she and Jack were having problems."

"Oh, no! That marriage means so much to her."

"Yes, it worries me." Aunt Eileen paused to pull a long knife from the butcher's block stand. "We've really got to eat those tomatoes tonight. I'll slice them for the salad. But, about Jack . . . He's involved in a new business venture, and Kathleen doesn't like his partner."

"Ah, I see. What kind of business?"

"Well, it does sound kind of flaky." Aunt Eileen brought out this piece of her childhood slang with a flourish. "It's hunting for Drake's treasure."

"Sir Francis?"

"Him, yes, the pirate or privateer or whatever he was. He's supposed to have had Spanish gold onboard when he landed up at Drake's Bay. This fellow, the one Kathleen doesn't like, has found some old documents or something. He thinks Drake might have buried some treasure along the coast somewhere."

"Well, there's only a thousand miles or so of California coast. Good luck!"

"Yes, it sounds like a really crazy idea."

We paused while Aunt Eileen ran the knife through the screeching electric sharpener. Eileen's knowledge of history tended to be more than a little flaky itself. As far as I knew, Drake's treasure had gone safely back to England for queen and country. If he had withheld some of it for himself, as some people thought, why would he have buried it on the other side of the world from his home base?

As for Jack, I wasn't surprised that the idea would appeal to him. His filthy-rich family had left him with no need for a real job. He lived with the constant danger of being bored. Treasure hunting would have sounded exciting as well as potentially profitable.

When the knife was sharp enough to suit her, Aunt Eileen wiped it clean on a checked dish towel, then went on talking while she lined the tomatoes up on a wooden cutting board shaped into the silhouette of a pig.

"Jack met this person through some of his other business contacts," Eileen said. "His name's Caleb something—I'm not sure if Kathleen told me his whole name or if she even knows it."

"Caleb? That's not a name you hear real often."

"Kathleen thinks he's from New England because he sounds like the Kennedys to her, the politician ones, I mean, not our cousins. Anyway, she says he smells funny, and the dogs don't like him. I don't know how much weight to put on that."

"I'd trust it," I said. "Kathleen's sense of smell isn't what you'd call normal."

"Well, that's certainly true. At first Caleb wanted to rent Jack's boat to go out deep-sea fishing."

"Since when does Jack rent out his boat?"

"He hardly needs to with his family's money, no, but I suppose Caleb didn't know that. But they did go fishing, and they became friends, and this other business came up."

"The buried treasure bit sounds all wrong to me."

"Yes, I agree." Eileen began slicing tomatoes with the vicious precision of a pirate. Juice ran on the cutting board.

I felt the odd trembling sensation in my hands that I occasionally get when I've heard something important. It's as if my fingers want to reach out and grab the information physically. Whoever Caleb was, he would bear keeping in mind. I would have asked more, but I heard Uncle Jim's truck come trundling up the steep driveway. In a minute, Jim himself came in, a tall man, not truly fat, but big all over, with gray hair streaked with its original red. He'd slung the jacket of his gray suit over one shoulder. A blue tie dangled out of one trouser pocket.

"How was your day?" Aunt Eileen reached up on tiptoe to kiss him on the cheek.

"Lousy," Jim said with a shrug. "One of the old L Taravals got stuck in the damned tunnel, and we had to run diesel feeder lines. I got it all cleared up okay eventually." He glanced my way and smiled. "Hi, honey. Where are the boys?"

"Upstairs with Ari," I said. "Talking, I guess."

In a few minutes, though, they all came down. Aunt Eileen had finished the salad, and Uncle Jim had just poured himself a juice glass full of whiskey when I heard them pounding down the back stairs, the ones that led right into the kitchen. Michael and Brian walked in first, a pair of cousins, though they looked enough alike to be brothers, with their dark blue eyes and straight black hair. Brian, however, stood a good head taller.

Ari shook hands with Jim, declined his offer of whiskey, and sat down next to me at the table. He leaned toward me and murmured.

"Interesting information from Mike. Remind me to tell you if I forget."

For dinner that night, Aunt Eileen had cooked her killer pot roast with potatoes and carrots. At least she served it with a salad, something I could eat in quantity. I did take a slice of meat and some carrots. Ari pointedly slopped the mushroom gravy on both of them before I could protest. I held him off before he added a potato chunk. For some minutes no one spoke, merely ate, led by two voracious teen boys. Eventually, Uncle Jim turned in his chair and waved a fork at me.

"Wanted to ask you," he said. "What about that damned gate to wherever it is?"

"Still no word on what the government wants done to it," I said. "I'm sorry. I've been bugging my contact about it at regular intervals."

"Well, you can tell them this. If they don't do something soon, I'm going to fill that damned room with concrete. That'll put an end to it."

Michael's head jerked up. He stared at Uncle Jim nervously, then tried to cover his slip by reaching for the platter of pot roast.

"Ask me to pass it to you, dear," Aunt Eileen said.

"Sorry. It's hella good, Aunt E."

She smiled and handed him the platter. Ari glanced my way and winked. I took it as meaning that yes, Michael had been slipping through the gate to visit his girl.

"What beats me all to hell," Uncle Jim continued, "is why the damned thing had to be right here in my house. Of all the bum luck!"

"No, not luck," I said. "Consider our family, all of it, over the generations. It's perfectly logical that there would be one here. It's not like it was the only one in San Francisco."

Uncle Jim grunted and speared a chunk of potato with his fork. I had the distinct feeling that I'd spoken truer than I knew. Mike was watching me, I realized.

"Mike," I said, "have you read those e-mails I printed out for you, the ones from our expert on the deviant levels?"

"NumbersGrrl, you mean?" Michael wiped his mouth on his crumpled napkin. "Yeah, they helped a lot. I did a little Web surfing, too, trying to find something about worldwalkers, but I only found a couple of fiction books."

"Here's one possibility. Look up a man named John 'Walking' Stewart. Late eighteenth century."

"Okay. Why?"

"He supposedly walked from England to America without bothering with a ship."

Mike blinked at me for a moment, then his mouth framed a silent O.

"He also believed," I went on, "in the transmigration of molecules and atoms from one body to another, but his main trick was covering long distances in short times just by walking."

"Are you having a joke on us?" Ari glared at me.

"No. Guys like Coleridge and Wordsworth wrote about him, so there's evidence. He'd disappear from one location, then turn up thousands of miles away in a year or so, but he always traveled on foot. He claimed that the atoms in your body could dissolve in one place and re-form in another, or something like that."

Uncle Jim leaned forward. "Wait a minute," he said. "This business about the atoms. Is that where Flann O'Brien got the idea about the Irishman and his bicycle?"

"Probably," I said.

"Flann O'Brien?" A bewildered Ari glanced at Aunt Eileen. "Another relative?"

"No, dear," Eileen said. "A novelist, and that's just his pen name, a very strange novelist who wrote a book called *The Third Policeman*."

"What is it, a murder mystery?"

Since Aunt Eileen had taken a bite of salad, I answered for her. "Sort of, but a comic take on one, and a lot weirder than usual. The narrator has this idea that over the years an Irishman and his bicycle exchange so many atoms that one becomes part of the other."

Ari stared at me. "A novelist," he said eventually. "No wonder I don't read fiction."

Uncle Jim's face turned pink from suppressed laughter. He made a great show of cutting his massive chunk of pot roast into tidy slices. Michael pushed back his chair and stood up.

"I'm going to write this down, okay?" he said to Aunt Eileen. "I'll be right back. Walking Stewart and then the writer guy."

"The book's in your uncle's den," Aunt Eileen said. "Remind me later, and I'll dig it out for you."

"I will, Aunt E. Thanks. Seriously."

Michael hurried up the staircase to the upper floor and his bedroom. Aunt Eileen watched him go with a slight smile.

"Anything to get them to read," she murmured in my direction.

"That 'them' means me as well as the boys," Uncle Jim said. "But I got to admit, I enjoyed that *Third Policeman* book, even if O'Brien was a Unionist." He glanced at Ari. "I'm betting you know what that means, working for the outfit you do and all."

"Oh, yes," Ari said. "Interpol does keep an eye on some aspects of the Irish situation."

I felt a sudden nag of premonitory fear. Aunt Eileen raised an eyebrow and lowered it again—quickly.

"There are some potatoes left," she said. "Brian, Ari, what about finishing them up?"

"Thank you, but I've had more than enough," Ari said. "Everything was very good."

Brian grabbed the serving spoon and loaded potatoes onto his plate. Gravy followed in profusion.

"Basketball practice again today?" I said to him.

"Yeah, it makes you kind of hungry." Brian's voice became solicitous as he continued, "Nola, you sure you don't want that last potato? And there's some beef left."

"What is this?" I managed a smile. "A conspiracy to make me eat?"

"More of a unified effort, dear," Aunt Eileen said.

I debated. If submitting to a lecture on my supposed eating disorder would keep the conversation away from the family secrets, Irish Politics Division, the annoyance would be worth it.

"I really do eat more than you all think I do." I allowed a slight surly tone to creep into my voice. "It's not like I'm starving to death."

"No," Ari said. "You just look like you are."

"Good point." Uncle Jim waved his fork in Ari's general direction. "You tell her."

"He does," I snapped. "Constantly."

Aunt Eileen gave Ari a beaming smile of approval. "This all started when Nola was a teenager," she began.

"Well, hey," I broke in before she could make the inevitable segue to my father's disappearance, an event that everyone in my family blamed for every single thing that ever went wrong ever after. "I was such a fat kid."

"No, you weren't," Uncle Jim said.

"He's right," Aunt Eileen said. "You were a perfectly normal size for your age. It's your wretched mother who started in on you because you weren't really thin, just normal."

"Ah," Ari murmured. "The dragon."

Brian suppressed a chortle and dropped his fork onto the floor. I welcomed the distraction. Unfortunately, it didn't last.

"I should get out a photo album," Aunt Eileen said to Ari. "And show you Nola's high school pictures."

"Please don't." The sound of my voice shocked me: a small desperate plea that threatened tears. I grabbed my water glass and drank. Everyone stared at me.

"All right, dear, I won't." Aunt Eileen stood up. "Everyone who's done hand me their plates. Nola, would you get the glass dessert plates down from the cupboard? You're taller than me, and I can't quite reach them."

Dessert turned out to be one of Eileen's irresistibles, as I called her fancy desserts, a chocolate cream pie in this case. Mike came back downstairs just as we were serving. He'd always had a good nose for chocolate in any shape or form. I took a slender slice to quell talk of my supposed disorder.

When everyone had finished dessert, the boys cleared the table under Uncle Jim's direction, not that they needed it, and began to load the dishwasher. Ari retrieved his sport coat from the back of the chair and brought something out of an inner pocket.

"That lining's torn," Aunt Eileen said. "I can fix it for you while you're here."

"Would you?" Ari said. "Thank you." He handed her an oblong white box. "I picked this up for you."

I don't think I've ever seen such a successful gift. As soon as Aunt Eileen realized that the rosary came direct from the Holy Land, she oohed and aahed and grinned until everyone had to smile with her. Ari relaxed. He even let Uncle Jim pour him a splash of whiskey and soda. I was oddly conscious of that gun he carried, especially when Aunt Eileen began mending his jacket for him. It set him apart, although no one but me knew about it.

I found myself remembering a long string of family dinners for various birthdays or anniversaries or holidays—heartwarming, perfectly normal family dinners except of course they were being given and attended by O'Gradys and O'Briens, none of us what you'd call normal, all of us set apart, too. We'd all learned to hide young, and so had Ari. In a way, I thought, we all lived on our very own deviant world level. It was not a happy thought.

When the time came to leave, Michael walked with us to the front door.

"Something I wanted to ask you," Michael said to me. "When are you going to get a real cell phone?"

"What's wrong with the one I have?" I said.

"It can't text. Epic fail!"

"Sorry, but I don't text. There's no way to secure those messages, because they all end up stored on a server somewhere. The Agency strictly forbids them."

Michael glanced at Ari, who nodded a confirmation. I'll admit to feeling annoyed that my pup of a brother doubted my information, but I decided that the slight was too slight, as it were, to argue over.

On the way home, while I drove, we discussed what we'd learned from our various conversations. I told Ari about the bothersome Caleb, and he told me about his conversation with Michael concerning Lisa, his girlfriend in the deviant level. She saw Mike as the best thing to ever come her way, an accurate observation considering the profession she'd been forced into.

"She never said this outright," Ari said, "but Mike got the impression that she was hoping he'd take her away, into his world."

"I can't say I'd blame her for wanting to leave hers."

"No more can I, but it's not possible, is it? For any length of time, I mean. What if she were involved in some sort of an accident? Would she heal up properly?"

"I don't have the slightest idea. I'll have to ask Numbers-Grrl. If anyone knows, which I doubt, it'll be her."

"Good. Do ask. Now here's the interesting bit. At some point in these conversations, Lisa said something along the lines of 'other people have gotten out of here permanently.' When he asked her what she meant, she changed the subject. She seemed frightened, as if she'd made some kind of slip."

"Very interesting, for sure! I wonder if Michael can find out more? He might as well do something useful, since there's no way we can stop him from going there."

"Unfortunately, that's true. I didn't even bother to ask him to stay away from that level. I don't want to make him start lying to me." Ari paused, staring out the windshield as we came down the sweeping curves by Laguna Honda. "I did raise the subject of marijuana. Michael handed his supply over to me, and he promised me he'd stay clean from now on."

"Good," I said, "and thank you. What about Brian?"

"He and Michael solemnly swore that Brian had never smoked any. Brian's afraid it would interfere with his athletics. Breathing hot smoke and all that."

"It would, yeah. What are you going to do with the stash now that you've got it?"

"Put it down the garbage disposal."

"That should get rid of it." A premonition crept over me. "Although I have this feeling it could come in handy, somehow. Not to smoke, don't worry. To bargain with or something."

"I don't want contraband in our apartment."

"How much is it?"

"No more than half an ounce."

"Nothing to worry about. The San Francisco police won't even bother anyone over that amount. Look, am I ever wrong about stuff like this?"

"No." The word squeezed out of grudging lips. "But hide it, will you?"

"Of course."

"Good. I have a question. I was thinking about the dinner conversation. That sofa your aunt has in the lounge. Isn't it a bit odd that it's orange?"

"She got it on sale, and she's an American." I nearly slipped up and added: in our family, we leave Irish politics to the men. Instead, I said, "If I remember correctly, the orange color wasn't moving, so the furniture guy knocked three hundred bucks off."

"That's a nice amount, yes."

Once we got back to the apartment, Ari handed me a plastic bag containing my brother's attempt at rebellion, enough cheap shake for maybe four joints. I tucked it under a pile of sweaters in the middle drawer of my dresser. As I was shutting the drawer, I noticed a blue cardboard box, roughly two inches thick and five long, lying on the top of the dresser. I sketched a quick Chaos ward, which had no effect on the box at all. I felt no SAWM concerning it, but since I'd never seen it before, I decided against touching it.

"Ari?" I said. "Would you come take a look at this?"

He walked into the bedroom and considered the box. "Oh," he said. "That."

"Yeah. That. Do you know what it is?"

"Yes. Perfectly harmless."

"It's one of your devices?"

"No."

"Then what is it?"

"Well." He looked away. "Actually, it's for you. Um, I got it for you, and then I thought you might be offended, so, well, I put it there."

At that point, I realized he was embarrassed. Yes, it was slow of me, but I'd never thought of him as capable of embarrassment.

"Offended?" I said. "Why?"

"Because it's a gift. I didn't know if you'd take a gift from me."

He shoved his hands in the pockets of his slacks and looked at me with his head tilted a little back. My first impulse was to say, "No, I won't," but luckily my second impulse was to think, "you bitch!"—so I shut up. He'd brought a gift for the woman he was sleeping with. What was wrong with that? Why did I want to hand it back to him with a sour remark? The moment stretched to a cold, nasty interval while I dithered.

"Sorry." Ari reached for the box. "I'll just put it away."

I reached out and caught his wrist. "No, don't," I said. "I'm sorry. I'm being rude. I don't know what's wrong with me sometimes."

He hesitated, then said with a perfectly straight face, "At times I've found myself wondering the same thing."

"You bastard!"

He grinned, his normal, no-tigers-need-apply smile, and handed me the box. I opened it, peeled off the thick layer of cotton packing, and felt myself smile, too.

"This is really beautiful," I said. "Thank you."

"This" was a pin in the shape of an olive branch in full leaf made of beaten gold, as soft and silky as only real gold can be. When I took it out, the leaves rustled, barely audible. I held it up against the rust sweater I was wearing, not a successful match.

"It'll look really good on the teal sweater," I said, "or the dark blue blouse."

Since he'd moved to stand behind me, I could see his reflection, smiling in relief more than pleasure. As I put the pin back into the box for safekeeping, I remembered Venus' advice that I needed a better mirror. I realized I did look a little gaunt in the bright light of the floor lamp.

"We could go out for breakfast tomorrow," I said, "if you want."

Ari slipped his arms around my waist and kissed the side of my neck.

"Good idea," he said. "So I'd better make sure you work up an appetite."

Being so thin had one big advantage. He could pick me up and carry me to bed.

In the morning we did go out to eat, but since both of us had work to do, we hurried back to the apartment. Ari took his twin leather cases of devices into the bedroom and shut the door to do something mysterious. Occasionally I could hear him talking on the phone, but always in Hebrew. I fired up my computer system and logged on to the Internet.

I had a set of news links that I surfed every day, because they specialized in local "human interest" stories. Now and then, hints of Chaos activity appeared in this welter of trivia, the kind of incidents you'd never find in the major television and paper news sources. Several of these sites reported on the rogue wave at Ocean Beach. As I'd intuited, the young girl had drowned.

"That makes me sick," I said to Ari later. "She was only twelve, just starting her life."

"Very sad, yes. Accidents will happen."

"It wasn't any accident."

"Oh? But I don't suppose that Satan had anything to do with it. Or are you going to tell me that Satan actually exists?"

"No." I managed to smile at that. "There are Chaos forces that have been personified as Satan, but there's no guy with the horns and the tail."

"Always nice to know. But you did get a feeling of agency, if I remember correctly."

"Yeah, but I'll bet that the agent was some human being, fooling around with stuff they didn't understand. That's the trouble with Chaos forces. They're chaotic. Which means they're really hard to control, especially by people who are kind of unbalanced to begin with."

"Who else would want to play with them?" Ari said. "I really don't understand this talk of Chaotics. It doesn't make sense."

"Of course it's not going to make sense."

"But what do these people want? They must have goals."

"Their goal is pretty much to keep from making sense."

Ari started to say something, then scowled at me.

"Well, what do you think Chaos is?" I went on. "When you talk about making sense, you're talking about finding a pattern to their actions, some kind of organized activities, right, leading somewhere?"

"Yes, of course."

"That all falls under the heading of Order. Chaos exists to keep the principles of Order from forming that kind of pattern. Pattern and Order lock out new possibilities. Chaos releases the energy that makes possibilities—" Here I got stuck for a moment. "Makes new possibilities possible, I guess it is. A world dominated by Order would be dead, sterile, with everything locked into place once and for all. A world dominated by Chaos would be a madhouse, with lots of energy flowing around to no good ends whatsoever. That's why I serve Harmony, that elusive balance point."

"Definitely a good cause, of course. I suppose that's enough to get on with."

I returned to my computer. I brought up my notes on the Sea Cliff coven, as I was thinking of it. I'd spotted only seven members at the one ritual I'd seen. With three of them dead, the job of tracking down the others should have been easier, but I'd not picked up any traces of them during the past weeks. I did have one line of inquiry that I'd never followed up, because it required the help of the San Francisco police force. Now that Ari had returned and could reestablish his link with the long-suffering Detective Lieutenant Sanchez, I could pick up that loose end.

"Do you remember the car our two loathsome perps drove to the Romero funeral?" I asked Ari. "The black Jaguar."

"The stolen car, yes."

"What if it wasn't stolen? I find it hard to believe that anyone would park an expensive car like that on the street and then not activate the alarm. You know it must have had one."

Ari smiled tigerlike. "Right you are," he said. "Yet the police report never mentioned anyone hearing an alarm."

"And it's a quiet neighborhood, Pacific Heights. The sound should have carried. They fine people over there for making loud noises."

"Really? Oh, wait, you're having a joke on me."

"Not on you. On the people who live in that neighborhood."

He looked relieved. "I'll call Sanchez," he said, "and see if I can get authorization to question this fellow."

Ari wandered into the kitchen and called Sanchez from his cell phone. I heard him speaking; then he appeared in the doorway.

"Sanchez needs a secure e-mail address," he said. "He's got some scanned paperwork to send through. Do you have one that doesn't rely on your agency's encryption system?"

"Yeah, actually I do."

I wrote the address down on a sticky note and handed it to him. He relayed it to the inspector, then signed off and rejoined me.

"Sanchez has no objection to our following up this lead," he said.

"Did Sanchez ever question this guy himself?" I asked.

"No," Ari said. "He did read the patrol officer's report on the theft, of course, once the car turned up at the funeral."

That official form and a couple of others appeared promptly in the queue for the particular e-mail address I'd given. I printed them out and read through the patrol officer's first report on what appeared to be an ordinary case of a car theft—or almost ordinary. Once the police found the car, the second report recorded two incriminating details.

"It says here that the car alarm hadn't been disabled." I handed Ari the printout so he could read the rest for himself.

"So you were right to wonder about that. Odd of Sanchez to not follow that up."

"I wonder if following it was going to lead him to some politically important people."

Ari looked at the report, quirked both eyebrows in surprise, then considered. "I'd hate to think that of Sanchez," he said eventually, "but you never know. I'll have to report back to him, and perhaps I'll find out then."

CHAPTER 3

WE DECIDED TO QUESTION WILLIAM FROST EVERS, the owner of the black Jaguar, that afternoon. We spent some time first discussing our strategy. For this interview, I'd play the assistant. Ari put on his navy-blue pinstriped suit with a white shirt and a red-and-gray–striped tie. I wore a dark gray pantsuit with a navy-blue silk blouse and a big black shoulder bag, all of which looked official as well. Before we left, Ari opened his sample case and put a casual handful of small devices into my bag. The case itself he locked into the trunk of the car.

Evers, a lawyer, specialized in divorce cases. He had an office in Embarcadero Center, a cluster of pale concrete blocks dwarfed by a nearby hotel, one apparently inspired by Babylonian ziggurats. These commercial towers stood down at the end of California Street, right close to the Bay itself. From the outside, the Center buildings looked bleak, but once you got inside, the spaces opened up into terraces and shops, escalators and little flower beds. Here and there hung massive modern tapestries to add warmth to the efficiency.

Evers' office sat on the fourth floor, toward the end of a narrow corridor right by an elevator, providing his clients a quick escape should they see someone they knew prowling around. The wood veneer door opened into a small reception room, carpeted and painted in pale gold and guarded by a pretty blonde secretary behind a formidable dark wood desk. A nameplate identified her as Miss Kowalski. She looked up from her computer monitor and gave us a bland smile.

"Good afternoon," she said. "May I have your name and the time of your appointment?"

"We don't have an appointment." Ari took out his Interpol ID and held it out. "We want to talk with Mr. Evers."

"I'm afraid you'll need an appointment—" The secretary glanced at the ID and stiffened. "Well, I'll tell him you're here, Inspector Nathan. May I ask what you'd like to talk to him about?"

"Just clearing up some routine odds and ends about the car he reported stolen." Ari paused for effect. "At the time of the Sea Cliff murder case."

"Oh, yes, I see." She started to reach for the elaborate phone next to her computer, then stood up instead. "I'll just tell him."

She beetled through the door behind her desk. I caught a glimpse of an inner office—wood paneling and a Persian carpet—before she shut the door behind her. Not more than a minute later she beetled out again, but this time she left the door open.

"Mr. Evers will see you, sir," she said.

"Thank you." Ari nodded at me to follow.

We walked around the desk and into Evers' office, spacious and bright from the rank of windows at one side, even though dark wood paneling covered the other three walls. A heavy desk and brown leather chairs sat near the back wall. Opposite the windows stood a rank of glassed-in bookshelves filled with clothbound volumes of the state and federal legal codes. Evers himself was standing in front of the desk, a man of medium height, beefy around the middle, wearing a soft gray suit that fit him perfectly and a violet-and-blue–striped button-down shirt, open at the throat. Compared to his fleshy face and the crow's feet at the corner of his eyes, his smooth reddish-brown hair looked suspiciously thick and evenly colored.

Evers gave Ari a fixed smile, started to speak, then noticed me. The smile disappeared and his thin lips parted, just briefly before he pasted the smile on again. He'd recognized me. I felt a slight familiar vibration from him, but I knew I'd never seen him before.

"Do sit down, Inspector." Evers had a soft, dark voice. "And Miss—er, or is it Inspector, too?"

I handed him my cross-agency government ID. When he glanced at it, a vein started throbbing at his right temple. He handed it back with a shaking hand.

"This case," Ari said, "has ramifications."

"So I see." Evers swallowed heavily. "Well, uh, have a seat."

Ari settled himself in one of the leather chairs. I perched on the edge of mine. Evers took refuge in the executive chair behind his desk and fixed his attention on Ari.

"As you may know," Ari began, "Interpol officers generally assist in cases as consultants and information facilitators. I came over to the States because the Silver Bullet Killer had committed two murders in Israel. Unfortunately, I became more involved than, perhaps, I should have."

"Er, yes," Evers said. "I remember the TV news."

"Good." Ari gave him a thin sliver of a smile. "Now, I'm here today because at one point the Silver Bullet Killer seemed to have stolen your car. I've read the police reports, and I'm wondering why the car alarm never sounded."

"It, uh, well, I must have forgotten to turn it on. Stupid, huh?"

"When the police recovered the vehicle, they found the keys lying on the back seat. Someone was stupid, yes, and careless as well."

Evers wilted, sagging against the tall black leather back of his chair. His SPP stank of a terror greater than a simple fear of the cops.

"What I wonder," Ari said, "is why you loaned your car to Johnson and Doyle. Who exactly did you think they were?"

"Just friends." His voice cracked on the implicit confession. "I had no idea what—they said they wanted to impress a client—I swear to God, I had nothing to do with the murders."

Ari glanced my way.

Since his SPP indicated that Evers was telling the truth, I nodded an okay.

"No one is accusing you of anything—" Ari began again.

Evers leaned forward and interrupted him. "If I'd known, I never would have had anything to do with them. I'd have gone to the police right away." Cold sweat ran down his jowls. "Poor little Elaine, strangled like that! Oh, my God, I've had nightmares for weeks!"

"I can well believe that," Ari said. "Now, could you—"

"Don't you see?" By then, the sweat was soaking the striped collar of his shirt. "Johnson gave me the creeps— always. Doyle was a smooth character, sure, but Johnson— scum, I knew he was scum, but—" He caught himself and gasped for breath.

Ari was considering him with a mild look of surprise, probably at this sudden outrush of the truth. The obvious occurred to me.

"You haven't found another source for the Persian white, have you?" I said. "How long had you been snorting it? Long enough, I bet, to really miss it now."

Evers jerked back into his chair. He leaned his head against the backrest and closed his eyes. He'd gone pale so fast and so thoroughly that it reminded me of those late-night TV ads where the demonstrator pours the miracle product into bright red water and turns it white.

"It's the ultimate middle-class high, isn't it?" I went on. "No needles, no mess, like snorting coke except it calms you down after a high-stress day. No wonder you handed over your car keys when they asked. Exposure would have ruined you."

Evers nodded.

"And now you have a medical problem," Ari said. "I suggest you consult your physician. No doubt it can be kept confidential if, of course, you cooperate."

"What do you want to know?" Evers was speaking so softly that I could barely hear him.

"Were you involved in Doyle and Johnson's occult activities?" Ari said.

Evers opened his eyes and nodded a yes. At that point, I realized why he recognized me.

"Does the phrase 'adest daemona' mean anything to you?" I said.

His eyes snapped open wide. "Who are you?" he said. "You're not a government agent. You're not really shaped like that, are you?" He swiveled his head toward Ari. "Are you real? Or are you another one? The chief of them all?"

"I beg your pardon!" Ari said in his best frosty British voice.

"Doyle warned me about this." Evers' voice shook on every word. "They come when you expect them not. They slither into your life like poisonous serpents. They—"

"That's quite enough." Ari slid to the edge of his chair, ready to spring. "Have you gone mad?"

"He's asking if we're demons." I broke into the exchange. "He thinks we might be tourists from Hell."

"Do you really?" Ari was staring at Evers.

Evers tried to speak but only gabbled. He turned toward me and held out both hands. I tried a reassuring smile.

"You're just having a hard time with withdrawal," I said. "We're real human beings, not satanic underlings. Look." I made the sign of the cross. "In the name of Jesus Christ. I couldn't do that if I were a demon."

Evers relaxed, although he continued sweating. "But you mentioned the daemona—how could you know?"

"It's a common phrase when people fool around with this kind of thing. Does it mean something special to you?"

He shook his head no, a lie of course, but then, I'd lied, too.

"Now," I continued, "was it Doyle or Johnson who was the leader of your coven?"

"Neither. It was the hooded man. He had another hood over his head under the robe's hood, I mean. I think it was just a piece of pantyhose, but, anyway, we never saw his face." Evers kept staring at me. It took him so long to blink that my own eyes ached. "We never knew his name. We called him Brother Belial. Please, I—"

"I believe you." I'd been anticipating that the real leader would mask his identity. "His voice, what was it like?"

"Deep, and he spoke real slowly, one word at a time. I thought at the time that he must have been loaded to talk like that. He was tall and skinny as a rail, even in the robes. I can tell you that much."

"All right. So you never heard his real name?"

"Never. He wouldn't let anyone touch him, either. He insisted that our vibrations would grate on him, because he was so attuned to the etheric somethings or other. Doyle said he was just paranoid about germs, but he only said that behind Brother Belial's back."

"I see." What I could see was that the leader was neurotic as hell, a poseur, or both. I suspected both. "So in this group we have you," I said aloud, "Johnson, Doyle, Politt, the hooded man—who were the others?"

"What others?" Evers forced out a brittle smile. "It was just the five of us."

"This kind of group generally has seven or eight members."

"Ours didn't. Just five." He spoke firmly, but with an odd querulous overtone to his voice, as if he were thinking, "Why don't you believe me, dammit!"

"Okay," I said and glanced at Ari to signal "over to you."

"Your car was in Johnson's possession during the time he attempted another murder," Ari said.

"I know." Evers was whispering again.

"Do you know anything about the blue Toyota sedan?"

"Only that it belonged to Johnson." The color was beginning to return to Evers' face. "Or, wait! There was an article in the paper that said it was stolen."

"Just that, yes. Did Mrs. Politt also use heroin?"

"No. Doyle wouldn't let her. He was living with her, at least when he was around. He'd disappear for a couple of weeks and then come back."

"With more heroin to distribute, yes. We know that part of the story." Ari stood up and shot me a glance. "I think we've learned what we can here. The occult silliness isn't a legal matter."

"Right," I said.

As we started for the door, Evers got up, but he stayed behind his desk. His color had returned to normal, and as he said good-bye, his voice sounded stronger as well.

At the door I glanced back and said, as casually as I could, "By the way, was one of the other coven members named Caleb?"

"No, they were both—" Evers said, then caught himself. "Oh, shit!"

Ari smiled, I smiled, and we returned to the chairs. Evers slumped down in his and covered his face with both hands.

"You might as well tell us their names," Ari said. "It will save you a great deal of future trouble. If they're not relevant to the investigation, nothing will happen to them."

"Yeah? Well, they're not." His voice sank too low to sound defiant. "Look, none of this is going to get on TV, is it?"

"Not if you cooperate." I paused to take a notebook and ballpoint pen out of my shoulder bag. "The names and contact information, please."

Evers gave it. I wrote down the names, phone numbers, and addresses of two women, friends of Elaine Politt, according to Evers.

"All right," I said. "Since we're still here, I want to know a little more about this so-called coven's activities. Were you all involved in selling heroin?"

"No!" Evers leaned forward and slapped his hands palms down on the desktop. "I was one of the suckers who bought it, that's all. My girlfriend told me over and over to leave it alone. I should have listened to her. Uh, God, how many men say that, after they make stupid mistakes?"

"Too many," Ari said. "Go on. What was the coven to you?"

"A stupid amusement." His voice had dropped to a whisper. "We did stupid things, like the curses. Write someone's name in blood on piece of paper and then send it through a shredder."

Ari leaned forward. "Where did you get the blood?"

"From meat packages, those little plastic trays, y'know? The blood collects under the steaks or whatever."

"A modern update for an old idea, huh?" I said. "What else? Invoking spirits, I suppose."

"Yes. They were supposed to tell you the secrets of the universe." He winced and shook his head. "I don't know why I believed any of it."

"You were loaded," I said. "That's why. What about—" I paused to pretend I was trying to remember something.

"This is probably not very important, but what about weather magic? Were you trying to command the spirits of the wind, for instance?"

"A lot of hot air." Evers tried to smile. "That's what those spells commanded. But there was some talk about elemental spirits, water, fire, and air, yeah, air was one of them. There were these tablets we studied."

"The Enochian watchtowers?" I said.

"Yeah. Doyle talked about John Dee a lot, but what he said didn't match what I read about Dee and Kelley. Doyle thought he knew everything, but he obviously hadn't studied the history very carefully."

Or else, I thought to myself, the history in his world level was different from ours. Aloud I said, "So you studied the elemental tablets."

"Yes. Elaine was really keen on the water angle. She loved living near the ocean, and so she wanted to contact the water spirits."

His last remark made me wonder if I'd just found an important clue. I was willing to bet that someone in that coven had done or was still doing something that troubled Fog Face. Maybe one of them would know something about the murder of the child down at Ocean Beach.

"About these spirits," I said, "did Doyle ever talk about making blood sacrifices to them?"

"You mean human sacrifices?"

"Yeah, particularly children."

"No. Nothing like that!" Evers slammed his hands on his desk again. "Hell, I wouldn't have put up with it for a minute if he had. I may be a goddamn junkie now, but I never would have gone along with anything like that."

I believed him. My important clue vanished.

"All right," I said. "Well, I think I've heard what I need to."

I put the notebook back in my shoulder bag and glanced at Ari. He stood up, and I followed.

"Thank you for cooperating," Ari said to Evers. "You may receive a follow-up call from Inspector Sanchez."

Evers stayed slumped in his chair, and we left for real.

Out in the corridor, we paused by the elevator. Ari

opened my shoulder bag and took out two devices. One teardrop-shaped bit of metal looked something like an ordinary earphone, but much smaller. I realized that Ari could have combed some of his hair over it, and no one would have noticed. The other device, a small square gray box, looked like nothing I'd ever seen. He clipped the one onto his left ear and held the other out in the direction of Evers' office.

"What are you doing?" I said.

"An illegal wiretap, of course. Shush."

As much as I disliked being told to shush, I did and kept a watch on the corridor. In a few minutes Ari made a small mutter of satisfaction and removed the earpiece. He put the devices back into my bag.

"As I thought," Ari said. "He called both women and told them we'd been to see him. Unfortunately, he didn't say anything incriminating, and neither did they. He did, though, call one of them Sweetie."

"Which may be why he didn't want to tell us their names."

While we waited for the elevator down, I had the distinct feeling that someone was staring at me. I turned around, looked in all directions, but saw no one. Once the elevator car arrived, the feeling disappeared.

As soon as we returned to the apartment, Ari phoned Inspector Sanchez to report in. I sat down at my computer desk and contemplated the blank screen of the monitor. In the past, I'd occasionally seen clues and pictures appear when the system was down—just image objectification, of course—but it stayed stubbornly dark. Still, Evers' remark about spirits and the secrets of the universe nagged at me.

"That's done." Ari strode back into the living room. "Sanchez will follow up on the other two coven members."

"Damn! I was hoping to interview them myself."

"So was I, but I think we're being put in our place. I doubt if they have anything valuable to contribute, so I suppose it doesn't matter."

"Let's hope. I—" I paused, staring at him. "Grimoires."

"What?"

"Sorry. The Collective Data Stream just reminded me

that I've got some grimoires. You know, books of spells and magical lore."

Ari rolled his eyes but said no more. I got up and went to my bookshelf, where I kept two scholarly editions of late medieval grimoires hidden behind a row of books on nutrition.

"You used a couple of words that triggered this," I said to Ari. "Put in place, valuable—they made me think of hidden treasure. If I'm not mistaken, that's one of the things spirits are supposed to do for you, finding lost treasures."

Sure enough, when I leafed through the first grimoire, I found a passage describing a guaranteed way of discovering buried gold. Since the spell began with biting out the heart of a living dove, I ignored the rest of the details.

"This Caleb guy," I said, "the one I told you about when we were coming home from Aunt Eileen's."

"The treasure hunter?"

"That's him, yes. I'm wondering if he's our Brother Belial, and he was looking to invoke some spirits that could help him find it."

"You could call your sister and ask if this fellow's tall and thin."

"Brilliant idea. I'll do that."

Kathleen, however, sank my hopes of a quick ID on the hooded man. Caleb Sumner was short and pudgy, she told me, and had a tenor voice.

"He pronounces some words kind of funny," Kathleen said. "I mean, he keeps dropping his R's like some New England people do, but beyond that. When he says light and night, it's sort of like loit and noit."

"When he's answering a question, does he say 'yeah yeah' instead of just 'yeah'?"

"Yeah, he does."

"I bet he's from Martha's Vineyard."

"The island? No wonder he's so good with boats, then. Jack says he really knows his stuff. Other than that, he's a total dork, if you ask me, not that anyone does." Hurt crept into her voice. "Jack won't hear a word against him."

That bit of information struck me as odd, because Jack

was normally suspicious of everyone who tried to befriend him. Like many rich people, he worried that these potential friends were trying to get into his bank account.

"Does Caleb come to the house a lot?" I said.

"Not a lot, not since Woofie Five bit him." Kathleen paused for a laugh. "Really hard on the ankle, which was all the poor little love could reach. He's the Yorkie mix."

And as nasty a canine critter as you could find, or at least, so I remembered him. In this case, however, I was prepared to cut Woofie Five some slack.

"Did Caleb do something to set him off?"

"No. It was just the bad vibe." Kathleen hesitated, thinking in her usual slow way. "Aunt Eileen told me that you're still going with that British guy. The one from InterCop or whatever it's called."

"Interpol, and his name's Ari Nathan. He's Israeli. He just sounds British. Actually, we're looking for an apartment together."

Kathleen squealed in honest delight. "Oh, that's great news!" she said once she'd finished squealing. "Congrats!"

"Well, it's not like we're engaged or anything."

"I could guess that, knowing you."

"What do you mean by that?"

"Just your fear of commitment. That's what Sean calls it, anyway."

"Well, he could be right about that."

"It's probably because we lost Dad."

"Oh, don't you get all psychological on me!"

Although she didn't laugh, I swear I could hear her smiling, it was that loud.

"Anyway." Kathleen paused again. "But, Ari, if he's a cop, he must know what criminals are like, right?"

"It comes with the job, yeah."

"I wonder if he could take a look at Caleb for me. You're coming to the party Sunday, aren't you?"

"Yeah, for sure. Will Caleb be there?"

"You bet. Jack insisted. Ari could tell me what he thinks of him."

"Better yet, Ari could look him up on a database if we

can get his fingerprints on a glass or something, which should be easy if you're serving finger food."

"I gotta say, Nola, you always have awfully useful boyfriends. I hope Ari's not the jealous type, though. Caleb's mentioned a couple of times that he wants to meet my sister, though maybe he was just joking around. Trying to flatter me, y'know."

An alarm went off like a foghorn in my mind. All I said was, "You get a lot of that, yeah. Are your sisters as beautiful as you?"

"Yeah, just like that." And to give her credit, she sounded honestly disgusted. "I get real sick of it."

"I bet. What time Sunday?"

"Around four or five. See ya then."

With that she clicked off. I told Ari the news.

"Odd all around," Ari said. "But then, anything to do with your family tends to be. I'll have a legitimate reason to ask for a match on this fellow's prints if we can get them. This Drake's treasure business—it sounds to me like some sort of confidence game."

"Getting Jack to put up cash, you mean, and then disappearing?"

"Precisely that. From everything you've told me," Ari went on, "your brother-in-law sounds frightened of him."

"Yeah, he does, and that's not like Jack at all."

"Which reminds me. I meant to ask you about this boat of his. I'm assuming it's not a commercial fishing craft."

"No, though it's big enough to go pretty far out to sea. It doesn't have sails, just an engine, but it's got a cabin and a galley. I don't know anything about boats, or I'd tell you what kind it is."

"Have you ever gone out on it?"

"Only when it's been docked down at Tiburon. Sometimes Kathleen throws parties on it. I get seasick too easily to want to go very far on the thing. Why?"

"No real reason. Just curious."

More warnings sounded in my brain. Thanks to his guns and his muscles, I tended to forget that Ari could be just as sly and sneaky as I could. He was probing for something, and Jack and his father had more than a few old secrets that

I didn't want found. Something must have shown on my face, because Ari smiled in a vague sort of way.

"Well," he said, "what's on the agenda for today? Apartment hunting?"

"For sure. The sooner we're out of this place, the better."

Besides the usual problems with finding an apartment in San Francisco, I had one particularly difficult requirement. Having Chaos masters out to kill me was one thing; putting innocent bystanders in their way, quite another. I wanted a unit over a business that would be closed and uninhabited at night, the most likely time for any attack.

That afternoon we had a real stroke of luck. Under a heavy gray sky that threatened rain, we were driving back and forth on various streets down in the Sunset district when I suddenly knew we should turn down 48th Avenue. Whether it was the forces of the Balance or the Collective Data Stream, I don't know, but the tip paid off.

Just a couple of blocks from Ocean Beach, we found a building that held two flats, both empty. Most of the houses on that block stood cheek by jowl in the standard Sunset district style, but this particular house stood between two wide driveways, both leading back to a graveled yard and a row of ramshackle garages. A "To Rent or Lease" sign displayed a handy realtor's phone number. When I called, the realtor was more than glad to meet us at the property.

While I looked over the inside of the building with the realtor, Ari prowled around the outside and sized up the neighboring apartment houses as well as the building itself. As I walked through the two flats, the realtor, a skinny dour sort in a gray suit and a pale green turban, kept peering out of various windows to keep track of him.

"May I ask what your partner is looking for?" Mr. Singh said eventually.

"I don't know," I said. "He's a cop. They're suspicious by nature, cops."

"I suppose this is so." Mr. Singh hesitated, then shrugged. The upstairs flat turned out to be a very typical San Francisco railroad flat, though a nice one with hardwood floors. It had a modern kitchen opening off the back door steps, which seemed solid when we climbed them. From the kitchen, a narrow hall led to a sizable bedroom and bathroom and eventually to a big living room with a squared-off bay window that let in afternoon sunlight. When I sampled the vibrations, I felt nothing but the usual lingering traces of domestic bickering and laughter, probably from a large family.

Downstairs, however, struck me as peculiar. From the upstairs flat, we went down the front stairs and out of the front door to a glassed-in porch and the door into the downstairs flat. It opened into an oddly shaped room with a closet that implied it had once been a bedroom, except that on the far side it opened directly into a tiny living room with the obligatory bay window. Beyond that, a hallway led down to a minuscule bathroom, a randomly assembled kitchen, and a huge proper bedroom with windows looking out to the graveled yard and the garages.

"This place is put together kind of weirdly," I said.

"Yes, I am afraid that is true." Mr. Singh paused to look out of a bedroom window at Ari, who had opened one of the garage doors and was peering inside. "What is he doing now?"

"I can only guess." I finally thought up a plausible reason for all the prowling. "But he's getting a new car this week."

"Ah." Mr. Singh smiled in relief. "Of course. He wishes to ensure it will be safe. With the lower flat, you would also gain access to the garage directly under the building, but the rain does run under that door. The outside garages are quite sound. The property management firm had our maintenance man look all the garages over."

"His name isn't George, is it?"

"No." His puzzled frown reappeared. "Why—"

"Just a thought. Sorry."

Mr. Singh led the way into the narrow beige kitchen— beige walls, stove, refrigerator, the works, all the same ugly yellowish tan. The paint and the counters looked brand-new, as did the stove. While Mr. Singh scowled out the window at Ari, who was taking pictures of the back of the house with his cell phone, I opened myself up to the vibrations. Immediately, I smelled gas and felt despair. I shut down fast.

"Someone killed themselves here, didn't they?" I said.

Singh winced, then forced out a weak smile. "You are very astute," he said. "I am afraid that this is true. A very sad case, a woman who had taken many drugs, or so the police told us."

"I see. That's why it's been standing empty so long."

"Yes, many people who rent here in the Sunset are arrived from China. They will not take a house where someone has recently died."

"I see. Well, that won't bother me, particularly. I'd only use this flat for business, if the zoning's okay with that, anyway. I'm moving into Internet marketing, and I'd like a separate office and storage space."

His dour mood lifted. "The zoning will be no problem. May I ask what you will be selling?"

"Souvenir objects from the Holy Land—Israel, that is." Although I was lying at the moment, it occurred to me that I'd found a good cover story. "Thanks to Ari, I have connections."

"Ah, of course. And then you would live in the upper flat?"

"Yes, and I assume nothing horrible happened there."

"Nothing, no, that I know of, and I have handled this property for many years. Perhaps if you rent the entire building, the owners can be persuaded to give good terms on the lease."

Although we made a formal commitment that afternoon, the owners, of course, wanted a credit check. On a handshake, Mr. Singh promised to call us as soon as he talked with them. We left him to lock up the building and returned to our car.

"Let's go straight to the old apartment," I said to Ari. "I want to do an LDRS on Evers. Something keeps nagging at my back brain."

But at the apartment we found Mr. Hansen the glazier there, busily glazing, while Mrs. Zukovski, swathed in her pink tracksuit, sat on my computer chair and watched him. He'd taken both side panes of glass out of the bay window as well as the remnants of the shattered main pane. A chilly wind blew through the living room.

"You might have told me that he was coming today," I said.

"I didn't know until he got here," Mrs. Z said. "He had a cancellation."

Hansen turned from the window and smiled. "Sorry. I got all the way down to the other job before they bothered to tell me I couldn't come in."

"Very rude of them," Mrs. Z said. "So I thought I'd just keep an eye on things."

Meaning, no doubt, that she'd been going through our stuff while Hansen worked. It was a good thing I'd put all the papers pertaining to the case into a locked drawer in my desk.

"Uh, I hope you're going to get that done before the rain hits," I said.

Hansen stuck his head out of the glass-free window and considered the cloudy sky. "Sure looks like it, don't it?" he said. "Sure been a wet year."

"It has, yeah," I said. "Everyone was worrying about drought, and it turns out that we've got water to burn."

Hansen laughed and nodded. "Yeah, we sure do. I'm glad of it, yeah, but it's sure caused a lot of trouble down the coast."

"Like Pacifica, you mean?"

"Yeah, that's it, all right. All them fancy buildings, red-tagged now." He paused to scratch his scalp with one dirty fingernail. "Well, I'll be getting the windows done in a couple of hours here."

Rather than sit around and freeze while Hansen finished, we left. Once we got outside, I paused on the sidewalk and considered my back brain. The nagging sensation had disappeared. "We could go sit in the car," Ari said. "You could do your LDRS there."

"Not necessary. I've missed my chance at whatever it was."

"That's too bad." Ari glanced at his watch. "It's four-thirty. Let's go have an early dinner."

We walked across the street to the Persian restaurant. Since they featured a salad bar, I'd gone in there a couple of times. Nice people ran it, the son and daughter of refugees from the fall of the Shah. That afternoon, in the slack time between lunch and dinner, a young skinny guy with a long blue apron covering his gray slacks and white shirt drifted over to take our order. I remembered him as a cousin of the owners.

His English, when he asked if we'd like something to drink, was not the best. Not a problem—Ari spoke to him in a language that sounded a little bit like Italian to my ignorant ears. The waiter grinned in relief and answered in the same. Needless to say, I let Ari order for both of us.

"Is that Farsi?" I said once the waiter had gone off to the kitchen.

"Yes," Ari said. "A dialect of it, anyway."

"How many languages do you know?"

"It depends on how you define a language." He looked away and frowned while he thought about it. "Five European ones, then Hebrew, of course, and Farsi. I can get by on the street with Dari, but I can't claim I know it. Then there's Arabic. It has a lot of dialects. Most speakers of one can't understand the others, but everyone who's been to school can understand the standard version. I know the standard and the Palestinian dialect well, and then I can get by with the Egyptian version."

I was impressed. I only know three languages, if you don't count Latin, which I don't, since there aren't a lot of people around who want to speak Latin back.

The waiter returned with rose-flavored sodas and a tray of appetizers, a more generous selection than I'd ever seen before. With the place so empty, he hovered at the table for a while, talking with Ari. Both of them laughed now and then—at jokes, I supposed. After he brought the main dishes, he lingered some more, and this time Ari began asking him questions in between bites, which the waiter answered at some length.

It dawned on me that the boy had no idea that he was talking with an Israeli, because as far as I could tell, Ari's accent was identical to his. I smiled and looked vacant in what I hoped was the proper public manner for the girlfriend of an Iranian guy. At the end of the meal, Ari paid in cash, not a credit card with his giveaway name on it. He left a good tip, too.

We walked outside just as the rain started. As we scurried across the street, dodging cars, I saw Hansen loading scrap glass into the back of his truck. Brand-new glass gleamed in the bay window of my apartment.

"All done," Hansen called out.

"Thanks!" I said and waved.

We managed to avoid Mrs. Z as we went upstairs. I'm sure that she needed to lie down and rest after writing the check for the windows. As soon as we got inside the apartment, Ari strode over to the new windows to examine the workmanship. I turned on the heat.

"What was all the conversation about?" I said. "In the restaurant, that is."

"I was asking him how Johnson got up to the roof," Ari said. "The night you were attacked, no one in the restaurant would tell the police anything. It made me wonder if they'd assisted him."

I experienced a retroactive frisson. "Uh, had they?"

"No, or at least, I doubt it. The waiter was too forthcoming. The Shah's Iran was a police state, and this new regime is no better. One gets used to acting ignorant around authorities. They saw Sanchez as a threat and told him nothing."

I was planning on running various Agency procedures that evening in the hopes of picking up traces of the coven members and through them, of the hooded man. I changed into work clothes, a pair of jeans, and a green top with a watercolor print and a deep V-neck. When I booted up my computer for a routine run on TranceWeb, I found nothing new in my inbox.

"I still haven't gotten that file on Reb Ezekiel," I said.

Ari muttered something in Hebrew, then took his cell phone out of his shirt pocket. "I'll see what I can do to speed things up," he said. "The sodding thing should have come through by now. I wonder if someone's intercepted it."

"Could be, but I'll bet the bureaucrats just haven't cleared it yet. It has to come to the Agency via the State Department and the two guys there who know we exist. I—"

His cell phone went off with a loud burst of sour Bach.

We both yelped. He clicked it on and wandered into the kitchen to answer the call in private, but he reappeared almost immediately.

"It's Sanchez," he said to me. "Evers apparently committed suicide this afternoon."

I murmured something unladylike. Ari alternated between listening to Sanchez and relaying the details.

"He drowned in the bay right by the Ferry Building . . . around four o'clock . . . jumped from one of the piers . . . witnesses . . . they said what?"

A long pause while I squirmed in curiosity. Four o'clock—just about the time when I should have been doing an LDRS on Evers. Thanks to Hansen, I'd missed the chance, not that I could have reached Evers to warn him. By the time we'd headed for the Persian restaurant, Evers must have been dead.

"That doesn't seem possible," Ari continued. "Yes, yes, I know you're not having a joke on me . . . a rogue wave? But he did jump . . . ah, then the wave came . . . heroin addiction, certainly but . . . yes, O'Grady's lot will be interested in this. Tomorrow? Very well . . . nine o'clock, then."

He clicked off the phone and returned it to his shirt pocket.

"We're going down to Sanchez's office?" I said.

"No, we're meeting him at the Ferry Building. Early, of course, while the chain of custody's intact."

"The what?"

"While the police are still in charge of the site, the tape up, officers there, and so on. Once they've left the scene, even for five minutes, any evidence anyone finds isn't valid in court. So since Sanchez wants to go over the site in daylight, they'll have to keep it sealed off all night."

"Good. I want to see where the murder happened."

"I take it you don't think this was suicide."

I walked over to the windows and stared out at the rain-dark sky. Off to the west, the clouds glowed silver and gold from the setting sun. For one brief moment, I could see in the swirling glare the horses and the chariot of the sun, rolling toward the horizon with Apollo at the reins. The Collective Data Stream tugged at my conscious mind.

"No," I said. "I think someone pushed him in, one way or another, and then the wave finished the job."

"A natural wave?"

"No, not there, with the water hemmed in by piers and breakwaters and ferries. It would take a howling winter storm to raise enough water to force someone under."

Ari slammed his right fist hard into the palm of his left hand. "I should have seen this coming," he said.

"So should I, and more likely me than you. In fact, since I didn't see it coming, I wonder if the murderer got the idea at the last minute, a totally unplanned impulse."

"True Chaos behavior, then?"

"It could be, yeah. Or panic."

I wished I could speak with the recently dead, the way that psychics do on TV, but that's fiction. I couldn't get Evers' side of the story. As much as I'd disliked him during our brief meeting, no way did he deserve to die, especially not by drowning a few yards from dry land.

CHAPTER 4

B ETWEEN THE TELEVISION NEWS AND THE IN-
TERNET, we got the public version of Evers' supposed suicide before we went to meet Sanchez. That night
I read aloud the newspaper account off my computer screen
while Ari flicked around the television channels, looking for
coverage.

Plenty of witnesses saw Evers walking along the Embarcadero, a troubled man from the look of him. One witness
said he seemed drunk, because his eyes were glazed, and he
staggered at moments. At the south end of the main Ferry
Building, he turned down the alley that runs between the
buildings toward the wharflike area that houses the Farm-
ers' Market on Saturdays. Before he walked out on the concrete jetty, he stopped for a moment and looked up at the
sky.

He started walking again, then broke into a run, stumbled and screamed, kept running across the market square.
At the wooden railing he hesitated again. One witness described him as looking like a baffled bull, turning this way
and that. Finally, he climbed the railing and plunged in before anyone could stop him.

He floated, flailing his arms, bobbing up and down, while
a good Samaritan on the jetty yelled at him to stay calm. It
took this would-be rescuer some seconds to strip off his
jacket and kick off his shoes, then climb the railing. He was
just about to dive in when the wave—a perfect arc of glassy

green water—rose up and swallowed Evers. The rescuer dove anyway, found Evers, and hauled him to the jetty, where other passersby helped pull both of them out.

"It's ridiculous!" Ari snapped. "Just one single wave, not a sign of any others, out of nowhere."

"Ridiculous, you bet. Also deadly."

"Here are more pictures." Ari gestured toward the TV with the remote. "Come watch."

He'd found my favorite TV news reporter, Vic Yee, interviewing the would-be good Samaritan, a young African-American man, still damp and shivering, who described himself as a strong swimmer. He'd once worked as a lifeguard at one of the local YMCAs.

"I've never seen anything like that in my life," the guy told Yee. "It looked like something out of the movies, you know, special effects."

"So this wave," Yee said, "broke and fell over the victim?"

"Yeah, just like a breaker on the beach. The weight of the water pushed him under and then the back current dragged him out toward the bay. So I jumped in and got him, but it was too late."

Yee turned and faced the camera. "The victim was pronounced dead on arrival at General Hospital. Police are withholding his name until they notify the next of kin."

Ari and I already knew the victim's name, of course. Ari clicked off the TV, then tossed the remote onto a pile of books on the coffee table.

"It's a good thing," Ari said, "that a lot of people witnessed this, or no one would believe it."

"You bet," I said. "But whoever murdered Evers gave his hand away with that wave. He must have been nearby and seen that Evers was about to be rescued. It strikes me as a desperate move."

"Let's hope someone noticed him, then. Or would he be noticeable? Waving his arms, muttering curses—that sort of thing. Well, assuming it was a he, not a she. We don't really know which."

"No, unfortunately. I'm pretty sure we can eliminate Satan as a suspect, however."

"Yes, and you're quite right: it does remind me of that girl who drowned at the beach."

"You bet. In this case, it sounds to me like our murderer had already ensorcelled Evers and told him what to do before he sent him on his run down the pier."

"What did he do to make the wave appear?"

I thought—hard—for a minute. "I'm only guessing, but I'd say he summoned more Qi and sent it flying at the surface of the water. If he hit the angle just right, it would scoop up a wave ahead of it. He'd have to move his hands a lot, yeah, but by then everyone would have been looking at Evers and the guy trying to save him."

"Summoned Qi?" Ari looked at me with a martyred droop of eyelids. "Very well, I'll take your word for it."

In the chilly morning, we headed out to inspect the murder site. We ended up parking under the Embarcadero Center complex that housed Evers' office, just a short walk from the Ferry Building itself, a huge gray edifice that stretches the length of a city block right next to the Bay. Until they finished the Bay Bridge, way back when, this building functioned as the transportation hub for the entire Bay Area. Now, while actual ferries still run to a few locations from the piers around it, it mostly houses restaurants and bars.

At the south end of the Ferry Building, we found chaos in full swing, the human kind, not the psychic version. Saturday was market day, but temporary metal barriers festooned with yellow police tape still barred the entrance to the walkway leading out to the market area. A line of uniformed police, truncheons out and threatening, stood in front of the barrier. Trucks loaded with fruit and vegetables had defiantly double-parked in every "No parking" zone available. Angry merchants stood on the street side of the barrier yelling at the cops. Pedestrians waving empty shopping bags milled around, confused and annoyed. TV trucks and men with cameras and sound equipment wandered through the melee.

When Ari showed his Interpol ID, a uniformed officer pulled the barrier aside just enough to let us pass. I glanced over at the huge window as we walked by the building's end wall and saw gawkers staring out in our direction. Since I can't throw wards through glass, I had no way of discovering if any were Chaos spies.

More uniformed officers wandered back and forth across the market square itself. I noticed that they were all staring at the ground as they walked. Bundled in a gray raincoat, Sanchez was pacing up and down near the wooden railing that edged the area. Beyond him stretched the Bay waters, dark green and flecked with white; choppy, certainly, but I saw nothing that could be described as a real rolling breaker. Still, open water lay right at hand for someone adept at handling Qi to fashion into a killer wave.

When Ari hailed him, Sanchez left the railing and hurried over to meet us. He was a tall man, with jet-black hair and thick eyebrows over dark eyes that glared at the world around him. He dispensed with any sort of hello.

"I've gone over your report," Sanchez said to Ari. "Evers sounds like a man on the edge to me."

"Edge of suicide, you mean?" Ari said. "I'm not sure I'd say he was that desperate, but then, he had a lot to lose if news of his addiction got out."

"And all that weirdo occult shit wouldn't have done his reputation any good." Sanchez frowned out at the Bay. "I don't mind telling you that he had important connections in local politics. I've been harassed over the phone a couple of times already."

"They want you to keep it quiet, huh?" I joined the conversation.

"Nailed down and shut up tight, yeah. They say it's because he was in the middle of handling a couple of very important divorces."

"I don't get that."

"Let me just say that the word blackmail's been thrown around." Sanchez paused for a small bitter smile. "People tell their divorce lawyer unpleasant stories about their spouses."

"So you haven't ruled out murder."

"You're quick on the uptake, O'Grady. Let's just leave it at that."

I had no intention of pressuring him, not yet anyway.

"Something else I don't get," I said instead. "Why seal off this area? What are your men looking for?"

"We don't know." Sanchez took off his rain hat and ran a weary hand through his hair before continuing. "Several witnesses swore they saw Evers reach into his pockets and throw a number of things onto the ground before he climbed the rail. No one saw them clearly, but one man thought he saw a plastic bag with white powder in it. If it was, I'm assuming it's smack. The powder, I mean, not what the witness said. We kept this area sealed off all night, so if it exists, it's still here."

"Have you found anything?" I said.

"A lot of trash. Used tissue, candy wrappers, that kind of crap. Who knows who threw it down? Oh, and one peacock feather. There must have been someone from Marin County here."

He laughed, I didn't. A devotee of the Peacock Angel had left a calling card. Murder, I thought, for sure.

"Anyway," Sanchez continued, "let me tell you what we know so far."

Because of those important connections, the powers that be had called in Sanchez immediately rather than leaving the investigation to lesser officers in Homicide. Normally, the police would have looked into a case of suicide only to dot all the i's and cross the t's on the report. Sanchez and his team had spent long hours the evening before, interviewing some eighteen witnesses who'd come forward to say they'd seen Evers on his last walk.

"Everyone," Sanchez said, "told us that he looked drunk or drugged. The autopsy report's not in yet, but I'm betting the blood tests show heroin in his system."

"Could be." I was betting against it. Ensorcellment leaves no traces that show up in laboratory tests, but I played along with Sanchez's theory because I wanted something out of him. "I wonder if the person who sold it to him was still close by."

"It's possible. Several witnesses saw the victim come out of the Ferry Building. He seemed to be accompanied by several other men. I say 'seemed' because there's so much foot traffic around here. We can't be sure that they were actual associates. They might have just been exiting at the same time."

"Yeah, for sure."

Sanchez took a small notebook from his inner jacket pocket and flipped it open. "One witness did see Evers stop to speak to a loiterer who'd been standing outside the building. Evers fumbled in his pocket and gave the man something. The witness thought it was money, because the man he spoke to looked like one of the homeless. The witness didn't see this person hand Evers anything in return, but I wonder."

"So do I," I said. "Dealers get very good at passing bags back and forth without anyone noticing."

Sanchez nodded and frowned at his notes. During this conversation, Ari had been standing nearby, listening, I'm sure, but also keeping a watch on the police officers searching the ground. Sanchez flipped a page in the notebook and smiled.

"Here it is," he said. "I've got an alert out for this homeless man as a person of interest. Even if he's not a dealer, he'll still have information we can use, assuming he's not too crazy to remember what happened." He cleared his throat and read aloud. "A white male about five foot eight, thin, maybe a hundred and twenty pounds, slightly stoop-shouldered. Long gray hair and beard, with long sideburns like an Orthodox rabbi—"

Ari spun around and walked over to stand just behind Sanchez.

"Probably brown eyes," Sanchez went on. "The witness wasn't close enough to tell eye color. The person of interest's face was wrinkled and tan, like he'd spent time in the desert, the witness said. He was wearing a pair of torn and faded black pants and a black suit jacket, also torn and stained in places."

"Any hat?" Ari said.

Sanchez flinched. Ari could move quietly when he wanted to, and the lieutenant hadn't noticed him come up.

"Yeah," Sanchez said, "a black Giants cap that looked brand-new."

"Huh," Ari said.

Sanchez looked at Ari and raised an eyebrow. Ari smiled and said nothing more. Sanchez turned to me.

"Do you want to interview Evers' secretary?" Sanchez said. "I'm going to his office."

"Will she be there on Saturday?" I said.

"Yeah, she offered to come in to meet me there."

"I do want," I said. "Thanks."

With Embarcadero Center so close, Ari and I headed off on foot, but Sanchez lingered to give instructions to the officers manning the barrier. Ten SWAT team members in riot gear had joined the line. We made our way through the mobs and crossed the street, which by then was totally blocked with farm trucks, Muni buses, pedestrians, and cars. Horns blared, drivers shouted. A distant streetcar clanged in rage.

As soon as we'd gotten far enough away to hear each other, I said, "Reb Ezekiel?"

"The description fits," Ari said. "Except for the choice of hat, but some kind soul might have given that to him. On the other hand, we could be dealing with coincidence. It's not an uncommon description."

"Not in Israel, maybe. What Sanchez called long sideburns aren't hot fashion items around here."

"That's a very good point. Let's hope the police can round this fellow up, and then we'll know."

In the Embarcadero Center, we rejoined Sanchez at the base of the elevator tower leading to Evers' office. During the ride up, I asked the lieutenant a few more questions and got some details about the men seen leaving the Ferry Building at the same time as Evers—all of them business types, all of them, it seemed, wearing gray or blue suits. One among them was indeed short and pudgy, and another was tall and rail-thin, but so were hundreds of thousands of men in the Bay Area.

At Evers' office, Miss Kowalski, dressed in a blue skirt suit and heels, was waiting outside the locked door, which the police had secured with tape the night before. While Sanchez showed her his police ID and made a few commiserating noises, I ran an SPP on her. Although she read as dazed, absolutely stunned at what had happened, and sorry for her former boss, most of her worry seemed to be directed toward finding a new job and an income. I couldn't blame her. Sanchez ripped the tape free of the door.

"You can open up now," Sanchez told her.

Kowalski nodded and took her keys out of her pocket. Once we were all inside, she sat down behind her desk in the front room.

"Mr. Evers' accountant will be in at two o'clock," she told Sanchez, "to look at financial matters, so if you need to speak with him—"

"I do," Sanchez said. "Was your boss in debt?"

"I don't know." She spoke carefully, choosing words. "He always paid me on time, and as far as I know, the rent here wasn't in arrears. But I got the impression that he was worried about his cash flow."

Heroin's not cheap, I thought to myself, especially the snortable Persian white.

"I'll come back to see the accountant, then." Sanchez glanced my way with a little nod to give me the okay to speak.

"When Evers left here," I asked, "was he meeting someone?"

"Yes," Kowalski said, "over at the Ferry Building. For a drink, he told me, but I don't know which bar exactly."

"Do you know whom he was meeting?"

"I don't, which is strange. Usually he told me who and whether or not I could interrupt him by phone if I needed to. I do know that the person was a man. Mr. Evers said something like 'I'm meeting him at four.'" She paused to hit a few keys, then swiveled the monitor around so we could all see it. "Here's his appointment list for yesterday. I can show you the entire year so far."

"Can you give me a printout of that?" Sanchez said. "A couple of copies would be good."

"Certainly, sir. He also received two calls on the landline here after he left for the day. I had the unit set to record. Do you want to hear those?"

"I sure do," Sanchez said. "If there's anything else you can tell me—"

"I will, and as soon as I think of it." She paused, her

mouth slack. "He was a good boss. He always treated me like a person, you know? Some bosses don't."

The phone calls told us nothing of interest. While Miss Kowalski was printing out Evers' appointments, the Homicide forensics team arrived. Sanchez handed me one copy of the printout, then made it clear that we could leave. Since the Forensic team was milling around, he followed us out into the quieter corridor.

"One last thing," I said to him. "Have you interviewed the two women that Evers named as members of his group?"

"I haven't had time." Sanchez hesitated briefly. "I suppose you still want to talk with them."

"Well, if it's possible. I don't want to poach on your territory, but it looks like you have your hands full here."

Ari started to butt in, but I silenced him with a scowl. I'd cultivated Sanchez for just this opportunity. I didn't want Ari's lack of manners to spoil it.

"Yeah, 'fraid so." Sanchez said. "Report back to me, will you?"

"Of course, and thanks! You know, I'm wondering if they should be kept under surveillance—for their own sakes, I mean. Do you think it's possible that the person Evers met for that drink threatened him somehow? Or frightened him so badly that he thought suicide was his only way out? If so, they might go after his associates next. Just a thought on my part, of course."

"A good thought, though. I'll detail a couple of men to keep an eye on those two ladies, yeah. Especially the one he called Sweetie." Sanchez suddenly grinned at Ari. "Not that I know how you got that information."

"Of course not," Ari said and grinned in return.

Sanchez went back into the office. We turned down the corridor. Standing by the elevator was a dark-haired young man in a pair of khakis, a white shirt, and a blue tie, an ordinary enough person to be in so large a complex, even on Saturday. He glanced at us, then away, in a perfectly casual manner. Unfortunately for the deception, though, a thin line of bluish light outlined his head and shoulders. I sketched a ward and threw. He grunted once like a wrestler slamming onto the mat, then disappeared in a fireball flash of azure.

"What?" Ari shook his head and blinked. "That light—"

"Was a Chaos illusion exploding," I said. "Did you see the guy standing there?"

"No. All I saw was a flash of light."

"Oh, yeah? There must have been a lot of power behind the critter for you to see anything at all. Tell you what. Let's take that other elevator back at the far end of the hall. I'm getting a strong SAWM."

"A semi-automatic . . ." Ari let his voice trail away

"Warning Mechanism, yeah. I'd just as soon not be in the same small enclosed space with whatever's causing it."

The location indicator over the elevator's bronze doors showed a car coming up to our floor. I never saw Ari draw the gun, but he was holding his Beretta, braced in both hands. He swirled around to aim at the elevator doors with the gun pointing to a spot at the height of a man's chest.

"Get back," he said. "Step back along the corridor."

I did. The car came to a stop. The doors slid open. I heard a faint burbling sound quickly stifled. The closest I could come to identifying it was the sound that an aerator makes in a fish tank. The elevator car looked empty, but my alarm was still going off.

"Do you see anything in there?" Ari said. "I don't."

"No," I said. "Let's not take chances anyway."

The doors slid shut, and the car began to descend, just as if an invisible hand had pressed the right buttons. Look, O'Grady, I told myself, it's more likely that a person on a lower floor just put in a call for the car. Oh, yeah? myself answered. Fat chance.

"Should we warn Sanchez?" Ari asked.

"It's not after him, whatever it is. Besides, would he believe us?"

"No." Ari holstered the Beretta. "Very good, then. Let's go."

As we walked down the long corridor to the other elevator, Ari kept his right hand hovering above the gun's approximate location. Every now and then, he turned and looked behind us. Maybe because of that, maybe not, we reached the other elevator safely and rode down to the underground garage without incident. I was real glad to drive out into the sunlight.

Since I was carrying my notebook in my shoulder bag, we had the phone numbers of the other two coven members with us. While I drove out California Street, Ari called the first woman on his cell phone and made arrangements to interview Mrs. Celia LaRosa. As always on the steep hills of San Francisco's downtown, the traffic moved so erratically, what with Muni buses and double-parked delivery trucks, that I had to concentrate to avoid being sideswiped. I missed about half of what Ari was saying, though I did hear him mention Inspector Sanchez before he ended the call.

"LaRosa sounds terrified," Ari said. "She told me to come straight over, because she and her husband are about to leave for France."

"A planned vacation?" I said.

"Not sodding likely. I can't say I blame her for wanting to leave town after what happened to Evers."

"Ah. That's why you warned her to notify the police. Think she will?"

"If she's smart. She didn't sound stupid."

The LaRosas lived on Washington Street, several blocks west of Divisadero, in a restored Victorian house, painted in tasteful greens and grays, and set back behind a luxury in the city: a few yards of lawn. The husband opened the door, a man of about sixty, skinny but not abnormally so, with a thick shock of gray-brown hair and a tidy mustache. He made sure to scrutinize both our IDs before he stepped back and let us come into the wood-paneled foyer.

"My wife's real upset," he informed us.

"I don't blame her, sir," I said. "Evers' suicide must have come as a real shock."

"It was, yeah. First Elaine, now this! I'm glad they sent a woman officer!"

Mrs. LaRosa received us in the living room directly off the hallway, a long narrow room that, judging from the still-visible seam about halfway along the pale cream ceiling, had been knocked together from two Victorian parlors.

Rose velvet overstuffed furniture sat around an Aubusson-style flowered rug. At the street end of the room was a bay window and at the other, set back in the pale blue wall, was a niche, tiled in dark green art nouveau tiles, that had originally held a gas heater. On the floor inside it stood a flower arrangement, yellow-and-white blooms around a central spray of red gladiolas.

The fashionably slender Mrs. LaRosa, wearing a pair of beige slacks and a pale blue blouse, perched on the edge of an armchair. Her champagne-colored hair in a perfect short coif and the location of her eyebrows, way too high on her forehead, made her seem older than she probably was. She should have waited a few more years for that first face-lift.

"Come in." Her voice shook on the words. "Do sit down."

Ari and I sat on the rose settee. Mr. LaRosa stood protectively behind his wife's chair. Ari took the notebook out of my bag, a pen out of his shirt pocket, and prepared to act like the assistant.

"I'm sorry to bother you at such a troubled time," I said.

Mrs. LaRosa forced out a smile and waved a feeble hand.

"I need to know when you first met William Evers," I went on. "And why you joined his occult study group."

"Damn nonsense," Mr. L muttered. Mrs. L ignored him.

"Evers handled my divorce," Mrs. LaRosa said. "This is my second marriage. As for the group, Elaine Politt was a good friend of mine. We belonged to the same bridge club. I joined because of her, not Evers."

"I see. Can you tell me anything about this Brother Belial?"

Mr. L snorted and coughed like a man hoping for an okay to interrupt.

"Very little," Mrs. L frowned and paused. "He was very tall and very thin, but he was always robed when we all came into the room, so I never caught a glimpse of his actual face. He always wore a stocking over his face, you see, like the bank robbers do, and then of course he had the hood of his robe pulled forward."

"Bank robber's about it," Mr. L put in. "I'm sorry, my dear, but you know what I thought of those people."

She winced and twined her fingers together. I figured that I knew, too, and that he'd been right. Aloud, I said, "Evers mentioned that there was something odd about Brother Belial's voice."

"Yes, it was very deep and very slow. You know, there were times when I wondered if he were a human being, he talked so oddly."

In the depths of my mind a little voice whispered, "Bingo!"

"I suppose that sounds silly," Mrs. L continued. "But you know, about his face, at times I wondered if he had one."

"Can you expand on that?" I said.

"Well, it was probably just the stocking he wore." She squirmed in her chair like a schoolgirl who's forgotten a crucial answer on a test.

"Your impressions could be valuable," I said. "No one will make fun of you."

"Thanks." She gave me a weak smile. "But you know, it never looked like he had features, facial features, I mean. His head seemed to be this smooth—" She gestured with her hands, a motion that defined a cylinder. "This smooth, well, thing under all the cloth."

"A mask, maybe?" I said.

"Or some sort of helmet." She looked away, then shuddered. "It made a very unpleasant impression."

Ari leaned forward and asked, "Did you know about the heroin traffic?"

"I did not!" Her nostrils flared, and her blue eyes opened wide. "I never would have stayed if I'd known that awful man was selling drugs."

"Which awful man?" Ari said.

"Well, both of them, really, Doyle and Johnson, but—" She paused again, and her hands began to shake even though she'd twined them together. "You're the officer who killed one of them, aren't you?"

"I'm afraid so," Ari said. "In the line of duty and all that."

"You deserve a medal," Mr. L put in. "In my opinion, anyway."

Mrs. LaRosa's facade cracked. Tears ran down her cheeks, tears gray with eyeliner that plowed little furrows into her foundation. LaRosa leaned over, put his hands on her shoulders, and rubbed them while he murmured a helpless "there, there, I'm sorry" over and over.

"I'm not upset over Johnson." Mrs. LaRosa choked out the words. "I keep thinking of Elaine, dying like that, and she loved him so much, Doyle, I mean, she really did, and he killed her."

She turned half away, then reached inside her shirt to pull a tissue out of her bra with delicate fingers. I waited until she'd gotten herself back under control.

"If there's anything else you can remember about Belial," I said, "when you're feeling less stressed, please call Lieutenant Sanchez. He'll see that I get the message."

"I'll do that, yes." Mrs. L forced out a smile. "I do want to know the truth about this. I feel so foolish, now, that I trusted them."

Agreeing with her would have been too rude, even though I wanted to. I stood up, and Ari followed. "We'll leave you alone now," I said. "Thank you for the information. And remember, if you think of anything to add, no matter how trivial it seems, please call homicide detective Sanchez down at the Police Department."

"We will," Mr. LaRosa said. "You can count on that. And they can always reach us by phone, even in Provence. I'll leave the numbers before we go."

We showed ourselves out. While we walked uphill to the spot where we'd parked, Ari stayed silent. Once we'd gotten into the car, he turned toward me.

"Do you think Belial was a human being?" he said.

"You're getting the hang of this, aren't you? At the moment, no, I don't. The question is: if not, then what?"

"I don't suppose there are actual demons involved in this case." He paused to buckle up his seat belt. "Um, is there such a thing? As demons, I mean."

"Well, it depends on how you define demon. What looks like a demon to some people might be a perfectly natural being in its own world. For all we know, Chaos masters live on some other world."

"You're having a joke on me, aren't you?"

"Unfortunately, no."

"Father was right." Ari rolled his eyes. "I should have been an insurance adjuster."

"You couldn't carry a gun everywhere if you were an insurance adjuster."

"I'll admit it; that was one of the things that influenced my decision. But these Chaos masters. I'm assuming they'll bleed if I have to shoot one."

"As far as I know, yeah. But then, I don't know much."

"How reassuring."

I smiled and started the car.

I've always hated the term "Chaos masters." It sounds like something from a golf tournament. For all we know, these "masters" don't exist as sapient beings. We may simply be personifying little vortices or knots of energy that strive to break up stagnant situations and other overloads of Order gone wild. The energy, however, is definitely real. It can form waterspouts and whirlpools of disruption that suck in the vulnerable and force them to do things that, left to themselves, they'd never even consider.

Like jumping into the bay fully clothed.

Still, in this particular case, we faced someone, human or not, who could pull a stocking over his face and put on a ritual robe. Whether he was a master or a minion—in fact, whether he was a "he" in any sense we'd recognize as a gender—were big questions.

We continued searching for answers that afternoon by interviewing the coven member called "Sweetie," or, in more ordinary terms, Caroline Burnside. She lived in the Cole Valley neighborhood on the uphill edge of the old Haight-Ashbury. As usual, parking there proved to be an aggravation and a half. Eventually, we found a spot of sorts. I could just squeeze the rental car between a monstrous black SUV and a pickup truck.

"By the way, I'll be getting the new car on Tuesday," Ari said. "I'm not sure if it'll be easier to handle or not."

"Am I going to be allowed to drive it?"

"Oh, yes. I made sure to ask."

We walked a couple of blocks to Burnside's address, a big white corner building housing a pair of flats above a laundromat. As we headed for the street door, I noticed an

obvious unmarked squad car, black and bulky, parked
nearby. A man in a sports jacket and open-throated white
shirt sat behind the wheel and read a newspaper. Ari
glanced his way.

"Sanchez's man, I assume," he said.

Since Ari stood between me and the car, I could throw
an unobtrusive Chaos ward. It bounced off the car door
with no effect. "Yeah," I said. "Must be."

When we rang the doorbell, Caroline Burnside buzzed
us in. A narrow flight of stairs, covered in ratty brown carpet, led up to the landing where she stood waiting. I'm not
sure what I expected Sweetie to be, but it wasn't the ama-
zon who greeted us. Dressed in a black tunic, caught with a
silver concho belt at the waist over a long black skirt, she
stood at least six feet tall, and was heavyset without being
fat, with broad shoulders and long legs. She had a shoulder-
length mop of curly blonde hair which she wore pulled back
from a square, strong-jawed face. Her voice, however, was
high and girlish, though I put her age at about forty.

"Hi," she said, "I'm Karo. That's what everyone calls me,
Karo like in the syrup."

Hence the nickname of Sweetie, I assumed. Ari and I
brought out our IDs, which she inspected with some care.

"Looks like you're real cops," she said. "Come in."

She ushered us into a room crammed with brightly colored stuff. It took me several minutes to sort out the sight—
piles of books on the floor, knickknacks and more books on
shelves and the mantel over the gas heater. Blue-and-
yellow paper lanterns, some with sun-and-moon faces, hung
from the ceiling. Patchwork pillows lay piled on the two
wicker chairs, on the floor in corners, and on the long cedar
chest that sat in the big bay window, which was partly covered by green-and-purple brocade swags of curtain. Karo
waved vaguely at the chairs.

"You can sit there, I guess," she said. "Just throw the pillows on to the floor if there's too many."

There were, and we did. Karo pulled over a huge red-
and-blue paisley floor pillow and sat on that.

"So," she said, "what do you want to ask me about?
Bill?"

"Evers, you mean?" I said. "How deeply addicted to heroin was he?"

Karo grimaced and looked at the floor. "Real bad," she said. "He kept fooling himself, saying he could handle it, because you snort Persian instead of shooting it, but he got to be a world-class junkie by the end."

"Do you think that's what prompted his suicide?"

She looked up and considered me. "I don't think he committed suicide." Her voice rang with defiance. "I think he was murdered. I just can't see how they did it."

"They?"

"Whoever it was." She shrugged. "I don't mean 'they' like in 'I know who it was and there were a couple of them.' Just they."

"Okay. What about this Brother Belial?"

"Bill told me he'd spilled the beans about that."

"He did, yeah. Celia LaRosa wonders if Brother B was really human."

"I heard her say that maybe a hundred times, but I didn't buy it. I think he was loaded, is all, and talked funny. And he always hid his face and wore gloves, so it was easy to make up stuff about him and what he must have looked like under all of it. Doyle always said Belial had a phobia about germs, but then, you couldn't trust a damn thing Doyle said, so who knows."

"I can see why everyone speculated about Belial."

"Elaine agreed with Celia, sort of. They used to like to scare themselves, giggling about demons." Her voice abruptly cracked. "God, poor Elaine! Last night I couldn't sleep, you know? I kept thinking, they got Elaine and now Bill, and what do you bet I'm next?"

I looked at Ari, who nodded a yes when I raised a questioning eyebrow.

"You've been given police protection," I said. "If you look out the window you'll see a plain black sedan—"

"The unmarked car, you mean?" Karo managed to smile. "They're always so obvious."

Ari winced.

"I thought they suspected me of something, like the drugs," Karo went on. "But I guess not."

"You know," I went on, "you can ask to be put in the witness protection program if you receive any sort of threat or see any signs of threats. If you feel you're being followed when you go out, for example."

"You think Bill was murdered, too, don't you?"

"Yeah." I saw no reason to lie. "But it's only a secondary theory at the moment in official circles. I'm not a member of the San Francisco police force."

"I noticed that from your ID, yeah." She turned slightly to look up at Ari. "Interpol, huh? There must be something real big behind all this, then."

"Heroin trafficking is always big," Ari said. "Especially high-grade heroin sold to middle-class customers."

"Oh. Yeah, I guess it would be. I wish Bill had never touched the shitty stuff." Karo paused to rub her face with both hands. "We used to fight about it, but Doyle—God, that creep Doyle, and what he did to Elaine! They said on the news that Johnson shot him. The one decent thing that super creep ever did in his life."

For a moment I thought she was going to cry, but she swallowed a couple of times and looked at me dry-eyed. "I bet you're wondering how I met Bill. It was through Elaine. I'm a tarot reader, and I did the cards for her a lot when she was getting her divorce, and so she invited me to the meetings." She paused for a twisted little smile. "Elaine kind of collected unusual people. But she was nice about it. It wasn't condescending. I think she was mostly real bored. Too much money, and everything was too easy for her."

"Do you know how she met Doyle?"

"In a singles bar on Union Street. She was real flattered that he was interested, because he was so much younger than her."

Nothing occult or unusual there. I realized I'd been hoping for some weird detail that would give us a new line of inquiry.

"Was there ever someone named Caleb associated with the coven?" I said.

"I never heard about any Caleb." Karo caught her upper lip between her teeth, thought, and let the lip go again. "No, sorry. It's a name I'd have remembered. You don't hear it much."

"All right. Anyone else?"

Karo looked away and thought some more. Finally, she shrugged and looked back at me. "Doyle did mention one other guy, but only in a real vague way. Something about the man who spoke to the Peacock Angel. You know about Tawsi Melek, right? It was on the TV news about the Silver Bullet Killer."

"Yes, we do know about the cult. Do you think it's satanic?"

"No. I wouldn't have had anything to do with that. It's stupid, Satanism."

"I was wondering if you'd ever heard anything about sacrificing children to this Tawsi Melek."

Karo's expression changed to authentic revulsion, wide-eyed and lip-curling. "No," she said. "I wouldn't have stuck around if they'd talked about that." She shuddered, then went on. "No, this angel was supposed to be God's right-hand man. Someone on the side of the Good and the Lovely, anyway. Doyle said there was someone who spoke to him and looked for converts. A missionary, kind of like those Mormons who show up at your door and won't go away."

I wondered if this missionary lived in our world or on Interchange, where Doyle came from. I suspected the latter. "Did he ever mention a name?"

"No. Sorry. But if you're looking for a suspect, I'd put my money on Brother Belial. He was the guy in charge."

"I'll take that under advisement."

I considered asking her about Evers and blackmail, then decided to leave that to Sanchez. I stood up, and Ari followed my lead.

"Thanks for your cooperation," I said to Karo. "If you think you've spotted trouble, call the police. Lieutenant Sanchez of Homicide is the name you want to invoke."

Karo laughed and scrambled to her feet. "Invoke," she said. "I like that. I'll keep it in mind. Don't worry."

As we were going down the stairs, I realized that of the

three coven members we'd interviewed, only Evers had recognized me from the ceremony I'd spied upon. He must have possessed a certain amount of psychic talent. Most likely, that very talent had made him vulnerable to whatever ensorcellment had driven him to his death.

A fourth coven member had survived, of course: Brother Belial. I could only hope that he, whatever he might have been, would fail to recognize me, too.

Chapter 5

WHEN WE RETURNED TO THE APARTMENT, Ari called Sanchez to tell him what we'd learned from the coven members. LaRosa had impressed both of us as an investigative dead end, but Karo interested me. Since people tell their tarot readers the damnedest things, she had plenty of chances to supplement her income by blackmailing her clients, some of whom she shared with Evers. On the other hand, I'd received a strong sense of honesty from her. Beyond the SPP, even, I couldn't see a criminal type living in a toy box like her apartment.

Sanchez would either hand this information over to the correct department or suppress it, depending on how much pressure the local powers that be put on him. Not my problem, either way, though Ari reported on the situation to Interpol, just in case there were "ramifications," as he called them.

"A great many people have been pressured into spying for one government or another," he said, "by blackmail."

"So you'll report it to your deep cover agency, too?"

He glared at me for a moment, then took his laptop into the kitchen to work in private.

I looked over the printout of Evers' appointments that Miss Kowalski had made for us. The first thing I noticed was that Evers' schedule began to clear out toward the end of February. New clients became scarce on the ground at that point. Perhaps, I speculated, his drug addiction had begun

to affect his work. The column for the day of his murder
contained only one entry, "unnamed man, 4 PM, Ferry
Building."

I went into the kitchen and gave the printout to Ari.

"See if you know any of these names," I said, "though I
don't suppose you will. I've put a red check by the names of
two municipal big shots."

"Thank you." Ari glanced at the printout and pointed to
the checked names. "Are these the men who are putting
pressure on Sanchez?"

"That would be my guess, yeah."

I returned to my computer. When I logged onto Trance-
Web, I found the file on Reb Ezekiel waiting for me. The
secret State Department office had finally connected with
the Agency and passed the information across, almost a
hundred and thirty pages of it. In a few places the text
jumped, as if something had been snipped out for security's
sake. The translator had also removed almost all the per-
sonal names and replaced them with a line of hyphens. At
first it referred to Reb Ezekiel, for instance, as J— W—.

Young JW's early career looked ordinary enough. He'd
been born into a Modern Orthodox family in Bradford in
the north of England, done brilliantly in the local primary
schools, then gone to a prestigious yeshiva for the rest of his
education, where he'd received his semikhah, his authority
to teach and advise about the laws, from the line of righ-
teous rabbis in his institution. He then spent two years in
the U.K. searching for a congregation to hire him. None
had, for reasons of "mental instability," or so the report put
it.

After this disappointment, JW emigrated to Israel,
where he hooked up with a group extreme even for the local extremists. He began to "seek wisdom in the desert," as
he called it, fasting for long periods and wandering around
like a wild man in the wastelands, some of which belonged
to Jordan. The authorities first took notice of him then.

He saw visions. He heard voices. He believed them all
uncritically, as rank amateurs always do. He also claimed to
have learned "spiritual practices" from these visions and
voices that enabled him to work "wonders." The climax

came when the ancient prophet Ezekiel came to him in vision and claimed him as his legitimate successor. From then on, the official report referred to him as Reb Ezekiel.

He wrote these experiences up into a couple of lurid books, which sold very well on the occult market. They brought him money and a small group of followers. On this basis, he returned to the U.K. and began to teach and recruit. When he had enough money, he led his by-then much larger group of followers back to Israel, Ari's parents among them, where they founded their kibbutz.

My poor Ari had spent his childhood in the midst of everything that followed. I felt I understood him a lot better after reading about the place where he'd lived his formative years.

Page after page of the report detailed the years that followed. Disenchanted followers had told the investigators plenty, not that the report gave their names. Many of the quotes reeked of bitterness, even in translation. I skimmed most of it that evening just to get a first impression. Later, I'd go over it in detail. The final pages, however, struck me as more important than the compilers of the report could know.

The defection of a woman called S— N——, and the details pointed to Ari's mother, had sparked something of a rebellion in the kibbutz. Reb Ezekiel had settled things down, then gone back out to the desert to fast and pray for new visions. He'd returned to the Negev Desert, which is when the government began to follow his movements in earnest. I hadn't realized just how many military bases, all of them restricted areas, lay in or near that stretch of terrain. A great many higher-ups wanted to know why this ex-Brit had taken to prowling around them.

Reb Zeke was gone about a month before he returned to his kibbutz. He staggered into the dining hall one night, half-starved, dehydrated, and incoherent. Sunstroke, perhaps concussion—for weeks afterward he'd acted confused, as if he'd forgotten the names of the people in the kibbutz as well as the details of its financial operation.

In time, everything came back to him, but his behavior changed in subtle, less than holy ways during the next couple of years. The report detailed each bout of secret drinking, each trip into Tel Aviv where he consorted with unclean women, i.e. the whores in the brothel where he'd eventually died. At first, the faithful put the disappearances down to the sunstroke or concussion incident; his place of death, however, made the hookers difficult to explain away.

I put the report through a second encryption, saved it, and cleared the screen, then stood up to stretch my back. When I glanced into the kitchen, I saw that Ari had attached a different keyboard to his laptop and was busily typing away. I started to sit back down, but I realized, thanks to a sudden line of cold running down my spine, that I was being watched. I spun around and saw a Chaos critter standing on the coffee table, a green-gray thing somewhat like a possum, except it had spiky scales instead of fur. As soon as I raised a hand to sketch out a ward, it disappeared.

"Good thing we're moving," I muttered. I was getting real tired of spies popping up everywhere.

I logged off TranceWeb, then walked into the kitchen. The screen on Ari's laptop displayed what looked like Arabic letters to me, though I couldn't be sure. Ari leaned back in his chair and smiled at me.

"Tell me about Armageddon," I said, "from an Orthodox Jewish point of view, I mean. The report mentions that Ezekiel believed it was coming, but it doesn't go into detail. I got the Christian version in school, but I don't know the Jewish one."

Ari's smile vanished. "Reb Ezekiel's version had very little to do with anything any other Jew believes. Alien invaders, mostly. In spaceships."

"You're the one having the joke now."

"I am not. I wish I were. I was only eight years old at the time, of course, when we were first told about this in the kibbutz school, so I probably heard only a simplified version. But alien invaders were going to appear in Megiddo, and we were going to repel them."

"Is Megiddo where the kibbutz was?"

"No. There's a proper kibbutz there already, and they wanted no part of Reb Ezekiel's revelations. It's an important archaeological site as well. The various academics involved weren't keen on having target practice going on near the antiquities. So he had to find land elsewhere."

I sat down in the chair opposite him.

"Oh, boy," I said. "And here I thought my hometown had a monopoly on that kind of thing."

"Belief in aliens, you mean?"

"Yeah, exactly. There are a lot of people who believe that the flying saucers are coming, not just in San Francisco, but the whole Bay Area, and down south in Santa Cruz, and then there's the Mount Shasta group, and—"

"That's enough, thank you." Ari paused for a look of profound gloom. "I take your point."

"Okay. According to the file your agency sent me, Ezekiel wandered off into the desert for about a month. You would have been about nine, I think. It was after your mother left. Do you remember him going off?"

"The incident when he had his stroke?"

"That's the one. The report calls it sunstroke or concussion."

"It was worse than that. Ezekiel was so muddled that at times he could barely remember where he was. He refused to get proper medical treatment." Ari thought for a few moments. "I remember the uproar, but not why he wouldn't let the doctors examine him. I probably wasn't told, actually. The adults did their best to keep things from the children."

"Too bad. Do you know if Zeke had any new visions during that missing month? The report doesn't detail any, but then, whoever's writing it tends toward scorn when it comes to psychic details. He thinks all the phenomena are just lies and scams."

"Do you think Ezekiel had genuine abilities?"

"Yeah, I do. A lot of the details ring true."

"That's a shock." Ari hesitated, then shrugged. "Well, you're the one who'd know. He was always having visions. I shouldn't be surprised if he'd had a sodding flock of them during the time he was gone." Ari paused to glare out at nothing in particular. "I wonder if his doppelgänger is as mad as he was?"

"Uh, I have a new theory about that. Brace yourself."

Ari's eyes narrowed. I decided that he was sufficiently braced.

"If Reb Ezekiel's in the city," I said, "it's not his doppelgänger. It's him."

"What?" Ari slammed one hand down on the table so hard that his laptop screen flipped down onto the keyboard. The machine beeped. He winced and began rubbing the slammed hand with the other. "Sorry. Shouldn't have done that. Nothing broken, I should think."

"Oh, good!" One of these days, I decided, I'd have to talk with him about that temper. "Look, he disappears for a month, and when he comes back, he doesn't remember half of his loyal followers. He doesn't know what bank the money's in, or when the crops were planted—none of the really important stuff. And then we have the personality change. The report makes it clear that while Zeke was a nutcase, he was a sincere nutcase. All he thought about was religion, his spiritual powers, and Armageddon. So he suddenly takes to drinking and screwing whores?"

Ari's eyes had gone very wide, and his mouth, a little slack. I figured he was following my line of reasoning.

"And then there's the clincher," I continued. "You told me that one of the things he claimed to be able to do was 'shorten the journey.' Right?"

"Right." His voice dropped nearly to a whisper. "Kefitzat haderach. So, what do we have?" His voice returned to normal. "He goes through one of the gates, and his doppelgänger comes back out?"

"That's the line I'm working on."

"So the doppelgänger's the one who died in the whorehouse." Ari nodded as if agreeing with himself. "And now for some reason the real Reb Ezekiel—well, they're both real, aren't they? I should say, the Reb Ezekiel I knew and loathed comes back out of wherever he's been. Let's see. I was eleven when the other one died. I'm thirty now. Took him long enough to return, I must say. Why, I wonder?"

"Why or how, I do not know." I smiled. "Yet. I'm hoping the police can find him. If not, maybe I can. I'd like to meet this Stein guy. Possible?"

"Very. I have his contact information with me. Hang on

a minute." Ari took his cell phone out of his shirt pocket. "I'll just ring him and see what he says."

Stein answered his phone immediately. Ari said something in Hebrew, then grinned. I could just hear a man's voice answering in the same language. He sounded on the edge of laughter, glad to hear from an old friend. After a few exchanges, though, they switched to English. At that point I did my best to stop eavesdropping. They kept the phone call short, anyway, and arranged for the three of us to get together for dinner that evening.

"A question," Ari said after he'd clicked off. "Do you think Reb Ezekiel is part of the coven?"

"No, but I don't think he isn't, either. I need to know why he's turned up. It might have something to do with you and Itzak Stein being in the same town. There's a weird karmic gravity that operates on these things, or you could call it a critical mass. You two might be attracting him, but that's only a metaphor. Don't take it literally."

Ari's eyes went glazed, as they so often did when I was trying to explain the psychic truths of the universe.

"There are other possibilities, too." I stopped trying. "His appearance could be a random coincidence, or it could be a true synchronicity, or he could be involved with our Brother Belial. I need to know which."

"Very well. That makes sense, as much as any of this ever does."

For our meeting, I wore a black dinner suit of satin-backed crepe and a teal silk blouse, accented with the pin Ari had given me. Itzak Stein had made reservations at a Cajun place on upper Fillmore Street, because it had private booths left over from the 1930s, with real mahogany walls that ran up nearly to the ceiling and a narrow doorway opening out to the main dining room of the restaurant. As long as we talked in a quiet tone of voice, no one was going to overhear us.

Just in case, though, Ari took a little black box that looked like a light meter out of an inner pocket of his sport coat. He passed it along the walls to check for bugs while Stein laughed at him. He was about Ari's age, Itzak, a stocky fellow with curly brown hair and brown eyes behind wire-rimmed glasses, not unattractive and not good-looking, either, except when he smiled. He had a great smile.

"Some things never change," Itzak said to me. "Good old Ari, as suspicious as always!" He grinned at Ari, who sat down with his back firmly to the booth's back wall, opposite the door. "I'm not surprised you ended up a cop." Itzak glanced at me. "Did you know that Ari was an M.P. in the army?"

"Military police?" I said. "No, but I'm not surprised."

"I wasn't, either," Itzak grinned, then looked Ari's way. "Interpol and you, a marriage made in heaven."

Ari forced out a small smile that signaled he was used to this line of teasing. "And I'm not surprised you ended up working with computers," Ari said. "You were always divorced from reality."

"One up to you! I'm afraid I am. I like life better that way. Reality generally sucks."

The waiter appeared, and Itzak ordered an amazing number of oysters for the table's appetizers.

"I see you're not keeping kosher," Ari remarked.

"Are you?" Itzak said. "Huh, that'd be a cold day in hell."

They shared a grin. Itzak ordered a cocktail for himself, though Ari stuck with mineral water, as did I. I half-expected Itzak to tease Ari about it, but he seemed resigned. We all studied the menu in silence. I finally found a dish I could eat if I dumped the potatoes onto Ari's plate and scraped the fancy sauce off the chicken.

"The desserts here are really good," Itzak said to me.

"I'll have a bite of Ari's," I said, "when the time comes."

"What's this? He's starving you? How cheap is he?"

Ari opened his mouth to object, but the waiter reappeared. We ordered. I waited till he'd left again to open the subject that really interested me.

"Tell us more about your sighting of Reb Ezekiel," I said. "What made you call the consulate and report it?"

"My parents." Itzak paused for a smile. "I called them first thing, and Dad insisted I should tell someone official. So I called the consulate to see if they could find Ari for me. We'd lost touch over the last couple of years, but he was the absolutely only person I could think of who might be 'official' and interested, too."

"So," I said, "you knew he works for Interpol?"

"Oh, yeah, we send e-mail now and then." Itzak grinned at Ari. "I don't know why you periodically drop off the face of the earth."

"Simple laziness," Ari said. "I apologize."

"Anyway," Itzak went on. "I told the receptionist she could contact him through Interpol, but she didn't seem to get anything I said. Especially she did not know why I thought this data point was important. So I hung up, but lo! a higher-up called me back about ten minutes later. He understood, all right, and told me he'd get the information into the right hands."

"I know who that was, yes," Ari put in. "Good move."

Oysters appeared, and the drinks. The waiter retreated once again. I ignored the oysters, raw and slimy as they were, but the two men scarfed them right up.

"So, anyway," Itzak continued, "another reason I chose this place. I first saw the old bastard not far from here, down at Fillmore and Geary. He was panhandling, it looked like. At first, I didn't believe it could possibly be him. So by the time I decided to talk to him, the bus had arrived, and he got on it and sped off."

"Heading which way?" I said.

"In." Itzak glanced at Ari. "That means, toward downtown, where there are social services abounding."

I made a mental note to ask Father Keith if someone answering Zeke's description had ever shown up at St. Anthony's Dining Room, the Franciscan mission to the homeless. "Can you give us a description?" I asked. "I want to see if it matches up with something a police officer told me."

"Sure. About five eight, skinny, shaggy gray hair, and long peyes." He glanced my way. "Peyes are what the unenlightened call 'sidelocks.' "

"Ah," I said. "I didn't know that."

"Mr. Secular here won't have told you, probably." Itzak grinned at me. "But back to the rebbe, he was wearing torn-up black clothing, except for a Giants cap that looked new—"

"That's plenty. Thanks."

Itzak paused to devour the last oyster, then continued

his story. He'd seen Reb Zeke twice more downtown, once
near the bank offices where he worked.

"I hailed him that last time," Itzak finished up. "He
screamed and ran, nearly dashed into traffic to get away. I
don't know why. I can't see how he could have recognized
me. The last time he saw me I was maybe ten years old."

"It's more likely he ran because he didn't recognize
you," Ari said, "than because he did."

"Yeah, I bet you're right." Itzak looked my way. "So
you're interested in all this, too? Don't tell me you're another cop!"

I rummaged in my bag and brought out my cross-agency
government ID. Itzak groaned as he handed it back.

"I should have known," he said. "Obviously, you guys
were meant for each other. Although, with a name like Nola
O'Grady, you can't be Jewish."

"Nope," I said. "I think he forgives me, though."

"A thousand times over," Ari said. "Other than that one
major flaw, she's perfect."

Itzak and I laughed, Ari smiled, but I kicked Ari under
the table, though not hard. He kept smiling as if he'd felt
nothing. The waiter trotted in with the main courses, and a
busboy materialized as well with a pitcher of ice water.
While the men ate and I nibbled, I asked the occasional
question. Since Itzak and his parents had a decently close
relationship, he'd heard bits and pieces of information
about life in the kibbutz as the adults had seen it.

"May I ask you where they live now?" I said. "I'd like to
debrief them."

"In upstate New York. But they're talking about coming
out for a visit sometime this summer. If you're still interested, they'd probably be willing to sit down and talk."

"They don't mind unburdening themselves, then."

"No, probably because they left early on, before Fearless
Leader's great disappearance. Do you know about that?"

"Zeke's month in the country?" I said.

He laughed. "Yeah, just that. When Ari's mother left, it
hit everyone hard. She was one of the inner circle, after all,
privy to the old boy's secrets and all that."

Ari looked up from his blackened catfish. "She was?"

"You didn't know?" I said.

"She never talks about those years, not to me anyway." Ari paused for a swallow of water. "Except she did apologize to me once, for staying so long and subjecting me to the place. I told her she needn't apologize. I understood how much it meant to her. She couldn't have foreseen how it would all turn out."

Ari's mother began to sound like someone I should know.

"Makes sense," Itzak said. "My folks call their stint on the kibbutz their romance with Israel, the whole idea of Israel." He looked my way. "A lot of American Jews go through that."

"I take it you don't share the feeling," I said.

"No." Itzak considered for a moment. "I'm a typical Reform guy, go to temple on the big holidays and when I feel I need to remember what I am."

"I have Catholic relatives who do the same with church," I said.

He grinned at me. "Yeah, I bet."

"You belong to a congregation?" Ari said to him. "I'm surprised. I can't stand the thought of going to temple after all of Reb Ezekiel's claptrap."

"It was claptrap, yeah. Not Judaism, Ari, but bullshit. That's why I can't reject the ceremonies and the observances wholesale. He was a raving lunatic, and what he taught us had nothing to do with the Torah."

"Well, there you have a point. Maybe two."

"What I'm wondering," I said, "is why you both hate Reb Zeke so much. Still, I mean, after all these years. Did he beat you or something?"

"No way!" Itzak said. "Our mothers would never have put up with that."

"I don't know if I'd say I hate him," Ari said. "But he disrupted my parents' lives and mine." He nodded at Itzak. "It was even worse for you."

"'Fraid so," Itzak said. "I was just old enough to be aware we were moving when my folks sold up everything and moved to Israel. When we came back, they were broke and depressed. It took them a couple of years to get back on their feet. That's probably what I can't forgive the rebbe for—the disruption, like Ari called it."

I nodded. I could understand that.

"It wasn't so bad, really, when we were all believers," Itzak continued. "I liked learning to shoot, and Ari here was incredible at it. A natural sure shot, I think the term is."

"Oh, yeah," I said. "I've seen him in action."

I felt cold, remembering. Ari raised an eyebrow in my direction. I managed to smile, but I laid down my fork.

"Too spicy for you?" Itzak said with a nod at my plate.

"Oh, no," I said. "I'm just not very hungry. But go on, this is fascinating, hearing about your lives."

"The work wasn't bad, either, for the children," Ari said. "Tzaki and I took care of the goats."

"Let me guess," I said. "Tzaki's the nickname for Itzak."

"Right," Ari said. "I'm regressing, I suppose. But they're surprisingly intelligent, goats. I got to be rather fond of them."

"So I've heard," I said. "It's funny, but I've never thought of you as a farm boy before."

"Only for those first few years." Ari suddenly smiled. "Tzaki, do you know what I remember as the best part of the day?"

"Let me guess," Itzak said. "Blowing away targets with six different kinds of rifle?"

"No, not that! The showers at the end of the day." Ari turned to me. "After school, you'd do your chores and have your weapons practice and all that, and it was hot. It was a good kind of heat, Nola, a dry heat, but still, you'd be sweaty and covered with dust, a layer of mud, really."

"Right!" Itzak broke in. "And then you had a shower, cool water just pouring down."

For a few minutes they ate in silence, as if in tribute to the glory of being clean at the end of a hard day. I found myself remembering how Kathleen and I used to whine about having to clear the table and load the dishwasher after my mother and Maureen had cooked the dinner. Little did we know how good we had it!

"But anyway," I said, "something must have left scars."

"It was what happened after," Itzak said, "once we returned to normal life, or that's how I think of it, anyway, normal American life in my case, normal Israeli life in Ari's. The other kids thought we were weird, and you know how kids treat someone they think is weird. We learned real fast to keep our mouths shut about where we'd been."

"Not fast enough in my case," Ari said. "I ended up expelled from the first school my father put me in."

"For what?" I said.

"Fighting."

"So, what else would it be for Ari?" Itzak said. "I was too much of a coward to hit first. I only hit in self-defense, and so the teachers cut me some slack."

The waiters returned and began to clear. Itzak ordered dessert for all of us, including a bourbon-laced pudding that looked as if it contained two days' worth of calories. The men dug in. I had a bite of each kind and left the rest to them.

"So, anyway," Itzak said after some minutes. "It took me a long time to come to terms with my charming childhood years."

"I can see why," I said.

"And coming to terms with the formalities of Judaism was part of that." Itzak glanced at Ari. "I take it you never have."

Ari shrugged and looked sour.

"But, you see," Itzak waved a fork at him, "you don't have my problem, because you're Israeli. You can be as secular as all hell, and it doesn't matter. I'm an American first and a Jew second, and sometimes the Jewish part threatens to fade away. Temple's important to me."

Ari said nothing, but he nodded, thinking it over.

"You're a hard-core sabra," Itzak went on. "Or more than that, even. You were raised to die for Israel."

"True," Ari said. "And someday I will, I suppose."

The blood in my body threatened to freeze. No, I wanted to scream. No way, not if I can help it, no, no, and no. My reaction shocked me so badly that I tried to keep it to myself, but since Itzak looked stricken, he must have noticed. He fumbled around and made a weak joke, while Ari calmly went on eating pecan pie. Itzak came up with a better joke, and I managed to laugh, which changed the mood back to pleasant for the remainder of the meal.

We drove back home through traffic sparse enough to let me mull over the things Stein had told us. That Reb Zeke had kept an inner circle intrigued me. This talk of secret knowledge opened a line of investigation that I wanted to pursue. When we stopped for a red light, I glanced Ari's way.

"One thing that really interested me," I said, "is the news that your mother ranked high in the organization. I'd love to find out if she knew things Reb Zeke kept from the others. Your agency's report mentioned that she lives in London. Do you think I could videoconference with her?"

Ari couldn't have looked more horrified if he'd found Cthulhu floating in our bathtub.

"You don't want me to talk with your mother," I said.

"Nothing of the sort." He paused to compose himself. "But she's already been interviewed, several times, in fact, for the report you have."

The light changed, and I let the matter drop. The Agency had other operatives in London. They could get the information I wanted more easily than I could pry it out of Ari.

When we went to bed, Ari fell asleep right away, but I lay awake for a long time, listening to the voices of the night. They only come to me sometimes, these voices, the muffled sounds of people talking in a distant room. I've heard them ever since I was a teenager, though at first I thought they meant that I was crazy or going that way. Eventually, I learned to stop worrying and start listening. Sometimes I hear music, too, but not like those songs that play inside your head, earworms some people call them. No, this music I hear outside my head, as it were, though it plays softly, and the songs have muddled words.

Once I realized what being an O'Grady means, I saw that the voices and the music were usually instances of the IOI procedure, images that objectify the odd bits of insight and intuitions that every person collects throughout a day, though few know they're doing it. Every now and then, though, the voices replay memories. A couple of times, I've heard my parents fighting in that mysterious other room.

Despite what my mother wanted everyone to believe, their marriage was no paradise.

That night, something different came along. The voices spoke to me about buried treasure, Spanish gold and Inca silver, and emeralds the size of robins' eggs, torn out of the earth but buried there again, somewhere close, somewhere just out of human reach. I heard waves washing up on sandy beaches or muttering on graveled ones. The waves were searching for treasure, too, but not eagerly, unlike all the human beings who'd dreamed of treasure for centuries. Uncover it and be rid of it, they seemed to say.

The voices formed into a single voice. I began to hear a man speaking. Another psychic, I realized suddenly, was thinking about treasure, obsessing about that Spanish gold, the emeralds as green as the depths of the sea. Caleb? The name formed in my mind before I could block my thought. The voice abruptly stopped. I picked up a trace of fear, then nothing from that source.

I got out of bed without waking Ari and padded naked and barefoot into the living room. The curtains over the bay window turned a faint lavender, then dark again, then lavender, as the sign from the Persian restaurant across the street blinked on and off. I switched on the desk lamp by my computer, found a pad of sticky notes, and scribbled a few words about Caleb. I had no worries about forgetting what I'd just experienced; I merely wanted to ground it so I could go to sleep.

When I turned off the light, I stood by the desk for a moment to listen to the inner world. The treasure hunter had definitely signed off, but someone else, or some thing—I felt a distant mind, but not a human mind, unless it was a human mind so twisted that it no longer felt human. At first I turned cold, thinking it was hunting for me. Yet as I listened, Caleb—or whoever the treasure hunter was—returned. I could hear nothing as concrete as a voice or even a muffled sound of voices, but I could feel the Other Thing's satisfaction. A curtain of silence fell and covered both of them. I'll admit it, I was glad.

I heard Ari get up and go into the bathroom. I scurried back to bed and slid under the warm covers. When he came back, I turned into his arms and stayed there for the rest of the night.

In the morning, though, he got up before I did. I was dimly aware of his leaving the bedroom before I fell back asleep. The smell of coffee brewing finally jerked me awake enough to take a shower. I put on a pair of jeans and a white Giants T-shirt, then followed the scent of coffee into the kitchen.

Ari was sitting at the table reading a fat book. When he saw me, he smiled and shut it with a paper napkin for a bookmark. I recognized the cover—a "learn Latin" text for adults.

"You want to crack the family code, huh?" I said.

"Yes. Do you mind?"

I hesitated. In a way I did mind, but only because it was another symptom of how serious he was about our relationship. I remembered how cold I'd been over the gold pin he'd given me, and how my behavior had hurt him. I never wanted to do that again.

"No, of course I don't," I said. "If you need help—"

"So far it all seems perfectly clear, especially compared to English."

"Just about any language is clear compared to English."

He smiled at that. I got myself a mug of coffee and sat down at the table. He continued reading for a few minutes with a self-absorbed seriousness that surprised me. Twice, he flipped a couple of pages back to check some point, then returned to his original place in the text with a little nod. At what looked like the end of a chapter, he shut the book again.

"It's about as complicated as the Hebrew of the oldest parts of the Tanakh," Ari said. "I'm not surprised. So many ancient languages are."

"I take it that modern Hebrew's a lot simpler."

"Oh, yes. We couldn't run a modern society otherwise."

The "we" came so easily that it reminded me of a truth I tended to forget. He wasn't British; he wasn't even European, much less American, despite his perfect accent and his jeans and leather jacket. He came from a country so different that I had trouble conceptualizing what it would be like, to live under siege in a place that ancient Romans had once claimed to own, even though it had a history old before the Romans ever got there.

And I found myself wondering if it was really Ari I wanted to keep at a distance, or Israel.

Chapter 6

WHEN IT WAS TIME TO LEAVE FOR KATH-
LEEN'S PARTY, I changed into a flowered skirt in
blues and rusts and a teal silk top with a draped neckline. I
put my ID and a lipstick into a small beaded bag with a
strap long enough to sling across my body bandolier style. I
considered taking a swimsuit, but even though the pool
would be heated, the weather outside looked so gray and
grim that I decided to skip the water. Ari, it turned out,
could swim but had absolutely no interest in doing so. He
wore jeans and a blue shirt and carried his gray pullover
sweater over his shoulders.

"Once we've moved, though," he said, "I do need to find
a gym to join. Something near the new flats, assuming we
get them, of course."

Even on Sundays, which lacked an official rush hour,
traffic swarmed on the Golden Gate Bridge. Marin folks
drove in to sample the delights of the city, while city folks
drove out to the country and suburbs to get away from the
same. We had some slow going through the rainbow tunnel. Still, we reached Kathleen and Jack's around four
o'clock.

The Donovans' house had originally been a Victorian
farmhouse. Although the farm was long gone, it sat on four
acres of prime San Anselmo land a couple of miles beyond
and behind Red Hill. Thanks to Kathleen's menagerie, Jack
had surrounded the entire plot with an eighteen-foot-high

chain-link fence, which he kept securely locked. We parked on the graveled strip out in front, then rang the electronic buzzer on the gate.

Jack trotted down the flagstone walk through rhododendron bushes to let us in and to meet Ari. He was a tall man, Jack, with a shock of wavy dark hair and pale blue eyes. In his early thirties, he was still handsome, but he had the fleshy neck and stippling of broken capillaries across his cheeks that announced a very Irish drinking habit. Eventually, I supposed, he'd look like Uncle Jim. That night, he was wearing his usual jeans and a heavy red cotton canvas shirt.

"It's going to be chilly later," he remarked. "I'll get the heaters going out back near the pool."

I introduced him to Ari, and Ari to him, and they shook hands companionably. Still, I noticed how the two men sized each other up. Jack had good reason to be suspicious of my new partner's job with Interpol. The British accent wouldn't sweeten Jack's mood, either. Ari smiled so pleasantly that I was sure he was up to something.

"So," Jack said to Ari. "You're another guy who's gotten involved with an O'Grady girl. I don't know if we're brave or stupid."

"Probably both," Ari said. "But she has her compensations."

Jack laughed, Ari smiled, and I considered mayhem.

"Ah, come on, Nola," Jack said. "We only tease you because you're usually right." He glanced Ari's way. "She saved my dad's life a while ago. She insisted he needed to see a doctor, and damn, she was right about that! A couple more weeks, the doc said, and the cancer would have spread. Lights out."

Ari winced. Both men turned solemn.

"How's he doing these days?" I said.

"Pretty good!" Jack brightened again. "The doc says he's in remission, all right. It's been a year now since he finished the chemo. We're going up to the vineyard next week to celebrate with him. The real problem is getting him to rest enough. You know what he's like."

"I sure do. He's too used to storming around in charge of everything, flinging orders right and left."

Jack laughed again. "That's it, yeah. Well, come on in. Everyone's out back."

The house metaphorically smelled of money, with its hardwood floors, Persian rugs, wood paneling, antique furniture, and original paintings by American Impressionists. It also literally smelled like cat boxes, no matter how often Kathleen and her housekeeper changed them. Kathleen had acquired two more strays, bringing her cat collection up to twenty. We tromped down the long hallway in a cloud of scattering felines, some diving into side rooms, others darting up the long staircase to the second floor. While they could go outside at will, in chilly weather they stuck to the central heating.

"Out back" at the Donovan house was not your usual backyard. Kathleen loved to swim, she loved to cook, and she loved to be outside. Jack had accommodated these three loves with a fifty-foot-long swimming pool and its surroundings. Off to the left side stood the cabaña, as they called it, which was actually a small cottage with a bathroom and all the necessaries. To the right stood what amounted to an outdoor kitchen, with a gas-powered grill and a portable bar and refrigerator unit powered by electricity from underground cables. Fruit trees, shrubs, and flowers grew thick and lush all around.

Kathleen herself was standing by the pool. She was wearing a pair of cut-off jeans over a modest tank suit in a light blue that set off her dark blue eyes. She'd pulled her long black hair back into a single braid, and she wore no makeup, a stark style that on her looked gorgeous. She trotted over to join us, followed by a small mob of mutts. We hugged.

"I was just going to get the guys inside," she said with a wave at the dogs, who swarmed around her like surf around a rock. "And I guess I'd better get dressed."

"Are you cooking tonight?" I said.

"Nah, I hired the usual caterers. They should be here any minute."

"I'll go wait on the front porch," Jack said. "Let 'em in and all that. Besides, I left my beer out there."

He strode off before Kathleen could even agree. I

glanced her way and raised an eyebrow. She shrugged with a faint look of disgust.

"I invited a lot of people, not just Caleb," Kathleen said to Ari. "So he'll be distracted, and we can snag his drinking glass or something."

"That would do," Ari said. "But why don't you just leave the matter to me?"

"Okay, I'll be glad to." She glanced around. "I'm keeping watch for Jack. He'd be furious if he knew."

"Nola tells me he's afraid of this person. He doesn't look like the sort of man who scares easily."

"He isn't, or he wouldn't have married me." She grinned at him. "The family, y'know?"

"I happen to like your family."

Kathleen's expression turned beatific, much like Aunt Eileen in a matchmaking mood. She patted Ari's arm. "I'm so glad Nola found you."

The dogs in the pack began to whine and shove each other. A golden retriever yawned and snapped. One of the Dobermans started sniffing Kathleen's bare leg. She kicked him, just lightly, and made him back off.

"I'll get them inside," Kathleen said. "Oh, and Ari? Thank you."

Kathleen rounded up her pack and began shepherding them toward the house. I noticed Woofie Five, gray, fat, and whiskery, bouncing along behind the big dogs on his short little legs.

"That's the dog that bit Jack's business partner," I said to Ari.

"Evil-looking creature," Ari said.

With the dogs stowed, Kathleen reappeared wearing a Jean Paul Gaultier dress in a subdued tropical print—but an original, not one of the department store numbers— over her bathing suit, though she had, mercifully, taken off the cut-off jeans. She'd unbound her hair and let it fall uncombed and wavy down her back. Since we stood a good distance away, Ari stared at her. Men always did, and I tried to ignore my burning jealousy.

"Your sister," Ari said, "is really peculiar. Sorry if that's offensive, but she is."

•

The jealousy cooled off and died. "We're all really peculiar," I said. "That includes you."

"I'd never deny it."

The caterers, Maria Elena and her husband, Diego, arrived soon after, both dressed in spotless white. They
brought with them helpers, a parade of boxes of food and
liquor, bottles of mineral water, and several enormous jugs
of orangeade. While this culinary mob set up a long buffet
table near the cabaña, Jack hovered nearby with a bottle of
beer in his hand. A few at a time, the other guests began to
arrive, about twenty adults in all, couples with young children, mostly. The kids hit the buffet like locusts while parents fussed and kept up a running chatter of "say please,
don't grab, say thank you."

When the kids gravitated toward the pool, Jack changed
into baggy swim trunks and an undershirt to play lifeguard
for the evening, a maneuver that let the other adults circu-
late, drink, and eat in relative peace. It also saved him
from having to make casual conversation, which he hated
doing.

"I thought kids weren't supposed to swim so soon after
eating," I said to Kathleen. "That's what Dad always told us,
anyway."

"I remember, yeah," Kathleen said. "But all that's
changed. I guess it never really mattered, according to the
doctors."

The cool night began to darken the sky. Jack got out of
the water long enough to put on the outdoor lighting, including the lights housed inside the rim of the pool. The
water turned into liquid turquoise—a seething mass of liquid turquoise with the kids jumping and splashing. Kathleen began glancing around and biting her lower lip.

"I don't see you know who," she whispered. "I hope the
little jerk gets here."

One of Maria Elena's helpers, a girl of maybe sixteen,
came trotting over to announce that the caterers needed
Kathleen's instructions about the arcane matter of reheat-
ing chiles rellenos. Kathleen hurried off just as Caleb arrived. I spotted a man answering his description moving
through the crowd, mostly men, around the bar. A quick

check showed me the disciplined aura of a person who's learned to control his natural talents.

"That's got to be him," I said to Ari.

Ari considered the distant Caleb. "I'll have a closer look," he said. "Do you want some food? No, of course you don't. Why do I ask? I do, however, and I'm going to go over to the buffet."

"Well, if there's salad—"

"Salad's not enough. You're not a leaf-eating chimpanzee."

On this wave of impeccable logic, Ari strode away. I stuck my tongue out at his retreating back. As I waited, I began to feel someone watching me, though no SAWM or ASTA went off in my brain. The natural suspect, Caleb, was sipping a drink and talking with Kathleen some distance away. He had his back toward me.

I turned around and saw a little girl of about five, with blonde curls and big blue eyes, dressed in a dripping wet pink bathing suit. She stood with her hands on her hips, studying me.

"Do you have worms?" she said.

"Say what?" I said.

"You're so skinny. We went to Mexico, and my aunt ate some bad candy, and she got worms. And she got skinny, and she kept getting skinnier and skinnier until the doctor killed them. The worms, I mean. With pills."

I gaped. A woman in a pale green dress spun around and shrieked, "Daphne! What are you asking the nice lady?"

"Does she have worms?" Daphne said.

"Ohmigawd!" The woman, whom I assumed was Daphne's mom, grabbed the child's arm. "Don't say things like that!" She looked up at me with eyes filled with honest anguish. "I'm so sorry."

"It's okay," I said. "Not a problem."

The woman groaned and dragged the protesting Daphne away. I remembered the Goddess Venus saying, "Get a better mirror." Not all mirrors are made of glass. Maybe, I decided, I could eat a little more, just now and then.

I started toward the buffet, but Kathleen strolled over, Caleb in tow. She introduced us, then announced that she had to discuss dessert with the caterers and hurried off again. Caleb and I stood near the pool and smiled the moronic smiles of people who have just met at a noisy party.

Kathleen's earlier description of Caleb—short, pudgy, smells bad—did not predispose me to think highly of him. In person, however, he turned out to be maybe 5'9", a few pounds heavy around the middle, and scented with musk-and-ginger aftershave. Facially he was good-looking, with humorous eyes and a tan; overall, I found myself thinking of William Shatner in *Star Trek*'s first TV season, not that I have any idea of how Captain Kirk smelled.

I was also positive I'd seen him before. I just couldn't place where. I did know I'd merely glimpsed him from a distance, but that I'd seen him at all struck me as important. For a few minutes we watched Jack teaching one of the younger kids how to float on his back. Caleb allowed as how he was impressed.

"He's got more patience with kids than I ever will." His voice, while light, certainly didn't squeak in the upper register, but he had the New England "havahd yahd" accent, all right. "Sometimes I think he should teach school."

"Yeah, I've had that thought, too."

I smiled; he smiled and moved a step closer. He glanced away, but I felt the touch of his mind on mine—an SPP. He had talents, then, just as I'd suspected. I refrained from defending or answering, and in a few seconds the touch vanished. Let him wonder, I figured, about any talents I might have.

"Jack must have told you," Caleb said, "that we've got a business venture going."

"Kathleen mentioned it, actually."

"I know she doesn't approve, so you don't have to be polite about it. Do you think Drake's treasure is just a myth?"

"Yes and no," I said. "He had one, yes, but I believe he gave it all to the queen of England, so no, I don't think any of it's still around here."

"Well, that's what the academic establishment wants us to believe. They can't think outside the box, and they're too damn lazy to change their lecture notes when new information comes along."

I had no idea of how to respond to that. I was saved when a woman called my name from across the babbling sea of guests.

"Nola! Is that really you?"

I looked and saw Mira Rosen, an old friend of mine from college. She'd gotten her M.S. in psych at the same time as I'd finished mine. I waved madly and yelled back, "It is! How cool to see you!" I turned to Caleb. "Excuse me. Someone I haven't seen in years."

He nodded and headed in the direction of the bar. I made my way through the chattering partygoers toward Mira, who waddled her way toward me. She stood about five foot one and normally barely topped a hundred pounds, but that night she was vastly pregnant. Her belly hung over her blue maternity shorts; her navel peered out from under her white maternity top.

"Good grief," I said, "are there twins in there?"

"No, only one," Mira said. "I bet it's a boy. I wouldn't let them tell me, after the sonogram, you know, but I'd bet anything it's some hulking brute of a boy child."

"I heard you and David got married last year, but I didn't know you guys had already decided to reproduce."

"I blame my husband. All his idea. I had nothing to do with it, nothing, I tell you!"

We shared a laugh. Mira paused to swig from the bottle of mineral water she was carrying. "Kathleen told me you were back," she said. "What's this about a steady boyfriend?"

"He's around here somewhere." I paused to survey the crowd and saw Ari talking with the bartender over at the portable bar. When Caleb came up beside him, Ari walked away.

"Over there." I pointed. "The dark-haired one. We just got a place together."

"Ooh. Good-looking! But I bet he's got issues."

"What makes you say that?"

"The way he moves, like he's ready to spring on his prey. And a cop, Kathleen says?"

"With Interpol, yeah." I wished that Kathleen had kept her mouth shut about that aspect of Ari's personality. I didn't want Caleb putting up his guard. "So what's going on with you besides the baby? Are you going to go back to work?"

"You bet. I didn't suffer to get that damned degree for nothing. I've got an arrangement with another therapist. He'll be on emergency call for my clients for three months, and I'll do the same for his when he goes to Europe this summer." She made a wry face. "I'm thinking of going back for the doctorate, though. I really want to work with autistic adults."

"Why the adults?"

"Because that's where the challenge is. These days a lot of people are working with the children. I've heard fellow professionals tell me that if you don't get them young, there's no hope. I don't give up on people that easy, thank you very much."

"I've never known you to, that's for sure."

"You know, that kind of work is something you'd be real good at."

"Oh, come on, I don't think so."

"Consider your family. You grew up learning how to take care of really annoying people."

We shared another laugh.

"It won't be an easy job, of course, but I like that aspect of it." Mira had another swig of mineral water. "What are you doing these days?"

"Well, uh, not much. I just lost my job, thanks to the recession. I was working for a marketing firm, and it went belly up."

"As they all deserve to do. Nola! Marketing? With your brains?"

With that, I came up against one of the drawbacks to working for the Agency; namely, the need to lie to people you'd rather treat honestly. I forced out a smile. "Why is it," I said, "that everyone feels they get to tell me what I should do?"

"I can't help it. I went to college to be a busybody. But okay, I hear you. I'll shut up."

"But let's get together, okay? When you can, anyway. You're living in Marin now?"

"Yeah, not far from here, or I wouldn't have been able to come at all." Mira glowered at her enormous midsection. "Once this creature deigns to make his appearance, I'll give you a call."

"I don't have anything to write my number on, but Kathleen can give it to you."

"She already did. Do me a favor. Look at my ankles and tell me if they're swollen. I can't see them."

I looked. "Yeah, they are."

"Time to go. I'll round up David before he gets his paws on a margarita. I can't drive like this."

I walked with her until she spotted her husband, blamelessly free of margaritas, talking with a couple I didn't know. We said good-bye, and I went looking for Ari. I finally met up with him near the back of the house. He was carrying an open cardboard box that had once held a bottle of Drambuie. I pointed to it and made a questioning noise.

"It's not got liquor in it," Ari said. "Something more interesting. Diego gave me the box to keep it clean. I'm going to go put this in the car for safekeeping."

I noticed that he'd draped the contents with a white napkin.

"Okay. How will you get through the fence?"

"Jack told me he hired a parking valet to handle the cars and the gate. And no, I won't let the cats out."

Ari strode on toward the back door, since the best route to the street lay through the house. Over by the side of the party area stood a pair of wooden benches in front of a dormant bed of annuals and right near one of the big patio heaters. I sat down to survey the party in comfort. I'd barely settled myself when Caleb appeared, carrying a drink in one hand. He plunked himself down next to me with a smile. The drink smelled like scotch and water. So did he.

"I was thinking," Caleb said, "how much I'd like to get to know you better."

"Uh, really?"

"Really." He took a sip of his drink. "And I'd like to talk to you about our business venture, too."

"Ah. We're back to Drake's treasure, huh?"

"Yeah yeah. This is going to sound crazy, but look, everyone in your family has talents, don't they? Psychic talents? Jack's always teasing Kathleen about them." He smiled at me over the rim of his glass.

I should have known, but I sent an inward curse Jack's way. "Well," I said, "if you believe in that stuff."

"Oh, I do, and I'll bet you do, too. Look, Kathleen mentioned that you were out of work. What about joining our venture? A psychic would be a handy person to have around. When it comes to locating the goods, the hard data's minimal, and the sources are real old."

"So you think I could help you find it?"

"Just that. Gold has psychic vibrations, you know. It's the archetypal form of the element of earth. Don't tell me you don't know what I mean by elemental earth."

"I do know, sure. This isn't the kind of place where I want to discuss things like that, however."

"You're right." He looked down in contrition. "I tend to have a big mouth. Sorry."

I considered. Discussing the alleged business venture, playing along with him in his scheme—I saw the chance to learn more about him in safe circumstances.

"We could have lunch," I said, "over in the city, and discuss your offer."

"That sounds good. Pick a restaurant you like, pick a day, I'll be there." He reached into his shirt pocket and brought out a business card, black lettering on white, and handed it to me.

"Caleb Sumner," it read, "Oceanography Degree, Sidereal Navigation Certificate."

"Impressive." I put the card into my beaded bag. "Is there much call for sidereal navigators these days?"

"No." His expression turned sour. "Thanks to the goddamn GPS systems. I used to get work as yacht crew all the time. Not so much anymore."

"That's too bad."

Caleb nodded and had another gulp of scotch and water. The nearby patio heater hissed loudly, then returned to its steady hum, but not before Caleb flinched and muttered at the sound.

"Lousy weather this year, isn't it?" Caleb said. "I'm not used to pool parties that need heaters."

"Yeah, sure is, but we need the rain."

"That's what everyone says." He smiled. "I'm still not used to California, period. Drought's never an issue back home in New England. Everything stays green in the summer."

"Yeah, but you pay for it with all that snow in winter. Of course, not all of our weather's perfect." I paused for effect. "Lately we've had to worry about rogue waves, for example."

Caleb went very still. He stared at me over the rim of his glass. I pretended not to notice.

"You've got that degree in Oceanography," I went on. "So I bet you know the answer to this. I've been wondering lately, what causes them, the rogue waves, I mean?"

Caleb's hands began to shake so badly that the scotch sloshed in his glass. He set it down on the ground, then pretended to cough.

"Sorry," he said. "Down the wrong pipe." He slapped both hands over his mouth, so that they covered part of his face. Sweat broke out on his forehead.

"Heavens!" I grabbed a tissue from my bag and held it out. "Are you choking? Need help?"

He shook his head no and continued his fake cough. Eventually he took the tissue and wiped his mouth.

"Guess I'd better not finish that drink," he said. "Diego makes them pretty strong."

"I'd say so, yeah."

I looked away while he composed himself. For a couple of minutes we sat in silence. I watched the guests swirling around the buffet in case I saw someone else I knew. I didn't.

"You know," Caleb said, "your sister's very beautiful, but it's a beauty like a work of art, museum worthy, kind of distant and cool. Jack's built her a museum here, really. It sets his art treasure off perfectly."

I thought of all the cat boxes in the house but managed a polite smile. Caleb smiled back while Qi oozed from his aura. I perceived it as long wisps like tendrils of fog, reaching for me, but my own aura held steady, and my own Qi stayed where it belonged, inside my magnetic field.

"You have a much more interesting kind of beauty." He edged a little closer to me on the bench. "Fiery, and no museum could ever contain it."

At fifteen, I would have swooned over this line. Unfortunately for Caleb, I was twenty-six. "Yeah?" I said. "My boyfriend says something like that, too."

Caleb's smile froze. The tendrils of Qi snapped back to his aura. Over his shoulder, I saw the boyfriend in question approaching.

"Here's Ari now," I said. "I'll introduce you."

At his first sight of Ari, Caleb slid back to his original position on the bench. Ari stood a bit less than six feet tall, but he could loom over people when he wanted to. He strode over and turned, looming, to Caleb, who suddenly did look short and pudgy. He didn't smell bad, however, to my normal nose, though Kathleen would have sniffed fear in the air.

"Ari," I said, "this is Caleb Sumner. He's been telling me about a possible job."

"Hi," Caleb said. "Pleased to meet you."

"How do you do?" Ari looked him over briefly and turned back to me. "Do you want to eat here, or should we just go home?"

"We could leave soon," I said. "If you'd like."

Caleb picked up his glass, then finished the drink in one long swallow. As we walked away, I glanced back and saw him heading to the bar.

Kathleen had gravitated to the buffet, where she was helping Maria Elena put out rows of paper bowls containing little flans, each swimming in a thin clear caramel sauce. A lot of calories per, I figured, but they did look delicious.

"We're thinking of leaving," I said to Kathleen. "We've had a long day, and Ari wants to get home to get some work done."

Kathleen smiled at the hint in that "work." "But you haven't eaten anything," she said to me.

"I will at home, I promise. I've got salad stuff—

"No, no," Maria Elena said. "I have an empty box right here. Let me make you up a care package."

"Good name for it," Ari said. "She looks like a refugee."

Since we were in public view, I couldn't kick him, but I thought about it. He stepped back fast, as if he felt it coming. The caterer moved up and down the long buffet, stuffing a big white cardboard box with miniature tacos, baggies of guacamole, rice, a bowl of chicken in salsa verde, and the like. My traitorous stomach growled.

"I saw you talking with Mira," Kathleen said. "I'm real glad you connected."

"So am I. It's great seeing her again. She wants to move into working with autistics, she told me."

"God, she's so motivated! I guess it's a real problem, lots of kids born with autism."

"It is, yeah. No one's sure why, either."

"I think it's because they're actually dinosaur souls."

I stared.

"Well, look," Kathleen continued. "Everyone talks about overpopulation, right? And how there's more people on earth now than there ever were before. Even if you add up all the people that lived before, ever, there's still more people now. So that means everyone human's been reborn already, so where are all these kids coming from? They must have souls. And so I figure it's the dinosaurs incarnating again. After all, we did take over their planet."

Ari dropped to one knee and pretended to be tying his shoelace. Out of the corner of my eye, I could see his shoulders trembling.

"That's a really interesting theory," I said. "I'll have to think about that."

Maria Elena popped the box of food into a plastic bag and handed it to me with a straight face. An amazing woman, she was. Ari stood up again and took the box.

"I'll carry," he said. "Thank you so much."

As we walked out, we passed Caleb, who rushed over to say good-bye. Although Ari loomed, Caleb spoke only to me.

"Let's make that business lunch date soon." He stressed

the word "business." "Jack and I would both like to have you onboard."

"I'll do that, for sure," I said. "I could use a new job."

Ari said nothing as we walked away, but he appeared to be in a pleasant enough mood. Once we got into the car, I left the interior light on and put the keys into the ignition.

"Caleb really was sounding me out about working with him and Jack," I said. "If I go to lunch with him, I'll have a good chance to size him up."

I waited for a reaction. Ari merely nodded his agreement.

"Well," I went on, "I wasn't flirting with him or anything."

"I never thought you were."

"Oh, okay."

Ari grinned at me. "What's this? Disappointed I'm not making a scene?"

"Bastard." I switched off the light. "Let's go home."

He chuckled in his usual grudging way and buckled his seat belt.

We drove back to the apartment without encountering any traffic slowdowns, a good thing, because the smell of the food Maria Elena had given us tormented me the whole way. I decided that I really could eat some of it, since I'd skipped both breakfast and lunch. Eventually, we found a parking place. Before I locked the car, Ari retrieved the Drambuie box from the trunk, and I took Maria Elena's bounty.

"What's in that box, anyway?" I said. "I take it that it's got Caleb's prints on it."

"A sherry glass. I thought about various ways to get the prints, but the bartender seemed like the reliable sort. So I explained that I was a police officer and showed him my ID and all that. He agreed to help."

"That was good of him."

"Well, he was reluctant until he found out whose prints I wanted. He remarked that Mrs. Donovan had had some trouble with Caleb at the last party. Apparently, Caleb knocks back the scotch and gets obnoxious."

"He was working on it already tonight."

"I thought so, yes. So, when Caleb went to the bar, Diego put out a bowl of nuts. They're oily. Caleb took a few, as anyone would. Diego then asked Caleb if he'd like to try a new brand of sherry and poured him a little, which our mark sampled. Then, of course, Diego gave Caleb a clean glass for his next drink."

"And you've got the old one."

"Just that. I hope the ride home hasn't smudged or smeared the prints, is all. I'll bring them up while you eat."

Since Ari had no desk of his own, he ended up spreading his equipment over the kitchen table. I went into the bedroom and changed out of my party clothes into jeans and a Giants T-shirt, then leaned against the refrigerator and ate a couple of miniature tacos and some guacamole while I watched him work. Before he'd put the glass into the box, Diego had made a little cage of soda straws around it, which had kept the napkin wrap at a safe distance.

"He did a good job," Ari said. "I get the impression he's been asked to gather evidence before."

"Maybe that's because he's a bartender," I said. "Are you sure those aren't his prints, though?"

"He wiped the glass before he handed it to Caleb, and he held it by the base. Caleb took the barrel between thumb and forefinger. I was watching from the shrubbery."

"Say what? On your hands and knees?"

"I was standing over by the shrubbery, not crawling around in it."

On the table Ari had spread out a newspaper and laid out a couple of brushes, a packet of index cards, and a box of something that looked like bits of tape on paper backing. He had a fine black powder in a container similar to an old-fashioned compact for makeup. He dipped a fat kolinski hair brush in the powder, tapped off the excess, and delicately began powdering the glass. When I squatted down to eye level, I could see the thin black lines where the powder stuck to Caleb's oily fingerprints.

"Brilliant," Ari said. "Let me get some pictures of these."

I stood up again and decided that I could have a few bites of that seductive chicken in salsa verde. When I got a fork out of the drawer beside the sink, Ari looked up from his work.

"That's the ticket," he said with just a hint of a joke in his voice. "Dig in. Have lots. Do it for America!"

"Oh, shut up!"

He smiled and did so, then picked up his tiny digital camera.

"It's best to snap them, if you can, before you try to lift them," he said. "In case something goes wrong."

He grabbed a paper towel, tore off part of it, and stuffed it into the inside of the glass to provide a background. For some minutes he fussed with the light, the camera, and the sherry glass until he managed to get some snaps that weren't ruined by reflections.

"The computer can work from digital images as well as it can from scanned paper," he remarked. "Maybe better."

"It's done by computer these days, huh?"

"Yes. It's the Integrated Automated Fingerprint Identification System, which as you can doubtless guess we call the IAFIS. Your agency doesn't have a monopoly on odd acronyms." Ari paused, hands on hips, to survey the glass and his equipment. "You know, if you're tired, you could go sit down. This is all rather routine work." He glanced my way. "Unless I can persuade you to eat something more?"

"I've had plenty, thanks." I wiped my hands on the remains of the paper towel he'd torn up. "I do want to sit down, yeah, and pick up my e-mail. Did you get enough to eat at the party? Finish this stuff if you want."

"I just might. It's quite good."

The only e-mail of any consequence came from NumbersGrrl, who'd attached a background document on deviant level/world theory. I figured I might understand half of it. I was logging off when Ari came in, wiping a mixture of fingerprint powder and guacamole onto his jeans.

"I'm finished," Ari said. "I need to send the photos off, is all."

"Okay. Where are you sending them, or shouldn't I ask?"

"An Interpol regional office. How fast the prints get into the system depends on how many other requests have come in."

"How long will it take to get an ID back? Weeks?"

"No. It's not like DNA. Shouldn't take long, overnight at the most."

"Y'know, sometimes I'm really impressed by what computers can do."

Ari smiled at that. "It takes a human tech to make the final determination. The machine normally spits out five or six close matches. In this case, we know our suspect's alleged name. We merely need to know if he has a record. Once the clerk picks the right print, the system will tell us that."

"I bet he does have a record. There's something too boyish about Caleb to be true. Boyish and kind of contrived."

I was planning on putting off my lunch with Caleb until late in the week, after the information on the fingerprints came back, but Ari received the report on the prints just four hours after he'd sent them off. I was thinking of going to bed, and he was working on his laptop in the kitchen, when I heard him whistle in surprise. I trotted in to see.

"What is it?" I glanced at the screen only to see Hebrew letters. "You sure have an automatic encryption system there, don't you?"

"If you want to learn some Hebrew, I'll be glad to teach you," Ari said. "It might come in handy one day."

I made a noncommittal noise, and he returned to looking at the screen. "I'll translate this for you," he said, "and print it out, but the essence is, yes, Caleb has a record. Caleb Sumner is his real name. He's still using it, I should think, because he served his sentence—eighteen months in a Massachusetts prison for blackmail—so I suppose people would consider him rehabilitated and all that. The sentence was light, but I'm assuming that was because of his age. He was nineteen at the time."

"Whoa! Not a nice guy, young or old."

"A petty criminal type, certainly. He'd had a few juvenile infractions, too. I can get the details from one of the American databanks."

"I thought juvenile records were all sealed."

"They are."

"Then how can you get them?"

Ari merely looked at me. I realized I'd asked a stupid question. "Never mind," I said. "I don't want to know."

Ari logged off and shut down the laptop. When he turned in his chair to look at me, I noticed his expression, solemn to the point of being stone cold.

"Nola," he said. "We've got to have a talk about your brother-in-law."

My heart thudded once. I sat down opposite him at the table.

"Caleb has to be blackmailing him," Ari said. "It's the only thing that would explain Donovan's actions."

"You're right, yeah. Why else would Jack cringe around that little jerk?"

"The question then is, on what grounds?"

His SPP gave me an impression of tremendous self-control without even a hint of what he might be controlling. As for the question, I could stay silent, give evasive answers, or outright lie. I decided on none of the above.

"Is he blackmailing Jack directly," I said, "or threatening Jack's father to make the blackmail stick? Jack would do pretty much anything to protect him."

"Possibly both." Ari hesitated, then gave a little "throw caution to the winds" shrug. "They were both involved in running guns to Northern Ireland, weren't they?"

My heart thudded again. His SPP returned to normal.

"What makes you think that?" I said.

"Oh, come now." Ari crossed his arms over his chest and glared at me.

"Okay, okay. Yes, they were, but Jack was a teenager at the time, doing what his dad told him to do. Remember that, will you?"

"I'm not a judge and jury."

No, I thought, just a cop, but it's my bad luck you're an honest one. Aloud, I said, "How did you find out?"

"I suspected Jack from the day we went out to Marin to interview your sister. Over Pat's death, if you remember. She made some odd remarks about firearms in relation to her husband. So I checked the files and saw various reports on Donovan senior." His smile was as thin as the edge of a knife blade. "His activities were one of those things that everyone knows, but no one can prove. No one ever caught the transfer boat with the guns aboard. When the Gardai finally managed to confiscate a shipment, there were no fingerprints on any of the contraband. Your FBI never saw the guns being shipped from the States. There was nothing that would stand up in any court."

Kevin Donovan had spread money liberally around to ensure that dearth of evidence. I knew that Ari would feel duty bound to report any charges of police corruption, so I kept my mouth shut about that. My stomach twisted so badly that I felt like vomiting, and it wasn't the salsa verde to blame. Ari cocked his head to one side and considered me with narrowed eyes.

"Nola, why do you look so frightened?"

"Are you going to report this conversation? Like a jerk I just gave evidence against them."

"Time to file charges ran out a long time ago. The statute of limitations applies to Customs violations, you know, at least in America. I suppose the British government might still prosecute, but I can't see your government extraditing the Donovans. I'm not even sure if what they did was a crime under American law."

"You're right, aren't you? Call me twice a jerk."

"Never that." Ari smiled at me. "I know how much your family means to you." The smile vanished. "But answer me one thing. Jack's not running guns to Gaza, is he?"

"Hell, no! Not to anywhere in the Middle East or to anywhere else, for that matter, not now. Why would he? They weren't doing it for the money."

"Good point."

"It was the old 'Erin go bragh' that caught both of them," I went on. "Once Jack's dad made his huge heap of cash, he was bored. Now, I can't see how building shopping centers is exciting, but Donovan père loved every minute of it. He took up kind of an odd hobby to replace it."

Ari's turn for the sigh—of relief, in this case. "Good. I wasn't looking forward to arresting your sister's husband."

"Would you have arrested Jack? If he'd been running guns to Hamas, say."

"I would have had to." He said it quietly, but I could hear

the steel in his voice. "I would have been sorry, but I would have. What would you have done?"

My first reaction was "I'd have dumped you so fast . . ." My second reaction was total paralysis, because somewhere in my weird brain I knew it never would have been that simple. Ari waited, watching me. I finally wrenched my mind back into gear.

"I don't know," was all I could say. "I honestly do not know what I would have done."

"Let's hope we're never in a position to find out."

I mistrusted my voice and nodded my agreement. My stomach continued to yearn for antacids.

"Jack must know about the statute of limitations," Ari went on. "I don't understand what Caleb could be holding over him. According to the records I've seen, Donovan's been an impeccable citizen ever since."

"As far as I know he has, too. Which brings us back to his father. He's in his 'pillar of the community' phase. Big man in the Knights of Columbus. Local charities adore him. When he had his cancer treatments last year, his church held special masses for his recovery. How would they all feel about a gun runner in their midst? Not everyone in that parish is Irish."

"Then exposure could create a very bad situation."

"Donovan senior isn't young anymore, and he's been really sick. If he ended up in the middle of a scandal, the stress could kill him."

Ari nodded. I could pick up his filing the data away in his mind. "I need to have a talk with Jack."

I must have winced or made some other physical gesture, because Ari looked offended.

"I'm planning on putting his mind at rest," Ari said. "Not making things worse."

"Okay. I guess."

"I suppose you're thinking that I won't be tactful."

"Yep. That's exactly right."

"For you, I'll try."

"I'll come with you when you do."

Ari looked briefly exasperated, then shrugged. "Oh, very well! Now, don't mention Caleb's background to Kathleen until we've had our chat with Donovan. If she asks, tell her I'm still confirming the details of the case."

"That sounds nice and official, yeah."

I got up and went into the bathroom. I grabbed the bottle of heartburn meds, shoved four of them into my mouth, and washed them down with a glass of water.

"What's wrong?" Ari was standing in the doorway and watching.

"My stomach hurts," I said, "from our little talk just now."

"I'm so sorry." He sounded perfectly sincere. "I didn't think it would upset you."

I considered throwing the bottle at his head but thought better of it. "What matters now," I said, "is doing something about Caleb. Can we get him arrested for blackmail?"

"If Donovan's willing to file charges, certainly."

"That's a pretty big if."

"I'm fairly sure that American law offers protection to blackmail victims."

"Yeah, but is it enough? If Jack's dad were in blooming good health, maybe, but he's not. What if something got out?"

"That's what Caleb's counting on, isn't it?"

I nodded and felt a knot of rage replace the pain in my stomach. "Well," I said, "if Caleb's involved with Chaos forces, the Agency will take up jurisdiction if Jack won't go to the police."

"It already has, hasn't it?" Ari paused for a yawn. "Thanks to your promotion, here in San Francisco the Agency means you."

With another twist of my put-upon stomach, I realized that he was right.

CHAPTER 7

NOW THAT I'D MET THE LITTLE SLIMEBALL, I could keep track of Caleb with LDRS and Search Mode: Personnel scans. I used both on Monday morning, but with extreme caution to avoid letting him know he was being watched. He never noticed my prying psychic eyes, most likely because of the nausea and headache pain he was transmitting. At one point I got a clear image of him drinking a glass of water, clouded by some kind of hangover medicine. He turned to a toilet and began to throw it up again, at which point I shut down the SM:P as fast as I possibly could.

"I get the impression," I told Ari, "that he sucked up too much of Jack's scotch last night."

"I'm not surprised," Ari said. "He seemed the type."

"He's got a big mouth, too. By the way, Caleb knows something about those rogue waves, all right. He nearly choked when I mentioned them."

"Did he say anything incriminating?"

"No. He could barely talk at all. But you know, it doesn't seem likely that he could have murdered Evers, to say nothing of that girl who drowned down at Ocean Beach."

"True. Blackmailers and the like rarely use violence. They tend to be cowards, is why. The murders—Brother Belial's work?"

"Possibly. I'm just not sure of where he fits into the case. Let's face it; we don't even really know if he's connected to

Caleb. I overheard that one contact between Caleb—I'm sure now it was him—and somebody or something that might have been Belial, but I can't be certain."

Monday morning also brought business hours in DC, when Y would be in his office. When I passed the problem of Ari's mother's role in the Armageddon kibbutz on to Y, he told me he'd get someone right on it.

"E-mail me a list of questions," Y said. "I just happen to have a contact in MI5. It would probably be politic to tell him what we want. She's one of their nationals, after all."

"I'll send them today, for sure. The problem is, I don't have an address or phone number for her. And I get the impression that Nathan doesn't want to give them to me."

"The original workup we did on Nathan gave us her current last name, Flowertree." His image—we were talking in trance state—frowned briefly. "It's quite unusual, so between that and my contact, I think we can trace her. I'll let you know as soon as we do."

After I left the trance state, I made up the list of questions, encrypted them, and e-mailed them to Y's private account. I started my usual work routine for a Monday, surfing the Internet, looking for the odd bits of data that might indicate Chaos activity. I'd gotten a third of the way through my bookmarked sites when Mr. Singh the realtor called with good news. The owners of the building we wanted had run their credit check on the Internet.

"So this morning they had their results," he said. "You may sign the lease at my office if you still wish."

"We sure do," I said. "I'll bring a cashier's check with me for the rent and deposit and all that."

"Excellent. I will give you the keys then."

In honor of the occasion, Ari put on the blue pinstriped suit. I wore my tan corduroy skirt with brown suede boots and a white blouse with a red rose print, and a burgundy raincoat, because the sky that morning hung low and dark over the city. Once we'd signed the lease and had the keys, we drove out to the building because I wanted to decide where to put the furniture, and Ari wanted to look the place over for a mysterious project he had in mind. Rather than negotiate the driveway, I parked on the street. As we got out of the car, I saw spray-painted graffiti on the pale blue wall holding up the front steps.

The black paint of the artwork, if you can call it that, was so precisely applied that I knew it had been stenciled, not done freehand. A ring of stylized black arrows, each about ten inches long, emerged from a solid circle about two feet across, "Crud!" I said. "Don't tell me that they found me already!"

"Who?" Ari was staring at the tag. "It looks like a traffic sign of some sort. A roundabout with many exits?"

"No, it's a symbol of Chaos magic."

"They have their own sort of magic?"

"Yes and no, if you mean the Chaos masters we're looking for. They probably do, but I don't know if they're responsible for this or not. There are all kinds of schools of magic. If it's the one I'm thinking of, it's modern, it comes from the U.K., and it's not a threat."

Ari stopped staring at the symbol and began staring at me.

"What I'm wondering," I went on, "is if the Chaos masters are using this symbol now, or if some jerk kids found it on the Internet and have started tagging with it." I looked closer and found a surprise. Four arrows emerged from the top half, but only three on the bottom. The discrepancy made the symbol appear ready to roll over.

"It must represent some kind of unbalanced force." I told Ari. "Normally this symbol has eight arrows." I paused for a grin. "Of course, it might represent stupidity if the tagger just copied it wrong."

"Schools of magic? Um, if you could back up a bit—"

"Sorry. And no, I'm not having a joke on you. A lot of people in the Bay Area take magical studies seriously, usually ritual magic or Wicca, though, not the true Chaos magic, which is a mix of all sorts of different systems. Uh, do you know who Aleister Crowley was?"

"I've heard the name. A writer and a heroin addict, wasn't he? He called himself a magician, I believe."

"The heroin was incidental, but he was definitely a magician. One of his disciples, a guy named Austin Spare, laid down the theory for Chaos magic. The basic theory is that there is no theory. The goal is raising your consciousness to higher levels, and whatever works is okay, even drugs."

Ari growled, more in disgust than anger.

"Never mind," I said. "What counts now is getting this stuff off the building."

I got out the cell phone and called Mr. Singh with the news, though I didn't give the magical meaning. I described the graffito as "looking like a dead spider or something."

"Another one?" he said. "Very well, I will have the maintenance man come out and wash over it. This has been a problem for a very long time, not that we have seen spiders before. Mostly letters and obscene words. The owners recently have been clever. They have painted the lower reaches of the outside walls with the special paint to which graffiti will not adhere. It can be removed with soap and water."

"Wonderful! If you could do that soon—"

"I will call and send him."

Singh signed off. Before we went inside, I tried to snap a picture of the tag with my phone so I could add it to my files on this case. The phone beeped and refused to save. I tried taking a picture of the garage door instead. The phone worked perfectly. I put the phone away, then sketched a Chaos ward in the air with my right hand. When I threw it at the symbol, the ward shattered in a spray of electric blue lines and triangles. The graffito sizzled like fat in a frying pan. Ari yelped.

"You heard that?" I said.

"I did, yes."

"This could be real trouble. I don't want anything happening to the realty maintenance man when the guy tries to wash this off."

"What do you think might happen?"

"I don't know. That's the problem."

I called Singh back and told him that we'd just deal with the graffito ourselves.

"I'm going to do some cleaning in the upstairs flat anyway," I said. "So I'll have rags and soap and stuff."

"If you prefer, certainly," Singh said. "I have not yet called the fellow, so it is not a problem."

I clicked off. Ari took off his jacket, handed it me, and began to roll up his sleeves.

"Put that in the car," he said. "I saw some rags and a hose in the back garage. There's a spigot over there by the front garage door. Let's just deal with this now."

"Okay, but be careful about it. Hey, you're not wearing a gun."

He smiled and patted the waistband of his trousers. Silly old me!

I stowed the jacket while he fetched the supplies. Before I let him wash the graffito off, I threw another Chaos ward. This one held steady. The graffito gave out a miserable hiss and fell silent. When Ari trickled water onto it from the hose, a few blue sparks flashed, but the design began to dribble paint a second or two later. He wiped off most of it with a rag.

"It'll take soap to get that last bit of gray smear off," I said.

"Yes." Ari turned off the water and began to disconnect the hose. "What do you think would have happened if water had touched it when it was full strength?"

"Nothing good. A lot of sparks at the very least."

After Ari returned the hose and rags to the garage, we went up the outside steps and tried our new keys in the locks. Both worked, a good sign. We went inside the lower flat first, where Ari prowled around, looking into every closet.

"Uh," I said, "is something wrong?"

"Not that I know of," he said. "After that thing on the front wall, I thought I'd best see what there is to see."

"You know what just occurred to me? You never came inside the day we rented the place."

He stopped prowling. "I assumed you knew what you wanted. I can't say it matters much to me where I live, as long as the sodding windows aren't covered over and the gas doesn't leak and so on."

"Ah. Well, the upstairs flat's a lot nicer than this one. I'll show you around."

We found no more peculiar graffiti or other problems inside either flat. Whoever had stenciled the symbol outside had made no effort to break in. I wondered if they'd left the Chaos mark as a signal to other Chaotics or as a warning to me to back off. Maybe both.

After I decided where I was putting the couch and other furniture, I called one of my operatives, Annie Wentworth. I had Agency money for her, and she invited us over so I could pay her. Although she'd been promised the police reward money from locating Johnson and Doyle, she'd yet to receive it.

Annie was still living in the same shabby basement studio, if you could call it a studio, one long room of a converted garage out in the Sunset district, not far from the building we'd just leased. She had, however, added a few new pieces of furniture to the previous daybed and round kitchen table: a new bed for Duncan, her fox terrier; an armchair in front of her tiny TV; a glass display case hanging on the wall beside the framed posters of her grandmother's vaudeville career.

"What's all this stuff, Annie?" I looked into the case.

"Equipment from my grandmother's spiritualist act."

Annie joined me in front of the glass case. She was a small woman, way too thin for her faded jeans and gray sweatshirt thanks to recent rounds of chemotherapy for breast cancer. Her hair had grown back gray and dead straight.

"Grandma had a number of different acts, huh?" I said.

"Yes, indeed." Annie paused for a smile. "She honestly was psychic, so she hated to 'prostitute that talent upon the stage,' as she always put it. She did it when she had to, but she preferred her turns—that's what they called their acts, turns—to be something fake. You can see by this stuff that she couldn't really call up spirits."

"This stuff" consisted of a couple of small black metal boxes, a pair of black garters, each decorated with one small embroidered rose, and some lengths of twisted wire, also black. Behind them stood a worn and faded ouija board flanked by two silver candleholders in the shape of small dragons.

"You fastened the soap box to your thigh with a garter," Annie continued, "so you could press your legs together and make cracking noises. The wires went up the sleeves of your mysteriously embroidered black robes. You could hook the edge of the table with them and make it shake. And so on. On a dimly lit stage it was probably all very effective."

"If you believed in spirits in the first place," Ari said.

"You had to, yes." Annie grinned at him. "She also gave private séances in her hotel rooms after the show. Most patrons probably had had a few drinks by then, so a different kind of spirits came into play."

"Is that where she used that ouija board?"

"Yes. Everyone sat around the table and joined hands, except for her of course. That little pointer thing that goes in the middle of the board? You put just one finger on it, with the excuse that the spirits get carried away and might knock it off the table. You're guiding it to various letters, of course, but if you practice, no one can tell."

"If everyone joined hands," I said, "then there probably was a good flow of Qi around the table."

"Oh, yes," Annie said. "It would have been the only legitimate phenomenon of the entire night—and the only one her patrons couldn't see."

Ari snorted, and she laughed. "This must all be very hard to accept, Inspector."

"I'm trying," Ari said. "By Qi, I take it you mean the same energy that karate people believe in."

"It's similar, yeah," I said. "But you don't believe in it like something religious. You either accept the evidence for it or not."

Ari made a noncommital noise, kind of like "umph."

"How about some tea?" Annie said. "I even have some cookies. Oh, it's so nice knowing I'll have a little extra money in the bank. And the Agency payment certainly helps, too."

"I take it you're willing to keep working for us," I said.

"Of course. That reward money won't last forever." She took off her glasses and busied herself in polishing them. "I know just how fast money you count on can disappear."

When it came to the tea, Ari slopped milk into his mug, British style. When I tasted mine, I followed his example.

Annie did not mess around when she made tea; it was as dark as coffee. We sat around the kitchen table and discussed the current case, particularly Evers' murder, while Duncan begged for bits of cookie. I also filled Annie in about Caleb.

"I keep thinking that he's somehow related to the coven," I told her, "but I really doubt that he's the hooded man. I'm still not sure if we have one case on our hands or two separate ones."

Annie had a thoughtful sip of her tea. "Maybe it's not so clear-cut," she said eventually. "Maybe the cases aren't joined, but parallel. The hooded man could be the link, not Caleb."

"Yes!" I sat up straight in my chair. "Thank you! I hadn't looked at it that way."

"More tea?" Annie held up the teapot, then continued talking as she refilled our mugs. "Do you think Belial is a human being?"

"I'm beginning to have my doubts. Doyle told several individuals that Brother Belial was afraid of germs, but I'm betting he wrapped up to hide who he really was—or what."

"Why not both?" Annie said. "What was that H.G. Wells story? *The War Of The Worlds.*"

"Right, the Martian invaders who were killed off by the common cold. If this guy comes from some other world, who's to say he has any kind of resistance to our diseases?"

"Or us to his," Annie said.

"That's an unpleasant thought, but yeah, it should work both ways, unless his people are overly sanitary and real good at killing germs."

"Do you really think," Ari broke in, "that this person might actually not be human? Or are you just having a—"

"No joke," I said. "He could come from some other world level entirely, and who knows who lives on it?"

"You're serious, then?"

"Very. I know this must be kind of hard to accept."

Ari made a strangulated noise, started to speak, then scowled at me instead.

"Well, look," I went on, "we've had a glimpse of one

deviant level so far. There was something so strange about it that I'm ready to believe just about anything. Ari, you heard Mike's description. Annie, you've read my report?"

"Oh, yes. The nuclear war planet."

Intuitions nagged at me. "Well, that's what everyone who lives there believes, yeah."

"You don't?" Annie said.

"I don't know what I believe. When I got that one look at it, what with the giant mutant morning glories and all, I believed the nuclear explanation. But there was something so odd about it. It's hard to put it into words." I let memory images rise. "It all looked solid. But it didn't seem real."

"I should think it wouldn't," Ari said. "Not at first glance. It would take anyone's mind time to come to terms with what you were seeing."

"That's true." I knew that a concept lay just beyond my mental grasp, but the words for it refused to come. "You could be right. Maybe that's it, then. But as for Belial, who knows what he is? A human neurotic scam artist is the most likely explanation."

"Well, after all, if he was an alien," Annie said, "Evers couldn't have met him for a drink in a public bar. I mean, San Francisco has some rather odd inhabitants, but I do think people would have noticed an alien from another planet."

"You never know around here." I grinned at her. "But yeah, I'm sure you're right about that."

"When I do my usual searches, I'll keep my extra eyes open for anything really outré, though."

"And listen with your third ear, too."

Ari tensed with a cookie in hand and stared at Annie.

"A joke," I said.

He relaxed and gave the cookie to the dog.

When we left Annie's, I found myself thinking about Reb Zeke, as I'd started calling him. If I could get a look at the man, I could track him with Long Distance Remote Sensing.

"You know," I said to Ari, "there are particular areas where panhandlers and the homeless hang out. We could drive through them, and you could see if you spot Reb Zeke."

We took a long slow tour of the sleaziest parts of San Francisco, around Sixth Street and Mission, up through the Tenderloin, down again to cruise along Howard and from there, back to the portion of Mission Street that runs parallel to Market. We never saw a sign of Reb Ezekiel until we were heading home.

We were driving out on Fell Street beside the park area called the Panhandle, a narrow slab of trees and lawns—the "pan" of the handle is Golden Gate Park—dotted here and there with benches and the occasional piece of children's play equipment. We'd stopped for the light at Ashbury when I spotted a group of men standing near the concrete hut that housed the public restrooms.

Since we had an hour before the police cleared the parking lane to ease the rush hour traffic, I found a spot on the right-hand curbside just beyond Ashbury and parked the car. Ari got out and stood with his hands in his pockets while he looked across the street. I saw him smile the tigerish grin, then dart right out into Fell Street and start dodging cars. I shrieked. How he made it across alive I cannot say—good reflexes, I guess, and blind luck.

I got out of our car and stood behind it on the sidewalk to watch Ari making his way toward an elderly man, dressed all in black, who sat slumped on a bench, asleep. Standing nearby, sharing a joint or maybe a cigarette—I couldn't really tell from my distance—were three other guys who had the rumpled clothes, messy hair, and defeated posture of men down on their luck. On the other side of four lanes of busy street as I was, I couldn't hear what Ari said, but the elderly man sat up, looked at him, and let out a shriek that carried all the way across. He jumped to his feet. I could see him clearly enough to figure that, yes, we'd found Reb Ezekiel.

Reb Zeke began to back away. When Ari took a step toward him, he yelped again, then ran, surprisingly fast for someone who looked so old. He darted between a pair of eucalyptus trees, where I lost track of him. Ari started after him, but one of the smokers, an African-American man who must have been nearly seven feet tall, stepped in front of him and blocked his way. For a couple of minutes they argued. Every time Ari tried to step around him, the guy moved with him. The other two finished what they were smoking, so openly that I assumed it was just a cigarette after all, then ambled over to help keep Ari penned.

Eventually, Ari gave up. The three watched him go as he stalked away. He went back to the traffic light and crossed on the green, which I took as meaning that the survival instinct had reasserted itself. Scowling, muttering under his breath, he rejoined me at the car.

"What went down?" I said.

"The man on the bench was Reb Ezekiel. I would have had him if it weren't for the misplaced loyalty of his street friends." Ari paused for a deep breath. "When I called his name, he screamed."

"I heard that. Did he say anything else?"

"You can't take me back." He shrugged. "Whatever the old sod meant by it."

"Did he recognize you?"

"Of course not! It's like I told Tzaki, he hasn't seen me since I was eight years old. I tried to tell him my name, but I doubt if he took it in. He was in a complete and utter panic."

"And those other guys—"

"Saw immediately that I was a police officer of some sort. I suppose you develop an instinct for it if you live on the street. They were very polite." Ari growled under his breath. "But they wouldn't move. Leave the rabbi alone, sir, the tall fellow told me, he dunt do nothing wrong."

"He called you sir?"

"Yes. As I said, very polite. I tried to explain that I wasn't going to arrest him, but they didn't believe me."

"Well, let's get back in the car. We can drive around and see if we can spot him."

While I drove, Ari called Lieutenant Sanchez about the "person of interest," as he described Reb Zeke. Sanchez promised he'd get a couple of squad cars over to the area. As we hunted for our runaway, we saw a lot of police on the streets, but neither we nor they found our fugitive rabbi.

I did, however, talk with Lieutenant Sanchez later, once we were back in the apartment. He called to discuss a left-over question from the Silver Bullet Killer case, the sudden and inexplicable decay of the criminals' bodies after their deaths. I'd asked for information about the fate of the blood soaking Doyle's shirt. The report had arrived, and as I'd suspected, the blood had disappeared as if by magic or dry cleaning. The silk shirt stayed behind. He must have bought it in our world.

"Look, O'Grady," Sanchez said, "I realize that there are things you can't tell me. But do you know if the rapid decay was the result of something the military's working on?"

"I don't know, and that's the honest truth." I lied only because the truth would have been impossible to explain. "They don't tell me or my agency anything unless they're forced to, and it usually takes a Congressional committee to do the forcing."

"Crap," he said. "I was afraid of that."

"I don't think we'd be out of line to suspect them, how-ever."

"I have to agree with that. Okay, and thank Nathan for me, will you, for the tip on that homeless man. We'll round him up yet. A couple of uniformed officers found and inter-viewed the men who interfered with Nathan's attempt at capture. That tall Black guy's easy to spot."

"For sure. You know, if the street people are protecting your witness, it's no wonder you haven't been able to find him."

"Exactly. But those three, they were willing to talk about 'the rabbi' as they called him. Insisted he was harmless, a real loony, though, talking about flying saucers and some kind of alien invasion."

"Uh-oh. Do you think he'll have any useful information about Evers, then?"

"No, but I'll follow up anyway. Nothing new on the Evers case, by the way. I'm about ready to agree it was suicide and leave at that."

I could decipher the wording: the pressure from above to drop the case was becoming intolerable.

"Too bad," I said. "But that's how things go, sometimes."

"They sure do." Sanchez hesitated, then spoke in a voice dripping with false humor. "Just never mention the word blackmailer in this connection, okay?"

I pretended to laugh. "I won't, for sure," I said. "To go back to our homeless person of interest. Did his buddies mention why he ran when Nathan tried to talk with him?"

"He's convinced that some of the aliens are out to get him. So I guess he thought Nathan was one of the flying saucer people. Now there he just might be right."

With that he hung up. My alleged flying saucer person was at the moment sitting on the couch, flipping through the TV channels with the remote. I assumed he was looking for soccer games. When I caught his attention, he turned the sound off and listened to my rerun of what Sanchez said.

"Interesting, all of it," Ari said. "So Sanchez thinks Evers was a blackmailer?"

"I got that impression, yeah. If so, the theory runs, one of his very important victims might have taken steps to end the blackmail once and for all. The only trouble with that theory is that it's completely wrong."

"A trivial problem." Ari paused to smile at me. "This doppelgänger business—I wonder if I look like someone Reb Ezekiel knew in that other whatever it is."

"Deviant world level," I said. "If so, you're not a nice guy over there. Not that you're a nice guy over here, either."

"I try to avoid that, yes. Which reminds me. I really should be teaching Michael how to handle a gun."

I winced.

"I knew you wouldn't like the idea," Ari went on. "But he's going to need to know how to defend himself, especially if he can't learn to do what you do."

"Ensorcellment? It's a real rare talent, so yeah, you're right. I appreciate your asking me first." I managed to smile. "That's a yes, by the way. Better he learns from you than from José and the BGs."

"That's precisely what I thought. There's a gun club over by Lake Merced. I'll see about getting a membership tomorrow." Ari glanced at his watch. "They're doubtless closed by now." He stood up and stretched. "I'm going to go down to the deli and get takeaway for dinner. Do you want to go with me?"

"No, I'm going to run an LDRS on Reb Zeke while his memory's fresh."

"Shouldn't I stay for that?"

"Why? It's just a routine procedure. When you're at the deli, could you get some actual vegetables? They have salads there."

"I promise. I'll be right back."

"Okay. And I'm going to call Caleb and see about that lunch date."

But when I called the cell phone number on Caleb's business card, I only got his answering service. I left my name and number and a message about arranging our lunch. To emphasize the business aspect, I asked if I should bring a resumé with me—a silly question, since he claimed to want my psychic skills, but I figured it would set the tone. To underscore it, I added that Ari and I were moving to a new flat, and so I might have to postpone the lunch till the next week.

With that out of the way, I brought out my large-size pad of paper and a box of crayons for the Long Distance Remote Sensing operation, or as the old sources call it, farseeing. I sat at the kitchen table and picked up a black crayon to start with. I slowed my breathing, thought of Reb Zeke, and let my mind range out. My hand jerked once and began to draw. I kept the memory image in my mind and let my hand take over.

It picked up crayons, drew, laid them down again, then finally put itself back into my lap. When I looked at the drawing, I saw rough sketches of tall buildings looming like monsters over a small figure dressed in black. Here and there a scribble in a bright color indicated a sign or label on one of the buildings. Absolutely nothing indicated where in the downtown area Reb Zeke was. Still, San Francisco's a small city, some eleven square miles, is all, and the downtown's a small portion of the whole. Sooner or later, Sanchez's men were bound to find him.

As soon as I mentally spoke that thought, I received a subtle warning, not quite a full SAWM, certainly not as strong as an ASTA, but a warning nonetheless. I concentrated on Reb Ekekiel—no, he wasn't the source. Someone else was hunting me, even as I searched for Zeke. I put up an SH—a shield persona, as the Agency calls them, a barrier to mental detection. The warning vanished. I took the SH down so I could think.

Who? Belial? Or maybe the shadowy guy who spoke to the Peacock Angel? The more I thought about that question, the more puzzling it became. The Chaos forces must have already known both me and my location, judging from the projections and Chaos critters I'd seen: Fish Guy, the green possum thing, the fake office worker, the invisible presence in the elevator, and finally the off-balance magical symbol painted on the new flats. Since they knew, they could come after me if they wanted to, yet so far I'd only been aware of surveillance, not attempts on my life or even serious malice. My license to ensorcell might have been making them think twice, and Ari and his gun collection possibly was deterring them, as well.

Perhaps—the thought struck me—perhaps they didn't know about the Agency. I'd assumed they knew that I was committed to serving Harmony, the balance point between Chaos and Order, but I had no way of knowing if that assumption was accurate. They might have considered me a lone Chaos operative, out for what I could get in the way of power and money, just like them. In that case, they might see me as a competitor or maybe even a useful ally, at least for the short run.

Those ideas gave me such a solid satisfaction that I knew the Collective Data Stream underlay them. I expanded them: if they didn't know about the Agency, then they likely came from some other deviant world level, where it didn't exist. Instead of a "they," I probably faced an "it" or a "him," a single actor, the most likely candidate for Chaos master being Brother Belial rather than Caleb, who'd impressed me as a candidate not for master but for "in over his head."

One thing I knew for certain. I needed to stay on my guard. Friendly relations between Chaotics never lasted long.

Ari returned shortly after with a large brown paper bag.

He put it down on a kitchen chair, then picked up the drawing from my LDRS.

"All it tells us is that he's downtown somewhere," I said. "Not real useful at the moment."

"No, but at least you can locate him." He laid the drawing down again. "Tomorrow, when it's light, we could do some more hunting. Though if it rains, he'll be driven indoors somewhere."

I glanced out the window at a sky dark with clouds, scudding in fast from the ocean. "Well, if they leave the homeless shelters open," I said. "Sometimes they don't, even in weather like this."

"Pretty rotten of them, then. Let's hope they do."

The paper bag turned out to be filled with small white cartons, one of which held coleslaw, the only vegetable dish he'd bothered to buy. It was better than nothing, I supposed, despite the mayonnaise dressing. He set the cartons out on the coffee table in front of the couch while I brought plates and silverware from the kitchen.

"There's nothing worth watching on television," Ari said.

"I'm not surprised. I've got some DVDs. They're over on the bookshelf."

Ari rummaged through the collection while I inspected the deli food to see if there was anything I could eat besides coleslaw. I heard him snort and looked up to see him holding a boxed set of *Looney Tunes*, a present from my brother Sean a couple of years back.

"Cartoons?" Ari glared at the boxes as if he suspected them of holding explosives.

"Bring them over," I said. "I love Bugs Bunny. You must have seen some of these, right?"

"No."

"You really did have a deprived childhood, didn't you? Well, it's never too late."

Actually, it was too late. I had never seen anyone sit through the best of Bugs—"Wabbit Season," Marvin the Martian, and "What's Opera, Doc?" my absolute favorite and a great cultural monument—with such a stony face. Occasionally Ari did smile. Very occasionally. Mostly he ate pastrami and dolmades and olives, steadily and neatly, and pita bread stuffed with all sorts of fattening things. After twenty minutes of this, I'd had enough.

"Never mind." I pressed the remote and ejected the current disk. "Maybe you'd prefer the video of my uncle Harry's funeral."

"Well, sorry!" Ari gave me a nasty look. "I just don't see the point, is all, of watching things like this. Yes, some of the spoken lines are clever, but they're only drawings, not real people or situations."

"The point is having a good laugh and forgetting the troubles of the world."

"I can think of better ways to do that." He slipped an arm around my shoulders and smiled. "When you're done eating and all that."

I leaned away from him in self-defense. "And when you don't smell like garlic and vinegar." I risked a sniff. "And onions."

"I'll have a shower." He let go of me and sat back on the couch. "I got you some baklava. I never did get to lick honey off your face."

"I'll smear some on just for you." I wiped my hands on a paper napkin. "For now I'll put these disks away."

Yet as I was returning the boxed sets to their place on the bookcase, I had an inspiration.

"Just one more," I said. "See what you think of this."

I put the disk devoted to the Roadrunner into the DVR and went back to the couch. Ari watched politely for a minute, then smiled. All of a sudden, when Wile E. Coyote's Acme brand catapult flipped a boulder onto him rather than onto the Roadrunner, Ari laughed, not his usual polite attempt to share a joke, but a real deep honest-to-God laugh. He continued to laugh at assorted explosions, runaway jet skates, accidents with firecrackers, unexpected railway trains, and malfunctioning rifles. I wondered if I had a doppelgänger on my couch until I remembered the one other time he'd laughed in the same hearty way, at the thought that Johnson might have been bitten by a werewolf. Consistency—one of Ari's salient characteristics, all right.

"Oh, very well," Ari said at last. "You've made your point. Now these are really rather amusing."

I smiled and turned off the video equipment.

While Ari took the promised shower, I did one last bit of research. A hunt through the apartment turned up the copy of the New American Bible I'd gotten for my first communion. I'd kept it mostly because my father had given it to me, but it came in handy that night, as did all those irritating hours I'd spent in religion class during my school years. When your uncle is a priest, like my uncle Keith, you don't dare cut religion class. You're sure that God will know and tell him. I had a dim memory of the original prophet Ezekiel's visions, which somehow seemed relevant to the case of his self-described successor, Reb Zeke.

I sat down on the edge of the bed, under my reading lamp, and turned to the Book of Ezekiel. It took me about two minutes of reading the first chapter to realize that "relevant" didn't even begin to describe it. I read through the entire vision twice. A damp Ari, wearing nothing but a pair of jeans and the smell of his witch hazel aftershave, came in just as I finished. Normally the sight of him in that condition would have made it impossible for me to concentrate, but that night I managed to keep going.

"What are you reading?" he said.

"The Book of Ezekiel, Chapter One, verses one through twenty-six." I looked up to see him scowling. "What's wrong?"

"We had to memorize that in the kibbutz school. Lot of sodding nonsense."

"It sounds like it could be a description of aliens and some kind of space vehicle."

"That's why we had to memorize it, so we'd recognize the aliens when we saw them invading." He sat down next to me on the bed. "Let me see that translation."

"This is the standard Catholic version." I handed him the Bible. "Or at least it was when I was in school."

He frowned over the passage, then read aloud, "As I looked, a stormwind came from the north, a huge cloud with flashing fire enveloped in brightness, from the midst of which, the midst of the fire, something gleamed like electrum." He shook his head. "That's not right. It isn't electrum. The word's ḥashmal."

"What does that mean?"

"No one really knows what it meant back then. Reb Ezekiel thought it was the name of the landing vehicle's pilot." He rolled his eyes. "Quite doubtful, really. It's become the modern word for electricity." He turned back to the beginning, then frowned again. "The way they used 'river' here is another mistake. The word means a canal, the Chebar canal in this case, that ran from Babylon to Warka."

"Is that the famous waters of Babylon?"

"Where we sat down and wept, remembering Zion? Yes."

From the way he said "we," you would have thought he was personally remembering the experience. He reminded me at that moment of my grandfather, who could rattle off a list of every massacre the English had perpetrated upon the Irish, starting in the twelfth century.

"They've left out a bit." Ari pointed to a line in the middle of the vision. "Here where it's describing the four-sided creatures. Aliens, of course, according to the ridiculous doctrine under which I was raised. Let me think, how would the missing line go in English?" He paused for a long moment. "In and among the creatures, bits of fire were dashing about—something like that. Reb Zeke, as you call him, said those were flashing signal lights from the landing vehicle, reflecting on the armor of the aliens." He looked at me. "Do you want me to go on, or is this enough?"

"More than enough, yeah. You know, I was almost convinced myself that the prophet was talking about a spaceship and an away team. That vision is something else again. Wheels that can roll in any direction without veering, huh? And all those eyes! The creatures could be androids powered by force fields, and then their bases would be rimmed with sensing devices."

Ari got up and laid the Bible down on the dresser. "First Bugs Bunny, now this!" he said, all mock seriousness. "I think you need a distraction from your own mind."

He hooked his thumbs into the waistband of his jeans

and smiled at me. I began to feel warm all over. Sexual desire raises the level of Qi, whether those feeling the heat know what to call it or not.

"Yeah, I do," I said. "If you'll turn on that dim light on the dresser, I'll turn this bright one off."

He did, and I did. When he sat down next to me, the warmth turned into a fever, and his mouth burned on mine.

CHAPTER 8

I SLEPT SOUNDLY THAT NIGHT UNTIL DAWN, when I woke to use the bathroom, probably because the rain was pelting down outside. Ari stayed asleep, though he reached for me when I lay back down. I cuddled against his chest and dreamed about Reb Ezekiel, that he had something to give me. When I woke again, the rain had stopped. Ari was already up and studying his Latin lesson for the day. I joined him at the table for coffee and told him about the dream.

"It probably just means he can give me information," I said to Ari, "which we kind of knew already. But I still want to go out and look for him."

"Driving again?"

"Yeah, since I can't pick him up on a scan. A quick survey of the kind of places he might hang out in could turn him up. If we spot Reb Zeke, you can come at him from one direction, while I come up from behind. I'd hate to ensorcell someone who looks as frail as he does, but I may have to, if we can't physically pin him."

"That would work, yes. If I spot one of the men who were protecting him, I can call Sanchez. The police can pick him up, and they'll get the information out of him—"

"Yeah, sure!" I broke in. "The last piece of information we'll ever get, if the cops work the guy over or scare the bejeezus out of him. Look, I've got some ideas about this."

Eventually he agreed with them. I dressed for the job in

my tightest jeans, a low-cut black blouse, a pair of beaten-up black boots with medium heels, and my older brother's cast-off khaki trail jacket as a nod to the damp weather. As I was leaving the bedroom, I had a sudden inspiration. I took the plastic bag that held the remains of Michael's stash and slipped it into an inside pocket. Ari wore his usual jeans, a gray sweater, and his leather bomber jacket.

"You look like one of the homeless yourself," Ari told me.

"That's the idea," I said. "I need to stop at a liquor store to buy a couple of packs of cigarettes. They're almost as good as cash on the street."

I did, however, also withdraw some of the Agency's money from the nearest automatic teller machine. If I'd been down and out and desperate, I'd have wanted payback for information, so I couldn't blame the people who actually were in that condition. When I got back into the car, Ari gave me a grim look.

"I don't like this," he said. "I don't think you should go through with it, not without me there."

"I've been waiting for you to say that. Can you think of anything better?"

"No, since you don't want the police involved."

"It may not come to anything, you know, or we could get lucky and spot Reb Zeke himself, in which case I won't have to playact at all."

"Let's hope, then. But if things look too dangerous, I'm not letting you out of the car."

"You'll let me out when I tell you to, or it could ruin everything."

He glared at me, then shrugged and started the car.

Because of the plan I had in mind, I had to let Ari drive. He did try to avoid killing us or wrecking the rental car, driving at about half his usual speed, stopping at stop lights, and refraining from swerving in front of buses and trucks. I only shrieked twice. Back and forth we went, first to the Panhandle, then downtown along Mission Street.

We cruised past the filthy sidewalks around Sixth and Mission, turned up Sixth and surveyed the human misery standing or sitting among the alleys and cheap hotels. We returned to Mission via Market and Seventh, where the traffic had Ari cursing in several languages at once. At Fifth, we turned up past the Old Mint, a dirty stone takeoff on a classical temple. A couple of men were sleeping on the little lawn in front, but no one we recognized.

We finally hit paydirt on Market itself. The office workers had all gone inside to their jobs by then, and the store clerks had yet to arrive to open the fancy boutiques and department stores, so the broad street, gleaming with silver streetcar tracks, stretched out oddly empty. A few people wandered along the sidewalks; a few cars drove down the asphalt side lanes. We were traveling past the shining clean windows of Bloomingdale's department store when I looked across the many lanes to the opposite side of Market. The unusually tall African-American guy was sitting on the sidewalk near the cavernous entrance to the Flood Building, a multi-story pile of gray stone. Ari drove on a little ways and let me off at Fourth Street.

"Go back to Fifth and Mission and park in the municipal lot," I said. "I don't think things will get nasty, but you never know, and I want to know you've got my back."

"I'll be there if I have to leave the sodding car in the middle of the street."

In cold gray fog light I crossed Market and walked along the sidewalk under a row of plane trees that lifted bare branches to the damp sky. The tall guy was still sitting where I'd spotted him. He was wearing a pair of filthy slacks and a green parka that I recognized as old Army issue, dirty and faded. Darker spots marked the places where he'd once worn insignia, probably his unit number and service branch, that kind of thing. A dark patch on the sleeve formed the silhouette of a chevron of sergeant's stripes.

When I came up, he looked at me and quirked an eyebrow. His hair had gone gray at the temples, with a scatter of gray hair in the rest—First Gulf War vet, I figured. I leaned against the brass plaque on the Flood Building wall, right next to where he sat.

"Mind if I join you?" I said.

"Pretty girl like you?" He had a deep voice but pleasant. "Hell, no, I don't mind."

For a moment or two we stayed companionably silent, waiting for a pair of the well-dressed employed to go past, her wrapped in a pink wool coat, him in a fitted leather jacket and tweed slacks. They glanced at us and hurried on fast.

"Hey, Sarge," I said, "someone told me you know where the rabbi is."

"Yeah? They was wrong."

"I'm not a cop."

"Sure you're not." He laughed.

I slithered the rolled-up plastic bag of dope out of my jacket pocket, holding it tight against the cloth to keep it hidden. Once I held it securely, I casually relaxed my arm till the bag hung in his line of sight. He whistled under his breath and snatched it to stow it inside his own jacket.

"Okay," he said, "so you're not a cop. My mistake, sorry 'bout that. Why do you want to find the rabbi?"

"I heard he has something to give me." I handed him, openly this time, a pack of cigarettes and a folder of matches.

"Thanks," he said. "Let me light one of these, and we'll talk. You want one?"

"No, I don't smoke."

"Smart girl. Wish I didn't."

I squatted down next to him on the upwind side. My jeans groaned but, thank heavens, didn't split. He lit the cigarette and took a couple of long drags. "Okay," he said, "what's your name?"

"Nola." I decided against adding my last name.

Sarge grinned, exposing a couple of gaps between yellow teeth. "Okay, you're right about that. He's got a letter for you. I don't know who it's from. He just keeps talking about giving a letter to some chick named Nola O'Grady."

"That's me, all right. How are we going to get together? I don't have an address I can give you. My man won't like it if I do, y'know?"

Sarge nodded, took another drag on the cigarette, and considered the problem. "Not sure," he said at last. "I don't know where the rabbi is. Honest, I don't. He freaked because a cop came up to him and knew his name. That was yesterday. He's disappeared somewhere, but y'know he can't have gone far. I mean, he's got no money."

"Yeah, that usually keeps you close to home. He's sure got a thing about flying saucers, doesn't he?"

"Jeez. You get sick of hearing it sometimes."

"Do you know why he's so afraid of cops?"

"Ain't we all?" Sarge paused for a bellow of laughter. "But the rabbi, he swears up and down he got sent up for something he didn't do. He ain't going back inside, he tells me, not for nothing. Eighteen years, he told me, in slam."

"Where? Do you know?"

"Somewhere in Israel, or that's his story. How did you get all the way over here, then? I ask him. He never would say, just kept shaking his head. Weird. But it was the flying saucer people who put him away, he tells me, so who knows where it was?"

"Uh, right, or if it happened at all." Dimly I could see that everything I knew about Reb Zeke was hovering on the edge of making sense, albeit a very weird kind of sense, but I'd need more information before I could push it over that edge. "That's too bad, either way."

"Yeah. I'll tell him about you when I see him again. He's bound to show up somewhere, one of the places that feed us, a shelter or something. I'll tell him I saw you, and that you're looking for him so you can get that letter." He paused to gaze across Market Street toward Bloomingdale's. "Most dry days I hang out around here, if the cops don't roust me. The tourists, some of them part with a few bucks. You could come back here and find me, and maybe I'll have news."

"Good idea." I stood up, then took a twenty from my jeans pocket and held it out. "Thanks for the help."

Sarge grinned and took the bill, which disappeared so fast, with just the bare flick of his wrist and a shake, that I couldn't see where in his clothes he'd hidden it.

"Nice trick," I said.

"You don't want people seeing when you get something worth stealing." He laughed again. "I got plenty of free time to practice."

"There'll be another one of those if you find the rabbi for me."

"Cool." Again the gap-toothed grin. "I'll keep an eye out."

By then a sporadic trickle of pedestrians flowed along the sidewalk, and out in the street traffic was picking up. I glanced around and saw Ari on the other side of Market, waiting for the light to change at the crosswalk in front of Bloomingdale's. I realized a little late that Sarge might remember him from their encounter in the park.

"See ya," I said, "and the rabbi, too, I hope."

I trotted off toward the crosswalk and reached it just as the light changed. A small crowd hurried toward me, including Ari, who was walking behind a couple of well-dressed older men and a pair of young women wrapped in sleek trench coats and high-heeled boots—boutique clerks, I figured.

I moved back out of the way and leaned against the cold stone wall of the old Woolworth's building. The older men looked my way and nudged one another, but mercifully they kept walkng. The girls minced by, giggling, in a drift of heavy perfume. When I glanced down the street, I could tell that Sarge was watching me. He was close enough to see what I was doing but too far to recognize Ari, especially considering Ari's clothing, so different from his police outfit of yesterday.

Still, caution demanded I come up with a new wrinkle on my original plan. I opened the jacket and pulled it back on my shoulders to reveal the low-cut blouse. When Ari reached me, I smiled and said, "Hey, good-looking, want a date?"

Ari stopped, looked me over with a perfect poker face, and said, "How much?"

"Depends on what you want."

"Let's discuss it. I'll buy you some breakfast."

"Thanks." I slipped my arm through his. "Sounds good."

I glanced back to see Sarge giving me the thumbs-up sign. He stood to get a share of whatever money this supposed john paid me, if he could deliver the rabbi and his mysterious letter.

Ari and I did go out to breakfast, but over on Irving Street near the apartment in a narrow diner, a throwback

to the Fifties with its chrome and beige Formica. The place
reeked of decades of frying bacon. Ari ordered pancakes
and chicken sausage. I had a scrambled egg and a glass of
skim milk. While we ate, I told him what I'd learned from
Sarge. The letter puzzled him as much as it did me.

"How does Reb Ezekiel know your name?" Ari said. "I
keep coming back to that."

"Yeah, me, too. The only theory I can come up with is that
he's immensely talented, psychically, I mean. This letter may
not be an actual piece of paper, you know. It could be some
message he saw in a dream with my name attached to it."

"Oh. Then I suppose it could be about aliens and spaceships."

"That's my greatest fear, yeah."

Ari poured syrup over the stack of pancakes and dug in.
I nibbled at my egg and considered the problem from several possible angles. Zeke might have picked my name up
from the aura field if he could access that, and I suspected
he could. His images of the Prophet Ezekiel must have derived from it. He might have run across Brother Belial or
Caleb and gotten my name—and the letter—from them.
The running across might have been physical, or it might
have occurred in a trance state. Caleb knew who I was, and
just maybe that meant Belial did, too.

"I wish you'd eat like a normal person," Ari said.

I snapped myself back to the present moment. "Say
what?"

"You've been picking at that one sodding egg for ten
minutes."

I realized he'd gone through most of his breakfast.

"Did you want to leave? I don't have to finish it."

"No, quite the opposite. I want you to finish it. And have
some of mine, too."

"This is plenty."

"No, it's not."

We stared narrow-eyed at each other while a waitress
hovered in the aisle beside our booth. She looked nervous,
as if she expected us to start shouting. It occurred to me that
we were on the edge of doing just that. As much as I disliked giving in, I refused to cause a scene in a public place.

"Okay," I said. "I'll shovel it in. If you don't want that last pancake, I'll take it."

He smiled, a tight little expression, and put it on my plate. The waitress smiled in open relief and drifted away to attend to other customers. I shoveled food as promised.

When we left, Ari shoved his hands in his jacket pockets and said not one word. Passersby stepped aside to let him go by or walked around him in a wide arc. When we reached the car, I drove, and he said nothing then, either. Nor did he speak as we went upstairs to the apartment. I let us in, then shut and locked the door behind us. I turned around to find Ari scowling at me with his arms crossed over his chest.

"What's wrong now?" I said.

"I don't appreciate having my partner act like a common prostitute."

"It was just my cover. Besides, you sure picked up the cue easily enough."

"I assumed you had a reason of some sort for the charade."

"It's not like I ever was a hooker, if that's what you're worrying about."

"Of course it isn't! Don't you think I have more respect for you than that?"

I caught myself on the edge of escalating the quarrel. "I don't get it, Ari. What's wrong?"

"I just told you."

"No, you didn't. I mean, I don't think that's the only thing. I don't get why you're so pissed off."

"What? You're the one who's so bloody psychic."

I thought I understood. "It's all getting to you, isn't it?" I said. "All these things that you thought didn't exist. It must be kind of like culture shock—"

"What a sodding condescending thing to say."

My mental calm tore like wet paper. "Then what's so wrong? You sulky son of a bitch!"

He stared at me, his mouth a little open, as if he wanted to speak but couldn't find words. I stared right back, but I wondered why I wanted to attack despite the SAWM inside my head that was screaming retreat. I felt Qi gathering around me like a cloud of biting flies, sharp and tormenting—his anger, I realized, not mine.

"What are you going to do?" I said. "Hit me?"

Ari tossed his head like a frightened horse, took a deep breath, and stepped back. "Never," he said. "I'm sorry."

The SAWM died away. The cloud of Qi drew back and began to disperse, but slowly, one fly's worth at a time. I felt so physically hot that a rivulet of sweat ran down my back. I took off the heavy jacket and tossed it onto the nearby computer chair, then ran my hands through my hair to lift it off my damp neck. Ari watched me with eyes that showed no feeling at all. I let the hair fall and wiped my sweaty palms on my jeans.

Ari took off his jacket and hung it over the back of the chair with a careful, almost fussy set of gestures, centering the jacket, smoothing the sleeves, turning the collar down. Anger management, I said to myself. They taught him how to calm himself. I'd spotted the techniques before, but I hadn't considered their implication. For the first time, I realized just how dangerous a man he was.

"It takes me over sometimes," he said. "I try not to let it. The rage, that is."

"Yeah, I guessed." My voice sounded reasonably steady to me. "But do you have some kind of gripe to air?"

"I don't know." He walked over to the couch and flopped down on it. "Nola, I'd rather cut off a hand than hurt you."

I hesitated. Prudence dictated that I sit on the computer chair with the coffee table between us. Prudence has never been my strong point. I sat down next to him on the couch and felt Qi begin to swirl around us, a turbulence in the air. He leaned back, slumped down with his legs stretched out in front of him, and rested his head on the top of the cushioned back of the couch.

"There was someone, though, wasn't there?" I tried to choose careful words. "That you did hit. Only once, probably, and a long time ago."

He stared up at the ceiling while he talked. "Oh, yes. We were both in the army at the time." He hesitated again, just briefly. "I slapped her across the face. She struck up and broke my jaw with one punch."

I gained a sudden respect for Israeli womanhood.

"She outranked me, too." Ari turned his head and gave me a twisted little rueful smile. "I remember sitting on the floor of the hotel room in a great deal of pain and watching her call a doctor on the telephone. I can still see her standing there afterward, rubbing her sore knuckles and saying, 'Oh, by the way, our affair's over.' I'd already assumed that, actually."

The stormy Qi began to smooth itself into a flow.

"What did your superior officers have to say about all this? It couldn't have been the first incident."

"It wasn't, just the first involving a woman. They gave me a choice. Learn to control the temper, or be discharged. I learned. If I hadn't been such a good marksman, they probably would have court-martialed me for striking an officer, but they didn't want to lose my rifle. They wanted me to reenlist when the time came, you see, and move from military police to the special forces. As a sniper."

I saw a Possibility Image in my mind: Ari in battle gear, lying stretched out on a flat roof in pitiless sunshine, the rifle cradled in his arms, his beautiful eyes narrowed as he watched a target below.

"Why didn't you?" I said. "Become the sniper, I mean."

He returned to staring at the ceiling. The gray fog light, dappled from the lace curtain over the window, threw shadows across his face. I waited, then waited some more.

He said, "I wanted to keep my soul."

For a couple of minutes we sat without speaking. Outside the N Judah streetcar rumbled past. A car alarm sounded, then stopped. Ari continued looking at the ceiling as if he were memorizing every stain and crack on it. I wondered how I could possibly want to stay involved with a man like him. Even though I'd just seen him take charge of himself and his rage, there could come a time when he'd choose not to control it. With a past like his, what could anyone expect from him but rage that now and then slipped its leash?

"Are you going to end this?" he said. "Our affair, I mean."

I hesitated and cursed common sense.

"I can't blame you," he went on. "We can still work together. I'll promise you that."

"I'm not going to end anything."

He turned his head and looked at me, just looked for maybe a minute. "You need my rifle, too," he said.

"It's more than that." I leaned over and kissed him, a quick brush of my mouth on his. "The rifle's just a bonus."

He sat up, and for a miserable moment I honestly thought he was going to cry. Instead, he put his hands on either side of my face and kissed me. The wave of Qi broke over us like warm water.

We spent a long time in bed that afternoon. He fell asleep, eventually, while I lay awake and wondered if I'd been stupid or smart. We had to work together indefinitely because both our agencies had decreed we would. Trying to do so without sex would be impossible, I decided, because without that outlet his rage would take him over sooner rather than later. It was a nice psychological explanation and utter crap, of course, because the truth was simple: I didn't want to give him up.

I was expecting that neither of us would refer to the incident again, but he rose above my expectations. For dinner, we ate the remains of the deli food from the night before, while a soccer game played on the TV with the sound off. About halfway through, Ari turned to me.

"Do you want to know what set me off this morning?" he said.

"You know what it was?"

He nodded.

"Yeah, I do want," I said. "Because I don't want to trigger it again."

"It was the way you took over the entire maneuver. I raised objections; you ignored them. It was obvious you were in charge." He smiled, rueful again. "And then you had to go and be right."

"Oh." My first thought: so, now you know what it feels like! Aloud, I said, "Yeah, I can see why that would get to you."

"But I'm not making an excuse for my later behavior. I take full responsibility for that."

I was willing to bet that those lines were right out of the manual for whatever program he'd been in. That he remembered them gave him high marks by my reckoning. "You could have told me right then," I said.

"Yes, I should have. I'm too used to working alone. I tried to tell you that when we first met."

"Well, I'm used to working alone, too."

"But you're the head of an operation now, aren't you?"

Exactly what I'd taken on hit me hard. I was no longer a single operative consulting now and then with a pair of part-time stringers. Small as my team was, it had become just that, a team, and I needed to learn how to lead it. I had a brief moment of panic where I considered handing authority over to Ari. I squelched the idea and the panic both.

"Yeah, I am the head of this op," I said. "I've got a lot to learn, but I'll learn it. Y'know, I've never been part of an army unit or even a sports team. This is all new."

"But you've been part of that peculiar mob you call your family." His smile took any sting out of the words. "You can draw on that."

He was right. I could. I kissed him for it, too, despite the garlic and onions on his breath.

Although I checked the messages for both my cell phone and my landline several times that evening, Caleb never returned my call. When I tried an SM:P for him, I ran into a psychic wall. I could assume that he'd put the hangover behind him and regained his strength. I did get a vague impression from an LDRS of a dimly lit room without any visible furniture in it, but I received no indication of where the room was.

Kathleen, however, called me midevening. When I asked her if she knew where Caleb was, she told me no. Jack was watching TV in his study, with no plans to see Caleb until later in the week.

"I think maybe Jack saw through Caleb a little bit," Kathleen told me. "Caleb got so drunk at the party Sunday that Jack insisted he stay over. And really, I hate him, but I didn't want him to get killed on the freeway or something. So he threw up all over the bed in the green guest room, and ended up sleeping in the blue guest room, where at least he didn't barf again."

"He's a really heavy drinker, huh?" I said.

"He is, yeah. He wasn't as bad when Jack first met him. But this last week, he's been awful. I think that's why Woofie Five bit him at that other party. He smelled weird from all the scotch."

"Drowning his sorrows over something, maybe?"

The moment I'd said the words I knew how significant they were. What if Caleb had drowned that girl at Ocean Beach? He'd committed a crime before, but murder fell into an entirely different category. He could easily be falling to pieces with terror at the thought of going back to prison. At nineteen, a cute guy like Caleb would have found himself real popular with the hardened older cons, though not in any pleasant way. It was also possible, I supposed, that if he'd killed her by mistake, he might even be feeling remorse.

"By the way," Kathleen said, "Did Ari get those—"

"He's still working on the case. He needs to confirm some details, he tells me."

"Okay. I really appreciate him doing this."

The irony of it pinched my conscience, but I kept my mouth shut about the Donovan connection.

It took us Tuesday evening and all day Wednesday to pack up the old apartment. One good thing about moving: you find stuff you've forgotten you had. I threw out a bunch of chipped coffee mugs, an out-of-style torn skirt I'd never gotten to the tailor's, and my collection of "farewell, it's over" letters from old boyfriends, which I should have dumped years before. In the back of a closet, I turned up a digital camcorder I'd been given when I first worked for the Agency as a stringer during grad school. I was investigating ghost sightings and recording interviews. The camcorder had been state of the art, back then. I kept it because it would still be useful, I figured, for family holiday gatherings.

I took breaks now and then to run LDRS and Search Modes for both Caleb and Reb Ezekiel. I picked up no traces of Zeke, but now and then on Wednesday I caught a glimpse of Caleb, driving a car on a winding road that ran along the tops of cliffs overlooking the ocean—Highway 1, of course. I could never get enough of a mental impression from him to tell what he was doing there or where he was heading.

Late in the afternoon on Wednesday, I called my other former stringer, Jerry Jamieson, who worked as a specialized kind of hustler, a man who dressed as a woman. The type particularly appealed to customers from South America, though not exclusively, or so he'd informed me. Wherever they came from, the customers were willing to spend a lot of money on a specific sexual fantasy, of being the passive partner in anal sex with a man in drag. I may have been a psych major in college, but analyzing that particular desire lay way beyond me.

At any rate, I described Reb Ekeziel and told Jerry about the letter, but omitted any mention of deviant world levels, mostly to save time. Jerry had a skeptical turn of mind, probably due to his chosen profession, and I didn't want to get into some involved argument over their existence.

"So suppose I spot this old guy," Jerry said. "Should I glom on to him?"

"Only if it's easy. He has friends on the street, and you don't want to get them involved. If he's willing to have you buy him a cup of coffee or something, sure. If he runs, no. If he doesn't run, tell him you know Nola O'Grady. Call me either way."

"Will do, darling. I haven't seen any Agency money in too long."

"Well, we're willing to put you on regular payroll."

"That means obligations, doesn't it? Regular reports, following your orders, all that tedious middle-class behavior."

"Some, sure, but it's not like you have to wear a suit and work in an office. Think about it, and let me know if you want to sit down and talk."

"I will. I'm not getting any younger, after all."

I clicked off and returned to packing up the kitchen while Ari took apart the bookcases. Late that afternoon, Ari left for a couple of hours to return the rental car and pick up his new vehicle, which, he informed me, had been specially customized.

"Promise me you'll stay inside," he said. "I don't want you out on the street alone without me there to keep an eye on things."

"Don't worry," I said. "I've got too much to do here anyway."

"You look tired." He considered me for a moment. "When I come back, we'll go out to dinner. Make a reservation somewhere, and you can see how the new car handles."

I made reservations at a small Russian restaurant on Balboa Avenue, not too far from the apartment, but far enough to drive the new car rather than walk. I also called Caleb about our so-called business lunch. I'll admit to being relieved when once again I got the answering service for his cell phone. He was still on the road, I figured. I left a brief message, saying I'd play another round of phone tag later, and clicked off.

With that out of the way, I sat down at the kitchen table and tried another LDRS for Reb Ezekiel. No matter how hard I concentrated, nothing came to me but a profound sense of absence. Either Zeke had died in the night, or he'd gone through a gate to some other deviant world level. I returned to my computer and web-surfed all my news sites, looking for a story about a homeless man found dead.

I found no reports of such deaths, but I did see a string of stories about rogue waves. Like hammers in an invisible hand, they had smashed into the cliffs all down the coast, starting in Pacifica at high tide just before dawn and continuing down to just north of Santa Cruz. When the tide turned, they stopped. No one had been injured. No structures, only cubic yards of dirt and rock, had fallen to the sand below. I immediately thought of Caleb, driving south on Highway 1.

I shut down the computer to foil Chaos hackers and spent a few minutes gazing at the blank screen, hoping for images. None. As far as Reb Zeke went, I was stuck with the gate theory, which in turn led me to believe that more gates existed in San Francisco than the one in the Houlihan house and the one that had been in the park. The old problem nagged at me: why the Houlihan house, of all places?

Finally I soothed my frustration by getting dressed up. I decided to wear a dress, since I knew Ari would like it, and I put on makeup, too. If you're going to regress to your teen years, you might as well do it right and flatter your boyfriend's ego. I owned several dresses, an ugly black number for funerals, and then a flowered summer dress, which would have been too cold, and a soft blue silk-and-linen blend that fell straight from a shirred neckline. It had nice warm sleeves. I chose the blue and added the gold pin he'd given me.

When Ari returned with the new car, and I saw this supposedly wondrous vehicle, I was shocked. It sat glumly by the curb, a gray sedan, several years old, with dark gray upholstery. I spotted a stain from some kind of beverage on the back seat and a couple of worn tracks on the fabric that might have been made by a child's car seat.

"A Saturn?" I said. "They gave you a Saturn?"

Ari was trying not to laugh, or to be precise, to make the odd noises that served him as a laugh in all circumstances but watching Roadrunner cartoons. "It's been heavily modified," he said eventually. "What did you expect? A Jaguar? An Aston Martin? Something that would attract attention everywhere we went?"

"Good point. No one's going to look twice at this."

"Get in." He handed me the keys. "Try it out."

As soon as I pulled away from the curb, I realized what Ari meant by modifications. Even when we were moving at a fast clip the car barely vibrated. It was as heavy as a 1960's Cadillac, thanks to some sort of armor installed between the plastic Saturn shell and the upholstery, but with its upgraded power steering, it handled like a sports car.

Ari's mystery mechanics had also added a pair of buttons on the steering column next to the horn. Punch one, and the red light you were approaching turned green. Punch two, and all the windows but the windshield darkened; you could see out, but no one could see in. Ari also had a device to carry with him that would stop the car in case of theft, though doing so would destroy the transmission.

"It doesn't fire nuclear missiles, however," Ari told me. "Or walk on water."

"Bummer," I said. "It's too bad it won't come when it's called. You know, like Wonder Woman's invisible jet."

Ari made a strangled noise that seemed to signal disgust.

"Just a joke," I said. "What's wrong?"

"Wonder Woman?"

"Er, I guess you didn't read that kind of comic when you were a kid."

Again the strangled noise. I decided to let the subject die.

"At any rate," Ari went on, "are you going to let me drive on occasion?"

"On occasion, like when I'm not in the car with you. It's bad enough having Chaos masters out to get me. You don't need to help them along."

"Oh, come now! My driving's not that bad."

"Hah!"

"Everyone drives that way at home."

"Remind me never to drive in Israel, then."

"If that's even a possibility." His voice turned wistful. "I'd enjoy showing you the country, even if you didn't want to live there. We could go on holiday."

I fumbled through my mind for a joke to turn the moment aside. Couldn't find one. He'd mentioned marriage once, and I wanted to make sure it stayed at only once. For a moment he watched me, waiting. At last he looked away and said nothing more until we reached Katya's restaurant. After I parked, he helped me out of the car.

"You look wonderful tonight," he said. "I meant to say so earlier."

"Thanks," I said. "I'm betting you speak Russian, by the way."

He merely smiled. Once we got inside, however, his perfect Russian got us great service. While we ate blini with golden caviar for a first course, I realized the pattern to his "unusual flair for languages," as his resumé called it.

"The European languages you told me you know," I said. "I bet they're Russian, French, Greek, and Turkish."

"Very good on the Turkish. Yes, I think of it as European, too."

"That part of the world will always be Anatolia to me."

"My old-fashioned girl. Very old-fashioned, by about what, a thousand years? There's one more European language, though, that I speak. Let's see if you can name it."

I thought for a long time. "Can't," I finally said. "Unless maybe Albanian."

"English." He grinned at me. "It's a foreign language to me."

"God! I keep forgetting that."

"Good. That means I'm speaking it properly." He reached for the last pancake on the plate. "I don't suppose you want that."

"No. I'm saving room for my main course."

"I'll hold you to that. Why did you ask about the languages?"

"It just occurred to me that the ones you know all have a bearing on Middle East politics. No Swedish or Irish for you."

"True. That's a nice bit of logic."

And a good thing about the Irish, too, but I kept that thought to myself.

Chapter 9

ON THURSDAY, WHEN THE TIME CAME TO MOVE, my local relatives offered to help except for Father Keith, who had church duties. Kathleen and Jack, however, had to beg off. She called me early and explained that Jack had woken up "sick as a human," as she always modified the cliché. She took the dignity of dogs seriously.

"He says he's got a touch of food poisoning," Kathleen said. "I say he's hungover."

"Did you guys go out last night?" I said.

"He did." She put emphasis on the "he." "But I'm real sorry, Nola. I wanted to help."

"Oh, it's okay. I don't have a lot of stuff anyway. Was he out with you know who?"

"Yeah. Who else?"

She paused, and in the background I could hear Jack's baritone growling at her. "My sister," Kathleen's voice sounded as if she was holding her phone away from her mouth. "I'm telling her that we're copping out on her."

Jack growled again, a little louder.

"He says he's sorry, too," Kathleen said into the phone. "I thought maybe the sea air would—"

This time Jack spoke loudly enough for me to hear. "Would you hang up that damned phone?"

"When I'm done talking," Kathleen said.

I had never heard them sound on the verge of a fight before.

"I'll let you go," I said. "He probably needs some love and Alka-Seltzer."

"I wanted to ask if you'd like a puppy." Kathleen pointedly ignored both my offer and the remark. "Or maybe a bonded pair. Tuesday, y'know? I took in some darling terrier mixes that some jerk dumped by the side of the road. I had the vet check them out, and they're in great shape."

"No, I can't. The lease was real specific about that. No pets." Actually, I was lying. I'd learned over the years that outright lies were the only way to fend off Kathleen's efforts to load me up with dogs and cats.

"I don't see how you can live in a place like that."

"Er, well, y'know. I'd better go, Kath. I've got to pack up the stuff in the fridge."

I clicked off to find Ari watching me. "Caleb's back," I told him. "But I'll wait till he calls me."

"You don't want to seem too eager, no," Ari said. "By the way, I've put in a request for detailed information on Caleb to the Massachusetts Attorney General's office. They should get back to me soon."

"You really must work for Interpol."

"Of course I do, as I keep telling you. Would I lie to you?"

"Of course you would, if you needed to."

Ari looked so annoyed that I dropped it. I had reasons for wondering. According to my own Agency's workup on Ari, he left Interpol for long periods of time to go off and do something for an Israeli undercover group that wasn't part of Mossad, unless maybe it was. Its true status was as mysterious as the "something" Ari did for it. Our agent had run into the proverbial stone wall when he'd been trying to put together a report on Mr. Nathan. I doubted if Ari believed that sleeping with him gave me the right to ask outright for more information, so I didn't. I was, however, beginning to get some ideas.

Early on Thursday morning, Ari and I made one run over to the new flats with several boxes of fragile things like glassware and our laptops. It was a good thing we did, because the Chaos magic symbol had returned, along with some typical graffiti, the F-word, and a tag insulting everyone of Chinese descent.

"I'll go get the hose and those rags," Ari said.

I threw a Chaos ward at the symbol with no result at all. Apparently, the paint was only paint this time around. Before we left, Ari washed everything off of the wall. Neither of us wanted Aunt Eileen to see the obscenities.

Aside from that nasty little incident, the move went as easily as moves ever do, which meant tiring and confused but possible. Even without the Donovans, we had enough warm bodies. Uncle Jim took Thursday off and allowed Michael and Brian to miss a day of school. Aunt Eileen, my older brother Sean, and his boyfriend Al also showed up. We got all the stuff out of the apartment, into the upstairs flat, and arranged in a single long day, except of course for the inevitable boxes of small items that only I could put away.

We even had a surprise helper. Around one o'clock, Itzak Stein turned up. He'd taken the afternoon off, he told me, to help Ari install the security system.

"Security system?" I said.

Itzak gave me his charming smile. "Did you really think Ari could live without one? Mr. Suspicion Writ Large?"

"More fool me, yeah. Well, then, thank you."

While the rest of us unpacked and fussed with furniture, Ari and Itzak scurried around, hammering insulated staples, stringing wires, placing routers, and generally putting together elaborate electronics inside and out. At one point I walked into the bedroom to find Ari frowning at my old camcorder. He was turning it around and around in his hands.

"Something wrong with that?" I said. "It's not going to blow up or anything, is it?"

"No, it's just very unusual." He set it back down on the dresser. "I've never seen one quite like it."

"That's because I got it from the Agency. There's a guy there who does stuff to stuff."

"Interesting. Do you need me to move some furniture?"

"No. I think everything's pretty much in place."

Toward the end of the day, Uncle Jim ordered pizza and soft drinks for everybody, and salad, too, at my insistence. While we waited for the order to arrive, I went into the bedroom to start hanging clothes in the closet. Michael followed me. With him came a little Chaos critter, a scaly blue cross between a lizard and a meerkat, with yellow claws and snaggly brown teeth. He called it "Or-Something," since we had no idea if it was male or female, alive or some sort of artificial construct. Whatever it was, it could walk the worlds and carry messages between them. Normally, the Chaos masters use them as spies, but this particular creature had come over to the side of the Balance, mostly because Mike fed it. It sniffed at the folded blankets and promptly pissed on the mattress.

"Fail!" Michael said. "Clean that up!"

Or-Something whimpered, and the puddle of green slime dried up and disappeared without leaving a stain.

"Nice trick, bro," I said.

"Thanks." Michael rummaged in his jeans pocket, brought out a couple of linty M&Ms, and gave them to the critter. "It can learn stuff, but you've got to be seriously patient with it."

"Yeah, I bet. How does it make the mess disappear, or do you know?"

"I think it just dumps it in another world, probably the one it comes from, wherever that is."

"So it can move things between worlds?"

"I guess." Michael shrugged and held out his hands palm-up. "It can't talk, so I dunno for sure."

I opened a cardboard box of Ari's clothes and set it on the bed where I could unpack more easily. Or-Something started to sniff the cardboard in a suspicious manner. When Michael snapped his fingers, it disappeared, much to my relief.

"There was something I wanted to ask you," Michael said. "About Lisa."

"Which one?"

"The one in the deviant level. I've sort of broken up with the one here."

"Just sort of? You mean: she doesn't know it yet."

He winced. I spent a few seconds rejoicing that I was no longer a teenager.

"But anyway," Michael said, "the one there, y'know? I was wondering if I could bring her here."

"Say what?"

"Help her start a new life, y'know? She's stuck in that crappy world, working as a—a—" He braced himself. "A whore, really, a cheap whore, and she's too good for that."

"They're all too good for it, the women who get forced into prostitution. Look, Mike, when you say 'cheap whore' you're being really judgmental. She's got to do what she's doing to survive."

"Well, yeah, I know that. I just didn't think, like, you would."

"I'm not judging her. Women have worked in the sex industry practically forever."

"Thanks. But I still want her to stop doing it. She sure wants to stop."

"Good for you and her, but getting her the new life isn't going to be easy. She'll be an illegal immigrant. Her life's going to be one long juggling act."

"Yeah, but the family knows how to do that, because of—"

"Careful!" I paused to look around. "You never know who's going to be listening."

"Sorry, yeah."

Michael went to the bedroom door, glanced out into the hall, then shut it. I waited to speak until he'd come back to the closet. He handed me one of Ari's shirts from the box on the bed. I put it on a hanger.

"She'll even need a new name," I said. "She can't use Lisa, because there's a Lisa already here who's just like her. Who is her, really."

"She knows that. And I meant to ask you, what if she did come here, and then ran into the other Lisa? If they met and like maybe shook hands, would they explode or something?"

"I've got no idea. I'll ask NumbersGrrl."

"Thanks, yeah, she might know. Lisa's always wished she

was named Sophia, she told me. She read it in a book some-where."

"She can read, then."

"Yeah, when the gang girls take in a baby, they try to raise it right."

Except, of course, for expecting these children to end up hustling on the streets or running some other scam, but I kept that thought to myself. What choice did they have, re-ally?

"Anyway," Michael went on, "I thought maybe you could get her fake papers. Like, through the Agency."

"You do realize, don't you, that you're asking me to commit a felony?"

"A felony?" He gaped at me. "But if the Agency—"

"The Agency is not God. It has to operate within certain guidelines, for instance, the laws of this country. Getting fake papers for an illegal alien is frowned upon by your typical district attorney. As we all know."

"Well, yeah." He handed me another shirt to hang up.

"There's also a person whose permission you'd have to get."

"I already asked. Aunt Eileen talked about Mary Mag-dalene and then said yes. She'd never let a girl live like that when she could take her in and help."

"I should have known." I paused for a long sigh. "I take it Lisa wants to leave and come here."

"Who wouldn't?"

"You have a point, but look, if we do this, and I do mean if, buster, she's going to be the only one. You cannot bring your entire gang."

"I know that. Once she's here, I'll never go back. I prom-ise. It's too dangerous. You were right about that."

"Occasionally, my aged brain comes up with the right answer, huh?"

"You bet. It's not just the rads, though there's that."

"You told me about the cops and the gangs. Life there must be pretty violent."

"Unless you're rich. But—" He paused again, frowning at the floor, thinking something through. "I don't know what this is, like, all about, but José's been making some

weird hints, about something I could do and like maybe
make a lot of money." He looked up. "I just keep changing
the subject. I don't know why, but whatever it is creeps me
out."

"That creepy feeling's a warning. Your talents are coming online, all right. Doesn't Lisa know what José means?"

"If she does, she won't tell me, not yet anyway. No one
else is going to tell me anything, that's for sure." Michael
paused, then smiled like a man with three aces and a pair
of kings. "She's got all kinds of information you can use,
about the levels and gates and stuff. She told me she
wouldn't tell me until we said she could come through, but
I believe her."

I couldn't blame a girl in Lisa's position for bargaining. I
would have done the same in her place. I still felt like
smacking the clever little darling across the face.

Michael was watching me with large hopeful blue eyes.
So, what do you do when your baby brother—the one you
bottle fed, changed, pushed in a stroller, walked to his first
day of school, taught to ride a bike, helped with his homework, and so on down the whole cruddy maternal list—
comes to you because his first real girlfriend lives in
desperate circumstances and you can help get her out?

"Oh, all right." I took the bargain. "Let me see what I
can do. If the Agency ever sends a team to seal off that gate,
I want you and Lisa on our side of it, so we'd better get
moving."

"Thanks, Nola!" Michael beamed at me, then threw his
arms around me and hugged. "You're the best sister ever in
both of the worlds. I'm hella stoked! Seriously!"

I returned the squeeze, but I felt like a complete sucker,
not thanks to any psychic talent, but Just Because. As soon
as everyone else began eating, I filed a report with Y. I requested his help with getting Sophia a U.S. passport or at
least, a green card that she could eventually use to apply for
citizenship. I emphasized that the girl had crucial information to trade for the papers. Beyond that, as I told Michael,
we could only wait and see what the Agency decided.

Late that night, after the last of the pizza was eaten and
everyone had gone home, Ari and I sat on the old blue

couch and contemplated the big stack of folded-down boxes. Outside, the rain began with its usual cozy patter.

"I did something really stupid this afternoon," I said.

"Agreed to help Michael and his girlfriend, yes." Ari said. "I suppose this information the girl has will be worth it."

"It better be! He must have told—" A sudden suspicion appeared in my mind. "Or do you have the bedroom bugged?"

"No, of course I don't! The office downstairs is on the security system, but I've blocked off the sounds from our bedroom. Simple decency and all that. Can't have you scaring the neighbors."

I was too tired to kick him. "But about Michael—"

"Yes, he did tell me. He asked me if I could get the papers if you couldn't. Your brother's entirely too clever."

"You mean, he doesn't believe you only work for Interpol?"

"Exactly. I told him that if he let one wrong word slip, they'd find his body on a lonely hillside." Ari stretched his legs out in front of him, a somehow melancholy gesture. "I doubt if he believed that, though."

"Do you think you could get her the papers?"

"If she were Jewish, we could cover her under the Right of Return, but according to Michael, she's not. Why?"

"Just a vain moment of hope that I could pass the buck. Oh, well, if I end up in federal prison, will you visit me?"

"I'll do better than that." He put an arm around my shoulders and drew me close. "I'll smuggle you out of the country before they catch you. I know how to get a new identity for you."

"You're wonderful."

"I'm glad to see you recognize that."

He smiled, and I kissed him. We didn't do much talking the rest of the evening.

At ten o'clock the next morning, I was unpacking glassware in the kitchen when my uncle, Father Keith, the Franciscan priest, called me. His first words, not even a hello, were, "Is Michael using drugs?"

"He told you about Lisa?"

"He told me a strange tale about a girl of that name."

"It's all true, the deviant world levels, his sweetheart in one of them, the works."

"Did her parents really dump her in an empty lot when she was two days old?"

"They did, yeah, because of her club foot. It happens a lot over there."

Father Keith was silent for so long that I began to wonder if we'd lost the connection.

"Too bad it's true," he said eventually. "I'd know what to do if he were using drugs."

"Why did he call you, anyway?"

"To see if I'd make her a fake baptismal certificate."

It occurred to me that Michael was going to be a first-class operative at the Agency once he officially joined up. "Will you?" I said. "After all, you've done it before."

"My sins haunt me. How badly do you need it?"

"Let's just say it would be a great first step in a long process. You'd be helping save this poor girl from a life of sin. She's being forced to work as a prostitute."

"Yes, Michael made sure to cite the example of Mary Magdalene. Let me think about this."

He hung up before I could say anything else. The abrupt end to the call put me off guard when the phone rang again. I clicked on, expecting it to be Father Keith. Instead, Caleb said hello. It took me a moment to gather my mind. Once I did, I felt profoundly uncomfortable, even though Caleb sounded pleasant and businesslike.

"Sorry about the phone tag," he said. "I had to go out of town for a couple of days. Some unexpected business dealings."

"Well, we were moving, too," I said. "Not a problem."

"Good, good. That's always a real chore, all right."

I pinpointed the problem as the distinct feeling that someone else was listening in to the call. It was nothing so clear-cut as the sound of breathing, or even that slight hollowness of sound that occurs when an eavesdropper's on a second phone, but I felt it nonetheless.

"Now, about that lunch date," I said, "I'll be unpacking for the rest of today. Tomorrow? Sunday?"

"Tomorrow would be best for me. Where are you living now? Is there some place good nearby? We want a place that's quiet so we can talk."

"For sure. None of those bright shiny places where everyone sounds like shrieking parrots. We're in the outer avenues, near Noriega."

"Okay, then I know where we should meet." Caleb paused for a strangely high-pitched laugh. "How about the Cliff House? The dining room, not that burger place. It's about as old-fashioned quiet as you can get."

"Sounds good. One o'clock?"

"Perfect. I'll see you then."

We ended the call. I continued unpacking while I went back over the conversation in my mind in order to decipher my feeling of discomfort. In their elaborate security system, Ari and Itzak had included the "interference generator" that protected cell phones conversations and other wireless communications, which made a tap in unlikely. The listener, therefore, had to be in Caleb's mind, or attached to his consciousness one way or another as a psychic wiretap, as it were. The obvious candidate: Brother Belial.

I suspected that I was going to meet him at lunch, too, whether he was present physically or not. When I considered Caleb's odd laugh, I remembered that the Cliff House stood just down the hill from the place where Doyle and Johnson died. Either Caleb's sense of humor was even stranger than Ari's, or the thought made him real nervous.

Although Father Keith never called me back, a couple of hours before sunset, he did drive over in a borrowed red SUV full of werewolves. Since the moon would be full that night, the Hounds of Heaven, as they called their pack, had gone to Father Keith's protection the day before. All five of them sat decorously in their seats inside the SUV, each wearing a doggie safety harness, Lawrence in the front seat, JoEllen, Matt, Ryan, and Samantha in the seats behind. Each also had a leather collar, decorated with a dog license tag and a small silver cross.

Keith himself was wearing his floor-length brown Franciscan robes. He's neither tall nor short, a compact, solid-looking man with curly gray hair, tonsured of course, and pale blue eyes. When I went outside to greet them, I noticed the window of the downstairs apartment next door, which looked our way from right across the driveway. Instead of the usual drawn curtains, I saw faces plastered against the glass, staring.

"It's warm down in town today," Keith said. "Since I was coming all the way out here, I thought I'd take the pack to the beach for a run."

"Sounds good," I said. "What's with the crosses on the collars?"

"Just something to help them keep their focus. It's not easy for them, keeping the chaotic side of their nature under control."

I helped him unlatch the wolves from their safety harnesses. They bounded out of the SUV one by one, shook themselves, and began sniffing around the sidewalk and the steps like ordinary dogs, tails wagging, tongues lolling. Of course, they all looked like wolves, not dogs, and they were all larger than Great Danes and stockier than St. Bernards, especially Lawrence, the alpha male. When I glanced at the building next door, I saw that the neighbors in the upstairs apartment had also come to their windows to stare. I gave them the sorority girl wave, that is, hold your hand up straight and waggle only the fingers, but they didn't even have the decency to look embarrassed.

"Why not come with us?" Father Keith said. "We haven't had a chance to talk in a long time."

I hesitated, tempted by the thought of fresh air and exercise. "I dunno," I said, "Ari's at the gym, and I should wait till he gets back."

Keith raised an eyebrow. "What's this? He keeps you on a leash? I could get you one of those ornamented collars."

"Very funny! Ha ha. But no, I'm worried about rogue waves. Did you hear about that girl who drowned not far from here, and then the lawyer down by the Ferry Building?"

"I did. You don't think the waves were natural."

"I sure don't. I don't want another one coming for me."

"Well, it should be low tide now, according to this morning's paper."

"Okay." I realized that if a wave did erupt, I'd be able to confirm my theory, assuming I got out of the way in time. "I really should take a look at the ocean, anyway."

"I could pray to Maria Stella Maris for protection," Father Keith said. "Or we could just go to the park."

"No, let's try the beach. I'd better leave Ari a note. I'll run upstairs and be right back."

"Wait a minute." Father Keith leaned into the van and took a piece of paper out of the glove compartment. "You'd better put this somewhere safe inside. Oh, and get yourself a sweatshirt. The wind's going to be chilly."

The paper was a baptismal certificate for one Sophia Chekov, dated sixteen years earlier and artfully stained with weak tea to age the paper. He'd put a couple of crumples in it, too, and rubbed a little dust along one edge.

"Why is her birthplace listed as Kiev?" I said. "And why was she baptized in Italy?"

"Italy because I was there that year. Kiev because Michael wanted it that way. He's got a scheme in mind."

"I see. It's a good thing you joined the church. The criminal element would have been real glad to employ you if you'd given them the chance."

"Just go get the sweatshirt, will you? My wolves are getting restless."

Since the beach was so close, we walked. The Hounds formed up into a tidy pack and sauntered ahead of us until we crossed the Great Highway. On its western edge we climbed the low rise of dunes, covered in ice plant, sea grass, and assorted weeds, and looked down onto Ocean Beach itself. A cool wind smacked us with the scent of dead and decaying ocean critters that most people call the "fresh smell of the sea."

The tide, just at its lowest point, rolled white foam onto the long stretch of pale beige sand, littered with dead kelp and driftwood. At a distance to our right, far up the misty beach, a few people were strolling on the firm sand at water's edge. Otherwise, we saw no one but a flock of sandpipers.

At the smell and the wild view, the pack broke ranks. With yips and muffled howls, they raced down the rise, slipping now and then in the soft dry sand, and headed for the water's edge. The sandpipers threw themselves into the air and flew away. I noticed, though, that Lawrence hung back, trotting after the others with his tail and head held low, still mourning his slain mate.

"Be careful!" Father Keith yelled after the wolves. "Remember who you are!"

We followed more decorously. Down by the water the air felt a lot colder than it had on the city streets. I zipped up my orange sweatshirt, and Father Keith pulled up the cowl of his robe. When I looked out to sea, I spotted a thick gray line at the horizon.

"Fog's coming in," I said.

"It sure is." He turned to look north, where the pack had dashed into the shallow water. "Stay close!" he called out.

For an answer they bounded out of the water and raced off to the north. We followed, striding on the firm damp sand.

"Their idea of a joke," Keith said. "I've been learning some interesting things about werewolf psychology lately."

"I bet. Say, does anyone in your order—well—mind that you have wolves hanging around you once a month?"

"I've been consulting with the higher-ups about that. So far, they agree that five souls are always worth saving, no matter how unusual the souls are. It might even be possible to schedule a meeting at the Vatican, but I wouldn't count on that."

Always the lousy higher-ups, I thought, whether in my agency or his, taking their time with their damn decisions!

The wolf pack turned and circled back, this time with Lawrence in the lead. Seawater and sand crusted their legs and white bellies. They galloped up to us, leaping and wagging, then dashed off to the south. We turned around and followed.

"They can't help wanting to run like this," Father Keith remarked. "But I wish they wouldn't get so far ahead."

"There's something I want to ask you. The Wolf of Gubbio, that legend about St. Francis, you know? Is there any chance it was a werewolf?"

Father Keith laughed under his breath. "If you'd asked

me that six weeks ago, I would have said no and suggested you see a qualified therapist. Now, well, I have to say yes, there probably was a wolf, and yes, it probably was a were-creature. Look, the legend tells us that the wolf was huge, it was solitary, and it sought out human company by hanging around a town. It listened to what the holy saint had to say and made a bargain with him, which indicates a human mind."

"Sure does. I wonder if it had gotten itself stuck in wolf form somehow."

"Maybe. Or maybe the original story did feature a were-wolf, and the monk who wrote it down figured that such things were nonsense. Medieval people didn't believe every crazy idea that came along, you know."

Keith paused to shade his eyes with one hand and look for his pack. By then the wolves had gone a good half mile down the beach. The tide was coming in stronger, reaching white fingers a little farther up the sand with every wave. When I looked out to sea, I noticed that the gray fog line was beginning to rise up in tufts like drifts of smoke. The breaking waves crested into blue-green swells, crusted with rusty-red kelp floats, higher and closer to shore than they been when we'd arrived. I saw a lone surfer crouched on his board as he waited for the right wave.

"One crazy surfer out there," I said, pointing.

"Where?" Keith looked out to sea. "I don't see anyone."

The surfer caught a good swell and rose to stand on his board. He was too tall, I realized suddenly, to be a human being.

"It must have been a trick of the light," I said, "or maybe a seal. I don't see him now either."

But of course I did see the huge figure, surfing the billow high and easily. Olive-green kelp draped his body. His long purple hair flowed in the wind as he lifted something to his mouth—a conch shell, wreathed in strands of seaweed. The note sounded long and low as it echoed over the murmur of the rising tide. Far down the beach the wolves began to howl. When Triton blew his wreathed horn a second time, they turned and raced back toward us.

"That's odd," Father Keith said. "I thought I heard a musical note." He shrugged. "Must have been a car horn, out on the Great Highway."

As the wave began to break, Triton and his surfboard disappeared. I was disappointed, because I'd been hoping to see him traveling the pipe.

Whining, ears flat, the sand-crusted wolves surrounded us, pushing one another to get close to Father Keith. Samantha, the omega female, leaned against me. When I stroked her sea-damp head, I could feel that she was trembling and not likely from cold. Father Keith knelt on one knee and began murmuring under his breath in Latin to comfort his little flock.

"There, there," I whispered to Sam in English. "Triton won't hurt you. He saw you as Chaotics, is all, and was warning me."

She whined openmouthed and wagged her tail in a feeble sort of way, then sat down at my feet.

While I'd been gawking at Triton, I'd missed noticing that we had company on the beach. Two people had come down from the dunes, and they'd obviously seen the wolf pack. Up on the dry sand a man and a child stood staring at us. He looked around thirty, the little girl was maybe six, and they shared a sandy-haired, freckled Norman Rockwell kind of face that marked them as dad and daughter. They both wore jeans and the heavy jackets of locals, not tourists. At first I wondered if they were actual people or more Chaotic projections. I cast a quick ward, which had no effect on either of them.

When Father Keith stood up again, they apparently decided he was approachable, thanks to his holy-orders robe, most likely. They walked over to join us, though they stayed about ten feet back from the lolling tongues and white teeth of our pack.

"Uh, excuse me," the man said. "We were just wondering what kind of dogs they are. They're pretty big, huh?"

"Yes." Father Keith looked completely flustered. "They're uh um—"

"Caucasian Lion Hunting Dogs," I broke in. "A very rare breed in this country, though there's plenty of them in Georgia and Kazakhstan."

"No wonder I never heard of them." The man smiled, but the little girl clutched his hand tighter still. She leaned against him with the same gesture that Samantha had just displayed with me.

"They won't bite," I told her. "But you're right to hang back like that."

"Yep," her dad said. "Never go right up to a strange dog. You know, I didn't realize that there were lions in that part of the world."

"There aren't anymore," I said. "They were hunted to extinction a long time ago."

"There used to be lions all through the territories around the eastern Mediterranean." Father Keith could never resist a chance to teach. "In what's now Iraq and all around the Black Sea as well as Turkey."

"That's right!" the man said with another smile. "I saw some pictures once of an old wall or something."

"The Assyrian lion hunt reliefs, probably."

The man nodded, a contemplative gesture.

"We'd better go," I said to Father Keith. "It'll take us a while to dry them off enough to get them back into the car."

"I'm glad that's your job, not mine," the man said. "They're sure big. And pretty dirty."

With a pleasant wave, he and his daughter walked on past, heading for the water's edge. We went in the opposite direction, stumbling across the soft sand toward the rise of dunes and the Great Highway.

"Lying is sinful," Father Keith said, "but I'm glad you're so good at it."

"Thanks. Let's just hope he doesn't look the breed up on the Internet."

When we got back to the building, the first thing I noticed was that wretched Chaos symbol, blatantly back on the wall. The second thing was even more ominous. Ari was sitting on the front steps, simmering. That is, his arms were tightly crossed over his chest, his mouth was shut tight, and his eyes—glaring doesn't begin to describe it. When he rose and came down the steps, the wolves clustered around me in defense and growled.

"Uh-oh," I said. "I think I'm in trouble."

Ari managed to remain civil while I introduced my uncle. He even went upstairs to fetch some old towels so we could clean the wolves off. Once we'd gotten everyone back into the SUV and on their way home, I scooped up the towels and hurried up the steps ahead of him to the downstairs flat. He followed me into the front room, shut the door, then stepped in front of me before I could escape.

"I told you to stay inside," he said.

Before I answered, I tested the flow of Qi. At the moment, at least, he had his rage under control.

"Oh, come off it!" I said. "I didn't feel the slightest touch of ASTA or SAWM. If I had, I'd have stayed home."

"Oh? What if you'd felt them when you were already on the beach? How fast could you have reached safety?"

"No one was going to threaten me with the wolves right there."

"I noticed how they protected you, yes, but what if someone had a sniper's rifle? He could have killed you from several hundred meters away. The wolves might have brought him down in the end, but it wouldn't have done you one sodding bit of good."

"Well, okay. I overlooked that."

He snorted. The flow of Qi stayed steady and normal.

"But are you angry," I said, "because of the danger, or because I didn't follow your orders?"

"Oh." He considered this seriously. "Both, I think." He paused, then shrugged. "I'll go get the hose. When I got back from the gym, I found that Chaos mark waiting. I asked the neighbors about it, but they insisted they'd seen nothing."

"That's really odd."

We trooped outside again. I glanced at the downstairs neighbor's window, but they'd closed the drapes. So had the upstairs set. The Chaos symbol looked smug.

"Huh," I said. "Stenciling the thing on like that would have taken a while."

"So you'd think." Ari considered the apartment house with narrowed eyes. "None of them look like the type to have done it, but I wonder."

After I threw a couple of wards at the symbol, and it had

stopped sizzling, he washed it down with the hose. I wiped the resulting smears off the wall with the old towels.

"Give me those," Ari said. "I'll take them down to the launderette if you promise me you'll stay inside while I'm gone. Upstairs. Away from windows."

"Okay, it's a deal. I might even get domestic and cook something. Aunt Eileen stocked the refrigerator for us."

He mugged shock and took the dirty towels.

That evening I called Michael and told him that I had the baptismal certificate. He responded with a whoop of triumph, or at least, I took the whoop to be triumphant. It's hard to tell with whoops.

"That's only step one," I said. "We've got a long haul ahead of us."

"Well, yeah," Michael said. "But Aunt Eileen said I could bring her here now, so she wouldn't have to turn any more tricks. But she said you have to agree."

Even though I would have preferred to have all the paperwork in hand, I shared my aunt's desire to spare the girl more trysts with radioactive customers.

"Okay," I said. "But look, you can't go on having sex with Sophie in Aunt Eileen's house."

"I know that." He sounded so indignant that I knew he hadn't thought of it till that minute.

"Just making sure. And why the name Chekov? You didn't get that from *Star Trek*, did you?"

"Yeah, it's the only Russian name I could think of."

"Why Russian?"

"I was thinking about all the rads Lisa—I mean Sophie's been exposed to. What if she needed to see a doctor one day, and they noticed?"

"It seems likely they would, yeah."

"So she could be from Ukraine, I thought, you know, where they had that big nuke plant blow up whenever it was. It was near some city or something, but Kiev's the capital, so I figured she could have been born there."

"Your knowledge of foreign affairs is astounding," I said. "Okay, that makes sense. Sophia Chekov she is. But you'd better look online and see if you can find some CDs for learning Ukranian. It's not the same as Russian, and she'd better know a few words of the lingo, just the things she would have learned as a little kid."

"I'll do that for sure."

"Good. One last thing. You've got to break up with Lisa, the one here I mean. Tonight."

A long paused followed, then a deep pitiful sigh.

"You're right," Michael said. "It would only be, like, fair."

Later that evening, when Ari was muttering in Hebrew over his laptop as he filed some sort of report—and no, I didn't ask what or to where—I logged onto TranceWeb to pick up my e-mail. I'd set my computer desk up in a corner of the living room, where there was a phone jack for the scrambled DSL. NumbersGrrl, our expert in alternate world theory, had answered my queries. I read that first. She told me that every cell in the human body is replaced roughly every seven years. If Lisa-Sophie stayed here for that many years, eating our food and drinking our water, her substance would, as NumbersGrrl put it, "come into conformity" with the matter of our world level.

It looked like Walking Stewart was right about those atoms, after all. To be on the safe side, however, she suggested that we try not to let the two Lisas meet.

"Folklore," the e-mail continued, "says that if you meet your doppelganger, you'll disappear, and it'll take over your life. Or maybe you'll merge into one person, or maybe you'll both disappear, but it doesn't sound good no matter which. It could just be bullshit—or maybe it's some old kernel of truth."

I printed out the information for Michael, though of course I removed all the headers and routing information first. Despite all the firewalls on my system and his, I didn't feel safe in sending the message through ordinary e-mail.

I also received a short note from Y, saying that he needed more information before he could set about getting Sophia papers. I sent him her new name and the data on the baptismal certificate. The object of all this activity, Michael, called me later to report that he'd called the our-world Lisa and done the breakup.

"It was gross," he said. "She cried."

"I guess she really liked you. Did she want to know why?"

"Yeah. I told her I hella liked her, but that this old girlfriend of mine, she'd moved away, y'know? But now she was back in town."

"You'd better work out a good story with Sophie."

"I will, yeah. I just sent her a message by critter mail."

"Okay. We'll talk more later. Go do your homework."

Michael laughed and signed off.

Ari wandered into the living room just as I got up from my computer chair to stretch my back. He caught me by the shoulders and kissed me. I reached up and ran my hand through his hair. I loved the way the curls twined around my fingers.

"You look happy tonight," I said.

"True." He smiled at me. "You forgave me for being what I am. I'd love you forever for that alone, even without the tremendous sex."

I could only stare at him. If I had tried to speak, I would have stammered.

"No need to say anything," he said. "But I wanted you to know why I love you."

He let me go, then turned and walked off down the hall.

Watch it, O'Grady! I told myself. You're melting again. Be careful, or you'll end up really falling for this guy. He's got issues, Mira had said at Kathleen's party. So he did, and so did I, and I could see an emotional train wreck in my future if they ever met head-on.

Chapter 10

I SUPPOSE I FELT NERVOUS ABOUT MEETING CALEB for lunch. I woke up too early on Saturday, at any rate, and staggered into the kitchen to make coffee. I'd just poured myself a cup when my cell phone rang. I yelped and nearly spilled the coffee. On the fifth ring I answered it.

"Hey, Nola? It's me, Mike."

I sighed in relief. "You're up early for a weekend."

"Yeah, Or-Something just turned up. It barfed a letter onto my bed. I guess I shouldn't have given it all that strawberry ice cream last night. The barf looked just like—"

"I don't want to know," I said. "What was in the letter? Could you read it?"

"Yeah. It was from Sophie. She's kind of upset. Jeez, I hope she can get away after all this."

"You hope? What do you mean, you hope?"

"Well, she's got to lie to José. He's not going to want to let her go. She's in his stable. So I was wondering, like, if you and Ari could come over, when it's time to fetch her, you know? Because if Ari's there with a gun or something, then José won't cause trouble."

"Uh, Mike, just how much trouble are you expecting?"

"Maybe none. I dunno."

"I thought you said José was cool."

"He is, but he's had a hard life. Seriously. Y'know?"

I did know, which is why the obvious occurred to me.

"Have you thought about buying her from José? Trading him the kind of goods the gang can use."

Silence hummed on the phone for a couple of seconds, before Michael said, "Hey, that might work! But I don't have a lot of cash to buy stuff with."

I groaned, but I'd gotten myself into this, and Ari did have a fabulous expense account from his deep cover agency. I figured he could come up with the whole rent if I spent too much of my salary to pay my share. "I'll front you the money," I said.

"Cool! Then I can go over tonight and get Sophie to calm down. She's, like, hella worried."

"About these nighttime visits, bro, the ones in the middle of the week. How are you staying awake in school?"

"I've got study hall first period, and I sit way in the back."

I took this as meaning that he slept for an hour instead of studying. I decided I wouldn't complain about something so trivial, considering everything else my sneaky little junior agent had going on.

"I'll be over tomorrow after mass," Michael went on. "Ari's going to teach me how to shoot."

"I know," I said. "We can talk more then."

With Latin book in hand, Ari joined me not long after. We sat at the kitchen table and looked out the window at our new view of a driveway and the flat wooden side of the apartment building next door. The gray cold light told me that the fog hung thick across the sky.

"What time are you meeting Caleb?" Ari said.

"One o'clock." I paused for a yawn. "What are you going to do while I'm there?"

"Wait outside, somewhere where he can't see me, but close enough to intervene if I have to. After what you told me about Caleb's reaction to the rogue waves, I'd rather not let you do this at all."

"Let me?" I set my hands on my hips.

"Sorry. I'll amend that. How about this: I feel a real need to provide backup."

I considered arguing, but I had to admit that I agreed.

"Okay," I said, "I can accept that."

"Good. I've got a pair of sunglasses for you," Ari went on. "They have a video camera in the frame. Wear them in, then set them down on the table with the lenses pointing at Caleb. I'll carry the monitor with me. It looks like a cheap phone. No one will think anything of it if I sit somewhere and stare at it."

"Will the glasses record the conversation?"

"No, but the monitor will." He smiled briefly. "Although all I really want to do is keep an eye on how things are developing."

I spent the rest of Saturday morning working LDRS sessions and getting nowhere. I checked my Internet sources, as well, but again, no stories about a dead homeless man turned up.

"I wonder if Sarge has seen Zeke," I said, "I hope he's not going to stay away forever. I want to read that letter."

"So do I," Ari said. "If he's so afraid of returning to prison, he can't have gone back to that same world."

"He may know of other ones, or, come to think of it, he could have just gone back to Israel via GateExpress. This is not going to be easy. All I can do, I guess, is to keep looking for him. Regular scans and LDRS sessions should turn him up."

"Eventually, yes. You know your own business best."

"Thanks. How many gates are there in San Francisco, I wonder?" A fragment of a folk song came back to me. "Twelve gates to the city, alleluia!"

Ari grimaced. Singing was not one of my talents.

"That song derives from the Book of Revelation," I said. "From a description of the heavenly Jerusalem—four gates each to the north, east, south, and west."

"That makes sixteen."

"Oh. Yeah, you're right. I was never very good at arithmetic. Okay, three gates each."

Yet I wondered about that mistake, if maybe the CDS was sending me a message. A fragment of an old song floated to the surface of my memory. "Sixteen candles on her cake tonight".

"What?" Ari snapped.

"Uh, sorry about that. I don't know what it means."

He rolled his eyes. I filed the number sixteen away in my memory, just in case it proved significant.

"If there are other gates in San Francisco," Ari said, "they can't all lead to the same place, or Doyle and Johnson wouldn't have been trapped here when their escape route closed."

"You're right, yeah."

Around noon, I got dressed for my lunch date. Since theoretically I had a job interview in hand, I wore the gray skirt suit with a teal silk shirt and heels. I also took a small notebook in my shoulder bag to write down the details of Caleb's offer, should he make one.

When we left, I drove our souped-up Saturn. I got onto the Great Highway going north, which led us along the beachfront. Even though the fog hovered thick, and a cold wind blew in from sea, we saw a good sprinkling of cars in the parking strips. Bundled in heavy jackets and long pants, people walked along the tide line or played Frisbee on the sand. I even saw a few surfers in full wet suits. Just before the road began to climb up the hill to the Cliff House, I pulled into the parking area and let Ari out. He handed me a pair of wraparound sunglasses that appeared perfectly ordinary, though they weighed oddly heavy in my hand.

"I suppose you'd better put them on top of your head for realism's sake," Ari said. "This sodding weather! It's nearly April. It should be warm."

"When the fog goes out, it'll be warmer," I said. "Where are you going to be?"

"I'm not going to tell you, in case Caleb can pick that up." He gave me a brief smile. "I'm learning."

Rather than mess up my hair, I put the sunglasses on, then drove up the hill. The gods favored me that day, because I found a head-in parking place above the complex in the curve of the road. As I walked downhill toward the restaurant, I passed a sleek white sedan that looked oddly familiar. I stopped and looked it over, because I could feel a memory starting to rise. I'd seen it in a similar context—the ocean, the Great Highway, the day the girl had drowned. The car had zipped past me without slowing down when other drivers on the road were gawking at the police cars and ambulance.

I took out my cell phone and snapped a shot of the license plate. Ari could check with the Department of Motor Vehicles and find out who owned the white sedan. The driver of the car I'd seen before had been blond, just like Caleb. Had he driven on by without slowing down because he already knew what had happened to those children? I put the phone away and walked on, but I stayed on guard.

For a San Francisco landmark, the Cliff House lacks pizazz, at least when you see it from outside: a wide stretch of concrete sidewalk, and behind that, a low white building housing a couple of restaurants joined by a lobby and glass doors. It appears to perch right on the edge of the cliff; I've heard tourists say that that they weren't going in because it looked so unsafe. From inside, it appears even more precarious, because it's actually built down the side of the cliff. Several levels hang lower than the street.

The formal dining area sits on the lowest level, a two-story high room lined with floor to ceiling windows. It seems to float right over the ocean and the sand below. White linen cloths and chrome fixtures add to the oddly empty ambience the restaurant projects even when crowded. As I walked down the ramp toward the hostess station, I could look out over the heads of the Saturday lunch crowd to the sea beyond and the cold gray sky.

Caleb was waiting for me at a table beside a west-facing window. He'd dressed for the location in a pair of gray wool slacks, a white shirt with a striped tie, and a navy blue blazer with the crest of a Boston yacht club on the chest pocket. The blazer sat too loosely on his shoulders. Either he'd lost weight since it'd been tailored, or he'd bought it second-hand. Now that I knew his record, I suspected the latter.

As I made my way across to join him, he rose from his seat and smiled, then held out his hand and shook mine when I offered it to him. His palm was sweaty. I noticed half a glass of white wine sitting at his place with the uncorked bottle nearby. We sat down, and he picked up the glass for a sip.

"Would you like some wine?" he said. "A cocktail?"

"No, thanks," I said. "Mineral water will be fine." I took off the sunglasses and set them down, lenses toward him, on the table between me and the window. "I guess I didn't need to wear these today."

"Well, the glare from the damned fog can be annoying," Caleb said. "I was wondering if you'd had a chance to talk with Jack about our plans."

"I haven't, no. I haven't been out to see them since the party. They're going up to Sonoma soon, I think."

"Yeah, yeah. He mentioned that to me."

The waitress arrived to hand us menus and rattle off a list of specials, then fled before we could ask questions. For a few minutes we studied the menus in silence. I could feel that Caleb was running an SPP on me. I was annoyed enough to drop caution and turn it back on him. He looked up from his menu and laughed, a short bark of honest amusement.

"I think we both know where we stand, Nola," he said. "Can we skip the fencing?"

"Sure," I said. "It'll save time." I glanced around. No one sat at the table behind ours. The crowd in the dining room was thinning out. Eavesdroppers seemed unlikely. "We both have talents that could come in handy for your venture. We know that."

"Good." He smiled again. "Then we can get down to business."

The waitress, however, interrupted, bearing Welsh spring water in a dark blue bottle. She filled my glass, then smiled impartially at us both. I ordered a fancy salad and, as a nod to the chilly day, soup. Caleb turned in his chair toward her and began asking earnest questions about every main dish on the menu. I took the opportunity to study the view, a seemingly endless stretch of gray sea flecked with white foam.

The ocean surged around the massive hulk of Seal Rock, iced white by generations of seabirds. I could just make out a few dark specks that might have been seals in the water around it. Like white wings waves broke just offshore, then charged with swirls of foam onto the pale beige beach. Silvery horses rose out of the waves, tossing their manes, galloping onto the sand only to disappear. Some thirty yards out from land a chariot of green glass emerged from the water. A towering blue-green god held the reins of four moon-pale horses.

"Uh, Nola?" Caleb's voice cut into the vision. "Are you okay?"

Poseidon, horses, chariot, all vanished. "Oh, yeah," I said. "Just thinking." I glanced around and realized that the waitress had long since left the table.

"What were you seeing out there?" Caleb was smiling at me.

"Oh, just a vision of the horses of the sea and Poseidon. Sorry. I do that sometimes, see things I mean."

"Well, of course. That's why I'm so keen on having you join us. Do your visions usually have classical themes?"

"Sometimes, sometimes not. I see angels a lot, too. And every now and then I get a glimpse of strange goings-on."

"Oh, like what?"

"Well, once I stumbled across a local coven. They were meeting to glorify the Peacock Angel."

Caleb's fingers tightened on his wineglass. His smile turned rigid.

"And I heard about," I continued, "someone named Brother Belial who led that coven. Know him?"

The color drained from his face.

"I take it that means yes," I said. "Sorry, but you suggested we skip the fencing."

"Uh, um," Caleb lifted his wineglass. "Yeah, yeah."

I waited, smiling, while he drank the glass dry in one long swallow. He poured himself more while I had a couple of sips of spring water.

"So, okay." Caleb's voice had returned to steady. "You know about that silly coven, then."

"Yeah. I'm glad you agree, about the silliness, I mean."

"Rank amateurs! I went once, and that was enough." He rolled his eyes. "Chanting about demons."

"And throwing around enough frankincense to choke a horse."

While we shared the laugh of equals looking down on our inferiors, I remembered all over again why I disliked

Chaotics. For people who say they believe in total freedom, status means so much to them. Caleb leaned a little closer across the table and lowered his voice.

"But the being they called Belial has real power," he said. "As you obviously know. I wonder how."

"Let's just say I guessed."

Caleb had another long swallow of wine. The waitress returned with my soup and a small plate of sliced Harvard beets sprinkled with walnuts for him. The puree of white corn soup, finished with a float of truffle oil, occupied my attention while he crunched away across the table. Finally, Caleb looked up and wiped his mouth on his napkin.

"Without some unusual help," Caleb said, "we wouldn't have a snowflake's chance in hell of finding the treasure. It was buried four hundred years ago. Long time gone. That's why I evoked Belial. That's not his real name, of course."

"Does Jack Donovan know about your little assistant?"

"No." Caleb's lip twitched in a gesture too near contempt for my liking. "He wouldn't believe me if I told him. Of the earth, earthy, our Jack. Talking about spirits would just confuse him."

"What rank of spirit, or have you found out yet?"

"Oh, he's from a very high level, I'm sure. He told me that he came from several worlds away from ours. He gave me its name, one that indicates the sphere of the stars." Caleb glanced around. "I'd better not say it aloud here."

So Caleb thought Bro Belial was a powerful spirit, did he? Not a bad guess, if only spirits had actually existed. Since they didn't, I finished my soup and considered my next move.

"Are you telling me," I said, "that you set the coven up?"

"What? No, nothing like that. Once he was here, Belial made contact with them on his own."

"Ah. And he let you know, huh?"

"Of course. I'm his master."

My thought: oh, sure you are! Aloud, "One thing that puzzles me," I said. "The coven members all say that Belial wore robes."

"An illusion." Caleb grinned at me. "If they'd touched him, they would have found that out."

Which meant to me that Belial, robed or not, was a projection similar to Fish Guy and the fake office worker I'd seen in Embarcadero Center. In fact, he could have actually been inside those very projections. That he'd been able to speak through the hooded man form indicated he had a very high level of talent.

A busboy appeared to take away my bowl and Caleb's empty plate. When I leaned back out of his way, my napkin slipped onto the floor. The busboy trotted off without noticing. I bent down and retrieved it.

"I should have gotten that for you," Caleb said. "Sorry."

"Not a problem," I said. "It's the modern world and all."

"Well, but is the modern world any different than the ancient one? We all think it is, thanks to the gadgets and science and garbage like that, but at the heart, with what matters, nothing's really changed."

"The universal forces still rule."

"Exactly." He saluted me with his wineglass. "And a man's only what he has the courage to be. I use the word 'man' generally, of course. A woman's what she has the guts to be, too."

"Very true."

The waitress and a waiter came gliding over, carrying assorted plates. Caleb had ordered a number of items, most of them fish dishes of some sort, and my elaborate salad arrived with a small china pitcher of dressing on yet another plate. In between bites of his enormous lunch, washed down with the bottle of wine, Caleb told me more about his search for Drake's alleged treasure.

Like so many treasure hunters before him, he simply couldn't believe that anyone would turn a fortune over to the Crown without holding some of it back in a private stash. I had to agree that Drake was probably just as venal as most Elizabethan gentlemen, but my central objection came from the large number of failed attempts to find the goods. If Drake had buried something on Bay Area shores, the horde of treasure hunters who'd gone after it surely would have found it by now.

Caleb, of course, thought otherwise. He'd been reading accounts of Drake's voyage, studying old maps and modern maps both, and above all, as he told me in near whispers, he'd been invoking more spirits than one to help him in his search.

"I'll bet none of the other hunters knew how to do that," Caleb said. "I've got help from a higher level, as you know."

I nodded and looked thoughtful.

"But I've also called up a crew of lesser beings. They've promised me a great treasure," he went on. "A great treasure and the fame to go with it. I'll be a man of distinction, then." He paused to pour the last few drops of wine into his glass. "The difficulty, of course, is pinpointing the location. Spirits don't see the world the way we do."

"No," I said, "they sure don't." I remembered some of the content of my medieval grimoires. "They're tricky little buggers, too, you know. You've got to be wary about what they say, or they'll mislead you every time."

"Yeah, yeah. We've been looking for two months now and not finding a damn thing. That's why I thought we should bring you into this. Fresh eyes and all that. We're prepared to offer you a full third of the treasure when we find it."

"Nothing before that, huh?"

"Unfortunately, my resources are limited right now. Maybe Jack can—"

"No." I spoke firmly. "I don't take money from my sister's husband."

"Oh. Right. The family connection."

Caleb turned in his chair and signaled to the waitress, who'd been hovering some tables away. When she came over, he asked for the "afters" menu, which she supplied. For a man of limited resources, he was spending a bundle on this lunch. I suspected that one way or the other, Jack was paying for it.

"Would you like some dessert?" Caleb asked me.

"No, thanks," I said. "I don't eat a lot of sweets."

"Which is one reason you're so beautiful, so slim and graceful." He smiled in a sloppy sort of way. "You're really amazing, Nola."

"Thanks." It came out a lot drier than I wanted, and he winced.

"Not just flattery," Caleb said. "I mean it, you're amazing. You know, when I was looking for a partner in this venture, I checked out a lot of guys with boats. I finally chose Jack because I wanted to meet Kathleen's sister. You're even more beautiful than I thought you'd be."

"Well, then, thank you." I heard various inner alarms go off. "I will have some coffee, but just black for me."

"All right. I was thinking of having an Irish coffee in your honor, but all that cream . . ."

"Don't feel obliged for my sake."

"Just plain whiskey, then. Let's see what kinds they have."

While he ordered, I glanced out the window, just casually. One vision trance with lunch was enough for me, especially with Caleb's interesting slipup to ponder. He'd chosen Jack to get at me, had he? I suspected that Belial lay behind the decision, not my pretty face.

The waitress arrived with our coffees, his so heavily laced that I could smell the hot whiskey from across the table. I turned back to pick up my cup and nearly knocked it over.

Someone else had joined us. Not a visible person, no, not even an invisible physical presence—but an intangible someone or something, a guest of sorts at the table, had taken the empty chair next to Caleb, who knew it as well as I did. I noticed how he slid over slightly in order to give the guest plenty of elbow room, how he glanced sideways at the chair. I decided to call the game.

"Who's your friend?" I said. "Brother Belial?"

Caleb turned as white as the seafoam. The presence rose up, flowed my way, and vanished. I might have heard a very high-pitched, very faint bubbling sound as it rushed by.

"Uh, well, yes," Caleb said. "He wanted a look at you. Because of the venture, I mean, and all that."

"I see." I smiled, but I doubted if it was a nice smile. "Well, I hope he approves."

"How could he not approve of someone like you?"

If I hadn't wanted to pry more information out of Caleb, I would have thrown my coffee into his face. Flattery wasn't going to cover his gaffe, summoning his spectral friend to size me up! As it was, I had a sip of the coffee and put the cup down on the saucer. "I'll have to think about your offer, of course. My partner will probably have something to say about it."

"Ah, yes, the boyfriend." His voice dripped sarcasm. "Where is he today, anyway?"

"Probably working out at the gym."

"He struck me as that type. What does he do for a living? I hope it's something that lets him support you in style. A woman like you shouldn't have to worry about money."

"Oh, I love being in charge of my own finances." Something twitched in my mind. I paused to look around and saw Ari striding down the ramp by the hostess station. "Er, no, scratch my remark about the gym. He's right here."

As Ari stalked across the dining room toward us, Caleb gulped down a hot mouthful of whiskey and coffee. He nearly choked, grabbed his water glass, and drank. Ari was scowling at us, his mouth set in a thin line, but his SPP told me that he was frightened more than angry. Something had come up, I figured, and I'd better play along. I could count on Caleb being too drunk to run an SPP of his own.

"Oh, God!" I said. "He's really furious. Uh, thanks for the lunch! I'd better go." I grabbed at my bag and pretended to nearly drop it, then picked up the sunglasses. "Sorry."

Caleb got up, wobbling, just as Ari reached us.

"Business lunch, huh?" Ari said. "Wine. Whiskey. Some guy."

"Look, darling," I said, "I told you—"

Ari grabbed my nearer arm. "Let's go," he snapped. "You can make your excuses in the car."

"Now, here!" Caleb managed to put some authority in his voice. "I'm Jack Donovan's business partner. You've met me. You know that I'm making Nola a job offer."

Ari looked at him, merely looked, but Caleb sat down. I was aware of Brother Belial again, floating somewhere above the middle of the dining room, and watching us. He wasn't alone in that activity. The other lunchers were turning in their chairs and staring.

"Let's go," Ari snapped again. "I'm sick and tired of this! Stepping out on me every chance you get!"

A horrified squad of waitress, busboy, and maitre d' was making its way over to us. I felt a stab of guilt for upsetting them for nothing.

"Ari, for crying out loud!" I said. "I am so sick of you being so jealous. All right, let's go home! We can fight about it there and not ruin everyone's lunch."

The line of potential allies relaxed. Caleb summoned enough courage to say, "You have my cell phone number. Call me if you're interested in the job."

Rather than spoil the effect, I let Ari half-drag me out of the dining room and up the ramp to the lobby. As soon as we were outside, he came out with one of his half-smothered chortles.

"Nice bit of acting," he said.

"Yours, too. What's going on?"

"I'll tell you in the car."

In case Caleb had followed us out, Ari stayed in character by berating me in what was probably Farsi while we walked back to the car. I had no idea of what he was saying. I concentrated on looking oppressed. A scattering of people were walking downhill as we walked up. Most looked away and walked faster. Just as we reached the car, we passed a well-dressed older couple. The woman had covered her hair with a beautiful silk scarf in teal and deep purple, which is why I noticed them. The silver-haired gentleman, however, had noticed us as well.

He reached out and caught Ari by the arm. I yelped aloud. Startling Ari that way could prove fatal. Ari spun around just as the man began talking to him in whatever language Ari had been using. Much to my shock, Ari ducked his head and stared at the sidewalk, a subservient gesture that surprised me further, mostly because it seemed so well-practiced. Ari shook his arm free, but he muttered something that sounded apologetic. The fellow nodded in satisfaction, said a few stern words, and the couple continued on downhill.

I unlocked the car. As we got in, I made sure to take the driver's seat.

"What was all that about?" I said.

Ari buckled on his seat belt while he told me. "I was being reminded that the Qu'ran teaches us to respect our wives, not yell at them in public."

"It does? Maybe I should read it sometime."

"You should. The actual text is quite different from the Taliban's interpretation of it. You Americans seem to think that all followers of Islam are fanatics. That's not true."

"Well, yeah, I'm sure it's not. Besides, we have our share of gun-toting fanatics, too."

"So do we. I have to admit, however, that there are a great many more of theirs than ours." He smiled briefly. "Which is why we're glad to have some of yours on our side."

"I take it you've read the Qu'ran. Probably in Arabic."

"Of course. It always pays to study your opposition in any political process, particularly in a war." Ari sounded abruptly exhausted. "And that's what we've got on our hands, these days, a war, whether the rest of the world chooses to see it or not."

"We? You mean Israel, right?"

"Of course. I always mean Israel."

Behind us on the street a car horn sounded in staccato bursts. I glanced at the rearview mirror and saw an enormous SUV blocking the lane while it waited for the parking spot.

"Let's get going," I said, "before Caleb finishes lapping up his booze and staggers out."

I turned on the engine and backed out under cover of the SUV, then drove on downhill. As we cruised along the Great Highway, I noticed that the ocean had reached high tide.

"So how was lunch?" Ari said.

"Good food," I said, "but a nutcase for company."

"Caleb, you mean?"

"He believes that spirits are helping him search for Drake's treasure."

"A total nutter, then."

"Yeah, for sure. Where were you, anyway?"

"Upstairs in the cheaper restaurant. It was too sodding cold to sit outside, so I had a sandwich while I watched the monitor."

"Why the jealous boyfriend act?"

"Because of that white thing that showed up on the monitor. I don't know what it was, and I wasn't sure if you knew it was there. So I decided to get you out of that room."

"You saw it? Brother Belial?"

"Is that what it was?"

"Yeah, but I couldn't see him. I just sensed him."

Once we got back to the flat, I changed into my flannel-lined jeans and the rust-colored sweater. Although the flat had a decent gas heater, the wind had picked up. It whistled around the building as it drove the fog inland. Before I put my shoulder bag away, I returned the sunglasses to Ari.

"Did you record that video?" I asked.

"I did, and I'm glad now. The sound quality's not very good on these things, though. Here, I'll show you."

We sat down together on the couch. He took an oblong unit, all shiny black plastic, out of his shirt pocket. It looked something like an old-fashioned PDA, but it had no logo or ID marks on it. He pressed a few buttons, then clicked play. On the tiny screen the lunch table appeared in black and white. An image of Caleb followed; he sat down but was partially hidden by his wineglass. I could see about half of the empty chair next to him.

"I need to learn how to aim those things better," I said.

Our conversation began, though we sounded like mice with sore throats. The waitress came and went as we talked about the coven and Brother Belial. Finally, in the other chair a form appeared.

"Pause it!" I snapped.

Ari already had. "There," he said. "Nola, what is that?"

"I don't know."

Brother Belial seemed to be made of white smoke, translucent rather than solid, roughly humanoid with a chest, two arms, and a strangely cubical shape for a head, pocked with little depressions and slits. Thanks to the table, we could only see him from the waist up. Ari advanced the recording a few frames at a time, until my mouse voice squeaked, "Who's your friend? Brother Belial?"

The smoke form rose up from the chair, as I remembered the presence doing. Now, however, I could see his legs, or rather, his single leg. Belial flowed toward the camera with a flip of the leg like a dolphin's tail. The image disintegrated into a drift of "snow," like on an old-fashioned TV set, then disappeared. For a moment the screen stayed blank. Another snowstorm filled the little square, then resolved itself into the shape of the smoke-being once again, flying straight up and out of range. I could hear the bubbling fish tank noise more clearly on the recording than I'd done at the table.

"This doesn't make any sense," I said.

"What a surprise," Ari said. "Shocking."

"I mean, this is a digital recording, not camera film. Aura-based phenomena shouldn't register on it, not if they can't be perceived normally, at any rate. I couldn't see Belial in the moment, though I knew he was there."

Ari looked at me slack-mouthed. "I don't have the slightest idea of what you mean by any of that," he said.

"Okay. Let's start at the beginning. I saw nothing at all in that chair, and I was right there. I did intuit that some kind of presence had joined us. When I said 'Brother Belial,' I felt it leave."

"Very good, so far."

"Do you know what an aura is?"

"I know what it's supposed to be, yes. Reb Ezekiel was keen on them. He was always looking at the air next to a person and announcing something about their aura."

"Okay. Well, some people believe that in certain circumstances you can capture an image of an aura on a particular kind of film or plate. Whatever Belial is, I'd assume he's made up of the same substance as an aura. A magnetic field is the closest analogy. But the sunglasses don't use film. So that's why I don't know how the image ended up in your recorder's memory. Uh, did you follow that?"

"It's enough to get on with. What's that kind of photography? Krill—no, that's what whales eat."

"Kirilian, you mean. A person has to be in contact with the photographic plate to get an image out of that."

"Doesn't apply here, then."

We stared at each other, baffled.

"The only thing I can think of," I said, "is that we're not

dealing with a psychic phenomenon, but a technological one." My mind issued a hazy prompt. "Or maybe it's both. I know that doesn't make any sense. It's just all I can think of."

"I thought you said you sensed a presence."

"I did, yeah, which generally means a consciousness. Huh. I wonder if old Bro here has some kind of gadget that produces a wave or ray or something that can carry his mind."

"I still don't understand how that would produce an image in a digital memory chip. Or wait! You said something about a magnetic field. Do you know how a digital image recorder works?"

"No."

"Those little decorations at the corner of the sunglass frames contain a lens and a microphone. The lens is fairly decent, unlike the microphone. It focuses light on a CMOS imager that converts the light into voltages. The stronger the light, the larger the voltage. Those measurements are numerical, of course, and the monitor then converts that information back into a pattern of light and shadow."

He might as well have spoken in Farsi for all that I understood him. He recognized my blank stare.

"Let's put it this way," Ari said. "The CMOS process in those sunglasses could respond to his electrical field, or magnetic field if that's what it was, more directly and more easily than your eyes could. He must have been producing a field of varying strengths that could activate the imager in a similiar way to light."

"I think I get it," I said. "Since you were watching on the monitor, you were seeing that captured image, not him directly. "

"Exactly! And captured is the word we want. When you startled him, he flew toward the device, and it sucked him in for a moment."

"That says to me that he's a consciousness attached to some kind of magnetic or electric field."

"That flickering distortion we saw? I suspect it was Belial fighting to get free. What I wonder," Ari continued, "is what sort of field he's riding. It's nothing I've ever heard of before."

"Qi, maybe?"

Ari shrugged.

"Damn!" I said. "It would be Saturday! I need to run this by my handler and NumbersGrrl, too. Could you download that video onto my desktop, do you think?"

"Not directly, but I can copy it onto a DVD, and you can download from there."

"That'll do, yeah. I'll send it to them when I file a report, and it'll be waiting for them on Monday. We can use all the speculation we can get."

"Speculation? Yes, solid information would be too much to hope for."

Ari took the monitor into the bedroom, where he was using an end table as a temporary desk for his laptop. I scribbled a note on a post-it, "get more furniture," stuck it on the refrigerator, then took out my phone to call Kathleen.

I hesitated with my finger poised over her speed dial number. Jack had mentioned that they were leaving town to visit his folks for a few days. If I told Kathleen about Caleb's record now, I figured, she'd never be able to keep the secret until they returned. If Kathleen did blab, Jack would want to have it out with Caleb right away. I'd lose my chance to pry more information out of the little slimeball. I unpoised the finger and put the phone back in my pocket.

Ari came out of the bedroom and handed me a DVD in a paper sheath. I put it on my desk beside the keyboard and sat down on the chair, then swiveled around to face him.

"I should warn you," I said. "I want to string Caleb along for a few days to see if I can get more information out of him."

"Of course. Is he lusting after you?"

"Yeah. That's why I'm warning you."

"Mata Hari in blue jeans, that's you." He stepped back out of range before I could kick him.

"I'm not real good at the vamp routine. If I was going to be seductive, I should have started at lunch."

"And I shouldn't have frightened him. What about flattering his superior occult knowledge? Judging from what I heard of the conversation, he thinks he has some."

"As you like to say, brilliant! I'll try that." I made a sour face. "But later. A little Caleb goes a long way."

Before I downloaded the captured video, I ran a check on the DVD with our special Agency software. I wouldn't have put it past Ari to have loaded some kind of Trojan horse onto it along with the video of Brother Belial, just so he could browse on my computer if he felt the need. I'd maligned him. At least as far as the Agency's detection programs knew, the disk was clean, and the Agency had very good software at its disposal.

Life intervened and made it imperative that I keep in touch with Caleb sooner than I wanted. Detective Lieutenant Sanchez called Ari later that afternoon. Since I was concentrating on filing the report about Brother Belial, Ari went into the bedroom to take the call. I'd just finished sending the file and video off via TranceWeb when Ari walked back into the living room. He shook his head in annoyance.

"What's wrong?" I said.

"Too much pressure on Sanchez," Ari said. "He's calling the Evers case suicide and ending the investigation."

"Good."

"Good?"

"Imagine this scene. I sit in the witness box in front of a jury and tell them, swearing on the Bible, that someone used a flood of Qi to ensorcell Evers, then drowned him by scooping up a rogue wave with his or her psychic powers."

"Oh." Ari blinked at me. "Quite right. Not much use in pursuing the matter, then. But the thought of letting that sodding little bastard off—"

"He's not off the hook yet," I said. "And for all we know, it wasn't Caleb who killed Evers. What we need to do next is find out if he did. He knows something about it. I'd bet on that."

I picked up the receiver of my landline phone and punched in Caleb's number. Four long rings, and then his answering machine clicked on with a simple name, number, please leave message. I started talking in case he was screening his calls, but no luck. I left a fake apology for Ari's behavior and hung up.

"Where does he live, anyway?" Ari said.

"I don't know." I rummaged through the papers on my desk and found the business card Caleb had given me at the party. "This only has a phone number on it. Jack must know, if it matters."

"Not at the moment. I just wanted to enter it into my files."

I heard a tapping sound on the bay window. When I walked over, I saw Fog Face hovering just outside. In the dying light of late afternoon, he held out gray and misty hands and mouthed a single word, help, before he melted back into the murky sky.

Caleb never returned my call that night. I made several LDRS attempts, which failed. Either he was asleep, or his location was pitch-dark. Either way, I received only black scribbles. When I tried an SM:P for him, I ran into his psychic shield. I received a faint impression of terror, but the shield held steady enough to prevent me from discovering if he was afraid of me or of someone else.

Chapter 11

EARLIER IN THE WEEK, ARI HAD CONTACTED the local gun club over by Lake Merced, a short drive from our new building. Although they lacked the kind of firing range he wanted, they had put him in touch with a police-oriented facility a little farther south in San Mateo County. For his first lesson in handling a lethal weapon, Michael drove over to the flat on Sunday morning, arriving well before noon. Uncle Jim had taken the family to early mass, he told us, to get a start on the day.

"Where's Brian?" I said. "Ari would be glad to teach him, too."

"He says he doesn't want to mess around with guns," Michael said. "I can't figure that out."

I could. Mentally, I saluted Brian as a fellow sane person.

"When I drove up, you know?" Michael continued. "I saw some graffiti on your steps. A black circle thing, and then the Norteños tag."

"Norteños?" Ari said. "A street gang?"

"Yeah. Theirs is the red one, Nor Fifteen, but they use the Roman number for the fifteen. I dunno what gang has the black circle, but you can bet that the Norteños wanted to tag over it."

"We'll clean that off before we go," Ari said to me. "I'm very glad the landlords painted the building the way they did."

"Yeah," I said. "A real time and stress saver."

Ari packed his sports bag with the two pieces, wrapped in black cloth, of what I assumed was some kind of rifle, a couple of pairs of earmuffs, and two sets of goggles. The sight of the safety equipment soothed my nerves.

I went downstairs with them to deal with the graffiti. Someone had spray-painted a big NORXV above the unbalanced Chaos symbol. A thrown ward had no effect on the red gang tag. While I waited for Ari and Michael to fetch the hose and rags, I examined the circle and its fringe of seven arrows more closely. I'd noticed the crisp edges and the smoothness of its paint before, but not the face that suddenly appeared in the center of the black circle. A white man, egg bald, with blue eyes in a narrow face stared out at me. He looked faintly familiar, but I was too surprised to place him.

"Join us."

I heard his high, fluting voice as distinctly as if he were standing in front of me.

"Join us," he repeated. "You can't fight us and win. Join us and receive the angel's gifts."

I wrenched my gaze away and stepped back just as Ari and Michael returned.

"Let me throw a couple of wards at this sucker," I said.

The first ward shattered with a spray of electric-blue glare; the second made the symbol hiss and writhe; the third killed it.

"Did you see the thing move when I threw the second ward?" I said to Ari.

"No. Did it?"

"What about the face?"

"Face? No, I didn't."

"I didn't see anything, either," Michael said. "Except you waving your hand around."

"Okay, I guess the message was for my eyes only. While you're gone, I'm going to report this to the Agency. I wonder if I've just heard from the man who talks to the Peacock Angel."

"Should we stay here?" Ari said.

"No reason to. If they wanted to come see me, they wouldn't be painting stuff on the walls."

Michael and Ari washed the mess off, then drove off to the firing range. I double-checked on the Internet to make sure I was remembering the Chaos magic symbol correctly. It indeed should have had eight arrows emerging from the circle instead of seven. There had been seven members in Belial's coven, too. Connection or coincidence? I didn't know.

I filed a report on the talking graffito, then got down to work on other Agency business. I wasn't expecting to hear from my handler till Monday at the earliest, but he surprised me. When I logged on to TranceWeb, I found good news waiting for me, a message from Y, stating that he would do his best to get the secret office at the State Department to produce some papers for Lisa/Sophie. They owed him several favors, he reckoned, for taking Ari off their hands. His contact at State still remembered Ari's lack of manners and what he called "Ari's infuriating arrogance." Y promised he'd pursue the matter on Monday or as soon as his contact could accommodate a meeting.

As for my suggestion about bringing Michael onboard to see if he could find other gates, Y counseled caution.

"He's young, and you feel responsible for him," Y's e-mail said. "Think about it very carefully before you act. I can't say yes or no."

NumbersGrrl had yet to reply about the video I'd sent her. She had a life, I assumed, to live on weekends.

That left Caleb and his possible role in Evers' murder. The pressure on Sanchez had, in a sense, shoved the case into my jurisdiction, to investigate or drop in turn. My "to do" list was already too long to take on anything else, but murder is murder. No matter how unpleasant the victim, an unjust death upsets the Balance that I'm sworn to serve. I picked up my cell phone and called Caroline Burnside.

Karo not only remembered me. She was glad to hear from me. No one had bothered to tell her that the police had ruled Bill Evers' death a suicide.

"Damn them damn them damn them!" she said. "I know that's not true. Yeah, Bill saw that he'd gone too far with that Persian white shit. He also knew that he could get into programs and see doctors and get his life back. He could be really stubborn, but he wasn't dumb. Someone killed him. I'm sure of it."

"You could be right," I said. "That's why I'm calling you. But if I'm going to take up the case, you've got to be honest with me."

I could feel the silence on the other end of the connection turn to fear. I waited.

"About what?" Karo said.

"Blackmail."

Karo gasped.

"Was Bill putting a squeeze on some of his clients?" I said.

"What? No, never!" Her relief sounded too deep to be feigned. "Sorry, I didn't get what you meant at first."

"Was someone blackmailing him?"

Again the gasp, and finally, "Yeah, or so he said. But it was too weird, and I don't know if it was true, or if the smack was talking for him."

My hands began to itch, ready to reach out and grab the information.

"You don't have to worry anymore about protecting him, unfortunately," I said. "What did he tell you?"

"He was being blackmailed by a guy who knew about the coven and the drugs. You can imagine how well that news would have gone over with Bill's clients."

"I sure can. How did this person find out about those things?"

"He told Bill that Brother Belial himself had informed on him. But this guy didn't want money from Bill. He wanted dirt, news he could use, y'know? Speaking of blackmail like we were. People tell their divorce lawyers some pretty hairy stuff about their exes."

"This begins to make sense," I said.

"It does?" Karo sounded honestly surprised. "I thought maybe Bill was hallucinating."

"Heroin doesn't make people hallucinate. Why did you think that?"

"Here's the weird part. Please don't hang up on me." Karo paused for a giggle of pure anxiety. "Bill said this guy had occult powers. That's what he called them, occult powers. He is a master, Bill told me, and Brother Belial's his familiar."

"Did he ever tell you anything concrete about this guy? What he looked like, where he came from, his age, that kind of thing?"

"No, and he never told me the guy's name. Bill was pretty sure that the name the guy gave when he made his appointments was fake, anyway. But still, that's why I wondered if the guy really existed."

"Did Bill give in to this person's demands and supply him with material for blackmail?"

"Bill told me no. Maybe he was telling the truth, but I dunno, junkies lie. Y'know?"

"Yeah, I'm afraid I do. You wanted to believe him, but you couldn't."

"If only he'd cleaned up." Karo's voice began to shake. "God, if only he had. I wanted him to go to the cops about this guy, but he wouldn't because of the drugs."

It's impossible to do an accurate SPP over the phone. I had to rely on ordinary clues, the sound of her voice, the way her mind jumped back and forth, my former impression of her. I decided that she was telling me the truth as she saw it.

"I'm sorry he didn't." I put as much sympathy as I could into my voice. "If you can think of anything else that might be relevant, call me." I gave her my landline number. "Leave a message if I'm not answering."

"I will, yeah." She paused for a long breath. "Do you think you can get whoever it was?"

"I don't know yet. One last thing. Don't go anywhere near the ocean for a while. And be real careful if you go out at night."

"I haven't been going out at night at all," Karo said. "You mean I'm not just being paranoid?"

"That's exactly what I mean. And especially, stay away from the ocean." I had a rational lie all ready. "I have reason to suspect that the killer's stalking the coast. He may even be camping out on the beach at times."

"Oh, jeez! Okay. I won't. Oh, crap!"

I signed off, then wrote up the conversation for my files

and sent a copy off to the Agency. A blackmailer, and he claimed Belial was his familiar—the probability of there being two men like that, even in the Bay Area with its bumper crop of would-be occultists, was low. When I remembered Caleb remarking that his resources were limited at the moment, the probability dropped to zero. With Evers gone, he lacked fresh manure to sell.

Which raised the question, why would Caleb kill Evers, if Evers was his cash cow? Unless Evers was getting ready to do what Karo wanted and go to the police? I remembered him saying how much he wished he'd listened to his girlfriend. He might have been ready to take Karo's advice—too late. I remembered my feeling that the murder had happened on a sudden impulse. If Evers and Caleb had been having that four o'clock drink together, Evers might have told Caleb that the game had ended. Might, maybe, possibly—I didn't know, and it rubbed on my mind the way a stone in a shoe rubs a foot.

By then, it was almost time for the boys, as I was thinking of them, to return. I went into the kitchen to put together some sandwiches. As soon as I opened the refrigerator door, I felt someone staring at me from behind. I turned around and looked out the window on the side wall. No Fog Face, no one at all hovered outside. The feeling vanished as fast as it had begun.

I shrugged and went back to the counter where I had a loaf of French bread and the bread knife.

"Remember the angel's gifts," a voice said from behind me. It sounded high and lilting, to the point where I wasn't sure if it were a man or a woman speaking.

I spun around: no one there. I wondered if I were having a simple IOI, because sometimes the "images," that is, the intuitions I have, do materialize as sound, not sight. Still, this voice had presented itself to my mind as something completely outside of myself.

"Belial?" I said. "Is that you?"

I heard a quick laugh and a snort of scorn. "Belial?" the voice said. "Small fry. Calamari."

"Then who are you?"

No answer, no nothing. I could feel no presence in the

flat but my own. I shuddered all over, then went back to making the sandwiches, but I kept my big German steel cooking knife right at hand. When I heard Ari and Michael's voices on the stairs, I felt like cheering in relief.

Michael went straight to the bathroom, which gave Ari a moment to ask if everything had been all right during their absence.

"I guess," I said. "I heard someone talking to me, but I couldn't see him or anything. That's kind of common around here."

"Then why do you sound so worried about it?" Ari said.

"Do I? Well, yeah, it was kind of creepy, but I didn't get an ASTA or SAWM."

"Do you remember what I said about trusting your sodding talents too much?"

I did, and he had a point. If Cryptic Creep, as I named him to myself, was hoping I'd join whatever group he belonged to, he posed no threat—yet. If I kept saying no, as I intended to do, the threat might move a whole lot closer. When Michael returned, I changed the subject. I didn't want him worrying about something I couldn't explain.

The guys pitched into the sandwiches as if they were starving, though Michael talked almost as much as he ate. Guns, apparently, were his new love in life, though he did allow as how Sophie came first and guns, second. I listened politely to the details of how loud and smelly the guns were, though Michael didn't use those particular terms. After they ate, we all went into the living room. Ari and I sat Michael down on the computer chair, while we sat on the couch and faced him across the coffee table.

"Okay, bro," I said. "Let's discuss this crazy idea. I've heard from the Agency. They're going to try to get Sophie her papers. Now we have to get Sophie over here to use them."

Michael started to smile, then got up. He walked over to the window and turned his back on us so fast that I realized he was crying—in sheer relief, an SPP told me. When Ari started to get up, I grabbed him by the shirttail and yanked him back down. Ari opened his mouth to protest, but when

I pointed to my tear ducts, he got the message and stayed silent.

First love, I thought to myself. It's always the worst.

With one last sniffle, Michael made a great show of wiping his eyes on the sleeve of his T-shirt, then turned back with a smile that amounted to rictus.

"Sorry," he said. "It uh must be uh tree pollen or something."

"Yeah," I said. "Your eyes are red. Allergies."

Michael glanced around, saw a box of tissues on the floor by my computer desk, and snagged a couple. He blew his nose before he sat back down. Ari, bless him, picked the conversational thread right up.

"What's this José going to think," Ari said, "when you show up with a gunman?"

"He'll be real impressed, that's all," Michael said. "You'll be, like, my wingman. In that world, it'll mean I'm seriously somebody."

"I'm very glad," Ari said, "that you don't want to take up permanent residence over there."

"Yeah, it would suck." Michael considered this for a moment. "Y'know, I was kind of afraid that maybe the BGs weren't going to let me leave one of these days. That's another reason why I want to get Sophie out of there."

"Why wouldn't they let you leave?" I said. "That scheme of José's?"

"Yeah, whatever it is. Sophie can tell us once we get her here."

"I'm willing to go with you," Ari said, "but can I? Nola has some share of your talents. I don't."

"Crap." Michael slumped a little on the chair. "Yeah, maybe you can't." He straightened back up. "Although, if Sophie can do it, you should be able to. I guess we'll just have to try it and see."

"Michael Eamonn O'Grady!" I said. "Are you telling me she's already been through once?"

Michael turned bright red. "Just into Nanny's old room. I mean, why go to all this trouble if she couldn't make it across?"

"Okay, you're forgiven. Does she have talents?"

"She doesn't think she does, but she can see Or-Something."

"Once we get her here, we'll find out more." I glanced at Ari. "The question now is, when are we going to try this out?"

"The sooner the better, I suppose," Ari said.

Michael was looking at me with those "you're my second mom" begging eyes.

"Yeah," I said. "The sooner the better."

Which is why, at five o'clock the next morning, I drove Ari and myself over to Aunt Eileen's house. Ari carried his sample case inside, where Michael, dressed in his best jeans and a white shirt with an actual collar, was waiting in the living room. I could smell coffee cake baking and hear the occasional noise of Aunt Eileen working in the kitchen.

"Is Uncle Jim up yet?" I said.

"No," Michael said. "Bri's still asleep, too. You can wait in the kitchen with Aunt Eileen if you want."

"Wash your mouth out with soap," I said, and he grinned at me.

We trooped down the hall to the door that led into Nanny Houlihan's old sitting room, a storage area now that she'd gone to her heavenly reward. While Michael picked the padlock that Uncle Jim had put on the door, Ari knelt down and opened one side of his sample case. He brought out the long thin bundle wrapped in the black cloth, then unwound the cloth to reveal two pieces of what I assumed was a gun.

The barrel and the trigger holder—I don't know the real name for it—looked like a silver robot arm. While the barrel was a solid tube, the bright red stuff around it had holes in it. Ari snapped this part onto a silver handle or stock or whatever you call those things at the end of a rifle. It also had holes in it.

"Is that made out of Play-Doh?" I said.

Ari rolled his eyes skyward. "It was constructed on the model of a biathlon rifle," he said. "You know, the Olympic event. They make them with piercings to save weight, since you have to ski with them on your back. I had to have it custom built, of course."

"Why the of course?"

"Biathlon rifles are only twenty-two caliber." Ari spoke these words as if they explained something. "But they're very high tech."

"I can see that much."

"Ari?" Michael said. "Were you on the Israeli biathlon team?"

"There isn't one." Ari was putting bullets into the rifle as he talked. "Israel's a bit short on snow."

Michael blushed scarlet and opened the door to the storeroom—and that gate to another world. I marveled all over again that the thing lay right to hand. Logical, I suppose, given what my family was, but improbable all the same. Yet deep in my mind something nagged at me, a thought trying to rise, pointing out that there was a damn good reason if only I could see it. At the moment the gate looked fairly ordinary, with a tidy row of cardboard cartons, stacked four deep, along one wall and an open box of old magazines in one corner.

Or-Something materialized near the window and trotted over to sniff at Ari's pant legs, not that Ari could see the little blue creature. Michael brought a plastic bag of salami out of his jeans pocket and took out a couple of slices before stuffing the bag back in. Or-Something rose up on its hind legs to beg. From the other pocket Mike took a note and a rubber band. The note went around the meat, and he tossed the entire thing, rubber band and all, to Or-Something. The creature caught it in yellow claws and gulped it down.

"Go find José," Michael said.

As Or-Something dematerialized, the room began to change. The row of cardboard boxes turned transparent, then disappeared. The cream-colored wallpaper, printed with bunches of violets, slowly faded into yellow wallboard. The crisp white shade over the window turned to a piece of dirty sheet, hung at an angle. Ari swore in several languages.

"You can see the change?" I said.

"Oh, yes." He was whispering. "So it's all real. I never quite believed it till now."

We went over to the window, where Michael pulled the

sheet aside. I could see the old man's garden with its rows
of deformed vegetables and the tall stakes supporting enormous morning-glory flowers, purple and blue in the misty
dawn light. As the sun rose higher, the scene shimmered as
if I were viewing it through gauze. I could feel the warmth
of a real springtime breeze. The weather in this deviant
level differed from that in the world I knew. I made a mental note to ask NumbersGrrl if the difference was logical or
otherwise.

A gadget in Ari's shirt pocket began to beep with a shrill,
steady note.

"Rad alarm." Ari took it out of his pocket, stared at it for
a moment, then tapped it into silence. "Odd. It's not the mix
of radiation types I was expecting." He put the gadget away.
"Still, it's a good thing we're getting your girl out of here.
The leukemia rate must be very high."

"It is, yeah," Michael said. "Most people don't live a
hella long time."

I offered up a silent prayer to Whomever that we weren't
too late for Sophie. Michael hauled himself up onto the sill,
then swung his legs out of the window and dropped down.
Ari slung the rifle across his back and followed. Once he
stood on solid ground, he shaded his eyes with one hand
and looked around him.

"Nola," Ari said, "stay where you are. I don't like this
situation. Too many places for a hostile to hide."

"But—"

"You can watch from where you are," Michael said.
"Here's José now."

Out among bushes thick with warty green tomatoes,
someone moved, then stood up—José, all right, and two
other BGs, all of them wearing Giants hooded sweatshirts
and patched, dirty pants. José himself, a blond teen a little
older than Michael, was good-looking on the right side of
his face. On the left and down his neck grew a thick crust of
growths, as brown and scabby as dried mushrooms. His left
eye peered out of the crust. I wondered how good its vision
was. José and his deformities were real enough, no matter
how suspicious I was about the place he lived in.

"Hey, BG bro!" José waved to Michael with one six-fingered hand, then jerked a thumb in Ari's direction. "Who's this?"

"My wingman," Michael said. "Ari's his name."

"Hey," José said. "I always knew you had to be somebody big back at home. Good thing you brought him and that fancy heat he's packing. We've had a little trouble 'round here."

"Dodger gang spies?" Michael said.

"Who else? But there's one less of them in the world today," José paused to jerk a thumb in the direction of one of his bodyguards, "thanks to Little Sam here and his knife."

Little Sam, a hulking six footer, grinned to reveal a lack of front teeth. I felt more than a little sick at my brother's choice of friends. I could say nothing for several reasons. First and foremost, they had saved his life back when he could have lost it to one of those same Dodger gangs.

"Now," José continued, "what's up?"

"A bargain, maybe." Michael arranged a neutral expression. "I'm thinking of buying Lisa from you."

When José laughed, the layered growths on his face moved in vertical waves. "I thought that might happen, yeah, one of these days. Let's talk."

They all sat down on the ground, except Ari, who leaned back against the wall, rifle at the ready, and kept his gaze on the garden. Now and then he turned his head back and forth, scanning for trouble, I assumed.

The negotiations, however, went smoothly. When it came to bargaining, Michael had always been clever, not from a psychic talent but a normal gift for fast talk. I remembered how he used to trade away pieces of the elaborate school lunches I bagged for him, back when he was in grade school. He'd gotten extra cookies and snack cakes from other kids until I found out and began giving him peanut butter and jelly like the other schoolyard wretches got.

"I'll trade her straight over," José began. "For that rifle your wingman's carrying."

"No way," Michael said, grinning. "I wouldn't try taking it from him, either."

Ari made a small growling noise. I suspected him of enjoying the role.

"I'm not in the mood to die today, yeah," José said. "Okay. What about the usual? Coffee, chocolate, some more of those allergy pills and aspirins. A couple of car batteries."

"I can get all that," Michael said. "The question is how many pounds?"

As they argued back and forth, I began to feel anger rising in my mind, a slow tide that at first seemed inexplicable until I remembered that my brother was buying a woman, a human being, whom José considered his property to sell. I found myself thinking of the other gang girls. You can't buy them all, O'Grady, I reminded myself. One is too many, really, to bring over.

I'd run smack into another problem of working for the Agency. Agents tended to uncover more misery than they could cure. I'd been warned about it. Now I was seeing it. I hated it, but I was stuck with it.

As the negotiations dragged on, I kept checking my watch. Theoretically, Michael should have been in school by eight o'clock. Theory gave way to reality as the hands crept around to seven thirty. Between time checks, I soaked up the sunlight and warmth of this alien spring day and studied the view out the window.

Rather than the tidy houses and urban yards of my world, a thick tangle of plants and weeds covered the hill behind this version of the Houlihan house. When I turned my head to look, I saw no houses to either side of the vegetable garden. Thanks to the low population of the city, the Excelsior district had never been developed, or the Sunset, either. When we'd discussed his first trip to this deviant world level, Michael had mentioned how much of San Francisco looked deserted, a consequence, or so he'd been told, of radiation poisoning from the nuclear wars.

I ran an SM:General Location and got a very strange sense of place. The world, not merely this version of San Francisco but what lay beyond, struck me as oddly small, limited somehow. When I tried to access the CDS, I received no information. I tried letting images rise but only got one ridiculous picture of a hunk of Swiss cheese right out of a Tom and Jerry cartoon. I squelched that and gave up. I decided that the radiation was interfering with my talents. It was the only explanation, anyway, that I could come up with.

Finally, when it was 8:15 and too late to get Michael to that first period study hall, he and José stood up. They shook hands, then slapped each other's palms in a ritual seal of the bargain. In my mind, Michael's normal California high school moved very far away.

"I'll get the stuff today," Michael said. "I'll send the critter to tell you when we can bring it over."

"Fine." José nodded his approval. "I'll have Lisa here and ready to go, the lucky little bitch."

Michael smiled at the epithet, but I could see the effort it cost him.

After they shook hands once more, José and his two guards walked away, turning brave backs on Ari and the biathlon rifle. If Michael and Ari had wanted to take over the BGs, they could have done it right then. Instead, they climbed back through the window, Ari first, then Michael.

Michael turned to face the view through the dirty windowpane. He neither moved nor spoke, but the yellow wallboard began to sprout bunches of printed violets. The cardboard cartons first reappeared, then solidified. Last of all, the white shade replaced the dirty sheet. I could see Uncle Jim's garden through the unblocked strip of window below the edge of the shade. We were back.

"Do you know how you do that?" I said.

"Nah," Michael said. "Except I think about the place I want to go to. I wish I could learn more."

"Well, I'll ask my handler. Maybe we can find someone to teach you. NumbersGrrl only knows the theory behind it."

We trooped out of the room. Michael put the padlock back on the door and clicked it shut.

"By the way," Michael said. "Aunt Eileen knows all about this. She called school and told them I had a dentist appointment."

"You might have mentioned that earlier," I said. "I've been worrying for nothing."

"Sorry." He blushed and looked down at the floor, an

ordinary kid at that moment. "Say, do you guys want breakfast? The stores won't be open yet."

"Go ask Aunt Eileen if there's enough."

Yes, it was a silly thing to ask, as I knew damn well she'd cooked enough breakfast for all of us and more, but I wanted a moment alone with Ari to get his reaction. When Michael trotted off toward the kitchen, Ari knelt down by his sample case and began to unload the rifle.

"That was interesting," he said. "I've always wondered what it would be like to live in the Dark Ages."

"The young warlord selling one of his concubines, yeah," I said. "It gave me the creeps."

Ari put the bullets away in their box, then disjointed the rifle itself. He was just wrapping the pieces up when Aunt Eileen trotted in, wearing her turquoise capris with a pink blouse and, of course, the fuzzy pink slippers.

"Scrambled eggs and coffee cake," she announced.

"Sounds wonderful." Ari gave me a significant look. "Doesn't it?"

"Yeah," I said. "It sure does."

To keep peace in the family, I managed to get down a glass of orange juice, what amounted to a scrambled egg, and a chunk of cake with streusel topping along with my usual black coffee. The difficulty of eating so much shocked me. I had to force myself, one forkful at a time, to finish the coffee cake, even though it was delicious.

I could take solace in the amount of exercise we got that day, buying and boxing up the goods that Michael was trading for Lisa-Sophie. Our final stop was an auto supply store. While Ari and Michael went inside to buy a battery, I sat in a nearby coffee shop that offered free wifi and used my Agency laptop—and a double encryption program—to pick up e-mail.

NumbersGrrl had seen the video and read my report. She agreed with my guess that Belial had some sort of field-generating device that transported his consciousness across deviant levels.

"I've got no idea what it is," she wrote. "That's the problem. Let me ask one of my old professors at MIT. He knows

I work for the government and won't ask too many awkward questions. BTW, I'm also guessing that if you destroy that field, he'll flip back to wherever he came from. I don't think it'll kill him, but I bet it would give him a helluva shock."

Yeah, I thought, but he could just use his fancy device again and come right back—once he recovered. It occurred to me that I'd been throwing wards at his projections and shattering them. He'd probably felt enough of those shocks to be really pissed at me. A sudden SAWM confirmed the guess.

By the time we returned to Aunt Eileen's, Brian had gotten home from school. He helped us carry the cartons down to the storage room.

"You know about all this?" I said to Brian.

"Oh, yeah," he said.

"You know the family rules, right?"

" 'Course I do." He gave me a look of faint disgust. "Suppose I told someone about it. Think they'd believe me?"

"Not for a minute. Okay, I get it."

"Some secrets you can't help keeping."

This time I decided to revert to the Dark Ages myself and let the male persons handle the transaction without me. I sat at the kitchen table and watched Aunt Eileen, who stood by the counter and trimmed up the last of the season's asparagus.

"Ari knows what he's doing with guns, doesn't he?" Aunt Eileen asked. "I read somewhere that all Israeli men have to serve in the Army, so I suppose he did, too."

"Oh, yeah," I said. "He has marksmanship medals and everything. So you know that he's teaching Michael how to shoot?"

She nodded and continued slicing off the fibrous ends of the asparagus stems.

"I was surprised that Brian didn't want to learn," I said.

"So was I, and I was relieved, to be honest. But I don't mind about Michael. It's not like we're in the Old Country, where he'd go off and get killed by the Black and Tans." She glanced my way with a smile. "Your grandfather used to love to talk about the tribulations of the Old Country. He made it sound awful. Not, of course, that he was ever there himself."

We laughed, but not very loud or long. Aunt Eileen laid down the knife and picked up a vegetable peeler to continue trimming the thickest stalks.

"I meant to tell you," Aunt Eileen said. "I had the oddest dream last night about Jack Donovan's father. He was looking at a newspaper headline and shaking like a leaf."

"Could you read the headline?"

"No, though I did try." She laid the peeler down and wiped her hands on her calico print apron. "It was some local paper up in Sonoma County. That's where he's living, you know, at his vinyard."

"A prescient dream or a possibility image only?"

"Only a possibility, I think."

"Then don't worry. Ari's got everything under control."

Although she fixed me with the gimlet eye, I smiled and never answered. I wanted nothing getting back to Kathleen until Jack and Ari had their talk, not even a hint. Eventually, Aunt Eileen gave in.

"Oh, by the way," she said, "I picked up several sacks of vintage clothing at an estate sale. Most of it fits me, but there are a couple of things that are too small. Do you want to try them?"

"This girl Mike's rescuing is even thinner than I am," I said. "How about we clothe her first? She's not going to have much with her."

In a few minutes we learned how truly I'd spoken when we heard footsteps coming down the hall. I got up and went to the doorway in time to see Michael carrying a gray cardboard suitcase held together by wrapped string. Behind him came Lisa, or that is, as I reminded myself, Sophie now, with Brian and Ari bringing up the rear.

Sophie looked even paler and thinner than I remembered her, a waif with her short brown hair and huge dark eyes. She was wearing a faded, patched denim skirt that came to mid-calf and a pink sweater several sizes too large. And she limped, of course, stumping along with her club-foot in its heavy brown shoe and her normal foot in an ordinary oxford. Aunt Eileen took one look at her, then turned to me.

"You raised Michael right," she said, "after all."

"Thanks," I said. "I tried."

Once they all piled into the kitchen, Sophie stood looking around her at the beige Formica counters, the plain white appliances, the maple table, the cabinets with their oak veneer.

"It's all so beautiful," she said and began to cry.

Michael dropped the suitcase and threw his arms around her. Ari and I exchanged a glance. He jerked his head in the direction of the door, and I nodded. We slithered our way out of the kitchen without anyone particularly noticing.

"We can debrief her tomorrow," I said.

"I hope the information's worth it," Ari said.

"Doesn't matter. Aunt Eileen's never going to let her go back, not now that she's seen her."

Although the sky was clear and sunny over Aunt Eileen's neighborhood, back at our flat the fog had already come in so thickly that we could barely see across the street. The front wall had stayed mercifully free of graffiti in our absence. Cryptic Creep must have been busy elsewhere. Upstairs, I found messages waiting on the answering machine. Y's secretary had called twice and left the code words indicating he wanted a trance conference.

"It's four-thirty," I said. "Seven-thirty in DC. There's not much use in my going into trance now."

I could, of course, see if Y had left me an online message. I fired up my desktop and logged onto TranceWeb. Y had indeed sent me a brief e-mail.

"Papers are a Go. Trance me about courier delivery."

I pumped a clenched fist and murmured, "Yes!" Soon Sophie would be legal. The problem, then, would be what to do with her, though I figured Aunt Eileen would have ideas on that subject. I spent a moment hoping, with deepest sincerity, that Sophie wasn't pregnant. If she were, I doubted that either she or the baby would survive the birth.

I should have known that Aunt Eileen would have the same thought. She called later to announce, triumphantly, that Sophie was not "in the family way."

"I bought one of those drugstore kits," Aunt Eileen said. "They're accurate, aren't they?"

"I think so, yeah, from what I've read. That's a relief."

"Yes, though I wouldn't be surprised to learn that she's barren. It's an odd old word, isn't it, barren? But honestly, considering how she's been starved, it's a very real possibility."

"That's true." I felt further relieved. "As soon as we can, we need to get her to a doctor. She's never seen one in her life, I bet." I was thinking about STDs, but somehow I couldn't bring myself to mention them to my aunt. "What with all the radiation and the poor conditions, something might be really wrong."

"Jim thinks we can get her on our health plan, though that will take forever, knowing them. Well, we'll burn that bridge when we're crossing it. Which reminds me, Rose and Wally will be here soon. You know how vague they are about dates, but probably next week."

"That'll be great! I'm looking forward to seeing them."

After I hung up, I realized that I knew someone who would understand about the STD problem: Jerry. When I called, I found him at home. Monday nights were too slow to bother working, he told me.

"Yeah, I can see that," I said, "especially in this nasty weather. I have a question for you. My aunt's taken in a runaway girl rescue. This kid ended up working the streets, and she's never seen a doctor for a blood test or anything."

"Oh, shit!" Jerry sounded sincerely horrified. "You can't talk to the young ones, darling, about AIDS or anything else. They think they'll live forever. Probably none of her johns would have used a rubber even if she'd wanted to."

"Probably not, no. So is there a clinic—"

"There is. No questions asked. Want me to take her?"

"That would be great. You know the—uh—ropes."

Jerry laughed.

"And think about working for the Agency," I said. "You're not going to live forever, either."

"How true that is!" He sighed with great drama. "I'm free Wednesday. Call me around two P.M. The clinic opens late."

I got off the phone to find Ari standing nearby, watching me with a piece of paper in his hand.

"Yeah?" I said.

"From the DMV." He handed me the paper. "That white sedan you saw near the Cliff House? It's registered to Caleb Sumner."

Chapter 12

W E WOKE TUESDAY MORNING TO POURING
RAIN. When I looked out of the bay window in the
front room, I saw clouds so thick at the horizon that I
couldn't tell where they ended and the gray sea began. The
unusually wet year was continuing to give us water to burn.
Northern California could rejoice. I had a different take on
the weather.

"Crud," I said. "Sarge isn't going to be outside today. No
Reb Zeke, either, if he's even on our world level."

"True." Ari handed me a mug of coffee.

"Thanks. I'll drink this, and then I've got to contact Y."

Our trance session went fast, because Y was on his way
to yet another meeting.

"Okay," I said, "in your e-mail, you said something about
a courier."

"Yes. We're sending you the documents for your new
information source by courier. He'll arrive tomorrow at
SFO with the attaché case attached." Y grinned at his own
joke. "I'm sending the flight information in e-mail, but in a
very stripped form. This conversation is the context for the
numbers you'll find there."

"An actual courier? Why?"

"We've got funding for special couriers in our budget. If
we don't use it, we'll lose it. Can't have that!"

I supposed I saw the point.

"When will you be debriefing the new source?" Y said.

"In a couple of hours," I said. "I'll file a report as soon as we're finished. What's the code for my courier?"

"Waukeegan. Ask him if he comes from there. He'll say, no, I'm from Peoria. His name's Paul."

"Got it. Paul from Peoria. One last thing, any news about those questions I had for Ari Nathan's mother?"

"Not yet. My contact in MI5 is handling the matter, but he's had to bring in the Israelis. I don't know why."

"I do. At one time Reb Ezekiel was suspected of spying for the British government."

Y groaned. The image of an enormous jar of blackstrap molasses materialized next to him, then flickered and disappeared. "That means the matter could be very sensitive," Y said. "You know what that implies."

"Yeah. It could take months."

"You're learning the ways of bureaucracy, aren't you? And speaking of which, I'd better go."

Before we left for Aunt Eileen's, I had time to surf my usual Internet news sources. Two rogue waves had hit the coast south of Pacifica, but no one had been drowned or injured. The first wave had struck around five o'clock, close to the time when Fog Face had appeared at my window, and the second, around ten in the evening. Both waves had dislodged a considerable quantity of earth and rocks from the cliffs near Año Nuevo Beach.

"I'm beginning to wonder," I told Ari, "if Caleb's been doing some excavating with these waves, trying to turn up the treasure."

"Wouldn't it be easier to use a shovel?" Ari said.

"Not if Drake buried the treasure so deep that it's halfway down the cliff face."

"He wouldn't have buried it right at the edge of a cliff. It's a sodding stupid place to look."

"Only if the edge of the cliff then was where it is now, and it wasn't. The whole California coast has been eroding ever since the Ice Age ended. Eight thousand years ago you could have walked to the Farallon Islands, and now they're twenty-seven miles out to sea."

"I didn't know that."

"There was a ton of information about oceanic erosion

on the news back in January. Down in Pacifica, the sea un-
dermined a big apartment complex so badly that the buildings had to be condemned. When they were built, they were
something like a hundred yards away from the edge, and
that was only about fifty years ago."

"So four hundred years ago, Drake might have buried
his loot near the shore but not on it. I see what you're getting at."

Over at the Houlihan house, Sophie was waiting for us
in the living room. Dressed in new jeans and a lavender
blouse with a little collar and pleats down the front, she
looked fed, clean, and utterly dazed. She perched on the
edge of the brown armchair and clutched a paper notebook
with a mottled white-and-black cover.

"This is for you." She handed me the notebook. "I wrote
down everything I could think of. Michael said you'd want
to know about the gates and the weird things people can do
and just anything weird."

"I sure do." I took the notebook and realized that the
pages were actually sewn and bound rather than glued or
threaded on a wire spiral. "Where is Michael, by the way?"

"In school." She gave me a quivering smile. "People go
to school for a long time, here, huh?"

"Yeah, they sure do." I sat down in the blue armchair
facing her. "We need to see about getting you some education, too."

"I'd like that. I really would."

As usual, no one wanted to sit on the orange brocade
sofa under the portrait of Father Keith. Ari looked around,
found a wooden chair by the window, and brought it over
to sit next to me. I opened the notebook and flipped through
a few pages, written in pencil. Sophie had big round handwriting, perfectly clear if childlike. She wrote in long gasps
of run-on sentences, so the information, while fascinating,
lacked any kind of organization that I could see.

"I'll study this material later," I said and laid the notebook in my lap. "Thank you for this."

"You're welcome. I bought it with my own money when
Mike said I could come across."

"José let you have money of your own?"

"Oh, yeah, twenty per cent of whatever we earned. He's really cool, one of the best gang guys. I was lucky."

Lucky. Well, in a way she was. She was out of there. Sophie sat on the edge of the chair with her hands clasped together and looked around the room.

"It's so weird, y'know?" she said. "I thought, well, when I got here, it was like a dream, but it's not. It's solid. Back in the old place, that was like a dream. Nothing really made any sense, y'know? Everyone always said it was the rads or the drugs. We all kinda felt it, but now that I'm here, I really feel it."

"Oh, yeah?" I said. "Did you write about that?"

"No, but I will if you want me to. I mean, I owe you so much. Anything you want, I'll do."

I felt like saying, you don't need to grovel, but on the other hand, I was glad she was grateful. "Look," I said, "Michael can give you a notebook to write in. Tell me what never made sense in your old place. It doesn't matter if it sounds dumb. Anything you can think of, why it doesn't seem solid now. And while you're at it, tell me what kind of drugs, how easy they were to get or how hard or whatever."

"Okay."

Ari looked my way and raised an eyebrow. I couldn't have explained why those details were important, but I knew they were. Ambiguity, again, but I'd learned over the years to minimize the risk of letting valuable information slip away.

"So," I said, "you know about the other gates?"

"Everyone knows about the gates, just not where they are or where they go. The big Dodger gangs keep that all secret, you see, so no one can muscle in."

"Right. Did José want Michael to open gates for the BGs?"

"Yeah. And to work the coyote racket."

"Coyote? Illegal immigrants?"

"Yeah, getting people to Brazzy—Brazil, I mean—or some other clean country. There's like rads everywhere, but some places it's not so bad as Merrka. So if Mike could open a road, José figured, to like Strayla or Brazzy or even Fricka, then they could clean up."

"Makes sense. But dangerous, I'll bet."

"Oh, yeah. If the cops found out, they'd have shot them both and taken the road over for themselves."

Ari made a noise somewhere between a cough and a screech of outrage. Sophie flinched and shrank back into her chair.

"Sorry," Ari said. "I take it that the police in your world have very low standards of conduct."

Sophie stared, utterly bewildered.

"In our world," Ari said, "the police obey the laws."

"No kidding?" Sophie said. "Wow, that's really something, huh?"

Ari muttered a few Hebrew words. I got back to the subject in hand.

"Sophie," I said, "what about immigration between worlds? Are there trans-world coyotes?"

"You hear about that," Sophie said, "but I don't know if it's true. I wrote down all the rumors. It'd be real dangerous. I mean, you might end up somewhere worse."

"Hard to imagine," Ari said.

"But there's one rumor I think is true," Sophie went on. " 'Cause I saw it happen one night when I was working downtown. Cops from somewhere else bring prisoners through. I don't know where from, but I heard about it, and then this one night, real late, I was standing down on Ellis Street near Market—" She stopped. "Is there an Ellis Street here?"

"There sure is." I was thinking of Jerry. "I don't suppose it's much different than the one in your old level."

"Okay. So I saw these guys come out of a bar, two guys in uniform, I mean, and I thought, 'Oh, shit, cops!' So I got a twenty out of my pocket to give them so they'd leave me alone, you know? But they didn't even look at me. They were hauling along some guy in handcuffs. There was a streetlight, and you could see the weird color of their uniforms and the patches on them and stuff. They weren't our cops. So they shoved the guy into a squad car and drove off. And I was bored so I watched, and halfway down the block, poof! they just disappeared. They must have had a world-walker in the front seat."

"You're sure about this?" Ari said.

"Real sure," Sophie said. "I hadn't smoked anything, either."

"What was the color of those uniforms?" I had one of my CDS insights. I knew the color had meaning, not that I knew what it was at that moment.

"Green, kind of, but the streetlight was like yellow, you know? Our cops' uniforms look black in streetlight light, but they're really dark blue."

"Green under yellow light, huh?" I contemplated this for a moment. "Peacock blue, then, in sunlight."

"So your police," Ari said, "would have let this other force operate in their jurisdiction?"

For a second time Sophie radiated bewilderment. Ari tried again.

"Your cops would have let these other guys arrest someone?"

"For enough baksheesh, sure." Sophie smiled and rubbed her thumb and forefinger together. "That's all it takes."

Ari glowered at an innocent wall as if he were thinking of punching it.

"Fascinating," I said. "This clears up so many things!"

"Does it?" Ari said. "Explain."

"Later. I need to get my thoughts in order. Sophie, I'd like to talk with you again tomorrow, after I've read the stuff in the notebook. That okay?"

"Sure. Any time."

"Okay, tomorrow your papers will be here, so we'll bring them by and—"

I stopped because she started to leak tears. "My papers?" she whispered between sniffs. "You got me the papers? Mike said you could, but I didn't like believe him, because it was too good to be true." She covered her face with both hands and sobbed aloud.

I got up from my chair to attempt to comfort her just as Aunt Eileen came rushing in. She could hear a member of her family weeping from a mile away, I swear it. Eileen pulled a folded wad of clean tissues out of her skirt pocket and handed them to Sophie, then fixed me with the gimlet eye. "What have you been asking her?"

"Nothing's wrong," Sophie stammered. "I'm just so happy." She began to unwad the tissues, carefully pulling them free one layer at a time. "Nola, hey, I don't know how to thank you."

What I wanted to say was, just don't ever break my brother's heart. What I said aloud was, "Keep thinking about those gates, and if you remember something new, write it down."

"I will, for sure." She wiped her cheeks with one ply of a tissue, then folded it up as if she were planning on using it again.

"I'll see you tomorrow," I said to Aunt Eileen. "We'll be bringing by her papers. And a friend of mine will take her to a free clinic, just for a quick checkup. All that radiation, you know."

"Wonderful!" Aunt Eileen said. "When you get back, will you stay for dinner?"

Ari came to attention like a dog scenting steak.

"Thanks, we will," I said. "What do you have planned for today?"

"More shopping," Aunt Eileen said. "And then we're going to turn her into a blonde."

"Good idea," I said. "A real good idea, in fact. Make sure the beautician does her eyebrows, too."

Since the rain had slacked off to a drizzle, we drove home the long way round, via Fifth and Market. Sarge's territory, the entrance to the Flood Building, imitated a slice of a Roman bath with a two-story-high coffered ceiling and, at the back, huge bronze-trimmed doors leading into the building itself. In wet weather it would provide plenty of shelter for a panhandler. Yet, even though I cruised by in slow traffic, I saw no sign of him. At a stoplight, I ran a quick SM:P and caught a glimpse of him sitting half asleep in a church pew. Which church it was I couldn't see.

"He must have found a place where they leave the heat on," I said.

"Good," Ari said. "I can't believe the weather here. It's almost spring. Why is it so sodding cold?"

"And wet. Don't forget the wet. Usually things are dry-ing out and warming up by now, yeah. I don't know why. It's weather. Weather does what it wants."

Ari growled. The first thing he did when we reached our flat was to turn on the heat.

I spent the rest of that day going over Sophie's notebook. I separated out the tangled strands of information and organized them by category, then sent the Agency a comprehensive report. I included the perceptions of the deviant level beyond the gate that I'd made on the day we bargained for Sophie. I also retrieved and reread all the information NumbersGrrl had sent me on deviant world levels.

During all this, Ari was sitting on the couch, channel surfing with the sound off. I swiveled my chair around and caught his attention.

"When we were fetching Sophie," I said, "you took your rad alarm out of your pocket. You said something was odd, the mix of radiation or something?"

"Just that, yes. There was a very high concentration of X-rays and ultraviolet light."

"And?"

"That much ultraviolet makes me think something stripped off part of the ozone layer." He quirked an eyebrow. "Do you know what that is?"

"The thing the aerosols were destroying?"

"That will do to get on with. But the main point is, that type of radiation damage isn't typical of nuclear explosions. With fallout, what lingers is the secondary radiation, such as gamma rays. The percentage of gamma radiation was too low to indicate normal fallout conditions, if you can call a nuclear war normal, at any rate."

"Huh. That is odd, but you know, I'm not surprised. There's something real strange about that deviant level. Let me do a little more reading in Agency files."

When I finished, I was ready to float a few theories. The San Francisco of that level struck me as being a little less than real. People there talked about Africa, Brazil—countries in the southern hemisphere. Neither Michael nor Sophie had ever mentioned Canada, Europe, Japan, any of the countries of the north. And all that radiation, the purported traces of a series of nuclear wars, had turned out to be the wrong kind. What's more, neither Michael nor Sophie had ever mentioned a picture of a place destroyed by bombing. I called Mike to confirm these thoughts.

"Do you remember telling me," I began, "that the Germans had nukes ready to deliver in the 1930s?"

"That's what I was told, yeah. Why?"

"I don't think that's actually possible. Way too early."

"Y'know, I kind of wondered about those bombs, too. Everyone said there was nothing left of LA to see. But I don't remember why—maybe Sophie will—but I got this weird feeling like maybe it never had been there, but everyone thought it should have been there, and so they made up stuff about it being bombed. The Dodgers were in Sackamenna for the '37 Coast League championships. Isn't that kind of early, too? I mean, they would have been called the Hollywood Stars back then."

"Real true, bro. Way too early for the actual Dodgers."

"And if they were in LA, how come they weren't blown up, too, when the bomb dropped?"

"Look, Mike, the Agency will be asking the same questions. Can you talk with Sophie some more? Write down any answers or data you guys can remember or put together."

"Okay. And if you and Ari want to go there and look around, just let me know."

"Thanks." My stomach twisted itself into a cold knot over the idea of walking any distance away from the gate. "We'll be over tomorrow. We can talk more then."

Wednesday was one of those frantic days when you run one errand after the other. I wore my best jeans with the teal sweater and the black satin-backed crepe jacket, practical but with a touch of class, and carried a red umbrella. In the morning, Ari and I drove to the airport, where I met the Agency courier, exchanged passwords, and got the attaché case. Since Paul from Peoria had a return flight to DC leaving twenty minutes after the exchange, I left him to it and drove back to San Francisco. I woke Jerry up with a phone call and made arrangements with him.

When I got to Aunt Eileen's, I opened the attaché case. We found naturalization papers for Sophia Yelena Chekov, along with a document in Ukranian, which is close enough to Russian for Ari to tell us it was a birth certificate, and a long document in English and Ukranian purporting to be the ruling of a court giving her the legal status of emancipated minor on the grounds that her parents had abandoned her. A note from Y remarked that we should get her an American passport as soon as possible and a California state ID card, too.

"I'll put these in the safe until we need them," Aunt Eileen said. "Jim insisted that we have a fireproof place for the mortgage papers and things like that. Because of the earthquakes, you know."

The safe, a small round door in the wall, turned out to lurk behind Father Keith's portrait. The papers would be protected by sanctity as well as the steel door.

Thanks to her pale skin, Sophie made a smashing honey-blonde. She told me that Michael really liked the way it looked, her last truly happy moment of the afternoon. We took her over to Jerry's and picked him up. He'd washed his usual hairspray out of his blond hair and tied it back with a macho strip of leather, though he was wearing a woman's flowered rayon red dress over his straight-leg jeans. Sophie paid no particular attention to this fashion statement. I supposed that she'd seen weirder.

I followed Jerry's directions and drove them down to the VD clinic. While we waited, Ari and I drove around downtown, looking for Sarge and Reb Ezekiel and finding neither. With an SM:P, I did locate Sarge in a homeless shelter that was staying open in the rainy weather. He was playing cards with a couple of friends in the midst of maybe a hundred homeless guys. I could never have gone in and kept my cover story, not safely, anyway.

Finally, we returned for Jerry and a very subdued Sophie, who had a fistful of prescriptions for antibiotics and dusting powder, some of which she needed to share with Michael on the doctor's orders. She wallowed in shame and guilt while she told me about them until I told her to shut up, she was forgiven.

"But Aunt Eileen's been so good to me," she said. "I feel so bad about being so well dirty and sick, I guess. I shouldn't have taken a bath last night."

"Oh, come on," Jerry said. "Chlorine bleach works wonders on the fixtures. Nola, this poor child had never had a pelvic before. No wonder she's grossed out. I'm real glad we got her to the doc."

Every muscle in Ari's body went tense. He scrupulously pretended he couldn't hear a thing, even though he was in the front passenger seat about three feet from Jerry, in the back.

"I'll scrub everything I touched," Sophie said. "I promise. I just feel awful."

"You'd have felt worse if you hadn't seen the nice doctor," Jerry said. "Itchier, anyway. Count your blessings, little girl. You should have gone to the clinic months ago."

I winced, waiting for Sophie to tell him the truth, that in her world no such thing existed, but she said nothing, only sniveled into a tissue.

We dropped Jerry off, then stopped at a big chain drugstore on outer Mission Street to get the prescriptions filled. I let Ari drive around the block—parking was impossible— while I went in with Sophie. We saw a security guard just inside the door, a barrel-chested white guy who gave us a vague smile as we went past.

"Wow," Sophie said. "You must really be somebody, Nola."

"Huh?" I said. "Why?"

"He passed you right through and didn't shake you down."

"Sophie, things are different here. Honest. The cops don't shake you down. If one tries, you can report him."

Sophie's eyes went very wide. "Wow," she whispered. "Just, well, wow."

The young woman pharmacist acted totally blasé about the conditions that the prescriptions indicated, which allowed Sophie to regain a small portion of her sense of self-worth.

"Just make sure you wash all your boyfriend's underwear with bleach in the water," the pharmacist said. "Body lice don't like chlorine. You've got to destroy the eggs."

"Okay," Sophie said. "Maybe we should buy a bottle of that stuff, too, huh?"

"Good idea," I said.

And we did, two big plastic jugs of it, not a very romantic purchase, but a necessary one.

The real rain began just as we reached the Houlihan house—while we were still outside at the bottom of the hill, of course. We scurried up the steps and got in before we were soaked. The house smelled like dinner. I actually salivated.

"That does smell good," I said.

Ari smiled and agreed. Sophie tipped her head a little to one side and sniffed. "It does," she said, "but what is it?"

"Fried chicken," I said. "And apple pie. Ever had them?"

"I've had some chicken, a couple of times. But I don't know what pie is."

When the time came for dessert, she decided that she liked it a lot.

We left Aunt Eileen's after dinner, because my mother called and announced she was coming over. Mom never actually waited to be invited when it came to visiting relatives. She merely gave an ETA. Michael hid Sophie in his room, and we fled.

I also wanted to put some time into tracking Caleb and Ari was expecting some important e-mail. Once we got back to our flat, I checked the answering machine: nothing from Caleb. I ran an SM:P only to find it blocked. I threw some Qi behind my probe and got a faint image of Caleb sitting on a bare wood floor and reading a book by flashlight. Although he was occupied, someone began pushing my probe away. Belial? The Cryptic Creep? I broke off the attempt.

I turned around to tell Ari only to find him nowhere in sight. I had a peculiar moment of panic, where I thought that everyone I needed to see or speak to had suddenly disappeared. I took a deep breath and realized that Ari had merely gone into the bedroom. From the sound of clicking keys, I deduced that he'd started working at his laptop. Not precisely at Sherlock Holmes' level, but the deduction did dispel the panic. I went in and saw him sitting on the edge of the bed with the laptop on the end table in front of him.

"Just checking e-mail," he said. "We've got to have another talk."

"What now?" I snapped. "Jack again?"

"No," Ari said. "Your father wasn't in the States legally, was he?"

I turned around and stalked out of the bedroom. Although I seriously considered grabbing my jacket and leaving, the rain hammered on the roof and swept across the street in gusts. Besides, I reminded myself, it's not like Dad's still around to arrest. I flopped down on the couch and scowled across the room at the bookshelf. Ari followed me in, but he stayed standing. He shoved his hands in his pockets.

"I suppose you're angry with me," he said.

"Whatever makes you think that?"

"Look, I'm trying to help you sort out the situation. That's all. I can hardly arrest a man who disappeared thirteen years ago."

"I did have a similiar thought."

"Good. I'm not an immigration official, either. I'd have no jurisdiction in a case of illegal entry."

My mood turned a small degree sweeter.

"I asked Sanchez a favor," Ari said. "He looked up the file on your father's disappearance for me and sent it over this afternoon. I thought I might find more information for your family from Interpol files if I had some concrete search terms."

Although Ari paused as if he expected me to say something, I refused on general principles. He sat down on the couch and turned toward me.

"Was he an illegal alien?" Ari went on. "The police had no proof, but one of them was suspicious enough to write down an odd remark of your mother's. In a case like this one, it's possible that someone from the missing person's background is responsible for the disappearance, so she was questioned about your father's history. Your mother told the officer that as far as she knew, Flann was born in Boston, but he never talked much about his family there. It made me wonder."

To lie or not to lie—what did it matter, with Dad gone for thirteen years?

"Yeah, he was an illegal," I said. "He was actually born in Ireland. You're good at what you do."

Ari smiled. "Do go on," he said. "How did he manage to get into the States?"

"It's easy, if you're white and European, particularly if you come to a city where there are a lot of legit immigrants from your country. They're your support system."

"And your family would have provided that."

"Oh, yeah. After Dad married my mother, in fact, it was Jack Donovan's father who gave him a good job and promoted him and all the rest of it."

"No wonder you were determined to protect the Donovans."

"You bet. When Dad disappeared, Kevin Donovan gave my mother a job, too, and paid for the training she needed to do it. Bookkeeping, that is. That's how Jack met Kathleen, at an office Christmas party."

"I noticed that there's nothing in the report about consulting the I.C.E."

"This was before they started fingerprinting everyone who visits the States."

"True. Still, I was surprised that the local police didn't follow up on their suspicions."

"Oh, they did, kind of. They consulted the public records in Boston. They found so many O'Gradys that they gave it up. Besides, half the cops in this city are Irish."

"And they'd let that influence them?"

"Maybe, yeah. I wouldn't know for sure."

Ari didn't exactly snarl, but his mouth twitched as if he wanted to.

"On top of that," I continued, "Dad was born right about the time that home births were popular. I remember Mom telling the cops what little she knew about his mother. Mrs. O'G was heavy into hippie stuff like natural foods and herbal medicines. He'd been born at home, and the certificate never properly recorded."

"I see. The report did mention a baptismal certificate from a Boston church."

"Yeah, he did have one of those."

"So once he arrived here, he was reasonably safe."

"Just that. He met Uncle Jim down at the Irish Cultural Center, and Jim kind of took him under his wing. This was before Jim and Eileen got married. Dad lived in the Houlihan house for a while, in fact."

Ari said something that, oddly enough, I couldn't hear. I leaned toward him, but I found myself sitting on a chair in the gray library, where shelves full of books shot off in all directions, even straight up. I'd been there before. The angel with the pince-nez was standing at the dark oak lectern, thumbing through a massive leather-bound book. When I cleared my throat, he looked up and waggled his wings.

"Family history, family future," he said. "Don't you remember?"

"I remember you telling me that, but—"

"Where does your brother get his talent?"

The bookshelves began to turn, slowly at first, then faster and faster, a gray whirlpool spinning around me, so fast that they turned into a swirl of lamplight.

I was sitting on the blue couch. Ari had his arm around my shoulders.

"I'm back." I was so dry-mouthed that I nearly squawked. "I need to get some water."

"Stay where you are. I'll fetch it."

While he went into the kitchen, I considered the angel's message. Ari returned with a glass of tap water, which I drank off in a couple of big gulps.

"Well?" he said.

"My dad opened that gate in the Houlihan house." I leaned forward and set the mug down on the floor by my feet. "That's where Mike gets his world-walking genes, isn't it? From his father. No wonder the gate opened so easily for him."

Ari sat down with a long hard sigh. "Now that I know those things actually exist," he said, "that makes sense."

"And that's why the gate is ever so conveniently there," I continued. "I should have seen this before now. I still hate thinking about Dad being gone, I guess. We all really loved him." I managed to keep from crying, but only just.

"I wonder if he was a very illegal alien, then, from another Ireland all together. That would certainly explain why he didn't bother getting a proper green card."

"Even if they issued them on some other deviant level, it wouldn't have been valid here."

"It's a good enough theory to get on with, then."

"Yeah. Huh, I wonder if Mother knows more. I doubt it. If she did know, she would have repressed it, anyway. She desperately wanted to be normal. I guess she still does."

"Do you think he came from that same level that Michael's been visiting?"

"Not necessarily. Sophie talked about people going through it to somewhere else. If it's true about the nuclear wars, which I doubt, there's not much of Ireland left there, anyway."

Ari held out his hand. I put mine into it without even hesitating. His clasp still felt warm and comfortable. I slid over close and rested my head on his shoulder. I could feel his deep relief even without running a formal SPP.

"I wonder why Dad left home?" I said. "Maybe he was born in a trashed Ireland."

"He could have had a good reason to come here, in that case. Although I've only seen that one world, and I'd like to think it's not typical."

"Let's hope it's not. What I really wonder is where did he go when he left us? Did he return home and why, if he did? He always seemed happy enough here."

"Maybe he didn't have a choice. Someone might have come to fetch him, such as that level's version of the Gardai."

I sat up straight and pulled my hand away. "What makes you think the cops would be after him?"

"Your reactions to this conversation." Ari was watching me with no trace of a smile.

Family history had run me right into his trap. I must have looked furious, because Ari grimaced.

"Nola, I'd have no authority to cause trouble for your father no matter what he did back in wherever he came from." Ari held out his hand again. "Even if he were here right now. Please don't hold this against me. I didn't mean to open old wounds."

"They're more like old abscesses. They've never really healed." I laid my hand in his. "Okay. You're right. I know that Interpol's a big deal, but I bet it's not a trans-deviant-level authority in the greater multiverse."

"Very doubtful, yes." He smiled at me.

My backbrain registered an odd twinge, but I could make no sense out of it. His SPP showed me that Ari was telling the truth as he saw it. If he said he couldn't arrest my father, then he couldn't.

"I'm mostly curious," Ari went on. "I don't suppose you'd care to tell me why he was a fugitive."

"I don't know. No one wanted to tell us kids anything."

"I'd suppose not."

I was about to tell him what little I knew when a SAWM stopped me. The family conditioning ran too deep. What with overhearing things, plus asking Aunt Eileen when I was old enough, plus a vision or two, I had pieced together a story. I suspected that he'd shot and killed a pair of British soldiers who were beating up a buddy of his. Dad was IRA to the core back when that meant something. I'd often wondered if his real name was even Flann O'Grady.

"If he'd been on the run, no one would have told me," I finessed the truth. "He might have just come here for the chance at a good job and a better life. That's what most immigrants want. Back when he arrived, Ireland was still a very poor country."

"What do they call it now?" Ari smiled so easily that I knew he wanted to believe me. "The Celtic tiger, that's right."

"But you can see why no one wants to talk about him much. It's also why the whole family learned to be so close-mouthed. From the time we were, like, two years old, we knew we had to keep our mouths shut about the family talents in general and about Dad's country of origin in particular."

"Yes, I can understand that. Especially about the talents."

"And you know," I finished up, "if Dad was from some

other deviant level, we don't know what the situation's like in their version of Ireland. I wonder if the whole island's still occupied by the Brits. I remember him talking about our Republic of Ireland with a reverent tone to his voice, as if it was some kind of miracle."

Ari slumped back against the couch cushions. "Just when I think I'm used to all of this," he said, "and to your family, I learn something new, and I'm gobsmacked."

"You know what?" I said. "Sometimes I feel that way myself." I stood up so I could retrieve my cell phone from my jeans pocket, then sat back down. "I've got to call Michael. He needs to know this right away."

It took Michael a few rings to answer his phone. He'd been in the bathroom, he told me, taking the first round of the pills Sophie had brought home. He sounded proud about needing them.

"You haven't told Aunt Eileen, have you?" I said.

"Only about the crabs. Like, that's seriously gross, so I didn't want her to have to touch my sheets, and she wanted to know why I wanted to wash them myself, so I had to tell her that. She was okay with it. She said she wasn't surprised."

"Well, good for you! Listen, I've got some big news. I figured out who put that gate in the Houlihan house."

"Yeah?" His voice turned eager. "Who?"

"Dad. That's where you get them, bro, the world-walking genes."

I heard a choking sound, then silence. "Mike? Are you okay?"

"Yeah. Jeez, I wish I'd known him. I can't even really remember him, y'know? I can sort of see his face, laughing about something. That's all."

"Yeah, I wish you'd known him, too. You were only three when he—"

"I'm gonna sign off. I'll call you later."

The line went dead in, I was willing to bet, a trickle of tears. You could have broken the news better, I told myself. Yet when I tried to think of fancy ways of saying it, I decided that out with it and blunt was the only way it could have been told.

"Well," I told Ari, "Michael is growing up every which way at once."

"We all have to, though I must admit, you O'Gradys have a more difficult time of it than most. It must have been particularly difficult for you."

I got an impression that he was waiting for me to go into detail about those miserable years. "Yeah, it was," I said. "I hate remembering it."

"I can understand that." He put his arm around my shoulders. "I feel that way about my childhood."

We shared a sigh that was not nostalgic.

"Anyway," I said. "I'm beginning to think Caleb has no intentions of returning my phone calls. It's been days now."

"True. I wonder if he knows you've been given information about him."

"He might. He's got talents of his own. And his friend Belial does, too."

I remembered his invisible presence hovering in the restaurant, watching Ari's charade of the jealous boyfriend. What did Belial make of it, I wondered, and of me? Nothing good, I was willing to bet. Nothing good at all.

CHAPTER 13

BETWEEN CALEB AND REB ZEKE, I grew increasingly irritated with men who refused to show up on my psychic scans. Zeke, at least, was harmless. Caleb, who was not, presented the more pressing problem. When Kathleen called to tell me that she and Jack had returned from the wine country, I decided that the time had come for the big reveal.

"Ari's got the information you asked for," I said. "He wants to tell Jack himself, though I don't see any reason why you and I can't be there to listen."

"That's great!" Kathleen said. "I guess the information makes you know who look bad."

"Very bad. Do you want us to come out today?"

"Why don't we come in? I haven't even seen your new flat. Say, do you want a couple of living room chairs? They'll fit in the SUV. Jack's mom gave them to us, and I don't have room for them."

"Yeah, I sure do! Thanks. That way you'll have something to sit on when you're here."

Jack, Kathleen, and two very modern chairs with wooden arms and burgundy leather cushions arrived at noon. While Jack and Ari wrestled the chairs upstairs, I showed Kathleen the flat. She looked typically gorgeous in a pair of cheap jeans and an Anna Sui black-and-white print blouse with dolman sleeves. In the kitchen she noticed my post-it about getting more furniture.

"What else do you need?" she said. "I've got stuff just sitting in the attic."

"A desk for Ari is the main priority," I said, "now that you've given me those chairs."

"Okay, that's easy. I've got Dad's old desk. I pried it off of Mom because she was turning it into a shrine, and I didn't think that was, y'know, healthy."

Every now and then Kathleen could hit the target dead center.

"I'd love to have that," I said. "And you are so right about the not healthy."

"Okay. Just don't let Ari take it when you guys break up."

Then again, there were times when she could score a real miss. Still, I could see why in this case. Breaking up with boyfriends had been something of a hobby of mine.

"I won't," I said. "Don't worry."

With the chairs in place, we all sat down in the living room. I ran a quick SM:Danger and then an SM:Personnel just to make sure that neither Caleb nor Belial was spying. They weren't. Jack was watching Ari so apprehensively that I figured Ari had hinted at bad news. I was right.

"Okay," Jack said, "out with it."

"I did some research on your business partner," Ari said. "Do you know he's a convicted felon?"

Jack stared at him for a long moment, started to speak, then stopped and stared some more.

"A blackmailer, as a matter of record," Ari went on. "As a teenager, he mowed lawns for pocket money in his small town and collected information on his customers while he did so. He was particularly good at spotting adulterous affairs and then extorting cash from the guilty parties, which he spent on alcohol and drugs. He was sent to juvenile facilities twice for possession of cocaine. At nineteen, he became too ambitious and tried to blackmail a local politician who was something of a womanizer. This victim went to the police. He figured, quite rightly, that if the scandal got out it would only increase his status among male voters."

Jack had turned bright red. His hands clenched into fists.

Kathleen leaned forward in her chair and put a hand on his knee.

"Your blood pressure," she said. "Honey—"

"I'll strangle the little bastard," Jack said. "So he's pulled this shit before, has he?"

"Yes, and he served a sentence of eighteen months for it. Who's his target this time? You or your father?"

"Dad, of course. I've got nothing to lose, now that the statute of—wait a minute, how do you—" Jack ran out of words. He returned to staring at Ari, this time with the helpless smile of a man who knows he's put his foot in too deep to pull out.

"Interpol keeps detailed records on everything that comes its way," Ari said. "When Nola told me that Sumner struck her as a criminal type, I did a bit of research. From there, I wondered what information we might have on you, because your wife had told Nola that Sumner had some sort of hold over you. As you say, it's an old matter. But I gather it would hurt your father if it came to light."

Jack's red face returned to its normal heavy tan. Brilliantly done, I thought. Ari's explanation left Kathleen in the clear, put Jack at ease, and as for me, everyone in the family knew I saw 'things' about people.

"Rather than physically assaulting Sumner," Ari said, "I suggest you threaten to go to the police. There are protections for blackmail victims these days. With a prior conviction for the same offense, Sumner would be wise to say nothing to anyone to avoid prosecution."

"Yeah, he would, but will he?" Jack glanced at his clenched hands and relaxed them. "Wise isn't a word I'd use to describe him."

"Who knows?" Ari shrugged. "If you like, I'll go with you when you confront him."

"Right, you're an actual cop," Jack said. "You can't just arrest him, huh?"

"Sorry, no. It's out of my jurisdiction. If you like, we can file a report with your local police department. I can then act as a consultant, if they ask me to."

Jack tossed his head and laughed. "I can just see the crew

in San Anselmo trying to deal with all of this. But I wouldn't mind your company, yeah. I'm supposed to see this floating piece of shit tomorrow. I appreciate the help, but why are you putting yourself out like this?"

"It's a criminal matter. I'm a police officer."

"Right, of course, yeah. Sorry." Jack shook his head as if he were trying to dislodge an invisible hat. "Nola, thanks. It's been eating me up inside. I've thought about going to the police a hundred times, but I never felt I had the leverage over the little turd that I'd need." He smiled with a thin twitch of his mouth. "Now I do."

"Just be careful," I said. "Real careful."

Ari nodded his agreement. "Where are you meeting him?"

"Over at the Chalet for lunch."

The Chalet was a bar and restaurant just across the Great Highway from the ocean.

"Can you change that location?" I said. "You'd be better off meeting him somewhere inland. I can't explain why, but it's important."

"What's this?" Jack said. "An O'Grady moment?"

"Exactly that."

Jack glanced at Kathleen, who said, "Nola's always right when she has one of those."

"Sure, why not? I can find a restaurant that's just as convenient for the little turd."

"Where does Caleb live?" Ari said. "I'd like that information for my files."

"In Pacifica. He was living up on Esplanade Avenue in one of those cliffside apartment blocks, but thanks to the erosion he had to move." Jack paused for a snarl. "Too bad the cliff didn't cave in and take him down with it. I've got his new address right here." He took a cell phone out of his pocket.

I fetched an old-fashioned sticky note and wrote down the address when Jack read it off. Something about it struck me as wrong. I found out what when I used my Agency laptop to log onto the Internet. I tried Google and a couple of other map sites.

"There's no such place," I told Jack.

"Shit," he said. "I must have recorded it wrong."

"Not necessarily," I said. "He might have given you a false address." I remembered the result of one of my scans, the image of Caleb sitting on a bare floor and reading a book by flashlight. "What was his old address? Do you remember?"

"Yeah, 3––Esplanade. But that property's been red-tagged."

"That doesn't mean someone looking for a place to hide wouldn't creep back in now and then. Especially if he's desperate for money."

Jack quirked both eyebrows, then nodded agreement. "Good point," he said. "He's going to be more desperate than ever real soon now. I'm going to cancel his credit card as soon as we get home."

"If I were you," Ari interrupted, "I'd wait till after we speak with him. Otherwise he'll get the wind up. He might not keep your lunch date."

"Right." Jack nodded his way. "And I have a few things to say to him."

"I want to be present at that meeting," I said. "Can you tell him that I've decided to work with you on the treasure hunt?"

"Sure." Jack paused for a tight-lipped smile. "Anything to set him up."

"He has reason to think I'm obsessively jealous," Ari put in. "So tell him I insisted upon coming with Nola."

"Okay." Jack grinned again. "I'm beginning to enjoy this."

"You can say that I hate the Chalet, too much grease, too many calories in everything." I thought about restaurants for a minute. "Why not the Boulevard over on John Daly Boulevard? It's an easy drive from Pacifica, but it's far enough away from the beach."

"One last thing," Ari said. "I'll need to contact the police force in Pacifica, since that's the address we have for him. I want the matter on record in case Caleb cuts up rough. Is that acceptable?"

"Whatever you want, pal." Jack suddenly laughed, a short bark that was colder than a snarl could have been. "I owe you big-time for this."

"No," Ari said. "It really is part of my job."

Jack and Kathleen left under a clearing sky. The rain clouds scudded off to the east to drop unseasonable snow on the mountains. I watched them go while Ari phoned various local police departments and made appointments.

By two o'clock, sunlight gleamed on the damp streets. My luck turned with the weather. A quick LDRS showed me Sarge sitting just inside the entrance to his territory downtown. I told Ari the news, then changed into the tight jeans and a red T-shirt that had shrunk in the dryer. I applied some bright red lipstick, too, and wore the black high heels.

"You look like a slut," Ari announced.

"Good. That's what I'm supposed to be. Besides, I'll be wearing Sean's old jacket again. It'll cover most of me."

Ari managed to drive us down to Market Street without causing an accident. He dropped me off at Fourth Street, then drove off to park the car in the public lot at Fifth and Mission. On Market, I hurried along the sidewalk, crowded with shoppers and workers on coffee breaks. As I passed under the row of plane trees, I noticed that some of them had swollen buds on their branches, a promise of leaves.

In his old green parka and filthy slacks, Sarge stood in front of the slice of Roman bath otherwise known as the entrance to the Flood Building. A black-and-white patrol car sat at the curb. A uniformed officer was talking to Sarge, and from the way he'd shoved his pale pink face right into Sarge's dark brown one I suspected the worst. As I came up to them, I heard Sarge say, "I told you, I'm waiting for a girl I know, and here she is now."

The cop looked me over with a twisted scowl around his mouth. "Yeah?" he said. "Okay, then, you can both move along."

He sauntered back to the patrol car. We walked up to the crosswalk that led over Market to Bloomingdale's.

"Am I glad to see you!" Sarge said. "I got that letter for you."

"You do? Where's the rabbi?"

"In San Francisco General. He's been back a few days, sick as a dog."

"What's wrong with him?"

"The pneumonia, I'm betting. He told me that the flying saucer people dumped water on him, and he got a chill from it. Or something like that. He wasn't making much sense by then."

"I guess not. How bad is it?"

"Real bad. Me and some of the boys got him down to Emergency last night. Finally. He didn't want to go, but he was coughing and spitting too hard for too long."

The light changed. We worked our way through the crowd of pedestrians coming across. On the other side, I looked back. The squad car and its driver, that overexcited champion of Order, had left.

"Ain't no use standing around in front of this store," Sarge jerked a thumb at Bloomingdale's. "They got private heat to roust us."

"Let's go down to Fifth," I said.

"Good idea."

We walked past the fancy indoor mall and around the corner under the scornful eyes of enormous fashion models, photographs, that is, three-times-life-size posters that covered the windows of the Westfield Building. Down on Fifth Street, we found a spot to talk by a loading dock, closed at the moment with a metal pull-down door. We stood in front of three normal-sized posters advertising gold jewelry. Out on the street, traffic snarled and honked. Pedestrians hurried by, glanced our way, then looked somewhere else fast.

Sarge reached under his parka and pulled out a beaten-up brownish envelope that had started life white. He handed it to me. I tried to say thanks but sobbed instead—just once. On the front it read "for Nola O'Grady" in my father's handwriting.

"What's wrong?" Sarge said.

"I thought he was dead," I said. "My dad."

"Jeezus!"

"Yeah." I stuffed the letter into an inside pocket of the jacket. From another pocket, I brought out a twenty and a pack of cigarettes. "Thanks." I handed them over.

"Thank you." Sarge grinned with a display of missing teeth. "Aint you gonna open it?"

"Curious?"

"Real curious. Look, the rabbi wants to see you, too. If you want to see him, you better go down there right away. He's pretty bad off. He kept talking about wanting to see you and someone he called Shira's boy. Know who that is?"

"Not for sure, but maybe."

"The rabbi told me that he went to Israel to look for Shira's boy but couldn't find him. So he came back here to give you the letter. I told him, no way you could get to Israel and back again. He didn't say nothing to that, and then the doctor made me leave, because they was going to X-ray him."

I took the letter out of my pocket. I wanted to read it. I was afraid to read it. Finally, I got up my courage and tore off a corner so I could slit it open with a fingernail. When I took out the letter, Sarge caught his breath.

"That paper," he said, "looks like the crap they give you inside."

"Sure does, yeah," I said.

Cheap wood pulp paper, lined, and the piece measured maybe four inches by six. At the top Dad had put a number—his number, I assumed, in whatever prison he was in. He'd covered every inch of the rest with tiny writing, except for one printed line at the bottom, which read "Moorwood H Block 814 Inspected 77."

"They sent him up, for sure," I said. "At least he's not dead."

"What did he do?"

"Long story." My hands began to shake.

"You read it." Sarge took a step to put himself between me and the sidewalk, then turned his back to me. "I'm too damn nosy."

I leaned against the cold damp stone of the wall behind me and read. "Nola, I'll pray to every saint I can remember that you get this. They're letting Reb Ezekiel out without the StopCollar on, so maybe he can get back. I'm sending it to you because you're the one with the brains in our cursed family. Tell your mother I never meant to leave her and you kids. I didn't think they'd come that far—"

"Oh, shit!" Sarge said. "That lousy undercover cop!"

I looked up and saw Ari striding down the sidewalk toward us. He had his hands shoved into the pockets of his leather jacket, but when I ran an SPP, I picked up annoyance, not rage.

"It's okay," I said. "Yeah, he's a cop, but he's one of my regular johns, too. I was supposed to meet him over on Market."

"I hope the bastard pays you."

"Yeah, he does. He's not one of those fuck me or get busted cops." I stepped away from the wall. "Hey, good-looking! Think you could give me a ride somewhere? Or are you on duty?"

"Off for the day," Ari said. "Where do you need to go?"

"San Francisco General. The rabbi sent me this letter, and he's in there with—" I glanced at Sarge.

"Pneumonia," Sarge said. "I hope you ain't gonna bust him for something."

"No," Ari said. "There's no warrant out on him. That's what I was trying to tell you that day in the park."

"Guess I should have listened. The way the rabbi freaked like that, I thought you was after him for sure."

"A reasonable supposition," Ari said. "But wrong."

"Look, Sarge," I said. "Thanks. I mean, jeez, really, thanks. I might have another twenty to give you later—" I glanced at Ari and raised an eyebrow. "Like, an advance on what you're going to owe me, huh?"

Ari pulled out his wallet. "Very well, but you'd better not run out on me now."

"Nah. You're the only guy I, like, look forward to."

Ari handed Sarge a twenty. "I must admit," he said, "it gripes me to see a veteran like you out on the streets. What's wrong with this sodding country?"

"I kind of wonder myself," Sarge said. "Thanks."

I started to read the rest of Dad's letter in the car, in between bursts of giving Ari directions. "I didn't think they'd come that far to fetch me, or I never would have let myself have the luxury of a family. I love you all, and I miss you. I can't tell you how much I miss you." At that point I began to cry. I put the letter back in the inner pocket and found some old tissues in another.

"I'll finish it later," I said.

"Good idea," Ari said. "We're nearly there."

While I was wiping my face, I blotted off the worst of that red lipstick, too.

San Francisco General Hospital sits over on Potrero Avenue on the fringe of the Outer Mission district. The red brick buildings with their 1930s Deco trim stand behind a green lawn and a wrought iron fence, topped with spikes to keep the druggies out of the dispensary. Reb Joseph Witzer, they told us at the public entrance, had been admitted to one of the wards in the new building, a huge gray concrete monster looming behind a parking lot. As we walked over to the front doors, I began to tremble, because despite the late afternoon sun, I felt cold, a deep numbing chill.

"What's wrong?" Ari said.

"I don't know. Some kind of warning, I guess."

As abruptly as it had started, the shivering stopped.

At first, the woman at the admissions desk refused to tell us the rabbi's location. Ari brought out his Interpol ID, which made her phone the head nurse of the shift to ask if Witzer could see visitors.

"Ari," I said, "is your mother's first name Shira?"

"Yes." He gave me a sharp look. "How do you know that?"

Rather than answer, I spoke to the guardian dragon. "This is the man the rabbi keeps talking about. Could you tell the head nurse that seeing him will help calm her patient down?"

She nodded and did. The ploy worked. We got permission.

We went up in the elevator, got lost, found the room eventually, a long narrow space, painted a cheerful yellow, with four beds in it. Two were empty. In the third lay an elderly African-American man who muttered and tossed his head back and forth. I noticed that he'd been strapped down. In the last bed, by the window, lay Reb Ezekiel. A small lamp clipped to one of the monitors above showered a pool of light onto the floor beside the bed. We could see, but he lay in comfortable shadow.

Dressed in a hospital robe, he looked more like a stick

of driftwood than a man. His gray hair, peyes and beard were long, combed back but matted with sweat. His scrawny hands clutched the blue blankets. Tubes in his nostrils connected him to an oxygen tank. He lay so still that I had a bad moment of wondering if he'd died, but his eyes snapped open, dark eyes glittering in a mass of fine wrinkles.

"Hah!" he whispered. "Not the other one. Shira's boy."

"Yes," Ari said. "And this is Nola O'Grady."

Ezekiel turned his head a couple of inches in my direction. He rested, breathing heavily, then whispered, "The letter?"

"I have it," I said. "Thank you."

"Good man, your father. He protected me." Ezekiel closed his eyes again. "From the gangs."

"What was he in for? Can you tell me?"

"Transport across the world line." Ezekiel coughed, a horrible rasp. I grabbed some tissues from a box on the side table and held them in front of his mouth so he could spit. "Not the accessory." He fell back against the pillows and gasped. "They never could prove the shootings."

A nurse came hurrying down the line of beds. She looked at me and tapped her wristwatch in a significant manner. I nodded to show I'd understood and dropped the tissues into the wastebasket.

"Ariel." Ezekiel opened his eyes again and looked at Ari. "They're coming. One of them is already here. And there are agents, human agents."

Once again, he coughed with that horrible rasp. I held the tissues and wiped his mouth for him. He smiled in thanks, then began to speak in Hebrew. Ari leaned close and murmured something in the same. Ezekiel went on speaking for a few minutes until he began to wheeze, choking, it sounded like, on his words.

"It's the fluid in his lungs," the nurse said. "You need to go."

"Right," I said. "Is it viral?"

"I'm afraid so."

I realized then, with a sick feeling in the pit of my stomach, that Reb Ezekiel would die before the night was out. I didn't need to be psychic to see it. Ari spoke another sentence or two to the old man, who smiled. We let the nurse usher us out.

Neither of us spoke as we left the building. As we were walking across the parking lot, I glanced back at the massive concrete slab. The west-facing windows gleamed with gold fire. I began to shiver again, so badly that I summoned Qi from the sunset air just to keep from fainting.

"Let's get you home," Ari said.

"Yeah," I said. "I guess this is some kind of premonition. Something not nice may be going to happen."

As soon as we were seated in the car, the cold shivers disappeared. Maybe they were just repeating the message about Reb Ezekiel's coming death, or so I told myself. The reassurance lacked conviction.

I read the rest of Dad's letter on the way back to the flat. "I can't tell you how much I miss you. When I get parole they'll put the StopCollar on me, so I'll never see you all again. I'm paying for something that's a crime here but not where you are, a serious crime, though it never harmed anyone. Forgive me. If I could explain I would, but I don't know if you'd understand or not. They took me away too soon. I don't know what talents you or the other children developed, though I'd bet even money that Dan's the most normal of all of us. Maybe Maureen turned out normal, too. Sean and Kathleen—they're the kind of people who always find someone to take care of them. You, I trust to take care of yourself. I worry about Pat in particular because of those lines on his palms. And Michael, my poor little Mike! The seventh gets the worst of it. I know. I'm one. I hope and pray to God that you're all well and safe. With all my love. Remember me. Tell your mother I'm sorry we fought so much. Dad."

I sobbed, I'll admit it. I read the letter again and sobbed all the way through it. Ari said nothing, just drove grimly on, the best thing he could have done.

By the time we reached our flat, I'd gotten control of myself. I washed my face and changed into a pair of jeans that fit so I could breathe and an indigo-and-white print blouse. I put the letter and my cell phone on my desk next to the computer, then flopped onto the couch.

"You look exhausted," Ari said.

"I am," I said. "But I should take the letter over to Aunt Eileen, so she can give it to Mother."

"Tomorrow will do." Ari sat down next to me. "It's been thirteen years. One day more won't matter."

"You've got a point there."

He was watching me in wide-eyed expectation.

"Okay," I said. "It looks like my father was a coyote, all right. He transported people across deviant levels. Apparently, that's a crime wherever he is. They have something called a StopCollar that he'll be stuck wearing when he's paroled. I'm guessing that it interferes with the world-walker talent. Maybe with others, too, I don't know. But he doesn't think he can make it back here. I got the impression that he's a couple of levels away, not just one."

"He seems to have befriended Ezekiel in prison."

"Yeah. I don't know what Zeke's doppelgänger did over there, but whatever crime it was, Zeke didn't have to wear the collar, so he could world-walk home once he got out. He took the letter as a favor, I guess, for Dad."

"What was the name of the prison? Did your father say?"

"Moorwood. It's printed on the paper."

Ari thought for a long minute or two. "I don't know of any prison with that name. I can look it up, but it sounds British to me. Except it can't be, because it's not."

"It's got an H Block."

"That's significant, yes. I suppose." Ari made his growling noise. "I don't know what we can believe anymore. A perfectly logical assumption here might have nothing to do with the reality over there."

"Unfortunately, that's true. What did Zeke say to you? Will you tell me?"

"Certainly. He thinks that the invading aliens have a spy here already. He says the spy followed him across. Brother Belial? Then Caleb might be one of those human agents he spoke of."

"He sure could. Zeke told Sarge some garbled story about the aliens soaking him with water. That could mean a rogue wave that didn't actually drown him. I'm seeing karmic gravity at work in this, pulling everything together into one big ugly mess."

"Karmic gravity? Oh, yes, you did mention that once. You were having a joke on me."

"No, I wasn't. It's actually a real principle. You can call it synchronicity if you prefer."

Ari said nothing in the first real act of tact I'd ever seen from him. His SPP radiated a firm belief that I was crazy in my own lovable way.

"Well, look," I said. "Gravity is a property of mass, right? You get enough mass together in a lump, and it'll exert a pull on other objects."

"After a manner of speaking, yes."

"Okay. So you get enough psychic mass together, and the same thing happens. You, Itzak, Reb Zeke, me, Mike, Dad's gate to another level, both of your jobs and my job— here we all are in San Francisco, and we've created a gravitational pull. On top of that, you and I busted the coven together. I ensorcelled Doyle, and you—uh, well—disposed of Johnson. That made a karmic link. All of this together pulled Belial right into our orbit."

Ari considered, then shrugged. I gathered he was unconvinced.

"I suppose we'd need to put my mother on your list, then," he said. "Ezekiel asked about her. He wants to go to London to find her, once he recovers. But he's not going to, is he?"

"Recover? No. Sorry."

"I'll have to call Tzaki and tell him that the old man's gone."

We observed a private moment of silence.

"I wonder," I said eventually, "if my mother will believe that the letter's really from Dad?"

"Judging from everything you've told me about her, I'd say no. Give the letter to Eileen, certainly, but let her decide what to do with it."

My first thought: I wasn't asking your advice. Second thought: but you're right.

"Okay," I said. "I'll do that. Michael needs to know, though. And soon."

"Of course." With a sigh, Ari stretched his legs out in

front of him. "Apparently, I have a doppelgänger. Reb Ezekiel called him Ari Nataniel. He thought I was him, that day
in the park." He paused for another sigh. "I rather dislike
all of this. Alien spies. Doppelgängers." He turned his head
and gave me the reproachful stare. "Werewolves."

"Life's hard, buddy," I said.

Ari growled and crossed his arms over his chest. I let him
simmer while I considered one of Dad's remarks in the letters, about the lines on Pat's palms. I'd never noticed them.
Now I wondered if they had indicated the lycanthropy
gene. If so, Dad would have been able to warn us before
Pat's first change. Doubtless, he could have handled the
problem a lot better than we all did. I began to feel personally aggrieved by the justice system of whatever world had
taken him away.

Ari abruptly spoke. "At the end of our visit, I promised
Reb Ezekiel that I'd stop the alien invasion. He badly
wanted to hear that. I wanted to give him what peace of
mind I could."

"That was really good of you." I remembered the cold
premonitions I'd had in the hospital parking lot. I could
think of a number of things they might mean and decide to
start with the most extreme.

"What if he was right?" I said. "If there's going to be an
alien invasion, stopping it would be a swell idea. I'm sure
the Agency will provide you with backup—me, that is."

Ari uncrossed his arms, turned toward me on the couch,
and opened his mouth. He stayed that way for another minute or two, openmouthed and reproachful. Finally he said,
"Do you really think that—"

"I don't know if there will be or not. I'm just saying. It
doesn't have to be flying saucers, y'know. That was his interpretation, but he was self-taught. I get the impression he
never understood the ambiguity principle."

"Which means?"

"The word, invasion, could mean anything from armed
aliens in flying saucers down to an uprush of psychotic images into his own consciousness from the unconscious mind.
There are all kinds of possibilities in between—illegal
aliens from deviant levels, terrorists, stuff like that."

Ari slumped down on the couch, rested his head on the cushions, and muttered something in Hebrew.

"I'm going to report all this to the Agency," I went on. "Huh, the higher-ups have been calling us the Apocalypse Squad. They thought it was a joke, but they're all psychics, too. Maybe they struck a target that they don't even know exists."

"My father was right. I should have been an insurance adjustor."

I always took the reference to insurance adjustors as a signal that Ari had reached overload on the subject of psychic truths. One more, and he might experience mental meltdown.

"Let's go have some dinner," I said. "I'll just call Michael first."

"Brilliant." He sat up straight. "And when the letter's been taken care of, we can go to bed early."

"Sure. After all, I owe you twenty bucks."

He glowered. I sighed.

"That's a joke," I said.

"It's not very funny."

"It really bothers you, doesn't it? When I pose as a sex industry worker, I mean. Why?"

"What do you mean, why? I should think it would be obvious."

"Strange. You're a holdover from the Victorian Age, and here I never noticed."

"Besides." The glower increased. "Sex industry worker? What sort of stupid euphemism is that?"

"It's the preferred term around the Bay Area. The women use it themselves."

Across the room, my cell phone rang. I stood up to fetch it, but Ari caught my wrist.

"Do you have to answer that right now?" he asked.

I considered as it rang again. "Yeah," I said. "It's Michael."

Ari let go of me, but his Qi felt ready to hit "boil." I went to my desk to answer the phone.

"Hey, Nola," Michael said. "Did you want to talk to me, like maybe a minute ago?"

"I sure did. Hang on a sec." I glanced back and saw Ari straightening all the books and papers on the coffee table. Anger management had kicked in. "I can talk now. What is this, you knew I wanted to talk with you?"

"I heard it loud and clear."

"It sounds like you've got another talent coming online, the family mental overlap."

"Epic cool! Better than a cell phone, huh?"

"Kind of. It'll be erratic at first, though. They all are. Look, I've got something here in my flat that you need to see. I'm trying to figure out when we can get together."

Ari stopped stacking the books by descending size and scowled at me.

"It's about five o'clock," I said to Michael. "Would you be up for a late dinner out? Say at seven?"

"I can't. It's a school night, and Aunt Eileen would raise serious hell. I could come over right now for a little while. I can borrow Uncle Jim's truck."

"Okay. How about you get here in an hour? I'll see you then."

We signed off. Ari appeared calmer, but I felt his Qi gather and begin to flow toward me. I registered an oddly neutral quality that could have flipped into either rage or desire. I stayed standing in case the Qi swung the wrong way.

"Where were we?" I said.

"I was merely pointing out that I dislike seeing you strut around in public in tight clothing." His British accent was getting thicker by the word. "You're not a prostitute, and I don't like you pretending to be one."

"I really don't understand that. I can understand how you'd be uptight if I actually turned tricks, but I never would. I mean, yuck!"

"The men seeing you don't know that."

I heard the ghostly voice of my old religion teacher from high school, Sister Peter Mary, whispering in my mental ear about the perils of slutty clothing.

"Aha!" I said to Ari. "Some other guy might think I'm a hooker and look upon me with lust in his heart. Is that what bothers you?"

"What man wouldn't be bothered by that about the woman he—" Ari paused for a fraction of a second, "he was involved with."

The pause and reboot bothered me. He'd really wanted to say that he loved me. I saw another stake drop into place in the picket fence of domesticity.

"Well?" Ari snapped.

"Well what? I did it because I needed street cred if we were going to find Reb Zeke. It worked, didn't it?"

"I have to admit it brought results." He scowled again. "But—"

He hesitated. I waited, hands on hips. I kept my own Qi neutral, but if I was going to lead this team, I couldn't let him steamroll me.

"What other kind of cover story would you suggest?" I said.

"If the need arises again," Ari said, "perhaps you could just pose as a drug dealer or some such thing." He paused again. "If you agreed."

"It would depend on the situation, but that's a possibility, yeah. We can work out the details when we need to. And speaking of details, I need to get started on my reports."

Ari looked as if he were thinking of saying more, then shrugged. "Very well. So do I."

I picked up e-mail from TranceWeb, most of it from NumbersGrrl. I printed those out, sans routing details, for Michael. When the doorbell rang, Ari let Michael in.

Ari ordered pizza and salad on his expense account credit card. We all sat down in the living room to wait for the pizza delivery. I'd been thinking over how to break the news about Dad, but I'd decided that once again, there was no easy way. I took the letter out of the envelope.

"Someone who can walk the worlds gave me this," I told Michael. "Unfortunately, he's too ill to teach you anything. He can't even provide more details, really, he's so sick." I held up the letter. "You won't recognize the handwriting, but it's from Dad."

Michael reached for it like a striking snake. I gave it to him, then sat down next to Ari on the couch to watch him read it, which he did methodically, slowly, and twice. When he finished, he nodded as if he'd made a decision and looked at me.

"Okay," Michael said. "How are we going to get him out of there?"

I realized that Aunt Eileen had spoken the simple truth. I had raised him right, after all.

"Well, we can't organize a jailbreak or anything," I said, "but he mentions being paroled. It comes down to getting the collar off, I guess."

"We've got to find him first."

The doorbell rang.

"There's the pizza," I said to Ari. "You need to go sign for it."

"Right." Ari got up from the couch. "And I don't need to hear you two discussing illegal activities."

I realized that I might have a future problem on my hands. I waited to point this out to Michael until I heard Ari clomping down the stairs to the front door.

"Listen, not one word more," I said. "What we're going to have to do is help Dad violate the terms of his parole."

"Oh." Michael looked stricken. "I guess that would seriously piss Ari off."

"Possibly. Leave all this to me."

"Sure." Michael waved the letter in my direction. "Can I keep this?"

"No, but I'll make you a photocopy. I want Aunt Eileen to have the original. It's up to her to decide what to tell Mom."

"Oh, right." Michael shuddered. "Mom."

Ari came back upstairs with the pizza boxes. I gave him a vague smile and went into the kitchen for napkins and plates.

We'd just finished eating when Aunt Eileen called Michael. She wanted him to come home and tend to his English homework. With my multifunction printer, I made two copies of Dad's letter, one for him, one for me, and gave him the original, which I put into the manila envelope of e-mails.

"Be careful with the letter," I said.

"You bet," Michael said. "Aunt Eileen's going to want to keep the real one."

Since Sophie had never seen a pizza, I bagged up a couple of slices for her, then walked Michael down to the front door and sent him on his way home. When I came upstairs, Ari was channel-surfing in the living room. We'd set up the TV opposite the couch. I was expecting that he'd be simmering, but he looked mostly bored as he clicked through the dismal offerings with the remote. I remained wary. Any minute, I figured, he'd start lecturing me on the need to follow the laws of whatever alien world had trapped my father.

"Come sit down." He clicked off the television. "Please."

I sat close to him but turned so I could see his face, not that his carefully arranged expression told me anything. His Qi read as neutral.

"Wherever your father is," Ari said, "is out of my jurisdiction. Completely and utterly beyond any sphere in which I'm authorized to operate as a police officer or in any capacity except one."

"Which is?"

"Your bodyguard." His mouth twitched in what might have been a smile. "I thought I'd best remind you of that."

"I'm glad you did. Thank you."

When he held out his hand, I took it. I knew that we'd completed a bargain, even though I couldn't find the words to define what that bargain entailed. I felt so grateful that another stake dropped into the picket fence, so quietly that I almost missed hearing it.

Chapter 14

I ENDED UP FILING MY AGENCY REPORTS EARLY the next morning. While I finished the last details, Ari phoned San Francisco General and heard that yes, Reb Ezekiel had died in the night. He called Itzak Stein to pass the news along.

"He said he was sorry to hear it," Ari told me afterward. "So am I, oddly enough. We may have been furious at the old man, but he was always part of our lives, even when we hadn't seen him for years."

"I can see that, yeah," I said. "My sympathies."

Ari glanced at his watch. "Our first appointment's in an hour. How far away is Pacifica?"

"Not very, but I'd better get my butt in gear and hurry anyway."

I put on the glen plaid skirt suit with the teal silk blouse, sensible low heels, and the official-looking shoulder bag for our quick tour of local police departments. Ari just wore slacks and took his sport coat rather than wearing the police suit. He had his Interpol ID; I had my cross-agency version. We introduced ourselves to various officers, who gave serious attention to our case of an internationally known blackmailer. All of them promised help when necessary.

After each stop, we lingered in the safe territory of the police station parking lot while I ran scans. I never got a clear focus on Caleb. I could pick up the edge, as it were, of his Shield Persona. Beyond that, he disappeared into a cloud of mist. Now and then I heard the bubbling noise of air rising in water that possibly meant I'd caught a glimpse of Belial. As far as I could tell, he was sticking close to Caleb. I could only wonder why.

"I don't like this," I said to Ari. "Something's wrong, but I can't find what it is."

"We'll need to be very careful then," Ari said. "I may have to make an arrest as we leave the restaurant. It'll be harder for Donovan to sort things out for his father, unfortunately, but if it's necessary—"

"Yeah, go for it. You might want to warn Jack it could happen."

"I will, yes."

After the official introductions, we drove home under a dark gray sky. Rather than meeting us at the Boulevard, Jack stopped by our place first. Thanks to the force of karmic gravity, he had Dad's old desk in the SUV with him, a solid oak number with drawers on each side of the kneehole. Kathleen had insisted he take it in with him. She'd supplied an antique oak captain's chair and a couple of needlepoint seat cushions to go with it. Ari changed into jeans for the furniture moving job.

While the guys unloaded the SUV, I changed into the gray glen plaid trousers with the teal sweater and a pair of blue suede athleisure shoes. After a quick look out the window at the sky, I also got out my burgundy raincoat. Between them, Jack and Ari carried the desk and the chair up the outside stairs and into the lower flat, which we were planning on turning into an office. With it came two big cardboard cartons of the things my mother had been keeping in it. Those they brought upstairs. I put them next to my desk in the living room for sorting later.

"I bet some of these papers are in Irish," I said. "If not all of them. I'll have to get out the dictionary."

"I'm surprised you're not fluent," Ari said. "I'm assuming your father was."

"Yeah, but the family didn't use it much. Not everyone's as good with languages as you are."

While Jack went over the strategy for the meeting with Ari, I went downstairs to take a look at the desk, just out of nostalgia. Dad had found it at a garage sale, and I remembered how he, Dan, and Sean had all struggled to load it into his truck and get it home. Made of solid oak, it stood over three feet high and had heavy drawers on either side of the kneehole.

The men had left the drawers piled up on the floor. I put them back into their proper places.

I had just finished sliding the last one in place when I felt someone watching me. I spun around and saw a transparent blue woman standing in the doorway to the living room. Long dark hair hung down to her narrow hips. She wore a long dress slit to reveal her heavy breasts. Since I had no talent for seeing ghosts and speaking with the dead, I assumed that I was merely objectifying the vibes of the person who'd committed suicide in the flat.

"There's one more drawer," she said to me.

"I don't see one," I said.

"Oh." She fixed me with a sad stare. "Too bad."

I raised a hand and smiled. "Go in peace," I said.

She smiled and disappeared.

Ari knocked on the door of the flat and called out that Jack had just left for the restaurant. We followed in the Saturn. Ari carried the Beretta in his shoulder holster under his gray sport coat. He also took his beaten-up old army trench coat. I made a mental note to replace that at soon as I had a chance.

We reached the Boulevard at 1:15, fifteen minutes early. I found a good parking place near the steps that led up to the entrance, then sat in the car and ran an SM:P on both Caleb and Belial. This time I received a misty image of Caleb driving on a wide street or narrow highway, on his way, I figured. Since he made no psychic response to my scan, I could assume that he hadn't noticed it. I felt no contact with Belial at all.

Jack had gotten a table for four in a quiet corner toward the rear of the open-plan restaurant. We sat down facing the door. The table stood in front of a floor-to-ceiling brown curtain near the kitchen and out of the main traffic aisle to the entrance, which ran slantwise between lines of maroon booths and banquettes. If Caleb decided to bolt and run, he'd have a difficult time making speed in the maze of chairs and customers.

"I'm starving," Jack announced. "The dog pack woke us up real early this morning, barking at a damn deer that came up to the fence. I had breakfast a long time ago. I've told the waitress we're expecting someone else, but we could at least order. Have you guys eaten yet?"

"No," Ari said, "and I'm hungry, too. We know, of course, that Nola isn't."

"Oh, shut up," I said.

They both grinned at me, the swine. When the waitress came over, they ordered, and I got a caffe latte, made with skim milk, of course.

And we waited. They ate, and I snagged a piece of Ari's toast and even put jam on it. At 1:45, I ran another SM:P. Nothing. The restaurant began to clear out. We waited a bit longer while they finished their food. At 2:10, I realized the obvious.

"He's not coming," I said. "You can call this an O'Grady moment or common sense, but something's tipped the little slimeball off."

Ari and I exchanged a glance. We both could guess that Brother Belial was most likely the "something." Jack, who knew nothing about the coven or my real job, started to swear like the ex-Marine he was, then stopped himself because the waitress was within earshot. She brought them more coffee. The busboy came and cleared the table. Just to make sure, we waited another fifteen minutes. No Caleb. Jack paid the bill.

"What now?" Jack said.

"Now we go to the police," Ari said, "and request they get a warrant for his arrest. For that to happen, you'll have to make a formal statement. Are you willing to do that?"

Jack sagged in his chair and looked away.

"If you make the complaint to the Pacifica police," Ari continued, "and you have that right based on Sumner's last known address, it's highly unlikely that anyone who lives near your father will ever hear of this. Blackmail victims have the right to remain anonymous."

"But will my father have to make a statement?" Jack said.

Ari drank the last of his coffee before he answered. "I'm not sure. Sumner never directly extorted anything from him. He played upon your fear of his being harmed and extorted money from you. Can you say how much, come to think of it?"

"Over eight thousand. Not counting the current credit card bill, which is probably plenty."

"We're definitely in the felony range, then. Blackmail's always a felony, I should say, but a clever solicitor can get the charges reduced if the amount is small. At any rate, you're the principal victim here."

"Sure am." Jack drummed his fingers on the tabletop. "You know, I want to talk with my lawyer about this before I go to the police. It's a cop out, I know, but shit, I just saw Dad, and he's getting frail. He's only seventy, but the cancer really took it out of him. I was hoping we could settle this without bringing him into it."

"That would have been best," Ari said. "It's your choice, but my advice would be to go to the police."

"If it was just me, I would, but it's not. Look, I'll do what my lawyer advises. I'll call him from here and see if he can fit me in today. If he says file a statement, I'll file. Shit!" Jack looked away again. "It would be Friday. I hope he's still in the office."

"So do I," Ari said. "Let me know either way, will you?"

"You bet. Hey, Nola, thanks. I appreciate your help."

Out in the parking lot, Jack called his lawyer, who was willing to wait to start his weekend if Jack came straight in. The Donovan business interests were keeping the law firm in luxury, I supposed. Unfortunately, "coming straight in," meant that Jack would have to drive to San Rafael out in Marin County. He promised us he'd call as soon as he and the lawyer had had their talk. We watched him drive away, then returned to our car.

Before I got into the Saturn, I ran an SM:P on Caleb. I received a faint impression of him driving with the ocean to his right, that is, he was traveling south. I focused in and put some Qi behind the scan. The image clarified into a grassy cliff top. He seemed to be parking his car.

"I wonder if he's gone back to Pacifica to collect his stuff before he runs," I said. "He told me he had maps and old books and important papers for his research."

"Good thought," Ari said. "We could go take a look, but I don't want you doing anything dangerous. If we apprehend him, leave him to me."

"Okay. And I don't want to go anywhere near the beach. Belial likes the beach entirely too much. I don't want to run into him until we've dealt with Caleb."

We drove west on John Daly Boulevard, which intersects with Skyline Boulevard heading south. While Pacifica lies reasonably near this intersection, I hadn't driven out that way in years. I ended up taking the wrong turnoff and finding myself in a maze of suburban development. I finally reoriented myself—or re-occidented would be the better word, because I found a place where I could see the ocean—on a long, mostly empty street named Palmetto Avenue. This I could follow south to Pacifica itself.

"We don't want to get too close," Ari said. "These situations are always difficult. We don't know if he's armed or not."

"Yeah, you're right. Here's a turnout." I slowed down and pulled over. "Let's park, and I'll get out and do another scan."

The turnout, on the eastern side of the road, proved to be the partially paved end of a decaying street. At one time, I supposed, a developer laid in the street, then for safety reasons broke off his plan to build houses along it. The west side of Palmetto abutted right onto the top of the sea cliff. Another bad winter like the one just behind us, and the blacktop would wind up on the sand below. Any houses built on the east side would have been next in line to go swimming. Even though we parked some fifteen yards away, I could hear the ocean fretting and gnawing at the base of the cliff.

We got out of the car. The strip of half-dead paving led east up a slight slope into a cluster of low-growing trees, bent and twisted by the perennial wind. I ran an SM:Danger and felt a warning at some distance.

"Something nasty's around here," I said, "but it's not strong enough to give me a SAWM or an ASTA."

"How close are we to Sumner's old address?" Ari asked.

"Let's see." I looked southward down the road. "Esplanade joins this road about a quarter of a mile down there. He'd be some ways along it, maybe another quarter mile. I'm not sure."

Ari swore in Hebrew and pointed at the sky. When I looked up, I saw a pale green Chaos light dancing just under the dark gray clouds.

"Isn't that interesting?" I said. "Let's go up a little higher. I don't want to go out on the cliff top itself."

"Quite right," Ari said. "It looks unstable."

Weeds and slippery iceplant covered the slope, but we managed to scramble up to the crest. Behind us, to the northeast, stood a small cluster of houses. When I looked off to the southwest, I could see onto Esplanade and a row of dark gray apartment houses that were barely clinging to the cliff. I pointed them out to Ari.

"Those look like the ones they've been showing on the TV news," I said. "The red-tagged ones."

The Chaos light, flickering like a green beacon, dropped away from the high clouds and danced over one particular long dark roof.

"Should we go investigate that?" Ari said.

"No, because this whole thing stinks. Real Chaos lights always come in pairs or clusters."

"We're being set up?"

"Exactly that. Can you call for police backup? Tell them your government contact's gotten information from aerial surveillance. She thinks that Sumner's hiding out in one of the red-tagged buildings."

"Yes." Ari pulled out his cell phone. "I'll do that right now."

The fake Chaos light disappeared, just as if someone had heard us. I did a fast SM:Danger but picked up nothing. An SM:P for Caleb placed him approximately a half mile away. Waiting for us in the deserted building? Possibly.

Far below the ocean muttered as the tide came foaming in over the rocks. While Ari called, I turned and looked down at the road where we'd left the Saturn. I was thinking only of leaving when I felt the first drops of water. Rain? I looked up, but I saw no rain, only clouds. More drops, more water from above—but my feet felt wet. I looked down and saw water welling up out of the ground where I stood. Water dropped from the sky. It oozed through my clothes, soaked my body, ran dripping from my hair. A trickle ran into the corner of my mouth. Saltwater.

"Say what?" I snapped.

Ari shoved the phone into his pocket and spun around. By then I was dripping wet, soaking with seawater that swirled around me in midair while the rest of the slope and the cliff top across the road stayed dry. Ari swore in Hebrew and grabbed my hand.

"Let's get out of here!" he said. "Back to the road."

I took a few steps toward him, but I was shivering so hard that I could barely walk. He threw an arm around my shoulders and guided me as I stumbled through the ice plants and weeds. The icy-cold water followed. It dripped, flowed, welled up with every step I took, just as if someone were pouring it from an inexhaustible pitcher. I had trouble breathing without choking on it.

I fought back. I raised a Shield Persona, then formed images of desert, dry, hot, parched, soaking up the water. I imagined a gust of wind that slammed into the downpour and blew it away from me. Abruptly the salt flow stopped. I looked around, dazed. We were still about twenty yards above the road, where our gray Saturn sat waiting. I heard a distant engine and the squeal of tires.

"Car approaching," Ari said. "I hope it's the police."

A sleek white sedan came racing down the road. With the screech of tires it pulled off and came to a stop next to the Saturn, but the driver left its motor running. He flung open the door. I felt an ASTA like a stab of ice to the heart.

Ari let go of me and drew the Beretta in one smooth motion. Caleb slid out of the car and stood up behind the open door. He raised both hands as if he were going to surrender. Ari lowered his gun and took a step toward him.

"Ari, no!" I screamed.

Caleb laughed aloud and flung his hands forward to release a net of Qi. I could see glittering strands like ice as it swept over Ari and bound him. I was expecting him to fall, but he took one step backward to brace himself, then froze in the tangled ensorcellment. I summoned Qi of my own in a ball of fire between my hands, but before I could free Ari, Belial attacked.

A wave of pain slammed into me and forced me to my knees. I felt it as claws, ripping holes in my shield. I threw my readied flaming ball, then thrust back with the image of lightning, dancing blue fire on the water that he commanded. The electricity flared. Water boiled. He screamed and pulled out his claws. I summoned more Qi, struck again, and shoved him back in time to see Caleb bringing some kind of pistol out of his jacket.

I had no time to gather enough Qi to both ensorcell Caleb and protect myself. From behind my Shield Persona I flung one last bolt of energy at Belial. He bubbled and retreated. I dropped the shield. With one hand, I managed to summon just enough Qi to form a tiny sphere, a weak sphere, but when I flung it at Caleb, it hit him so hard that I knew he'd failed to raise a shield of his own.

Caleb yelped and fell back against the body of the sedan. The net of Qi around Ari disappeared. Ari swore and fired. I had just time to hear a staccato of shots before Belial leaped on my mind again, as savage as a hungry shark.

I fought him off, symbol after symbol, electric bolts, parching desert winds, thrusting them into his mind, shriveling his ocean waves to a trickle. He backed off long enough for me to raise my Shield. Cold, freezing cold, I've never felt so cold, utterly drained of Qi, of body heat, of everything but a numb dim awareness that Ari had flung his arms around me, two ropes of warmth.

"Caleb?" I whispered.

"Don't worry about that now."

I heard a rumbling sound, the pounding of waves on earth. Ari swore again. He picked me up and slung me over his shoulder like a sack of dirty laundry, then ran, half-stumbling, for the road. My arms flopped, my hair covered my face, I could do nothing but concentrate on breathing, forcing air into my lungs one gulp at a time. The sound grew louder. What it meant finally reached me, a rumble, a thump and crash, rocks rolling somewhere, huge rocks if I could hear them over the sound of the battering waves.

Ari stopped and slid me around, catching me in both arms. I heard sirens rushing toward us.

"We're at the road," he said. "Not too close to the edge, I hope. The cliff is falling away."

He sat down and let me settle into his lap. He squirmed out of his sport coat and began to pull up his shirt.

"What are—" I couldn't finish the sentence.

"Warmth," he said. "You need it."

He flung the jacket around my shoulders, then pulled me against his bare chest. I could feel the heat from his body and began to soak up Qi, mentally forcing it through my skin. The sirens came closer, louder. They had almost reached us when Belial attacked again. I'd lost track of him in my exhaustion.

I had my shield up, or he would have killed me right then and there. I could hear him splashing and bubbling as he grasped my mind with his. I struggled and summoned the last of my Qi. I dropped my shield, sucked up the Qi from it, and threw a bolt of fire. He howled as he pulled back. One last bolt—I threw again, heard him scream, but he, as desperate as I was, struck back with every bit of Chaos force he could summon.

I saw an enormous wave fill the sky, emerald-green water tipped with white foam. It broke and roared as it plunged down. It swept over me, grabbed me, tore me out of Ari's arms, and thrust me down into an ocean that opened under me. The world turned green, light-shot and strung with lines of bubbles.

I'm drowning, I thought. Crud!

Interlude:
Aunt Eileen

A T ABOUT THREE O'CLOCK THAT AFTER-
NOON I had the first premonition. Nola, I knew, had
to be ill or injured. I tried calling her flat—no answer—then
her cell phone—no answer there, either. When Michael
came home from school, he told me he'd received a warning, too.

"Could you reach her by phone?" I said.

"No," Michael said. "This is hella gross."

I considered calling various hospitals to see if she'd been
admitted, but for all I knew, she might have merely sprained
an ankle or gotten the flu. My waking talents tend to be too
shapeless to trust in any detail. I had too much to do that
day to take a nap in hopes of a dream, which would have
been more accurate. Still, I felt more and more worried as
the afternoon went on.

When Ari finally called me, I'd just put dinner—a pair of
roast chickens and a stir-fry of mixed vegetables with rice,
of course—on the table. Jim told me to just let the answering machine pick up, but I knew the call was important and
grabbed the receiver. I had trouble breathing while I listened to the news. Jim, Sophie, and the two boys sat staring
at me. I relayed what Ari told me.

"Oh, Mother Mary, help us!" I said. "Something awful's
happened to Nola. She's in a coma. They're at the Kaiser
hospital on Mission Street in South City. The doctors are
calling it hypothermia, but Ari said, 'Like hell it was,'

whatever that means." I took off my apron and threw it onto a chair. "I'm going down. Go ahead and eat. I'll call when there's news."

Michael shoved his chair back and stood up.

"I want to go with you."

"They won't let that many people in the room, dear," I said.

"I'll make them let me in." Michael crossed his arms over his chest. "You've got to let me go."

"Michael, I said no."

"I don't give a damn about what you said."

Jim put his whiskey glass down on the table and got to his feet. "Don't you talk to your aunt that way." His voice was soft and controlled, which meant he was truly angry. "I won't have it in my house."

They stared at each other. Michael looked away first. He glanced at Brian, who winced, and Sophie, who mouthed a couple of words. I think they were "shut up."

Michael sat back down. Jim smiled and sat down himself.

"I'm sorry, Aunt E," Michael said. "I'm just hella worried."

"We all are, dear," I said. "You call Father Keith and tell him what's happened. Ari's so upset he could barely get ten words out."

I hurried upstairs to our bedroom to get my car coat and purse. As I was leaving, I saw the rosary Ari had given me in its special box on the dresser. For the comfort it offered, I put it into my purse. When I came back down, Jim followed me out to the car.

"It's that damn dangerous job of hers, isn't it?" he said. "For Chrissakes, be careful! What if there's an assassin prowling around? You never know what some foreign bastard's going to do these days."

"Darling, Ari would have warned me. He'll be right there, and after all, he is a police officer."

"Well, okay. He's probably armed. Good."

"Of course he's armed. It's sweet of him to try to hide it, but every time he's been here, he's been carrying a gun."

My poor darling husband looked honestly shocked. He hadn't noticed, but then, I'm not surprised.

"Anyway, I'll call as soon as I know anything," I said and got into the car.

Since the freeway would be crowded thanks to the evening rush hour, I went out Mission Street, which was busy enough but not as bad as the rush. Just past Daly City the traffic thinned out, which meant I could say a few prayers to the Holy Virgin as I drove. The rainstorm had broken up into long streamers of cloud scudding away in the sunset, all streaked red and gold. When we were children, Keith always called that kind of cloud the banners of the church militant, strange for a child, but there you are, that was Keith. We all called him Key, when we were children, short for "key to the mysteries." I suppose it's no surprise that he took holy orders.

Ari had told the hospital receptionist to be careful about whom they allowed to see Nola. They called the room to check, then gave me her room number, at the top of the green tower, they said. I followed the green tape on the floor to the correct elevator and from there found the private room with no trouble. When I walked in, Ari got up from the chair he'd been sitting in.

"You came down," he said.

"Of course. Did you think I wouldn't?"

He managed a twisted sort of smile.

Dressed in one of those flimsy hospital gowns, Nola lay on her back on the bed, which had been cranked up at an angle to help her breathe better. Wires hooked her up to monitors, and a tube from her left hand connected to an IV. Her face—I'd never seen her so pale. It was hard to tell her skin from the pillowcase. Her eyes, which were open, looked like green glass, just by contrast.

I walked over to the bed and began to brush away the wisps of hair sticking to her face. Her skin felt cool and as dead as damp paper.

"Nola darling," I said. "It's Eileen. I'm right here."

I could tell that she didn't hear me. I perched on the edge of the bed and took the hand that didn't have the tube in it into both of mine. Her fingers lay limp as a dead fish against my palm, but she blinked once and closed her eyes.

"What happened?" I said to Ari.

He shrugged and seemed to be fighting for words. All of that nice curly hair of his was matted down in some places and standing up in others. He needed to shave, too. He'd buttoned his white shirt up wrong, and it was stained with what looked like dirty water. His sport coat and trench coat lay on the floor with the holster and his pistol—whatever kind it was, I wouldn't know—on top of them.

"We were investigating that idiot friend of Jack Donovan's," Ari said finally. "He was camping out in one of those condemned apartment buildings on the cliff top."

"In Pacifica? I thought they had security guards watching them."

"They should have. But while we were scouting the situation, a rogue wave soaked her to the skin."

"You were on the beach?"

"Not exactly." Ari paused with a nod of his head toward the door. "I'll explain later."

"All right, I understand."

He looked away, and his eyes moved as if he were watching an inner movie. "We never should have gone out there, but she wouldn't listen to me."

"Nola rarely listens to anyone, dear. Well, not to anyone real, that is."

"So I've learned." He tried to smile and failed. "I was trying to keep her warm, but she went under. The doctors say it's hypothermia, because she was wet and cold. I'd already called in police backup, and they arrived just as she fainted. I suppose you'd call it a faint."

"Was it some sort of psychic attack?"

He shrugged again. "I'd assume so."

I could tell that other things had happened, things I probably didn't need to know. If I did need to, I'd dream about them, so I didn't press the poor man.

"What have they been doing for her?" I said instead.

"When we got to the ER, they wrapped her in electric blankets to get her body temperature up." His eyes began to move as if he were watching the scene all over again. "They told me that the IVs they gave her were warm fluid, and they gave her warmed oxygen, too. She should have woken up then. She didn't."

We heard voices out in the hall. Ari reached down and pulled part of his old Army trench coat over the gun to hide it. A woman wearing green scrubs came in with a dinner tray, glanced at Nola, and frowned.

"I don't know why they ordered her a dinner," she said. "Either of you want it?"

"No, thank you," I said.

Ari shook his head no.

"You need to eat," I said to him. "If you could leave that for him?" I said to the nurse.

She smiled and put the tray down on the slide-over tabletop or whatever you call those things that they use in hospitals to feed people on. It was on Ari's side of the room, anyway, and once she left, he did eat some of the rather awful looking chicken and noodles dish and the white bread roll. I don't see how anyone gets well on that food they serve in hospitals, I really don't.

Ari had just finished when the nurse returned and took the tray away. He leaned back in the chair and looked at me.

"If you want to go get something to eat in the coffee bar," Ari said. "They have one downstairs."

"I'm fine, dear," I said. "By the way, Father Keith will probably come down later."

"Good."

Ari turned slightly in his chair so he could look straight at Nola. I tried to rub some warmth into her hand, but after a few minutes I gave up and arranged her hand and arm across her chest in what looked like a comfortable position.

"Nola, I'm right here," I said. "So is Ari."

I received not the slightest sign that I'd reached her, but at least she was breathing steadily on her own. There was hope, I decided, in that and in the steady if slow beating of her heart, which I could see on the monitor above the bed. By then my back was aching, so I got up and moved over to the second chair, on the opposite side of the bed from Ari's.

For some while we sat and never spoke, while outside the sunset faded into night. I turned on the light beside her bed, then sat down again. Ari made an odd noise. When I looked at him, I realized he was choking back tears.

"You really love her, don't you?" I said.

He nodded a yes and wiped his face on his shirt sleeve. "It frightens me sometimes," he said, "just how much I do."

"She's frightened, too, not of you, I mean, but of how much she cares for you. She's had an awfully hard time with boyfriends in the past. They all ran away eventually, some quicker than others."

"You needn't worry about that now." He paused and looked away. "Their loss, my gain, and all that, but why?"

"Because of the rest of us."

Ari spoke without looking at me. "I like the rest of you."

"Well, you're as odd in your own way as we are in ours, so you fit right in. Whether that's a blessing or a curse for you, I couldn't say."

Ari smiled at that. I kept things light, because he was the kind of man who'd regret any emotional scenes later, and he had enough to worry about as it was.

"You really look exhausted. Do you think you could nap in that chair? I'll wake you if there's any change."

"Not in this wretched chair, no." Ari got up, stretched, then sat down on the floor and began to bunch his jacket into a pillow. "I've slept in worse places than the floor."

There was an extra blanket on a little shelf under the tray table. Ari took that, too, but he used it to wrap the gun. He laid it down right next to him. I'm afraid I was reminded of a little boy and a teddy bear, though I certainly never would have told him that. He used his damp trench coat for a blanket. Even with all the noise out in the hall—hospitals are always so noisy, I don't know why—he fell asleep right away.

I regretted not bringing some mending or a book, but I did have the rosary, so I took it out. I decided that the Five Sorrowful Mysteries were really the only ones appropriate, even though I would have preferred to meditate on the Joyous, and started off on the Apostle's Creed. For some reason, that night, I began speaking the Latin I'd learned as a child, rather than using the English versions as we're supposed to do now. It was comforting, somehow, to form those ancient words.

I had just finished the first set of three Ave Marias when

I heard someone come into the room. I looked up, expecting to see Keith, but I could see no one. Yet I could hear someone or something breathing, just very quietly. I think it was breathing. It sounded like a fish blowing bubbles in a tank. I heard the scuff of a foot or perhaps a flipper on the linoleum as it moved a few steps closer to the bed. It brought a waft of cold air with it, and a smell like ozone after an electrical discharge. I stood up, clutching the rosary in my left hand. It hesitated and began to breathe more quickly.

"Get out of here!" I said. "Ari, wake up!"

I heard Ari roll over with a grunt, but I kept looking in the direction of the thing at the door. I knew someone stood there, even though I saw nothing. The cold exhalation deepened.

All at once I was furious, not frightened. How dare this thing threaten my family! I held up the rosary and reminded myself that the cross had been carved from wood grown in the Holy Land. The fiend, if that's what it was, made a snarling sound. Because I couldn't think of anything else to do, I began to recite the Paternoster. I felt warmth beat back the cold.

"*Et libera nos a malo*, amen," I finished up. "You—you—" I thrust the cross in its direction. "Go to your room!"

I heard a whimper, a very high soft bubbling noise. The fiend ran. I felt the stirring of the air. The ozone smell vanished with it. Ari had gotten to his feet. When I glanced his way, I saw he was holding the gun, but loosely, pointing it at the floor.

"What was that?" Ari whispered.

"I have no idea, but it was something evil. I'm an O'Brien. I can always tell."

"I couldn't see anything."

"Neither could I, but I know what I felt."

"I'm not arguing with you, merely remarking. You chased it off, whatever it was."

During all of this excitement, Nola had never moved or made the slightest sound. I put the rosary into my skirt pocket, where I could reach it quickly if need be, and sat down next to her on the bed. I picked up her hand again and rubbed some warmth into it.

"Nola," I whispered. "You're safe now. You can wake up."

She never moved or spoke, but on the monitor her heartbeats grew stronger and quicker, just for a moment, before they returned to their slow, steady rhythm. I took the change for a good sign.

The big gun arrived about twenty minutes later, Father Keith, that is, wearing his friar's robes. We left Ari to watch over Nola and went out in the hall, so I could tell him about the fiend. He listened silently, making the sign of the cross now and then.

"Keep the rosary with you," he said when I'd finished. "I doubt if the fiend will follow you home, but let's not take chances."

"Key, you do think it was a fiend, then?"

"I think it was something evil, or a thing with evil intent at that moment, but I can't put a name to it. Fiend will do."

"All right," I said. "How long can you stay with Nola?"

"As long as I need to. I made arrangements. You go home, Leeni. Ari and I can keep watch here."

By the time I'd driven home, I felt exhausted, but I did eat dinner. Sophie had made the boys leave me some chicken. While I ate, Sophie sat at the table, her thin little hands clasped tight, her eyes full of tears for Nola's sake. Michael kept pacing back and forth by the phone. Brian leaned against the counter and watched Michael pace. Jim hovered around, nattering. Even though I knew they were simply worried, it got on my nerves so badly that I went to bed just to get away from all of them.

And of course, I dreamed about Nola, a very odd dream, even for me, not that I can remember all of it, but I know it had something to do with water and that little gold pin from Israel that Ari gave her, the olive branch with the rustling leaves. When I woke up, just at dawn, I was very tired, and my legs ached, just as if I'd walked a long way.

Chapter 15

I N THE MOMENT EVERYTHING SEEMED PER-
FECTLY LOGICAL. Belial the Chaos master had
trapped me in a small enclosed space and left me to starve
to death. The glass walls of my cage allowed me to look out
and see that water surrounded me, a glass-green ocean lit
dimly from above by the sun, or so I assumed. Once the sun
set, I'd die in darkness. I began to shiver, though not just
from the cold. Telling myself that the world turned dark for
everyone when they were dying didn't help at all.

I regretted never seeing my family again, but most of all
I regretted losing Ari. As I thought about him, remembering the touch of his hand along my face, it occurred to me
that I could at least try to escape. I turned around a couple
of times to look the glass cage over. The walls went straight
up, so far up that I lost sight of them. When I touched one,
it felt as slick as I expected, impossible to climb since I
wasn't a gecko. I was the only thing inside it, not a stone to
throw, nothing.

I saw something moving outside the glass walls. Three
female forms floated, waving languid hands, slender, pale
green women with pale blue hair that drifted like kelp in
the slow tide—Nereids, water nymphs, daughters of Poseidon. They reached out slender hands and knocked on the
glass wall.

For one short moment I panicked. If the glass broke, I'd
drown, but better to drown in sunlight and their company,

I decided, than to die in the dark alone. A Nereid with deep-set brown eyes, a slender face, and a sharp little chin sketched out the same motion I used for Chaos wards, then pointed at me. The others nodded their heads and smiled, urging me on.

I couldn't throw a Chaos ward through glass. I knew that, but the Nereids kept knocking on the surface and making ward-tossing motions with their hands. It occurred to me to wonder if the glass were really there. When I threw the ward, the glass walls shattered and disappeared. Although the water flowed in and covered me, I could still breathe. The Nereids clustered around, smiling, bobbing their heads in approval. One appeared to be talking, but I could hear nothing.

That's when I realized I was in a coma. The problem redefined itself. Rather than "escaping from Belial's clutches" it became "waking up." My last strike on that vicious bastard must have wounded him enough to drive him away before he could finish me off. If he recovered before me, he'd be back. I could be sure of that. I needed to get out of my own mind in time to fend him off.

The Nereids swam away. They headed straight up for maybe ten yards, then paused, treading water, and beckoned to me. I felt exhausted, stripped of all my Qi, but I tried to swim after them. Every stroke through the warm water cost me Qi, or so I felt at first. The water weighed down upon me like stones, piled up to the roof of sky. The Nereids circled around me, concerned, holding out their hands.

"I need Qi," I said.

"Water to burn," they said in chorus.

I felt like a fool. Of course—Qi pulsed in the water, the ocean, the very ocean that I'd started seeing as an enemy, back in the real world as well as here, trapped in my own mind. I should have realized, because of Fog Face if nothing else, that the ocean was what it was, neither friend nor enemy, but what you made of it. I drew upon it, called it into myself, and felt the Qi pour into my body. I could swim.

We spiraled up, around and around, on and on, until at last I broke the surface and floated, head and shoulders out of the water. Even though I knew I was only trapped in a dreamlike state, still I breathed deeply, blessing the air. The Nereids called out in some language that I took to be Greek, then dove down again and disappeared.

Ahead lay an island, a dark mass on the horizon. As I swam toward it, the shape of the land began to look familiar, similar to the shape of Mount Tam in Marin County. The line against the sky traced out a woman's head, sloped down into a neck, then rose again into her breasts and the rest of her torso. It occurred to me that the island was my own body, waiting for me to come home. Just as I crested a wave for a clear view, with a splash a presence rose up out of the water between me and the safety of the land.

Belial bubbled and splashed. I saw nothing, but I knew he was there from the sounds. I smelled ozone, like you smell after a lightning strike, and the water turned icy cold around me as Belial sucked up all the Qi. I had no weapons. I had to use my hands to stay afloat as I tried to tread water in a choppy sea. He bubbled again and reached out invisible tentacles. In his proper element as I was, I could intuit that he had tentacles, not hands. Once he touched me, he'd drain the Qi from my body, and I'd die. I could neither move nor fight. He came closer, reached out—then stopped, paralyzed. He shrieked, a high-pitched discharge of bubbles, and disappeared. I started swimming again, as fast as I could.

I reached the island and staggered out onto a rocky beach edged by a cliff, much like Pacifica, except this cliff was as slick and smooth as the glass walls of my former cage. As I walked along the beach, I wondered how I was going to reach the interior of the island itself.

The beach led me around a rocky point to a stretch of soft sand, littered with twisted branches from dead trees. I saw a fire burning, the flames all blue from the salt in the driftwood. Someone crouched on the far side. I hesitated, afraid that the Chaos master was waiting for me, but the figure stood up: an old woman, as bent and gnarled as the dead trees on the sand. As I walked up, I saw that she was holding a branch made of gold, with leaves of metal foil that creaked and rustled. Crepitabat brattea, I thought. The Sybil held up the golden bough, although this bough was an olive branch with gold leaves rather than the mistletoe of the legends.

"There you are, dear," she said. "Let's go back now."

She set off walking along the beach, and I followed. Slowly, the sky turned dark. A moon rose. Since I could see the moonlight glinting off the golden bough, I never lost sight of the old woman. We left the beach and traveled through a field of tall sea grass. We walked for miles until at last we came to a pair of elevator doors. The Sybil handed me the golden bough.

"Through there," was all she said.

I punched the button beside the doors. They opened onto an elevator with rusty iron walls. When I walked in, carrying the bough, the doors began to close.

"Thank you!" I called out.

She smiled. The doors closed, and we started up.

A jolt, a shaking—I was awake, lying in a hospital bed in a pale green room with monitor feeds stuck to various portions of my anatomy and an IV needle in the back of my left hand. Through the window, I could just see the gray sky of dawn. To my left, Ari lay asleep on the floor beside the bed. To the right, Father Keith—he'd pulled a padded chair up backward to the bed, then knelt on it, leaning on the back, to pray. His head rested on his clasped hands. I assumed he was asleep until he began to murmur the Latin words of a prayer to St. Paul of the Shipwreck.

My throat felt as dry as sand, and my voice rasped, but I managed to say a few words. "That's appropriate."

Father Keith's head jerked up, and he grinned at me.

"I figured you were too tough to kill," he said. "Thanks be to God that I was right."

"I had help. I don't know from what god."

"Don't worry about theology now." Father Keith got off the chair and muttered something under his breath when he straightened his spine. "I'm getting old. How did that happen?" He reached for the cord with the button that called the nurse, then hesitated and let it dangle. "Ari! Wake up! Someone's here to see you."

Ari sat up with a grunt, then scrambled to his feet. He glanced around and finally saw me, smiling at him. He did something I never expected: he wept, just two thin trails of tears but tears nonetheless. Father Keith muttered something about finding the men's room and trotted out. Ari leaned over the bed and laid a gentle hand along my face. The tears had stopped, and he smiled. For a long time we smiled at each other like a pair of idiots. I knew then that I was truly back in the physical world, not in some wishful dream state my mind had created, because Ari really needed a shower.

"Well," he said eventually. "You gave me a bit of a scare, there."

"Yeah?" I said. "I was terrified, myself."

He laughed, leaned over farther, and kissed me. He might have been smelly and stubbled, but I've never enjoyed a kiss more. He gave me a second one, every bit as good.

"Could you pour me some water?" I said. "I can see a pitcher on that tray thing."

When Ari handed me the full glass, my fingers were so weak that I nearly dropped it. He caught it and helped me drink. I gulped water and washed the taste of salt out of my mouth.

"How long have I been out?" I said.

"Just overnight." He put the glass back on the tray, then paused to glance out the door. "What happened?"

"I was in a coma. Fighting that sleazoid Belial drained every bit of Qi I had. Well, almost all. All and I would have been dead."

Ari winced and glanced away, then wiped his face on his filthy sleeve.

"You saved my life," I said. "Again."

"Keeping you safe is the job I was given."

"Just your job, huh?"

"Don't be stupid." He leaned over and kissed me on the forehead. "I just never know what to say in these situations."

"Well, I'll say thank you, and you don't have to answer that."

"I might add that you saved mine. I don't know what Caleb did to me, but if you'd not stopped him, he might have actually figured out how to use that gun."

I smiled and took another kiss.

"Which reminds me," I said. "What about Caleb? Did you—" I had trouble saying it outright. "Uh, is he dead?"

"No. He fired one shot at me and missed so badly that I realized he knew nothing about guns. He was holding the sodding pistol in one hand. The recoil jerked him off-balance." Ari's voice dripped contempt. "He scrambled back into the car when I fired. I was only aiming for the tires, to disable it so we could make an arrest." He shook his head, baffled. "I assume he did something to my mind, and that you made him stop. Just before I fired, I mean."

"Yeah, that's it, more or less."

"I felt like I'd been drinking all day." His voice shook with sheer indignation. "I missed the tires. I got one shot into his rear door and bounced a third one off the trunk when he drove back onto the road."

He'd missed his target for the first time in twenty years, I figured. "So he got away?"

"Unless the Pacifica police have him, yes."

"Don't be too hard on yourself." I leaned back against the pillows. "Most people would have stayed ensorcelled for hours. You snapped right out of it when I broke up the web of Qi. I'm not surprised you missed. I am surprised that you could stand up."

"You're only saying that to make me feel better."

"No, I'm not. Don't you remember how Doyle hit the ground? And how he looked afterward?"

He considered this. "Yes," he said. "I do see what you mean."

"You're amazing, Ari. You really are."

He scowled at me, then suddenly smiled. "Thank you," he said. "I still wish I'd shot out his tires, though."

Father Keith trotted back in, followed by a solid-looking nurse with a wonderful mass of curly sandy-brown hair, pulled back into a pair of metal clips. The nameplate on her blue scrubs read "Enderby." End or be, I thought. Yeah, that was the question, all right.

"Ari?" Father Keith said. "If you've got a cell phone, would you call Eileen and tell her that Nola's back with us?"

"And go out in the hall, both of you," Enderby said. "I've got to take her vitals."

"Where are you taking them?" Father Keith said.

"Not very far." Enderby's tone of voice implied she'd heard that joke too many times. "Out!"

The vitals turned out to be blood pressure, temperature, and other routine measurements. The nurse pronounced me fit to eat breakfast and sent in someone she called Doctor Poulis. I wondered why the doctor looked so familiar, with her deep-set brown eyes, slender face, and pointed chin, until I remembered the Nereid.

"Were you the admitting doctor?" I asked. "In the ER when they brought me in, I mean?"

"I was, yes. I just came back on shift and heard about the miracle."

"That's me, huh?" I knew that at times an unconscious person could be aware of their surroundings, but I'd never had it happen to me. The ego's suppressed, but the animal sees and remembers. "I'm recovering, right?"

"I'd say so, but hypothermia can be a funny thing. How are you feeling this morning?"

"Okay. Can I go home now?"

"I'd rather you stayed for a few tests and some more observation. I want to order blood tests to determine your various levels, like potassium and creatinine." She caught my wrist and took my pulse all over again. "I've got to admit that you look a lot stronger than anyone should after an extreme hypothermia incident, but still, another day here would be a good idea." She let go of my hand and smiled. "It'll give your boyfriend a chance to go home and rest. I take it he's the one who pulled you out of the water."

It took me a few moments to understand that Ari had planted a cover story. I hid the delay with a sob and a snivel. "Yeah, he was," I said. "It was really stupid of me, getting that close to the tide line. I know rogue waves happen along there."

"There have certainly been a lot of them lately." Poulis was watching the monitor above my bed. "One more thing. You need to gain weight. Not a lot, no, but you had no resistance to the cold because you're dangerously thin."

I started to argue, but she stopped gazing at the monitor to fix me with a gimlet eye worthy of Aunt Eileen. "I know, I know. Everyone worries about being fat, but abnormally low body weight is just as dangerous. I'm estimating that you fall in the second or third percentile for your height/weight ratio. That's abnormal. Anything under the tenth percentile is dangerous, and under five it's damned dangerous."

"How much should I gain? Five pounds?"

"Twenty is more like it."

"That's a whole dress size up! Maybe even two."

"My heart bleeds. One size at your size is nothing. Two would be about right. Do you want episodes like this to keep happening?"

"No."

"Then eat like a normal person."

From the hallway I heard applause. Father Keith and Ari had been eavesdropping.

"If you're really worried about getting fat," she went on, "join a gym. The extra food will put on muscle, not fat, that way."

"Okay," I said. "I'll do that."

When Dr. Poulis marched out, Ari and Father Keith cheered her on her way.

"Very funny," I said. "Ha ha."

Not that they heard me, I suppose, since they were still out in the hall. But what if I'd been a bit heavier? I wondered. Would I have had more Qi at my disposal to fight off Belial? That interesting thought made me remember my insight about the ocean: water to burn. No wonder he'd managed to overwhelm me, if he'd been drawing upon that vast reservoir of Qi. I could draw upon that reservoir myself—but I wondered if I could ever best him, even though I knew his secret now. Man or alien, whatever he was, he had power.

Out in the hallway, Nurse Enderby returned and began to talk to Ari. I heard her suggesting politely that he go home and clean up.

"No," he said, less than politely. "Not until Nola leaves with me."

"Sorry," Enderby said. "In your present condition you're unsanitary. I'm not letting you near her."

There was a silence that could be described as strained. I suspected that the eye contact between them was less than pleasant. I was betting on Ari, but the impossible happened.

"Oh, all right!" Ari snapped. He appeared in the doorway and blew me a kiss. "I'm going to go home and clean up. I'll come back in a few hours."

"Get some sleep first," Enderby said. "And a good breakfast."

Ari muttered something in Hebrew and left. I heard him stalking off down the hall. Father Keith slipped back into the room before Enderby could send him away, too, though he was doubtless clean enough to pass muster.

"I'm wondering if we should tell your mother," he said.

"No." My blood pressure raised itself a couple of points. "I'm not going to die, so she doesn't need to know."

"Is that the only condition you'd see her under?"

"Yeah, but don't tell her that. She might arrange it."

He opened his mouth as if to argue, then merely sighed.

Father Keith left when Aunt Eileen arrived a few minutes later. Came down a second time, she told me—she'd been there the night before, but of course I hadn't known it. When Enderby brought me a high-calorie breakfast on a tray, Aunt Eileen helped me eat it. My fingers showed an alarming tendency to drop forks and spoons.

"I'm very glad they'll be doing more tests, dear," Aunt Eileen said. "And you really do need to rest. Either Keith or I will be here on guard, so you won't need to worry."

"On guard?" I said. "What happened when I was out?"

"An invisible fiend tried to come into the room. Fortunately, I had the rosary from the Holy Land with me, and I chased it away."

She said all this in the calm, everyday sort of voice that she would have used to tell me that she'd dropped a tissue but picked it up again. I stared. Goggled at her would be more like it.

"Well, I don't know what else to call it," Aunt Eileen said.

"Uh, that's fine, yeah. Invisible fiend, huh?" I leaned

back against the pillows. Belial, probably. "Maybe I do need to have those tests done. The Agency will pick up the tab, after all."

"You're going to need your strength."

"Yeah. My thought exactly."

At that point I realized Nurse Enderby was standing in the doorway. "Invisible fiends," she said, in a matter-of-fact voice that matched Aunt Eileen's, "are not allowed to mess with my patients in my ICU. Don't worry about it."

If she could make Ari do something he didn't want to do, I figured that she'd have no trouble with fiends, invisible or not.

"Okay," I said. "I won't."

She gave me a smile—an oddly impish smile considering her strength of character—and left. The meaning of her acronym hit me. I was in the Intensive Care Unit. Intensive Care generally meant "you could die," as far as I understood the label.

"We were all so worried," Aunt Eileen said. "You do look much better today."

"Good. You know, I was kind of worried, too."

During the rest of that boring day, filled with tests that mostly involved making me uncomfortable with various machines or drawing blood the old-fashioned way, Belial never dropped by. I had plenty of time to think over our battle. I made a few notes about the encounter on a pad of pink notepaper that Aunt Eileen found in the gift shop. Each sheet had a cartoon kitty printed on one corner, but it was better than nothing.

The first note I made concerned Reb Ezekiel. When he'd talked about the flying saucer people getting him wet and chilled, he must have meant a similar attack to the one on me. The flying saucer people most likely meant Brother Belial, I figured, but the water and chills had been real enough. Either the rebbe had fought him off before Belial could drain enough Qi to put him in a coma, or something had interrupted our murderous little friend's attack. I was betting on the interruption, but I'd probably never know which.

The how of these attacks baffled me until I remembered Michael's critter, Or-Something, picking up its liquid mess and dumping it onto another deviant level. I was willing to bet that Belial had a similar talent, strong enough in his case to transfer seawater by the gallon. I wondered if the skill Belial shared with Or-Something meant they came from the same world. Small details added up to indicate that his species lived underwater: the single "leg," the tentacles, his skill with aquatic Qi, his need of a psychic mechanism to interact with creatures of the air, the Cryptic Creep's remark about calamari. Belial's ability to drain Qi, however, was a common Chaos weapon. So was Caleb's ensorcellment attempt.

One other detail came clear in my mind. I remembered the strange chilly premonitions I'd had when we went to see Reb Zeke in San Francisco General. They'd been warning me that I could end up in the hospital myself if I met the same being who had sickened Reb Ezekiel.

Toward the end of the afternoon, Ari brought me my Agency laptop in its canvas tote to replace the kitty notepaper. He was wearing the pinstriped suit and a clean white shirt. Aunt Eileen tactfully excused herself to go find the coffee shop. Ari leaned over the bed rail and kissed me. He was shiny clean and smelled only of witch hazel.

"Thanks so much for this." I patted the laptop. "I see you're going to consult with the Pacifica police."

"Yes," he said. "How did you know?"

"What you're wearing. No psychic powers involved."

Ari smiled. "I'll be meeting Jack Donovan and his lawyer there. He's going to press charges."

"Wonderful! That means they can issue a warrant for Caleb, right?"

"A second warrant, actually. He's a convicted felon, and he has a gun in his possession. That's illegal even in gun-mad America. They've already put out an all points bulletin on him."

"If he's smart he'll be miles away by now. Let me see if I can pick him up."

I set the laptop bag down next to me on the bed, then ran an SM:P. I received a strong, clear impression. Brother Belial must have been off recovering rather than helping Caleb hide.

"He's watching TV in a motel room somewhere," I told Ari. "But I've got no idea where or which one. It looks like a pretty cheap room, though."

"Donovan told me over the phone that Sumner had withdrawn a lot of cash from the credit card account he'd given him. He can probably travel for some days on that amount. Donovan doesn't know how much money from other sources Sumner has at his disposal. He must have other cards, too."

"Probably under assumed names, yeah. Say, was everything all right back at the flats?"

"Yes." He hesitated. "Except for one odd detail. The security system picked up some sort of energy discharge in the lower flat. According to the log, though, it happened just before we left to join Jack at the restaurant."

"Weird." I remembered the transparent woman I'd seen at that moment. She might have been some sort of manifestation rather than an IOI. "I'll investigate that once they let me out of here."

"Good, but for now, please rest." Ari glanced at his watch. "I'd better go, but I'll be back this evening."

"Okay. Just don't go too near the ocean."

"Does it matter? After all, the ocean came to you."

"Yeah, but let's not make it easy for the bastard. I doubt if he's got enough Qi left to pull that stunt again." Not right away, anyway, but I kept that thought to myself.

Ari kissed me, then walked to the door, where he paused and looked back.

"One last thing I've been meaning to ask you." He kept a perfectly straight face. "Is this what the Roadrunner does? Manipulate Qi?"

I laughed, and he grinned at me. "Yeah," I said, "that must be it."

After he left, Enderby unhooked me from the monitors, though the IV in my hand stayed, dripping assorted electrolytes into my bloodstream. Aunt Eileen returned, bringing big paper cups of coffee, one for me as well as for herself, bless her.

"This is the first chance we've had to actually talk," Eileen said. "Michael gave me that letter. Do you really think it's from Flann?"

"I do, yeah. The man who brought it to our world was a rabbi, and he was dying when I talked with him. He wouldn't have lied. Besides, there's the handwriting."

"Yes, seeing it gave Jim and me both quite a shock." She sipped her coffee and gazed out the window across the room. "I'm glad he's alive, but I really don't understand why he's in prison."

"I don't know, either. I think it's got something to do with world-walking. It must be illegal wherever he is."

"That's what Michael said, too." Aunt Eileen looked at me. "Michael's determined to find him."

"So am I, eventually. I have a couple of cases on hand here, though. I can't just drop everything and run off."

"I hope Michael realizes that." Eileen sighed with a shake of her head. "Honestly, Nola, I used to think, when you children were all little, that it was going to be such a blessing once you were all grown up and out on your own and all. Instead, I really think things have gotten—well, I won't say worse, just more complicated."

"Yeah. I have to agree." I realized that we were talking around the biggest problem the letter had brought us. "What about Mother?"

"I haven't told Deirdre yet. I *was* thinking about asking Sean. He's the one who calls her all the time, but I decided to ask Keith instead."

"I think that's the best."

"Thank you. I was feeling like a coward, but there you are, no one wants to tackle Deirdre in one of her moods. Keith can always think of it as a spiritual trial and get something out of it that way."

Enderby returned at this point in the conversation to tell me that I was through with the humiliating tests. She also plugged my laptop's transformer for the power supply into a nearby outlet, so I didn't have to worry about running down the battery. After Aunt Eileen left to go home and start dinner for the family, I managed to type a report to TranceWeb despite the tube in my hand. I sent Y an e-mail

stating that I was assessing the situation and would com-
municate further when I got my strength back.

Ari returned shortly after with the news that the blackmail charges against Caleb Sumner had been filed and pro-
cessed. The police had put out a state-wide alert and
notified the FBI as well.

"It sounds like they'll get him sooner or later," I said,
"unless he leaves the country or something." As soon as I
finished speaking, I realized that Caleb was going to do
nothing so sensible. "But he won't. It's the treasure. It's his
obsession."

"Good. Then we have a chance at him."

At dinnertime, Enderby came in with a tray full of awful-
looking food. I managed to choke down about half of it
with Ari badgering me to keep eating. When I was done, he
went down to the coffee shop for a meal that, he told me
when he returned, wasn't much better. Not long after Father Keith arrived. He told us that Aunt Eileen had shown
him the letter from Dad.

"I'll tell your mother," he said to me. "The blessed Francis always preached that tribulation is good for the soul."

"She won't believe you," I said. "Why tell her at all?"

"Get thee behind me, Satan. She deserves to know that
Flann's still alive."

With the matter in such good hands, I could rest. Nothing troubled my sleep but the usual noises of a big hospital. An hour before dawn, in fact, I woke up to the sound
of hollow metal things bouncing and clanging out in the
hall. Trays? Equipment? Garbage cans? I never did find
out.

Ari had managed to get himself next to me on the single
bed by lying precariously on his side with his suit jacket
thrown over him for a blanket. He slept, snoring, right
through the clanging of the metal things. Even though I had
the comfortable pillows and most of the bed, I couldn't get
back to sleep.

Someone or something tugged at my consciousness. For
a moment I froze, terrified, before I recognized the familiar
touch of Y's mind on mine. I realized that back in Washington the sun had already come up. I let myself fall into trance

and saw his image as if he were standing beside the bed. Everything and everyone else in the room turned misty and pale.

"I'm surprised to see you," I said. "It's Sunday."

"Something prompted me to log on," Y said. "So I read your report and e-mail. I take it you nearly drowned."

"I didn't, exactly, just got soaking wet. After he drenched me, I was so cold and shaky that it hampered my ability to fight. He damn near drained all of my Qi."

Y's image shuddered. "Do you want me to fly out?" he said. "Do you need reinforcements?"

At first I was shocked that he'd offer. Second, however, I felt shamed, that he'd think I needed help. "My bureau can handle this."

"Really?"

Common sense took over. "Okay, I don't know if I can or not," I said. "At the moment I'm in no shape to decide."

"Aha, the truth stands revealed in all her glory. Very well. Contact me as soon as you've made up your mind. When do they let you out of the hospital?"

"It better be today. I'll make sure of it."

Y smiled and disappeared. I woke myself up. I felt entirely too tired, considering I'd only been in a simple trance state.

When Doctor Poulis came in, I announced that I was going home. She made no objection, but she did warn Ari to make sure I took things easy. Thanks to that, he insisted on driving. Being in a car with Ari at the wheel was the opposite of taking things easy, but we managed to get back home alive, unmangled, and reasonably anxiety free.

As we drove up to our flats, I saw a sprawling blot of graffiti on the outside of the stairwell, the symbol of Chaos magic once again. Another tagger had sprayed over it in red: NorXV. Oddly enough, the black Chaos magic symbol, stenciled as it was, looked precise and tidy, while the gang marker was smeared and sloppy.

"Again?" I said. "These kids don't give up easily, do they?"

"Apparently not," Ari said. "I'll carry you upstairs and then wash it off."

"I don't need carrying. What is this, your secret Tarzan Complex?"

"Do you have to see psychology everywhere?" He glanced my way in annoyance and nearly drove into the apartment house next door.

I shrieked. He swore and straightened the wheel just in time. We managed to reach the garage safely; I got out of the car before he drove in, however, just in case he went right through the back wall.

By the time we walked back to the front of the building, I felt ridiculously tired. I just had enough energy to throw a couple of Chaos wards at that unbalanced arrow symbol. It hissed and died on my second attempt. I was so exhausted by then that sweat broke out on my forehead. The one-and-a-half flights of stairs ahead of me loomed like a small mountain.

Ari paused, looked me over, and picked me up before I could complain. To be honest, I didn't want to complain. He carried me up the outside steps, set me down to open the door, then carried me up to our flat. He put me down on the couch.

"I'll be right back," Ari said. "I just want to get rid of that sodding graffiti."

"Please and thank you," I said.

Ari took off his suit jacket and tossed it over one of the burgundy leather chairs. He also unstrapped his shoulder holster and took it off before he went outside.

"No use in frightening the neighbors," he said.

While he worked, I dozed, recovering from the ride home, I figured. The sound of my cell phone buzzing woke me. When I answered, it was Aunt Eileen, who called to tell me that Aunt Rose and her husband Wally had arrived.

"They're going over to see your mother tonight," Eileen said. "I thought we'd have a barbeque tomorrow, if it doesn't rain. Dinner in any case. Are you well enough—"

"Yes," I snapped.

"All right, dear. Four o'clock."

"We'll be there. I'm looking forward to it."

I clicked off, then put the phone down on the coffee table. I could hear the hose running as Ari worked outside, a trickle of water that sounded like human voices, talking softly in another room. I couldn't quite make out what they were saying. I remembered Belial's attack and shivered. Water to burn, water to chill, water to drown a victim—like Bill Evers, I thought to myself. Now that I'd felt Belial's malice, I was convinced that he'd murdered Evers with Caleb's help. What to do about it still eluded me.

I heard the front door open and someone's footsteps on the stairs. Even though I knew it was Ari, for a brief moment I thought I was going to see a stranger arrive. Ari walked in, unbuttoning his wet shirt.

"What's wrong?" he said. "You look worried."

"I see Belial everywhere," I said. "Why are you so wet?"

"The sodding hose leaked." He took off the shirt. "I'll hang this over the shower rail."

Even though he'd stopped running the water, the voices continued their murmured conversation. I heard Ari go into the bedroom and begin rustling around in the closet. I felt like yelling at him to be quiet, but even if he had, the voices still would have been incomprehensible. I knew that from prior experience. Ari returned wearing his jeans and a dark green shirt.

"Did the graffiti wash off?" I said.

"Easily, except for the leak in the hose." Ari sat down next to me on the couch. "I wonder if Caleb painted that symbol, the Chaotic magic thing. It still looks like a roundabout to me."

"I can see why, but—" I stopped in mid-sentence. "Interchange."

"That's what a roundabout amounts to, yes," Ari went on. "Though on the big motorways—"

"Yeah, I know." I held up a hand and interrupted. "Something just hit me. The deviant world level that Mike discovered. What if it's an interchange between a lot of worlds?" I remembered the cartoon image of Swiss cheese. "Full of holes that lead to somewhere else."

Ari was staring at me. Words continued to rise into my consciousness. "Twelve gates to the city, but there are only seven arrows on that circle, so the symbol's incomplete. So is that deviant level, incomplete, I mean."

"The way your mind works," Ari said, "never fails to amaze me."

"I find it kind of surprising, myself."

"Your theory might explain the radiation. None of this makes sense, precisely, but I do see a logical thread of some sort here."

"So do I. Jumping around between worlds might let loose a lot of weird radiation. I don't understand the science involved."

"Obviously."

"But doesn't it seem plausible? About the interchange."

"Plausible enough to get on with. I suppose then that those Chaos lights could be bursts of energy from the interchange itself."

"It could be, yeah. Huh, I don't know who's doing the stenciling, but I bet he's not doing it to give us useful clues."

"Clues? About what?"

"The interchange concept."

Ari sighed and said nothing.

"He probably never realized that I'd put it together," I said, "unless it's a kind of bait. He wants me to join him, whatever he is. I think. You know, this doesn't exactly make sense."

"How unusual."

"You don't need to be sarcastic. Hold on a sec."

I pried myself off the couch and went to my desk. I accessed TranceWeb and brought up my file of e-mails from NumbersGrrl. A quick search found the lines I was looking for. I read them aloud to Ari.

"Human minds hate cognitive dissonance. Our species will struggle to complete every broken pattern we find no matter how absurd the completing elements are. If the folks on that deviant level know about nuclear bombs from some source of information, nukes would give them the rationale they need to explain their predicament."

"It certainly is a predicament," Ari said, "with those rad levels."

I turned in the chair to look at him. "Yeah, there they are, trapped on the fragments of a world level, soaked in radiation from some lousy catastrophe." I turned back to the screen. "Let me just run this by NumbersGrrl."

When I logged on, I found e-mail, flagged Urgent, from Y. He reiterated that he'd come to San Francisco himself if I wanted. He could also send another agent if I needed specific talents that he himself lacked. I thanked him but told him that I'd have to wait and see if the police could catch Caleb Sumner. If we took that slimeball out of the equation, it would be much easier to solve.

As methodically as I could, I wrote a brief summary of my ideas about the interchange and sent that off to NumbersGrrl. I added a few bits of other information about the case, then logged off. When I stood up, I tottered in a sudden dizzy spell. Ari jumped up and hurried over. He caught me by the shoulders and steadied me.

"You should take a nap," Ari said. "Is there anything I can do for you? Get you some aspirin? Orange juice? A jumper?"

I needed Qi. His concern, his need to do something, anything, made him give it off in a steady drift. Feeling the energy came close to making me salivate. I had a moment of sympathy for vampires. Rather than draining him, though, the way a vampire would have, I knew how to balance Qi and restore both of us.

"There's one thing you could do," I said. "Come take the nap with me."

"You should rest, not tire yourself further."

"You're never tiresome."

I reached up and put my hands on either side of his face. When he kissed me, Qi poured over me and made me sweat. I channeled half of it back to him. He picked me up and carried me into our bedroom.

CHAPTER 16

I DIDN'T GET AROUND TO CHECKING TranceWeb
again until early Monday morning. Although I found
nothing new, I reread some of NumbersGrrl's e-mails. She'd
answered one question that had been nagging at me.

"I'm pretty sure that Belial escaped from Nathan's monitor," she wrote, "because the file hadn't been saved yet.
Recorded, yeah, but the recording wasn't saved with a file
name and location. My old prof at MIT is super intrigued
with all of this, BTW. We gotta play things close to the vest
from now on. He'd lie, cheat, and steal for the sake of Science though not for anything else."

I might have read more, but Ari stood next to my desk
and scowled at me. I finally logged off and swiveled the
chair around to scowl right back.

"What—" I began.

"You should rest today," Ari said. "And have a proper
breakfast. Remember what the doctor told you."

I suppressed the urge to say "yes, sir" and salute. "Don't
forget," I said instead, "that we're going to Aunt Eileen's
later."

"I haven't forgotten. I'll be checking in with the Pacifica
police and our FBI contact all day, though. I might be called
away if they have a solid lead on Sumner."

"I'll go with you. I want to be there when they catch the
little slimeball."

"Are you sure you're well enough?"

"Would it be smart for me to stay here alone?"

Ari blinked at me. "No, of course not," he said. "Sorry. But if we're already at the Houlihan house, you should be safe there."

He had a point, not that I was going to grant it. "Maybe," I said. "Look, I'm the one who has the best chance of spotting Caleb anyway. I should run scans for him."

"I don't want you tiring yourself out."

"There's nothing particularly tiring about running an LDRS or even an SM:P."

"Not unless you come up against someone who fights back. I happen to remember you telling me that the snap back felt like touching an electric fence."

He had another point, especially if Brother Belial had returned to help Caleb hide. I wavered, but I refused to give in to my fear.

"I'll try a general scan first," I said. "If that goes well, I'll zero in. If it doesn't, I won't."

"As long as you're careful. Shouldn't you eat first?"

"Ari, would you stop it?" I may have spoken a trifle loudly.

"No need to shout!"

I glared at him. He gave me a weak smile and wandered away.

On the general scan, I picked up nothing. When I tried to focus in on Belial, both with the LDRS and the SM:P, nothing was what I got again, not a single trace of him, not even a bubble, even though I repeated the procedure four separate times. Caleb, on the other hand, did appear on the SM:P. I saw him clearly, holed up in a cheap motel or hotel room while he studied pages in a book. Once, I saw him unfolding a paper map.

When I tried an LDRS to get a glimpse of the outside of the building, I could see nothing but a faint impression of white stucco and a red-tiled roof, a description that would fit half the motels in California. It's supposed to be Ye Olde Spanishy. On the non-psychic front, Ari had similiar luck. None of the law enforcement agencies involved had managed to find Caleb or his conspicuous white sedan.

"Well, that tells us he's in a motel with underground parking," I said. "Or maybe a covered lot."

"A sodding lot of good that's going to do us," Ari said.

I had to agree.

For the dinner at Aunt Eileen's, I wore my best trouser jeans and the green watercolor print top that Ari liked because it had a deep V-neck. As long as we were among family, I noticed, he didn't complain about my showing some skin. By then I felt well enough to drive. I insisted on doing so.

On our way down to the car, we stopped for a few minutes in the lower flat. I showed Ari the spot where I'd seen the transparent woman.

"That's near the security node that registered the energy discharge," he said.

"Somehow I figured it would be," I said. "Crud. I hope this doesn't mean that I saw a real ghost."

Ari rolled his eyes and sighed. "More things in heaven and earth," he said, "than are dreamt of in your sodding philosophy. Let's go."

When we arrived at the Houlihan house, I saw a small RV parked at the top of the driveway. Once upon a time the vehicle had been white with a blue racing stripe, but over the years Aunt Rose had painted it all over with flowers, peace symbols, random paisleys, and photorealistic tigers peeking out of psychedelic shrubbery. Ari stared at the thing the whole way up the stairs to the front porch.

"Aunt Rose," I said, "is the second-oldest O'Brien sibling. She turned eighteen in 1966. Brace yourself. She doesn't seem to make a lot of sense, even when she's really making sense."

"What?"

"Drugs. Her mind's a wreck, but what's weird is she still has her O'Brien talents."

Ari's shoulders sagged, but he manfully strode onward up the path to the porch. A grinning Brian let us in at the front door.

"Aunt Frog's in the kitchen," he said. "Mom and Sophie are cooking. Dad and Wally and Mike are all out in the yard roasting chickens."

"Aunt Frog?" Ari said.

"You'll see." I patted him on the arm to reassure him. "She likes the nickname, by the way. It's not an insult."

In the kitchen, Aunt Eileen, with a barbeque apron over her black capris and ditzy-flower-print blouse, stood at the counter cutting butter into flour in a big white bowl. Sophie stood beside her and listened while Eileen explained the process. They both looked up and smiled at us, then went on working.

Aunt Rose, dressed in her usual jeans and plaid flannel shirt, was sitting at the table. I'd always thought of Rose as obese, as vast and squat as the frog of her nickname, but with a sense of shock I realized that she was merely large, a tall, solid cylinder of a woman topped by a frizzy mop of pale gray hair. She had the usual O'Brien blue eyes, but her mouth was wide and thin in the lips, really kind of froglike. When she grinned at me, I could see that she'd lost a couple more teeth since I'd last seen her.

"Here's one of my favorite tadpoles," Aunt Rose said in her low boom of a voice. "Get well soon!"

Which was her way of saying, "I heard you were sick." I sat down opposite her at the table.

"I'm doing just that," I said. "This is Ari, my boyfriend."

"If you get lost, just ask a policeman, huh?" Rose grinned at him and held out a mottled hand for him to shake, which, to give him credit, he did.

Ari smiled, I smiled, Aunt Eileen stifled a laugh, and Aunt Rose said, "Reebeep, baby," then rolled off a few ribbits in her best frog imitation. Sophie giggled.

"You'll get used to her," Aunt Eileen said. "Coffee on the stove, Ari."

Ari fetched two mugs, handed me one, and sat down next to me. I caught a glimpse of his stony if pleasant poker face, but I avoided looking right at him. I might have gotten the giggles, too, but at his expense, not Aunt Rose's.

"Where's the wolfhound?" I asked. "Or did you already drop her off at Kathleen's?"

"Lassie went home, yeah," Aunt Rose said. "She's got a bone in the oven."

"Are the puppies purebred?"

"Papa was a rolling stone, wherever he wagged his tail was his home."

"Ah, too bad."

"A dog's a dog for a' that." Aunt Rose shrugged. "Kathleen will love them no matter what they look like." She rolled her eyes. "Ugly ugly ugly. Just my guess."

Sean and his lover Al arrived, then Kathleen and Jack. Al brought two homemade coconut cream pies. Aunt Eileen took trays of appetizers out of the refrigerator. I carried one of them out to the men by the barbeque. The family party swirled back and forth from the yard to the kitchen as various people got up, stepped outside to say hi, then stayed out there to talk while someone else came back inside. I noticed Ari and Sophie hang back at first, then slowly relax and join in the talk and the food and the drink. Ari even accepted a bottle of beer from Uncle Jim.

So early in the evening the talk was all the music we needed, but later, I knew, someone would put a couple of Chieftains CDs on the stereo system. First Uncle Jim would start singing along, and Sean would join him. One at time, the other Houlihans and O'Briens and O'Gradys who could sing would blend their voices into the music. When the CDs ended, they would keep singing until long after midnight.

I could remember a time when my whole family had attended these gatherings, back when my father was with us, and my mother and I got along, and Pat was a healthy little boy who ran around and played with his cousins. Now Pat was dead, my dad long gone. Maureen had moved away with her kids to put distance between her and my mother, and Dan was far away in the middle of a war.

Watching everyone, listening to the talk and the laughter, I wished that we could stay forever at one of these gatherings, that the music would never die away, that no one would ever have to leave because they worked the next day or because the kids were tired or any of the practical reasons that ended every party. Yet, of course, the evening always grew late. That night, in fact, I was the first one who had to go.

During the dessert my mind wandered away from the

conversations going on around me. Although my Qi was recharging rapidly, I still had a ways to go before I regained my full strength. I found myself worrying about Belial, whose Qi level would be recovering just as mine was. If I could challenge him when my strength was high, and there were no irritating distractions like that damned idiot Caleb, maybe then I could win. The thought of facing him again made my stomach twist in sheer terror. My one comforting thought came from Cryptic Creep, oddly enough, who had called Belial a "small fry." Comforting for the moment, that is—if Belial was a small fry, what were the big ones like? I decided I could think about that later. Much later.

I realized in the midst of all this brooding that Aunt Rose had walked over to watch me, her smile gone, her eyes heavy with thought.

"Many a mickle maks a muckle," she said, then smiled. "You gonna finish that piece of pie?"

"Nope." I held the plate out. "Here."

She grinned and scooped the plate up, then turned to glance at Ari, who was listening to Brian tell some involved anecdote about a basketball game. She pursed her lips and let out a loud, sharp imitation of a British police whistle. Ari spun around, and his right hand grabbed air about halfway to his gun before he stopped himself.

"A whiter shade of pale," Aunt Rose said. "Take her home, but not to West Virginia."

"Right you are," Ari said. "Nola, you need to rest."

"I can't argue with that."

When we got into the car, Ari sighed, a long drawn-out sigh as if he'd been holding his breath for hours.

"Well," I said, "now you know that not everyone in my family is glamorous."

"Yes," Ari said. "But you have to take the rough with the smooth."

I laughed, but the joke made me remember "Many a mickle maks a muckle." I suddenly realized why that particular proverb had floated to the surface of Aunt Frog's mind. Alone, I could never defeat Belial. But what if Annie and Jerry melded their minds with mine and loaned me Qi? I remembered Annie talking about her grandmother's séances, and how the Qi had flowed around the circle. Together, we could give this so-called master more of a fight than he could handle.

Even though Ari did the driving, I arrived home happy. There is nothing like seeing your way out of a trap to elevate your mood.

Before we could deal with Belial, however, I needed to get Caleb into the hands of the police. As I told Ari, we could never prove his complicity in Bill Evers' murder, but at least we could get him back into jail on the extortion and firearm charges.

"That will have to do," Ari said. "Pity. You're sure, then, that he was involved in the murder? We don't want to let some other guilty party go free by focusing on him if he's innocent."

"That's true, yeah," I said, "but I've never run across anyone else with the close connections to both Evers and Belial except for the two women who were in the coven. Do you agree that we can leave La Rosa and Burnside off our suspect list?"

"Yes."

"Okay. Look, let me run this down for you. See if it sounds reasonable."

"Very well." He sat down next to me on the couch. "Go on."

"Here's the likely scenario. Caleb bought Evers a drink or two to soften him up, then ensorcelled him so that Belial could fill his mind with evil thoughts. Evers was an addict. His law practice was failing. He'd taken part in some really silly fake occult stuff. He'd given a blackmailer information, which means he'd violated attorney confidentiality. He would have been reviled by the best names in San Francisco society if they had ever learned the truth. He might even have gone to jail."

"For the drugs if nothing else," Ari said. "He certainly would have lost his practice."

"Right, and he'd have been disbarred. Belial could have planted the idea that suicide would solve everything while Caleb escorted Evers outside for his run to the bay. That young lifeguard, the good Samaritan we saw on the news?"

"I remember him, yes."

"Well, he ruined the plan. When he tried to save Evers, it forced Brother Belial to take a direct hand in the murder with the rogue wave. And that's what tipped me off. If Evers had just drowned himself the way they'd planned, I might have just accepted the whole thing as suicide. They knew about us, because we'd just interviewed Evers. I felt someone watching us when we left, but I couldn't see anyone. They had to know I was a psychic, because Caleb told me that he'd picked Jack as a partner in order to get to know me. I'll bet Belial put him up to that. So Old Bro took a big gamble when he drowned Evers, and he lost."

Ari nodded, thinking it over. "What about that poor girl down at the beach?" he said.

"Her death might have been an accident. I'm sure as I can be that I saw Caleb and his fancy white car that day, so I'm placing him near the scene. Did Caleb mean to kill someone? Maybe not. It would have taken him a while to learn how to control the waves. We'll probably never know for sure why those two kids got swept into the water."

"What I'm wondering is if Belial wanted something to hold over Caleb."

"By involving him in a death? It could be, all right. The blackmailer blackmailed. Chaotics never really can trust each other."

"I see. You've certainly put together a plausible case."

My case would never stand up in any court, of course. Even if by some bizarre turn the police issued a warrant, how would anyone capture Belial to bring him to justice? His body—whatever that was like—existed safely tucked away on some other deviant level or even on some other planet. I had no idea of what was carrying his consciousness to our world, except that it had to be an energy field of some kind that would register on Ari's special sunglasses.

"It really bothers me, thinking of Caleb getting off so easy," I said. "Even if he gets twenty years, he'll be out of prison one day, while Evers and that child are dead forever."

"True," Ari said, "but the law can only do what it may do. If the law recognized psychic talents, we could at least file an accessory to murder charge on the basis of what you've just told me. But it doesn't, so blackmail and gun violations are the best we can do. Besides." He slammed his right fist into his left palm. "Who knows what will happen to him in prison?"

Sure, if we catch him, I thought. We had a decent chance so long as Belial stayed out of the picture. Because my scans had come so easily, I was tempted to assume that Belial had deserted his alleged ally. It was also possible that he was pretending to stay away in the hopes of catching me off-guard. At the moment I had no way of testing either assumption.

As long as Caleb stayed holed up in whatever motel he'd chosen and kept his car out of sight, the local police would never find him. They simply didn't have the manpower to search every motel and hotel in the Bay Area, which has hundreds of them, for a nonviolent criminal like a blackmailer. With Caleb's own talents, he would probably receive an ASTA if they were getting close to him or a SAWM at least. Warned, he could just skip out ahead of them.

Spotting him, therefore, was my job. Since I was officially a cross-agency government operative in the eyes of the police, Ari could call in any information I might garner. I began running regular SM:P and LDRS scans that evening, every hour or so. I saw Caleb reading, eating junk food, and making marks on a map of Northern California. The scans lacked the focus for me to identify his marks, although I could tell he was putting them on the coastline.

"My guess was right," I told Ari. "The treasure's keeping him here."

"Good. By the way, it's after midnight. You really need to get some sleep."

"I wish you wouldn't nag me."

"I'm your bodyguard." He gave me a smug smile. "And you're endangering your health."

I realized that my talents were beginning to fade out of sheer exhaustion. "Oh, all right," I said. "I'll go to bed."

That night I dreamed a kaleidoscope of images from the past few weeks. The last image woke me early on Tuesday morning. I opened my eyes in a bedroom filled with pale gray fog light. The clock read 6:15. Ari was sound asleep and snoring next to me. I elbowed him awake.

"Oof," he said. "What?"

"Caleb's on the move," I said. "Let's get up."

I threw on a pair of jeans and the same shirt I'd worn the night before. While Ari took a quick shower, I sat down at the kitchen table with my pad of paper and crayons. The minute I thought of Caleb, my hand grabbed a blue-green crayon and began to draw. The water and the tide line came effortlessly, followed by beige scribbles for sand. Clear enough, but exactly where on the thousand miles of California coast Sumner was remained a mystery. Most likely his location lay somewhere near the Bay Area, where Drake supposedly buried his gold, but that only narrowed the area down to a hundred and fifty miles.

I switched to an SM:P. I got glimpses of Caleb, burdened by a backpack, walking along the firm sand at the water's edge. He carried a long narrow object over one shoulder. A rifle? Not a good sign, if so. Again, he could have been anywhere on the coast of the greater Bay Area. Inspiration struck. I ran a Scan Mode:Object for his white sedan. While objects rarely provide the starting point for a scan, I had a deep emotional connection to that car because Caleb had used it during the attack. Nearly getting killed tends to set the vibrations in your mind.

The sedan showed up as a misty white blob, touched with glints of gold, roughly car-shaped, parked in a small lot surrounded by beach grass and weeds. I let myself drift into a light trance, which clarified the scan on my inner monitor. I could move only a few feet within the image, but that was enough to see the landmark I needed.

I left the trance state and ended the scan just as a damp Ari strode into the kitchen. He was wearing his gray suit slacks, a white shirt, and the Beretta in its shoulder holster.

"Got him!" I said. "He's on the beach near Mussel Rock in Pacifica."

"I'll call in the location." Ari took his cell phone out of his shirt pocket. "Get ready to go."

I put on a pair of running shoes and a sweater. I owned a black anorak with the initials of my supposed government agency prominent on the front and back. I used it as little as possible since I didn't really work for that group, but it seemed appropriate for this particular occasion. I grabbed my shoulder bag. Ari shrugged into his leather jacket. We trotted down the stairs and ran for the car. I pulled on the anorak before we got in.

"I'll drive," I said. "You keep in touch with the cops."

Those extra buttons on the Saturn's steering column proved their worth. Every time we drove along the Great Highway toward a red light, I pressed one, and the light turned green. Once we connected with Skyline, there were no more red lights, and I let the car show me her speed. Close to Pacifica, we had to leave the good roads behind and turn onto narrow access roads that led straight past the corporation yard of the local garbage company.

The cliff across the water from Mussel Rock, part of a county park, launches plenty of hang gliders on weekends and summer days. Under a cold gray sky, with a west wind driving in from the ocean, the only cars were Caleb's white sedan and a police cruiser. We parked on the far side of the cruiser. When Ari got out, a uniformed officer jogged over to confer with him.

I left my shoulder bag under the front seat but took the car keys with me when I got out. I walked over to the edge of the lot. Far below, the ocean murmured and swelled onto the sand. The tide, I realized was coming in fast. The rock itself, which is shaped like a mussel rather than harboring a lot of them, loomed black and spiky some distance from the beach.

The sea has eroded this stretch of coast into an alteration of deep inlets and jutting fingers of land. After our stormy winter, nothing but bare dirt and rock covered the faces of the cliffs, all of them unstable formations, especially with the tide rushing into the coves and foaming out again. Off to the south from where I stood, I saw a small figure. He had his back to the ocean and was staring at the jut of dark brown dirt directly above him. When I ran an SM:P for Caleb, it matched. I trotted back to the parking lot.

"He's down on the sand a couple hundred yards off," I said. "We'd better hurry. The tide's turned."

"I've already called in backup," the police officer said. "I'll call again and get a rescue unit out here."

"Brilliant," Ari said. "O'Grady, give me the keys."

I handed them over. Ari unlocked the trunk and grabbed a coil of bright yellow nylon rope. I noticed a neat arrangement of boxes and bundles before he slammed the trunk shut. He threw me the keys, and I put them in my jeans pocket. I could feel my heart pounding. Was Belial out there in the waves, sucking up Qi for an attack? I reminded myself that if he was, I could draw from the same source. Ari slung the coil of rope over one shoulder like a mountaineer.

"Ready," Ari said.

"Good," I said. "Let's go, Nathan."

We jogged along a dirt road that ran parallel to the cliff top, then cut over to the grassy flat. At the edge, I looked down and saw Caleb directly below us, holding a shovel, not a rifle. Grooves and holes on the cliff face indicated he'd already done some digging. He might have thought he'd found the location of the treasure. He'd also trapped himself inside one of the coves. He stood at the narrow point of a dangerous V of cliffs. Beyond the wide mouth of the V, the beach had already disappeared under water, which was growing deeper by the minute. As we watched, a wave came foaming into the inlet. The white line of water stopped barely two feet behind him. He seemed utterly unaware of it.

"Caleb!" I yelled down. "Start climbing! The tide's coming in."

At the sound of my voice, he looked up and shaded his eyes with one hand against the glare of sun through fog. The morning sun hung low behind us to the east. He may not have seen us. He may not have recognized us if he did.

"Get out of there!" I screamed. "You'll drown."

Caleb spun around just as another wave broke and came rushing into the cove. This one splashed on his heels. He dropped the shovel and ran the last few feet to the portion of the cliff directly below me, right at the point of the V. He looked up and around with frantic movements of his head. The wave receded. Caleb found some sort of handhold on the cliff face, grabbed it, and pulled himself up.

One hand at a time, one foot at a time, he scrambled up the cliff. Loose dirt and rocks fell away below him. Weighed down as he was by the backpack, he stopped some ten yards up to pant for breath. Distantly, I heard sirens announcing the approach of the police rescue unit. I ran a quick SM:Danger, which made me aware only of the incoming tide. I tried again with an SM:P for Belial and picked up nothing.

"Drop the backpack!" Ari called out. "Don't be stupid!"

Caleb shook his head no. While I'd been running scans, Ari had uncoiled the rope. He flung one end over the side of the cliff. It dangled, bright yellow against the brown, about thirty feet above Caleb's head.

"Try to reach it," Ari called down.

Caleb started his painful climb once again. I looked out to sea and saw Poseidon rising from the waves in his glass-green chariot. In the roar of the tide, I thought I heard him call a command. He vanished, but a wave rushed into the cove and bit into the bottom of the cliff. When it slid out, it took a huge mouthful of dirt with it. I heard Caleb cry out, but in triumph, not in fear.

Caleb stopped climbing, resting again I thought at first. He clung to an outcrop of what appeared to be stable rock with one arm and began to dig into the cliff with the other hand.

"Hang it up, you idiot!" I called out. "The cliff's falling apart."

"No!" His voice cracked and screeched. "I won't leave it."

"You're going to fall unless you climb—"

"I won't let you have it!" He screamed into the wind. "It's mine!"

A chunk of cliff the size of an economy car broke free and fell with a spray of pebbles and clods. A scatter of dirt dusted his shoulder as it passed him. The chunk crashed onto the beach below and splashed in the rising tide.

"Get up here!" Ari tried again. "Grab the sodding rope!"

Caleb ignored him and the rope. He wedged himself into a crack in the cliff face, clung to a projecting rock with one arm, and kept scrabbling in the dirt with the other. I heard police officers on the cliff top yelling as they ran toward us. So did Caleb. He yelped out a couple of incomprehensible words, shook his head, and kept digging with one hand.

A crumble of dirt broke loose just a few feet from us and plunged to the beach below. Ari grabbed my arm.

"Get back from the edge," he said. "We could be caught by a landslide any moment now."

I started to follow orders, but Caleb suddenly shrieked aloud in triumph. He sank his arm into the fissure up to the shoulder and pulled something free, a long dirt-stained shape that looked like an enormous bone. I stopped moving, but Ari grabbed me around the waist from behind. Before I could complain, he dragged me away from the edge.

Just as we staggered back to safety, the section of ground upon which we'd been standing gave way. I heard Caleb scream, heard a rumble like the sound of a wave—but a wave of earth and rock. Caleb screamed again, and the sound followed him down as he fell, twisting, shrieking, to the flooded shore below. Clods of dirt and lumps of—of something—tumbled down after him in a cloud of dust and a vomit of mud.

I caught my breath and my balance just as the first officers reached us. Enough of the cliff had fallen away that we stood near its newly formed brink. I could see all the way down to Caleb's body, lying flat on its back in a pool of seafoam. It was half-covered with dirt and rocks, as if the cliff had tried to bury its tormentor. Nearby lay the lumps of whatever it was that he'd given his life to find.

"What—"

"Bones of some sort." Ari shaded his eyes and peered down. "Fossils, I'd say. A treasure, certainly, but not, I suppose, what he had in mind."

I took a few cautious steps toward the edge for a better look. I could make a half-educated guess as to what I was seeing. The huge skull had fallen on to Caleb's chest with what must have been a crushing blow.

"Yeah, fossils," I said. "A mammoth or mastodon, I betcha. They used to be real common around here, y'know, in the Ice Age."

"Dangerous prey," Ari said.

"Yeah. Just think. Caleb is the first man killed by a mammoth in ten thousand years. Well, his spirits promised him he'd be famous. I'll bet he makes the *Guinness Book of World Records*."

The ground under my feet trembled again. Ari and I turned and ran back to solid earth and safety.

Since his heavy backpack weighed Caleb down, the police rescue unit recovered his corpse before the waves swept it out to sea. The backpack turned out to be full of books and maps, some stolen from research libraries back east, pertaining to Drake's treasure. The rare volumes were soaked through and ruined, of course, another small crime totted up on Caleb's tab.

Caleb's death was ruled an accident, another case of an unwary person trusting an ocean that could turn treacherous in a split second. A lot of people have died that way, trapped between a rising tide and the unstable ground of the northern California coast. The police could call it what they wanted, I decided. I knew better.

Karma. The Great Wheel turns slowly, but it never swerves.

Later that day, after we finished all the official procedures and filled out the forms, and I had reported to my real agency and Ari had contacted both of his, I called Caroline Burnside. At the news that one of Bill Evers' murderers was dead, she laughed aloud.

"I did a tarot reading for myself this morning," she told me, "and it looked like something good was going to happen. Chalk one up for my cards!"

By the time we got back home that night, the sun had set, and I felt ready to do the same. As I turned the car to pull into the driveway, the Saturn's headlights swept across the front of the building and illuminated a streak of red paint.

"More sodding graffiti!" Ari said.

"But no interchange symbol this time," I said, "just the Norteños tag."

"True. I wonder if that means something."

"Maybe. Whoever's been putting it up might have finally figured out that I'm not interested in his message. I hope so."

Ari said nothing until I finished guiding the car into the

garage. We got out, and I waited out in the graveled yard while he pulled down and locked the garage doors. We started walking toward the front of the building to get in, since we'd bolted the back doors from inside.

"About that symbol and the message," Ari said. "Do you really think someone sent—"

"Yeah."

"Do you have any idea of who it might be?"

"The only person I can think of is that guy Karo mentioned, the man who speaks to the Peacock Angel."

"Some kind of Satanist?"

"I doubt it. I don't much like him anyway. If it's actually him and not some other new and improved weirdo."

Ari stopped walking. By the glow of the streetlight in front of our building I could see his reproachful stare.

"Well, I've got to consider all the possibilities," I said. "Sorry."

He groaned aloud and started up the stairs. I followed and let the subject drop.

Chapter 17

I WOKE UP EARLY AND FOUND HERCULES standing beside our bed, a massive blond guy wearing a tunic with a lion skin draped down his back. He rested a wooden club on one shoulder. Ari stayed asleep even when I sat up and turned toward the IOI.

"Hi," I said. "Something you want to tell me?"

"Antaeus," Hercules said. "Remember how I disposed of him?" He winked at me and vanished.

Rather than try to go back to sleep after an apparition, I got up and took a shower. I crept into the bedroom to grab my flannel-lined jeans, warm socks, and the teal sweater. In his sleep, Ari turned over onto his back and began to snore. I dressed out in the hall, then went into the kitchen to make coffee.

While I watched the water dripping through the grounds, I remembered who Antaeus was, a particularly nasty Titan who derived his superhuman strength from his mother, Gaia, a.k.a. the Earth. As long as he touched the ground, he was invincible. Hercules lifted him above his head and held him there until he was weak enough to strangle.

Belial derived his strength from the ocean. If I could lure him inland, the odds would swing in favor of my team. The problem became finding the right bait. I spent half an hour and two cups of coffee trying to come up with an alternative, but in the end I admitted what I knew all along: the best bait was going to be me. If he stayed true to the Chaos master type, Belial would want revenge for his follower's death.

And once we had him, what then? I discussed the problem with Ari a little while later, once he'd gotten up and had his coffee.

"Belial's not really here," I told him. "What we're experiencing is some kind of weird linkup to his actual self. He's got some kind of vehicle for his consciousness, kind of like the powers of that casket thing in *AVATAR*. We don't understand either the link or the vehicle."

"True," Ari said. "We don't even know what he is when he's at home."

"Actually, I have a theory about that. A sapient squid from another planet."

Ari choked on his mouthful of granola. I tactfully looked away while he corrected the problem.

"Another planet," Ari said eventually. "A sapient what?"

"Squid." I returned my gaze to my partner and found him cleaned up and respectable again. "But I mean a cephalopod in general, not exactly a squid, but a similiar line of evolution."

"Oh. That makes it ever so much better."

I ignored the sarcasm and continued thinking aloud. "Even if his body were on this planet, how could you arrest him? Do you know how to scuba dive?"

"No. Sorry."

"And even if I could figure out how to terminate him," I went on, "it's against Agency policy unless he's directly threatening another sapient being's life. If I use myself as bait, he probably will be threatening my life, of course. He's already done that once."

"The more you natter on about this," Ari said, "the less I like it."

"I'm not real keen on it myself. But I can't allow a Chaos master to wander around in my territory causing trouble."

Ari started to speak, caught himself, and considered what I'd said for a couple of moments. "True." He spoke quietly without a trace of sarcasm. "You can't."

I caught myself before I said something gushy. "Glad you understand," I said instead. "Thanks."

It took some time and many phone calls before Annie, Jerry, and I finalized our plan. We needed to meet indoors for our séance to prevent an interruption from some curious bystander. Annie and I both lived too near the ocean. Jerry's roommate dealt so many different drugs that I refused to let Ari inside their apartment. We finally settled on a hotel room as the only alternative.

"I'm going to get a suite, because we'll need plenty of room on the floor," I said. "What about the place where we spent our first night together?"

Ari smiled. "You do have a sentimental streak after all."

"Actually, I was thinking that it was quiet and not too expensive."

The smile vanished. "As you'd say: whatever."

Since the tourist season had yet to start, I had no trouble renting a suite at the Daly City hotel for that night and the next. It came with wireless access, so I took my Agency laptop with me as part of our respectable amount of luggage. I also wore the glen plaid pants suit, a further touch of respectability. I didn't want the staff wondering what we were doing in that suite. Ari and I checked in late that afternoon. Annie and Jerry would arrive on the morrow.

"I need some time to bait Belial," I told Ari. "I've got to make sure he attacks when I want him to."

"Oh? How?"

"Running scans. Lots of them, simple ones at first. I'll start pushing him tomorrow morning."

Whoever had decorated the two rooms of the suite loved brown. We had pale brown walls and lots of dark brown furniture, relieved by white curtains and bedspread and the occasional touch of orange in a lamp base and throw pillows, all very restful and earthy—exactly the mood I wanted for trapping a restless soul who belonged in the ocean.

I began by taking my crayons and large-size pad of paper to the table for an LDRS. I picked up no trace of Belial, but then, I hadn't expected to. Next I ran an SM:P. Again, nothing. I repeated this procedure at intervals throughout the afternoon. After dinner, I stepped up the pressure by throwing Qi behind the scans. Eventually, somewhere around ten o'clock, I felt a faint stirring of interest out on the aura field. Although Belial came no closer, I knew he'd smelled the bait.

That night I dreamed of oceans, vast beautiful oceans with clear turquoise water, edged by white sand beaches. Plants in various shades of green and purple grew on the bottom of the sea, and enormous coral reefs spread out to the size of cities. Fishlike creatures in pinks and yellows darted through the water. In the dream, I floated on the surface and looked down on these marvels. When I woke, I wanted to believe that I'd seen Belial's home seas, but I distrusted the easy explanation. It never pays to take dreams literally, no matter how beautiful they are, unless of course you're Aunt Eileen.

We ordered breakfast from room service, then got to work with our laptops. I was filing a provisional report with the Agency when I heard Ari say, "What?" I looked up from the screen.

"This must be some sort of joke," Ari said.

"What is?" I said.

"Sorry. This e-mail. It says 'Tell O'Grady to keep him pinned until Javert can reach us physically.' This particular account comes through Interpol. They shouldn't know anything about you. The sender ID is typical, AOS14, but I can't find whoever it is on any directory."

"Isn't there any routing information?"

Ari hit a couple of keys. "Yes, a standard encrypted route for agents. It's the lack of information about the sender that's odd. I'll send tech support an inquiry."

"Please do." I paused to run an SM:D but felt no particular danger from any quarter. "That message is really strange."

It occurred to me that if we, however AOS14 defined "we," were waiting for Javert to reach us physically, then it was possible—and logical—that he'd already reached "us" psychically. I decided against speculating out loud. Ari could only handle a few psychic weirdities at a time.

I encrypted and sent my report, then logged off. "It's time to start harassing Belial again."

"Shouldn't you wait till the others arrive?"

"For our big move, yeah. For now I'll just be agitating him."

I ran a couple of high-Qi SM:Ps for Belial. The second one hit home. I received a clear impression of anger tinged with fear. I found his fear reassuring even though I had to admit that I felt the same emotion. When I tried to do an LDRS for his location, however, I picked up nothing but a tenuous, possibly inaccurate impression of a solidly raised Shield Persona.

Just before the rest of the team arrived, Ari checked his e-mail again. He snarled and looked up from his laptop. "I've heard back from tech support about that e-mail," he told me.

"Oh? What did they have to say?"

"That there's no such e-mail address for any agent." He scowled at the screen. "That's impossible. If this person could access that part of the e-mail system, he has to be an agent. I told them to look for a security breach." He glanced my way with an injured look worthy of a tragic actor. "They're accusing me of having a joke on them."

Maybe it was just the tension, but I laughed.

Annie and Jerry cabbed down to the hotel together. Since I'd given them the room number in e-mail, they came straight up. Jerry was wearing men's clothing for a change, a pair of chinos, an oxford cloth gray shirt, and a jeans jacket. Annie had put on a blue pants suit that actually fit her and a flowered blouse.

"New clothes?" I said.

"Well, I got this used." She ran a hand down the front of the jacket. "But I was so tired of slopping around in sweatshirts that I indulged myself."

Ari called room service and ordered breakfast and coffee for everyone while I got out the equipment we were going to use. I opened the special suitcase where I had my CDEP material, the Chaos Diagnostic Emergency Procedure, that is. After room service had been and gone, the others pitched into the food. I spread the black velvet cloth, decorated with a large pentagram painted in white, out on the floor, and placed the black candles at the four directions.

"I first made contact with Belial using this," I told the group, "so I think it's our best shot of attracting him."

"I agree," Annie said. "Jerry and I should sit to each side of you, probably on cushions so we don't waste Qi on the floor." She sighed. "I used to be able to get into the lotus posture, but those days are long gone."

Jerry grinned at her. "I think I can still do that," he said. "My job, you know. You have to be flexible."

Annie snickered. Ari's expression turned into a credible imitation of stone.

Next I got out the camcorder, the relic of my first days at the Agency. Despite our technician's modifications at the time, by then it was far from state of the art. For one thing, it recorded to a clunky-looking flash card rather than a thumb drive. Most likely that particular variety of memory wasn't even for sale any longer. Luckily, I'd been given several of them, one of which I'd never used. I handed the machine and the card to Ari, who had new batteries ready. While he tested out the camcorder, we talked through our plan—twice, just to make sure we'd anticipated all the possibilities.

"Okay," I said, "let's do it. Now or never and all that jazz."

I lit the black votive lights and lay down on the black cloth with my head between two of the points of the pentagram. Jerry sat in the lotus posture at my left hand, Annie on a couch cushion to my right. Ari went into the bedroom. He propped the door into the living room, where we were, open with a stack of phone books, then pulled a chair around to the side of opening. Although he'd be mostly hidden, he still had a good clear line of sight.

"When Annie says go," I told him, "start recording. When she says save, save the file."

"Yes," Ari said. "I know."

I stretched out my arms to either side. Jerry and Annie each took one of my hands.

"If the going gets tough," Jerry said to Annie, "let her start tapping my Qi first."

"I'm not that old!" Annie frowned at him.

"No," Jerry said, "but you've had cancer."

"He's right," I put in. "I don't want to risk your health, Annie. You're going to need it."

At the moment, the Qi balanced out normally. Feeling the reassuring flow between the three of us made it easy for me to slip into trance.

At first, I floated in a black void. I had the usual sensation of rising through the air while a daylight brightness grew around me. When I could finally see, I felt as if I were floating upright, not lying on my back. The glow revealed nothing, though distantly I heard the sound of the sea, murmuring on a graveled beach. I bent my mind toward the sound and called for Belial.

I became aware of him as a kind of psychic smudge on my inner horizon. I called again. He drifted toward me but stayed sensibly out of range.

"Hey!" I called out. "Calamari! Deep-fried!"

On a tide of rage, he swept toward me. I gathered Qi, shaped it into a lightning bolt, and threw it in his direction. I heard his snarl of fury echo through the bright void. In a churning vortex of water he surged toward me. I could clearly hear his fish tank bubble. Within it, words formed.

"Your kind eats my little brothers, ape girl! Squid, octopi! Hatred shall be your bitter sauce."

"My species will eat just about anybody," I thought to him. "Don't take it personally."

Once again he snarled and bubbled. "Let us have it out between us, thou and I!"

From his way with words, I gathered that he listened to Goth rock when he was on our planet. I answered in the same spirit, "Indeed, for the time has come to see who will be the greater master."

I threw another sizzling blot of Qi straight at him. Thunder cracked the inner sky as blue fire enveloped the waterspout, but his image held. In return, he thrust a long spear of ice straight for me. I dodged and summoned Qi. When he thrust the spear again, I sent a blaze of fire along it. The spear melted and disappeared.

The waterspout veered off, drew back, then with a howl of rage, it charged straight for me. I dodged, leaped, threw a flaming ball of Qi into its midst. Steam rose, but still he kept coming. I danced away. He followed. I pulled Qi from deep within and felt it replenish like a leap of flame along my left arm. Jerry was online.

I called upon the desert wind. It came, a scorching blast, and struck the waterspout. Drops scattered and dried. Belial pulled back and drew more Qi into himself. He appeared as a flood, like a breaking green wave—then screamed, again and again, a high-pitched shriek of rage, not pain. I held back my last bolt as the waterspout began to shrink, spiraling around and around like water going down a drain. I could hear him bubbling and sobbing as the vast vortex of water shrank down to the spray from a hose.

"No, no," he said. "You don't fight fair!"

"Tough," I said. "Grow up!"

I heard a sound like a kid slurping up the last bit of soda through a straw. Belial vanished. I woke myself up and found that I was still lying on the velvet pentagram. Annie was calmly pinching out the flames of the black candles. A sweat-soaked Jerry grinned at me.

"Oooh," he said, "better'n sex."

At that point I knew I was fully back. I sat up. Since Ari had walked into the room, I refrained from pointing out that in a nonphysical way, Jerry and I had had sex.

With a small smile of triumph, Ari handed me the camcorder. When I looked into the tiny playback screen, I saw a shape like a cloud of white smoke. Belial was twisting, turning, swirling around and around. Finally, he stopped and hovered, a wisp of trapped and exhausted mist. He raised the lumpish shape that I assumed was his head and pointed it in my direction.

"I know where your father is." His voice bubbled in my mind. "Let me go, and I'll tell you."

"I'll find him on my own," I said. "Sorry."

I hit "eject" and the flash memory card popped out into my hand. From Belial, I received a brief glimmer of panic, then an eerie sense of nothing at all.

"Is he dead?" Ari said.

"I doubt it," I said. "I think he's in a state that's a lot like deep sleep. He'll stay that way until we figure out what to do with him."

"Why not just delete the file?" Jerry said. "The little motherfucker's a murderer, after all."

"Yeah, but I don't want to be one, too."

"Ever high-minded, that's you, darling."

"Someone has to be around here." I glanced at the flash card. "I need to keep this safe till Javert gets here."

"Who?" Jerry said.

"I don't know," I said. "But someone sent Ari an e-mail saying Javert was coming for our friend Belial. Sort of like waiting for Godot, I guess."

"No, no," Annie said with a laugh. "Not Godot. *Les Miserables*. Javert's the police officer who keeps dogging Jean Valjean." She thought for a moment. "Well, he does in the book. I don't know if they had room for him in the musical. I've never seen it. They cost so much, those big shows."

"A squid cop!" Jerry rolled his eyes and grinned. "I wonder what kind of cuffs they use?"

"You would," I said.

"It's because of the tentacles." Jerry put false dignity into his voice. "You do have a dirty mind, darling. I was just wondering how many loops you'd need to cuff a squid."

"Plenty, no doubt." I got up off the floor and staggered over to the table, where I'd left my shoulder bag. "Would someone get me a glass of water?"

Annie trotted into the suite's bathroom. I put the flash card back into its silvery antistatic packaging and tucked it into a zipper pocket of my shoulder bag.

"Sit down." Ari pointed to the couch. "You're white in the face. I saved some food for you, and you're going to eat it."

"Great," I said. "You know what? I'm actually hungry."

CHAPTER 18

OVER THE NEXT FEW DAYS, ARI AND I WAITED for the mysterious Javert, but he never arrived. I began to think that the e-mail Ari had received was just a joke on the part of one of his colleagues or even someone in Interpol's tech support. Ari had assumed that no one in Interpol would know who I was. I figured that their internal security had investigated the woman he was living with as a routine matter. My Agency certainly would have.

Several times a day we checked the front wall of the building for graffiti. Although we saw the normal obscene scribblings, which Ari promptly washed off, it wasn't until Wednesday, just at sunset, that the unbalanced Chaos symbol made another appearance. While Ari asked the various neighbors if they'd seen the "artist" who'd drawn it, I waited on the sidewalk and stared into the circle with the seven arrows.

The face appeared: the oddly familiar-looking white guy with blue eyes and a bald head—a shaved head, I realized. During this manifestation, I saw stubble around the base of his skull. He spoke with the same high, fluting voice.

"You've got power," he said. "Good job on that squirt Belial."

"I take he was no friend of yours," I said.

"No, but he does have friends." The face paused for a high-pitched laugh. "I can't protect you unless you join us. Find the Angel, and you find me."

He disappeared before I could sketch a Chaos ward. I threw it anyway, but the graffito was only paint—no sizzle, no sparks, and Ari washed it off without any trouble.

I reported the incident to the Agency, then did some hard thinking about the manifestations. Ari and Michael could both see the graffito, but only I could see the face. The images and the voice, therefore, had to be psychic phenomena, not recorded messages or anything that physically existed. Somehow, Cryptic Creep could tell when I was looking into the circle, then contact my mind if he felt like doing so. I disliked this "walk right in" attitude of his. How he could contact me so easily presented a real puzzle.

"I can't keep a shield up all the time," I told Ari. "I won't be able to use most of my other talents if I do."

"That may be what he's counting on," Ari said. "From now on, just blast the sodding circles. Don't give him a chance to speak."

"I may have to, but I could be missing clues if I do. I don't suppose the neighbors saw someone do the tagging this time, either."

"No, or so they say. They must be lying."

"Not necessarily. He could be transferring paint onto the wall the same way Belial transferred seawater onto me."

"I hadn't thought of that. Very well, then. A question. If Belial could slosh water across the worlds, why couldn't he bring his sodding body with him?"

"He's alive. The water isn't. I bet that his body would end up a lot worse for wear if he tried to travel in it that way. He's obviously not a real world-walker."

"Obviously, is it?" Ari paused for a sigh. "I should have been an insurance adjustor."

I heard the signal and changed the subject.

On Thursday, Aunt Eileen drove Father Keith over to the flat to discuss the letter from Dad and the problem it presented. Just as I'd predicted, my mother had refused to believe that it was genuine. Ari took himself off to the gym so we could have a family conference. Aunt Eileen had brought chocolate chip cookies. I made coffee, and we ended up sitting at the kitchen table.

While we all sipped coffee and ate cookies—I made a

point of having a couple, doctor's orders—I took a good look at my aunt and uncle together. Immediately, I found myself remembering Cryptic Creep. He looked familiar, I realized, because he reminded me of my O'Brien relatives. Except for his peculiar voice, he could have been one of their siblings. Doppelgänger. Which member of my family, I wondered, did he duplicate? I shivered and turned my mind to what Aunt Eileen was saying.

"Now your mother's angrier than ever," Aunt Eileen told me. "She's annoyed that you came back without telling her. I asked her why, since she kept saying she never wanted to see you again. She just went off on a tangent and never told me."

"She wanted the pleasure of having me call her," I said, "so she could hang up on me. Maybe after she'd told me off."

"I'm afraid that sounds like her." Eileen addressed her absent sister. "Honestly, Deirdre!"

"But what about the letter?" I wanted to keep this unpleasant subject focused and get the discussion over with. "Did she think I forged it to annoy her?"

"No," Father Keith said. "She thinks Michael forged it to annoy her."

All three of us sighed.

"The real problem," Father Keith continued, "is the way she refuses to believe that any of us have talents. Especially herself, which is the height of ridiculousness, considering how easily and often hers manifest."

"Boom crash bang," I said. "I guess she doesn't do that at the office or when she's out with her friends."

"No, she doesn't," Eileen said. "Only around family. So it's all our fault. We must be doing it to tease her, or so she says."

Father Keith took a mournful bite of a cookie.

"If she refuses to believe that anyone could be a world-walker," I said, "it's no wonder she thinks the letter can't possibly be authentic. If someone had forged it, it would be a really cruel joke, after all."

"Now, that's very true," Keith said. "And let's remember that she is a seventh. Things have always been harder for her. Let's be charitable."

Aunt Eileen and I glared at him. He sighed again and looked up to speak to God. "Well, I tried."

"Speaking of sevenths," I said. "I'm beginning to get the impression that Michael is bilging out of school."

"Yes, he is." Eileen paused for a scowl. "He'll have to go to summer school. He's passing Spanish and second year algebra. Everything else—he'll be lucky if he gets one D among the Fs."

"I'll try to make more time to help him," I said. "Now that I know I'm back here for good."

"It's not a lack of homework help that's the problem." At that moment Father Keith's sour face reminded me of Sister Peter Mary. "It's that young lady of his. She offers a lot more entertainment than civics class does."

"Yeah, unfortunately," I said. "We need to figure out what to do with her, too. Home schooling would probably be best."

Father Keith nodded his agreement.

"You don't have to take care of Michael any longer, dear," Aunt Eileen said, "or of Sophie, either. It's hard to let them go at that age, but you have to. He needs to learn the consequences of not doing his homework."

"You're right, but I really was his second mom."

"Thanks to your mother. After your father disappeared, she demanded so much from all of you children. Yes, it was terrible for her, but she's not the only woman in the world who lost her husband."

I found myself remembering those awful months of Mother's alternate tears and rages, and how bitter she was about having to get a paying job.

"She wanted you older children to replace Flann," Keith put in. "It's no wonder Dan joined the army the day he turned eighteen."

"And Maureen married the first man who asked her," I said.

"Yes," Eileen said. "And it's also no wonder that the marriage didn't work out. I'll admit to being relieved when they divorced." She shot Father Keith a nervous glance.

"Officially, as a priest," Keith said, "I was horrified. As

me, the uncle, I was relieved, too. This new boyfriend—is he any better?"

"No," Eileen said. "The children are afraid of him. It worries me."

"She's got lousy taste in men," I said. "It's too bad Ari doesn't have a brother."

Aunt Eileen smiled. "It is, yes, and really, Nola, the only person you do need to take care of is your Ari. He's rather odd, but then, so are you."

We shared a laugh. Father Keith smiled at both of us.

"You don't mind that he's Jewish?" I said.

"No. It doesn't bother me at all." She looked away in thought. "If he were Protestant, it would be different. That would be a betrayal, somehow, after all our families have gone through over the centuries."

"All I'd ask," Father Keith said, "is that you let me preside over some kind of nonsectarian ceremony when you marry him. Times have changed. I'm not going to throw a churchman's holy howling fit."

"I am not going to marry him."

Father Keith snorted.

"Of course not." Eileen was trying to keep from smiling. "But does he know that?"

I felt a SAWM go off like a fire alarm.

"No," I said. "I'll have to have a talk with him."

"Good luck," she said, and she and Father Keith both laughed.

After they left, I wandered over to the window in the living room and looked out. The fog was blowing in thickly. Swirls of gray covered the sky and sent long tendrils over the roofs across the street. A familiar gray face drifted in from the sea, then paused just beyond my window. Illumination struck my brain.

"Javert?" I said.

The consciousness I'd been calling Fog Face nodded.

"I've got Belial pinned," I said.

The projection smiled at that.

"Was he the one who murdered that little girl?"

The smile disappeared, and he nodded a yes.

"And the lawyer guy?"

Another sad nod.

"Okay," I said. "I'll see about transferring custody over to your people."

I raised one hand in the sign of peace. With another grin he turned away, then frayed out into tufts of normal fog, sailing on the wind.

Like Belial, I realized, this being was a master at projected forms. Belial had managed to form the Qi he stockpiled into the shape of a robed figure. Somehow he'd been able to manipulate the air to produce sounds, too, in order to seem to be speaking. Javert had never spoken to me, but then, I'd only ever seen him through window glass. He'd just heard me speak, of course, unless he'd merely read the words from my mind. Their species, whatever it was, had to have talents beyond ours in some areas but only some. Their set of genetic mind tools must have lacked world-walking, since they'd been forced to rely on projections instead.

When they transferred their consciousness, though, they lacked hands, physical hands or tentacles to manipulate objects here on our world. Caleb had supplied those for Belial. Had he found Drake's treasure, he would have had the money to work with his so-called spirit to do whatever mischief Belial had planned. Nothing good—I was willing to bet on that—a plan dangerous or criminal enough for Javert to stalk him across the worlds. Javert, in turn, had needed my hands and my ability to speak in order to stop the malfeasance.

I'd just finished sending this new information off to the Agency when Ari returned from the gym. He brought with him a receipt for one of those apartment-sized washer/dryer combos. He'd seen one advertised on sale in a local appliance store.

"They'll install it next Tuesday," he told me. "I don't want you going down to the launderette alone."

The white picket fence gleamed on the green lawn of my mind.

"Thanks," I said. "But we could just go do the laundry together."

"Of course, but I hate those places, so why should either of us bother?"

He smiled and left to hang his sweaty workout clothes over the back porch railing. I logged off TranceWeb, closed down my system, and sat down on the couch. Ari returned with a bottle of a silvery gray sports drink and joined me.

"That looks like dishwater," I said.

He scrutinized the bottle, then shrugged. "It doesn't taste like it."

"Whatever. Um, Ari, we need to have a talk. I take it you're planning on staying in San Francisco for a while."

"Indefinitely, according to my superiors." He paused for a swallow of the bottled dishwater. "Both of them. I'll admit to both since there's no hiding it from you. There's a nexus of anti-Israel activity in this city, as I'm sure you've noticed."

"Well, yeah. I don't mean to pry."

"Pry?" He smiled, just a brief flicker of his mouth. "Good word, I suppose. Very tactful. It's one reason I love you."

I went tense.

"Don't you think I feel that?" he said. "The way you freeze up, pull away, turn into yourself, whatever it is, the minute I say something, too—oh, I don't know—too sentimental, I suppose it is. I don't have to be psychic to feel you pushing me away."

"I'm sorry." I felt like a bleating sheep, but the words crept out before I could stop them. "Ari, I've only known you—what? A couple of months? It's not long enough for either of us to know how we really feel."

"Where did you read that?" He leaned over and put the ghastly-looking drink down on the coffee table. "One of your college textbooks?"

I had to admit that my wording needed improvement. "Oh, okay. Let me amend that. Do you really think this relationship can possibly work long-term? Look, we're both really strange people, misfits, I guess I mean. We've both been wounded in strange ways."

"Who else goes in for our line of work?" He turned on the couch to look directly at me. "How many normal family men or career women do you see in your agency? I can't think of any in mine. There's too much lying, too much danger, the tedious kind of danger that's mostly waiting for the worst to happen. Only a misfit would take the job."

"That's true." I looked away and listened to my heart pounding in fear. "But I just don't see how we can make any kind of commitment to each other. Your country's always going to come first to you. I'll always be waiting for you to leave me. Not for another woman, I mean, but for Israel's sake."

"If I go, I'll take you with me."

"But I don't want to leave here. I've got my family to consider, and now, come to think of it, so do you. They've taken you in lock, stock, and barrel."

Ari smiled as if he was about to make a smart remark, then let the smile fade. "That could present a problem."

"It's not the only one, either. What am I supposed to do? Sit in some flat in Tel Aviv and worry myself sick while you're gone?"

"Gone?" He blinked at me in fake innocence.

"Yeah, gone! Wandering around the hill country pretending to be Iranian. What's your cover? Just a simple tribesman herding goats? What do you look for out there? Military installations? Missile emplacements?"

Ari whistled under his breath. "You do puzzle things out, don't you?"

"Hey, it's part of my job. What would happen if the Iranian military caught you? I bet you wouldn't live to reach a court of law."

"Probably not, no."

"Would I ever even know what had happened to you?"

"Probably not, though I assume you could guess." He grinned at me. "After all, you are psychic."

"Oh, great! And so one night I'll have a nightmare where I watch you get shot or beheaded. Only it won't be a dream. It'll be true. No, Ari. I won't live like that."

The grin disappeared. He sat silently for a couple of minutes, weighing things out in his mind, or so his SPP indicated. "Well," he said eventually, "I suppose I could compromise on my career choice."

"Career choice. What a phrase to use!"

He laughed. He actually laughed. "True," he said. "How about mission assignment, then? I can turn it down in the future. No one forces that kind of assignment on an operative. I've always volunteered for it."

"Know something? You're an adrenaline junkie."

"What?"

"Someone who's addicted to their own adrenaline, which starts flowing when they're doing something dangerous."

"I've never thought of it that way before." Ari paused in contemplation. "But it's a fair evaluation. Why else would I want to marry you?"

I decided that I must be psychotic to care so much about a man like him. He caught my hands in his and pulled me a little closer. His touch made me feel like melting. No, I realized that I'd already melted. Psychotic, I told myself. O'Grady, you actually love this guy. How could you?

"Nola?" he said. "Think of the Roadrunner cartoons. The coyote runs off the edge of the cliff, but as long as he doesn't look down, he doesn't fall. He can walk on the air. That's what our marriage is going to be like. Just don't look down, and we'll do splendidly."

"That's absolutely nuts!"

He raised my hands to his mouth and kissed each of them in turn. "No, it's a metaphor. It makes perfect sense."

"I'm not going to marry you. I'm not going to marry anyone."

"Oh?" He smiled his tiger's smile. "We'll just see about that."

Agency Talents and Acronyms

ASTA Automatic survival threat awareness

CDEP Chaos diagnostic emergency procedure

CW Chaos wards

CDS Collective Data Stream

CEV Conscious evasion procedure

DEI Deliberately extruded images (visible only to psychics)

DW Dice walk

E Ensorcellment

HC Heat conservation

IOI Image Objectification of Insight

LDRS Long distance remote sensing

MI Manifested indicators (of chaos forces)

PI Possibility Images

RSL Random Synchronistic Linkage (dice walking)

SAF Scanning the aura field

SM Search mode

SM:P Search mode: Personnel G:General D: Danger L: Location

SAWM Semiautomatic warning mechanism

SH Shield persona

SPP Subliminal psychological profile

UPC Unexplained personnel capabilities (occult powers)

Katharine Kerr

The Nola O'Grady *Novels*

"Breakneck plotting, punning, and romance make for a
mostly fast, fun read." —*Publishers Weekly*

"This is an entertaining investigative urban fantasy that sub-
genre readers will enjoy...fans will enjoy the streets of San
Francisco as seen through an otherworldly lens."
—*Midwest Book Review*

LICENSE TO ENSORCELL
978-0-7564-0656-1

WATER TO BURN
978-0-7564-0691-2

To Order Call: 1-800-788-6262
www.dawbooks.com

DAW 180

Katharine Kerr

The Silver Wyrm
The Novels of Deverry

"Prepare to get lost in the magic." — *Voya*

Book One
THE GOLD FALCON 978-0-7564-0419-2

Book Two
THE SPIRIT STONE 978-0-7564-0477-2

Book Three
THE SHADOW ISLE 978-0-7564-0476-5

Book Four
THE SILVER MAGE 978-0-7564-0587-8

"Much as I dislike comparing anything to
The Lord of the Rings, I have to admit on that on
this occasion it's justified." — *Interzone*

To Order Call: 1-800-788-6262
www.dawbooks.com

DAW 50